THE
BACKSTREETS
OF
PURGATORY

This edition first published in 2018

Unbound
6th Floor Mutual House, 70 Conduit Street,
London W1S 2GF
www.unbound.com

Lyrics from 'Carry Me' © Malcolm Middleton 2009,
The Domino Music Publishing Company

Text Design by Ellipsis, Glasgow

A CIP record for this book is available from the British Library

ISBN 978-1-78352-555-3 (trade hbk)
ISBN 978-1-78352-556-0 (ebook)
ISBN 978-1-78352-557-7 (limited edition)

Printed in Great Britain by Clays Ltd, St Ives Plc
1 3 5 7 9 8 6 4 2

THE
BACKSTREETS
OF
PURGATORY

HELEN TAYLOR

Unbound

Dear Reader,

The book you are holding came about in a rather different way to most others. It was funded directly by readers through a new website: Unbound. Unbound is the creation of three writers. We started the company because we believed there had to be a better deal for both writers and readers. On the Unbound website, authors share the ideas for the books they want to write directly with readers. If enough of you support the book by pledging for it in advance, we produce a beautifully bound special subscribers' edition and distribute a regular edition and ebook wherever books are sold, in shops and online.

This new way of publishing is actually a very old idea (Samuel Johnson funded his dictionary this way). We're just using the internet to build each writer a network of patrons. At the back of this book, you'll find the names of all the people who made it happen.

Publishing in this way means readers are no longer just passive consumers of the books they buy, and authors are free to write the books they really want. They get a much fairer return too – half the profits their books generate, rather than a tiny percentage of the cover price.

If you're not yet a subscriber, we hope that you'll want to join our publishing revolution and have your name listed in one of our books in the future. To get you started, here is a £5 discount on your first pledge. Just visit unbound.com, make your pledge and type **caravaggio5** in the promo code box when you check out.

Thank you for your support,

Dan, Justin and John
Founders, Unbound

For Malcolm, without whom I would be lost.

Will you carry me when my legs have gone?
Will you carry me home?
Will you pray for me as they're taking me?
Pray for my soul.

Malcolm Middleton, 'Carry Me'

BURNT UMBER

I

David with the Head of Goliath

Finn hauled up the jeans that were slipping down his arse and kicked open the door of his studio. The first thing he clapped eyes on was the blank canvas he'd shoved in the corner two days earlier. It was staring at him from under the eaves, gesso-primed and expectant and menacing him with its vacant expression. As far as Finn was concerned, it could fuck right off. It was just one other thing that was conspiring to do his head in. One more trial to add to the litany of tribulations he'd had to endure on this particularly shite of shite days. And, as if that wasn't enough, to pile injury on top of the insults, his studio was stifling. Heated by communal pipes that had come on automatically despite the unseasonal November warmth. Finn slung his jacket over the chair at his workbench and went to open the window. Air was required pronto before he suffocated on the heat and general crapness that was his life.

From the vantage point at the top-floor window, above side streets already dark from the shadows of surrounding tenement flats, the fire-damaged Mackintosh Building was just visible. In a lamentable attempt to stop the day's events replaying inside his head, Finn tilted open the window pane and breathed in the evening air. Work on the Art School had finished hours ago, but the air still hung with sandstone and steel and sawdust, and echoed with the clank of scaffolding and the shouts of the workies and stonemasons and carpenters who were crafting the life back into the place. But the facade was half hidden behind a casing of scaffolding. As if, Finn reckoned, the building itself was ashamed of its bruises of soot, its blackened scarred lintels and busted lead glass. It was too pitiful to gaze on for long.

Instead, he looked southwards, westwards towards the bloated evening sun, to where the city stretched to the river and beyond. On the horizon, against the sherbet sky, the city's few remaining tower blocks wobbled rotten-toothed style under the flossy clouds. In the old days, Finn knew, by the time those clouds had crossed the city from the airy open spaces and wealthy merchant villas of the West End to the claustrophobic slums of the industrial darkland in the east, slaves to the prevailing westerlies, polluted by the smoke and filth of the burgeoning urbanisation, they'd be sullied from their silver linings to their rain-loaded centres and couldn't help but stain whatever they touched. Sugar and tobacco. The dark twin souls that founded the city.

As the sun dipped towards the horizon, Finn gazed out over the fading metropolis hoping somehow the sight would lift his mood. Whatever its inglorious past, he felt a strong allegiance to his adopted home town. It hid its compassionate side behind the myth of hard men, cheap alcohol and the splendour of squalor and violence. There were few places that appealed to him in quite the same way.

Squalor and violence were all well and good, but it was clear to Finn that his diversionary tactics were failing. Even putting aside the day's events, he couldn't shift his mood. And it wasn't helped by his surroundings. This outstandingly nondescript studio in its equally nondescript building. It wasn't what he'd signed up for. He'd imagined himself cosseted in the sandstone and oak art nouveau masterpiece along the road (until some stupid fuck had burnt the place down), adding his own few kilograms to the weight of history.

Dismally, Finn pulled himself away from the window and turned back to face the studio, half hoping that while his back had been turned the place had undergone a transformation that would at least make hanging out there bearable. But, as usual, like every other time before that time, he found it in exactly the same mundane state as it ever was. Torn between the unappealing proposition of attempting some work or aggravating his depression further with a few pints down the pub, he wandered over to his workbench and poked around in the mess. The bench was scattered with tubes of oils and brushes he hadn't washed properly since his undergrad, and photos that he'd printed out and failed to sketch. He sharpened a desultory pencil or two, incapable of doing anything more productive.

In summary, it had been a bad day. One of many in the last few weeks. The trouble was that things weren't panning out the way he had expected. Term was disappearing and he hadn't produced any work he was happy with. Any work *full stop*, if he was being precise, and everything was conspiring to make sure it stayed that way. An hour earlier, sitting on the pavement opposite the building site in the late afternoon sunshine, drinking coffee-machine espresso and flicking ash from his roll-up at an out-of-season ant trail to see if he could make them do an about-turn, he'd told himself he could do this, he could manage, he could cope with the daily crap. It was just a matter of getting over himself.

That was until he stopped by his tutor's office to pick up his essay. Fail. Totally fucking unjust. The title was genius: 'Navel Gazing in the Twenty-First Century: How Art Stopped Speaking to the People'. He'd slipped the colon in for irony. If he'd learnt one thing on this course, it was that an essay title without a colon didn't cut it in academia.

Finn chucked the sharpened pencils back on the bench. He didn't need this extra pressure. The unpainted pictures that haunted his every second were making him feel more than bad enough. He scraped a chair across the floorboards and sat for a while with his back to the window, hoping inspiration might visit when he wasn't stalking it. From a distant playground, high-pitched yells of kids arguing over five-a-side floated through the open pane. Lazily, he stretched his neck over the backrest of his chair making his skull crunch against the frame. He envied those kids the liberty of their brutal childhood. Not for him, his mother had dictated, the grazed knees of inner-city asphalt. She'd had much more suburban ambitions for her son.

A burst of orange from the setting sun flared over Finn's shoulder and a draught flurried around him, blowing straggles of hair off his brow so they momentarily danced in the blaze. He dropped his arms by his sides to loosen the tension in his shoulders. Fail? It wasn't credible. Basically, the problem was that his tutor didn't get him. Rather than finding him subtly ingenious and modestly amusing, the woman had slagged him off, saying his essay was dismally thought out, his prose chaotic, his grammar poor. Putting his place on the course in jeopardy. Frankly, she was way off. Just plain rude. There was much more to his essay than saying modern art was elitist shite. If that's what she thought, she hadn't read it properly. Finn tipped back in the chair, gripping the seat edge, testing the limits of his balance. His fingers buzzed with pins and needles, and the skin over his knuckles was tight and bloodless. At that angle, everything looked upside down. Everything *was* upside down. By rights, he should be top of the class, not floundering in the fucking depths.

He stayed like that for ages, with his feet planted on the floor and his head leaning over the back of the chair, letting the cool breeze whisper over his face and listening to the last of the kids' shouts before they headed home for their tea. Of all the things that hacked him off, he'd say the worst was that his tutor had questioned his commitment. Honestly, she didn't know shit. He'd been infected by an obsession for the whole palaver since he was a boy and his wee granny – his Italian grandma on his old man's side – had opened his eyes to it all. Continental claptrap, his old doll called it, and reckoned his brain had been addled. An opinion that wasn't lessened when his granny died and Finn decided the most effective way to avenge her, the only way to honour her as she deserved to be honoured, was to completely piss off his social-climbing mother, subvert his turgid middle-class upbringing, show up the future doctors and lawyers that were his classmates and class enemies for the closed-minded, tight-arsed crowd-followers that they were, and commit entirely to the role of misunderstood artist. Which he'd done with a fervour until the pretence and the reality had become inseparable. Advanced Higher art, A; BA (Hons) Fine Art, First Class Honours; Leverhulme Scholarship for this course.

Master of Fine Art. It had a certain ring. Brackets Distinction, Finn told himself, if he could hold for five. He lifted his feet off the floor and for a moment – arms like wire coat hangers, legs stretched to bootlaces by the shadows spilling on the floorboards – he was perfectly balanced, until the weight of the junk in the pockets of his jacket pulled the chair backwards beyond its equilibrium. His stomach bounced past his heart and he slammed his feet down, managing to save himself at the last second. He glanced around. No witnesses, bar that fucking canvas. Distinction now questionable.

The last of the setting sun sank below the skyline and the studio plunged into shadow. Finn shivered. For reasons that were beyond him, his tutor hadn't appreciated his thesis that the only talent required to succeed these days was the ability to arse-lick the establishment and ignore the offensive taste. Not that he'd said it quite in those words. But you didn't have to look too far into the belly of said establishment to find the type of nonsense he was talking about. Works so far up their own rectum they'd more or less turned themselves inside out. Works that took no skill or proper thought, and which stank of mediocrity and after-the-fact justification. The type of self-reverential, self-referential excrement designed only to be understood in the context of the intention of the artist. Or in the context of other work. Exactly the kind of postmodern crap he couldn't be arsed with. Not that he couldn't shite-speak with the best of them. It was just that he didn't see the point.

What remained of the sparse daylight sidled around the patches of dirt on the studio window and through the open pane, and trickled over the back of Finn's neck and he sank into a melancholic stupor. He knew he should do something but he couldn't bring himself to move. Briefly, he considered phoning Lizzi because she usually had some words of wisdom when it came to matters of the psyche (although, in truth, they tended to sound as if they had been lifted straight from the pages of her course book, so he rarely bothered to listen).

The thing was, hard though it might be to believe from his current state, Finn wouldn't say he was generally morose by nature. Especially in this city, with its aberrant charms in such abundance. On cue, a gull squawked from the nearby pedestrian precinct. As vermin Finn had always contended that seagulls were totally underrated. In days gone by, whenever he arrived back in Glasgow after surviving a trip to his parents' place, their squawks had signalled his homecoming and the racket alone had served as relaxation therapy. More than once, he'd considered recording it and selling it as some kind of urban whale music. Or licensing the concept as an ad for VisitScotland. Where Trafalgar Square had pigeons, Sauchiehall Street had gulls. Ugly bastards that bullied the shoppers and scavenged the remnants of Happy Meals. The avian equivalent of neds, the ad would explain, in their light grey hoodies and matching sweatpants. If you thought about it, as a uniform it couldn't be more impractical. Except for the protection that any uniform gave: anonymity. *Can you describe the person who stole your handbag, madam? Yes, officer. Some wee shite in a grey tracksuit.*

Time was ticking on but Finn was at a total loss how to fill it. He rubbed his eyes, yawned, stared gloomily at his surroundings. The only thing of any interest to him at all was the stack of art books piled against the wall that he'd blown his scholarship money on. Truth be told, he'd only actually bothered to read the one on Caravaggio (an excellent and informative book, though missing one little-publicised but pivotal biographical detail of particular relevance to the Italian side of Finn's family), although the others served as an effective stool for visitors on the occasions the need arose. Without getting out of his chair, Finn stretched his leg to trap the Caravaggio under the sole of his trainer, and dragged it across the floor until it was within reach.

He leant down and heaved the book on to his lap. In a stupendously unimaginative and banal comeback to his arse-licking hypothesis, his tutor had accused him of being reactionary, just because he'd argued that art had reached its *apice* in seventeenth-century Rome. *Apice*. Finn savoured the Italian word. The language was part of his heritage. A quarter of it to be exact. He wasn't reactionary. He was simply loyal to his roots. He should have stuck up for himself. Told the woman where to stick her personal affronts. Taken a lesson or two in social niceties from the big man.

Finn ran his hand over the cover of the book. It was at times like these he wished he could have actually met Caravaggio. It wasn't only in his personal life that the man was a total headcase. When it came to his paintings, he was a genius, a maverick, a maverick genius, trailblazing through the Counter-Reformation, subverting the social order. His work was intimate, intense, incandescent. It transluminated painting, lighting the way for *il popolo*, so you stepped into the picture, became part of it, no longer kept behind the crush barrier by bouncers in the pay of snooty classicism and exaggerated mannerism. Finn paused for a second to reflect. Did you call those folk who worked in galleries *bouncers*?

The book was heavy in Finn's lap. He turned the cover and fanned the pages. It fell open at *David with the Head of Goliath*. In the semi-darkness, he examined the familiar painting. Despite the violent subject, he'd always found the image bizarrely tender. And he'd have had to have been completely gay-blind not to appreciate the astonishing homoeroticism. A version of David, sword glinting, naked torso pale – almost glowing – against the pitch background, holding the disembodied head of his conquest by its straggly black hair, and on his, David's, face, an expression of such detached compassion that you'd swear it wasn't him who had killed the poor bastard and chopped his head off. And Caravaggio as Goliath, staring into a chasm, his left eye wide, the right glazed over, mouth open in a death yell as if he didn't yet know that his number was up.

Given a choice for one to hang above the mantelpiece, handsome David and his ugly mate wouldn't be top of Finn's list. That said, the thing still spoke to him. Much like the painted David, Finn felt sorry for the big man. If you believed all the medical stuff, Goliath was probably over-producing growth hormone from a tumour or suchlike, sprouting upwards without the energy to sustain him. Which, from what Finn had read, meant even an asthmatic flea could have blown the lanky fucker over. Not a great physical triumph for young Davy at all, when you thought about it.

The temperature in the studio was dropping. Darkness was enveloping the room. Finn knew he ought to move – shut the window, turn on the light, work or go home – but the picture wouldn't let him go. He had to concentrate. It was telling him more than he could easily hear.

When he'd cast himself as the villain, Caravaggio hadn't spared himself. Not just because he'd portrayed himself in all his magnificent ugliness. It was the symbolism he'd used. The right eye – the eye of morality and virtuousness – unseeing. The left – not just the sinister left in Renaissance, Post-Renaissance art, but the side of the deepest emotions, of love, despair and all the unnavigable nonsense in between – still open, still pleading. It was more than an allegory, more than a self-portrait. It was a petition for mercy, an acknowledgement of his wrongdoing. This was his plea, for safety, for protection, a return from exile after the murder he committed in Rome. Finn could hear his cries. If you don't spare me, my genius will be wasted. Even in this purgatory, the artist recognised a greater obligation. Lizzi would probably argue that it was nothing of the kind. Rather that it was a confession of the artist's homosexual proclivity, that his boyfriend's sword was simply a massive shiny boner (although Lizzi would probably have framed it in different terms) and that old Caravaggio was begging to be punished. But then she read repression and Catholic guilt in almost everyone she came across. Flag-waving Proddies included.

In a distant office, a phone rang out. In the corridor, parting footsteps echoed off the plaster walls. All around, the joists of the old building creaked. It was relaxing, settling down for the night. Soon he would be the only person left, bar the porter on the front desk. Finn placed the open book on the floor at his feet and hauled himself out of the chair. Another day gone. Another day wasted. Taking care not to catch the eye of the blank canvas on his way, he went to the window and pulled it shut. Give or take a functioning organ system or two, he'd put that canvas as quite literally the personification of his artistic paralysis, he'd say. Brush-stroke by non-existent brushstroke, his portfolio was turning into one massive non-event. The original plan for his project had been vetoed by his tutor because she was under the impression he was taking the piss. Finn picked up his jacket off the back of the chair and shoved his arms into the sleeves, bewildered by the injustice of it all. His Bingo project was serious. More than serious. It was about community, poverty, friendship. It was about money being the new religion and the poor being condemned to a living hell. It was about false hope and real despair. He wanted to do the things that Caravaggio had done, subvert the social order, make the art-buying class indebted to those who would never have more than the poster replica, but apparently all he had succeeded in doing – if he listened to the pseudo-sociological gibberish that his tutor spouted – was patronise the very people he wanted to represent.

One last glance at David and Goliath before he closed the cover of his book, however, was enough to rally him. The fact was his tutor didn't know one end of a paintbrush from another. He didn't need permission from the uptight spinster to paint what he wanted to paint. He certainly didn't need assignments and essays and marks out of ten to show that he had talent. It wasn't as if Caravaggio had had formal training. According to Finn's own granny, he'd ditched his apprenticeship and spent his money whoring and brawling his way around town with his buddies.

Finn shoved the book into his messenger bag. The picture was clear. In black and white and in extremes of contrast. If he stayed here – in this straitjacket of fakery and privilege – he would never see the light. He should be out there with the people – grey tracksuits, Bingo and all – not hanging around here, being misunderstood and dragged down by all these pretentious losers. Fuck it. It was time he followed Caravaggio's lead.

For the first time in days Finn managed a smile. He slung his bag over his chest and – pausing only to kick over the unpainted canvas for no other reason save that it was asking for it – legged it out the place like his life depended on it.

2

Boy Peeling a Fruit

At much the same time as Finn was admiring young Davy's nude torso at the Art School, across town, in a side street two up from Partick Cross, Tuesday McLaughlin was attempting to gain entry to a tattoo parlour that was owned by Finn's best mate. The shop belonged to Rob Stevenson, a detail to which Tuesday was, for the moment, happily oblivious, intent as she was on finding a lawful way into the premises. The trouble was, from where she was standing, it didn't look too promising. The sign quite clearly stated the place was open for another hour, but it was closed, no question. For about the seventh time, Tuesday rattled the locked door and, when it still wouldn't open, shoved her face up against the window. The shop was full of stuff she'd have been happy to offload given different circumstances: shelves lined with old medicine bottles and volumes of faded red and green hardbacks; a round mirror speckled with age that would definitely make good money down the antique market; and, on the counter, gleaming under the protection of a fingerprint-free glass case, a set of brass weighing scales of a quality any dealer would happily pawn their weans for. But, as far as Tuesday could make out, if you were talking actual living breathing life, there was less than what you'd find in your average coffin-dodgers' coach trip. The only hope of someone who might be able to do the business was the limp skeleton hanging from a scaffold by a screw in its baldy head who appeared to be guarding the till, or the baby alligator perched on top of the stationery cupboard with glassy eyes and a stupid grin on its face. Strictly, Tuesday knew she couldn't complain if the shop was dead – it was the whole morbid thing it had going on that had made her choose it in the first place – but, frankly, if the sign said open, it should bloody well be open.

Frustrated, she rattled the door again. The lock was pretty flimsy, barely holding. If she still had her old ways about her, she might have considered it worth booting the door in and having a run-in with the skinny bloke at the till, if only for the scrap metal value of the chemical balance. Instead, as she left, she gave the door a half-hearted kick for old times' sake, and immediately regretted it when she stubbed her middle toe. Once the numbness had passed, it started throbbing like a tadger.

She was hopping on the white line halfway across the main road, waiting for a break in the traffic, when she heard a shout.

'Hey, missus.' Rob was waving to her from under a streetlight at the corner of the side street. A big bloke with a shaved head and tats on his face was Tuesday's take. Nobody she knew. Although with his steel toecaps and pumped-up muscles, she clocked him for the type who reckoned he was hard.

'Aye, you with the skinny pins. Are you coming in or what?'

Rush-hour traffic was passing either side, coughing out blue exhaust fumes around her. Tuesday shook her head. She'd lost the motivation. The shut-up shop had floored her. Whatever the opposite of psyched-up, that was her. Psyched-down or something. It would be easier to dis-appear into the going-home crowd.

'Nah, you missed your chance, doll.'

Mind made up, Tuesday waved Rob off, but before she managed to dive through the oncoming traffic, a black BMW came speeding up the main road. The driver was playing with his mobile, steering one-handed, swerving all over the place. For a second, Tuesday swithered on the mid-line, too late to make the dash. She couldn't believe it. He was practically on top of her and he hadn't seen a bone in her body. Fuck that. She wasn't having it. She held her ground and pumped her bunched fist from her forehead. *Dickhead.* The car missed her by a sliver. The driver beeped, leaving his hand on the klax – a wanker's lesson in road safety – and, as the car passed, the sound dropped a semi-tone and faded into the traffic hum.

'You okay?'

'Aye, fucking peachy,' Tuesday said, even though she wasn't. It did her head in, these fancy tossers who thought they were entitled to make her invisible because they lived inside their fuel-injection, leather-trimmed lives. But even though the near-miss had left her shaky, there was no way she was admitting as much to a bloke who wore his denims *that* tight.

'Come on. I've put the kettle on.'

Tuesday pulled a face and crossed back over, following Rob past the overflowing bins in the darkened side street. At the shop, he waited for her, holding open the door.

'Milk and three sugars,' Tuesday said, as rudely as she could. She may have been quarter his size but it didn't mean she wasn't capable of opening a door. Not that she was one of those feminist nut-jobs who got offended by basic manners, but this chivalry business annoyed the tits off her. In normal life, the only time a man held open a door for her was when the door in question was attached to a police van.

She was still working out how best to slag him off when Rob bowed elaborately and offered her his arm. 'Would the young lady care to enter my humble premises?'

Tuesday shoved his arm out of the way and pushed past him. 'If you don't mind me saying, pal, that's no fucking normal.'

He laughed and followed her in.

Close up the shop looked even better than it had through the window. Tuesday glanced around, taking it all in. Pretty phenomenal. Without intending to, she let out a low whistle. Front of house, a computer and music speakers were the only evidence of the twenty-first century. Otherwise, the place was entirely kitted out as a Victorian consulting room, complete with microscopes, anatomy charts and pickled specimens. There was a waiting area under the window lit with pretend oil lamps, a travelling trunk in place of a table, and through the half-open door at the back of the shop, she could have sworn it was a full-on operating theatre walled by the industrial white glazed tiles familiar from the back courts of warehouses and workshops all around the city.

'Some place,' she said, unzipping her puffer jacket. 'Lots of bottles.'

'Indeed,' Rob said. 'As you can see, we have products to meet your every requirement. From the *benign*' – he indicated a tin of Beecham's Pills, another of Allenburys Throat Pastilles – 'to – I hesitate to say *ridiculous* – let's say *safe-in-the-correct-hands* . . .' His hand swept past thick bottles with ground-glass stoppers and peeling labels. Tuesday had to strain to read names. Aquae camphorae, saltpetre.

'. . . to the *outright-hazardous-to-human-health*.'

Mercurous chloride, belladonna.

'Are thae ones poison too?' Arsenic, she knew.

He frowned. 'Well spotted. I'm probably meant to keep them behind bars. I ought to find out.'

'Aye, you ought to,' Tuesday sneered. He was doing that thing they did at the day centre. Feigning idiocy to get down to your level.

After a microsecond of hesitation, Rob finished his tour. 'Finally, the favourite of poets and physicians alike . . .' He made it sound like a big pronouncement, a fanfare, like Tuesday would guess what was coming before he said it.

'Eh?'

'Laudanum.'

Tuesday gawped as blankly as her irritation would allow.

'Opium for the upper class,' Rob clarified.

In response, Tuesday flashed him a look of contempt and pointed out that the bottle was empty.

He grinned at her inanely. 'Aye, well at least I cannae get done for possession.'

The line of chat was boring her already, so to liven things up she asked why Rob had pickled his dick. Puzzled, he glanced over to see what she was talking about. 'You mean the eel? I bought it in a supermarket in France when I bought the calf's brain.' He nodded at a jellied mushroom in a jar. 'It's amazing what you can buy in the pre-packed aisle over there.'

'I'll take your word for it.' In the last few years, the furthest Tuesday had been from Partick was the Underground station at Govan.

'I'm no sure, though, that bunging it in neat formaldehyde will stop it rotting.' Rob lifted the specimen jar off the shelf and wiped the dust on its shoulders with a cloth from under the desk. The liquid around the jelly brain was snot-thick. 'Maybe I should've consulted a taxidermist.'

'Aye, mebbe you should've,' Tuesday said, and wandered

over to the travelling trunk to pick up one of the folders scattered on it.

'I'm thinking about a tattoo,' she said finally.

'Well, you've come to the right place.'

Riled, she spun round, ready to match whatever aggro came her way. But straight off she registered Rob wasn't taking the piss. He was nervous, she realised. *She* was making him nervous. She was beginning to wonder if, in fact, she *had* come to the right place.

Casually, she flicked through the folder. 'These all yours?'

'Indeed. By my own dark hand.' He did a weird thing with his fingers.

'No kidding.'

'Aye. Rule number one. Original artwork only.'

'No bad.'

'Thanks.' Under his tattoos, Rob blushed. Tuesday sniggered. How awkward. The bloke clearly fancied himself as an artist. In what even to her was obvious as an abysmal effort to gloss past, Rob took the folder and opened the inside cover. The price list was stuck to the plastic. 'It's by the hour. A wee one will take an hour, max hour and a half. Big ones can take anything up to five or six. Longer for colour.'

Tuesday nodded. It was pricier than she had anticipated.

'When can we start?'

'Rule number two. First appointments strictly consults only. Don't want to jeopardise my stats.'

She just looked at him. He laughed. Nervously.

'My cadaver rate. It's exceptionally low. If I don't think someone's up to it, I scare them off deliberately.'

'Cadaver rate?'

'You know, the jessies who take a whitey at the sight of a needle.'

'Right.'

'Talking of cadavers and the like, did you meet Lister?'

'The skelly? Aye.' Tuesday didn't like the way Rob was looking at her, kind of squinty-eyed and troubled, even as he held out the skeleton's bony hand to shake hers. Suddenly, she panicked that he was going to refuse her.

But all he said was, 'We know each other, right?'

Tuesday breathed a sigh of relief. 'To be honest, doll, I'm pretty sure I've never seen you before in my puff.' She would have remembered. He had near enough a menagerie swimming, running, crawling around his neck, up his jaw, on to his cheek. 'It'd be hard to forget a face like that.'

'Fair point,' he said. 'I'm Rob, by the way. Short for Robin. But you knew that already, I take it, or you wouldna've come in fancy dress.'

She laughed. 'Fuck off.' The funny thing was, he wasn't that far off. The red puffer jacket had been her latest Oxfam steal and the leggings belonged to the Somali lassie who did the cleaning in the B&B and who changed into her work overalls in the reception toilets. The boots were her own. Discount sheepskin, tide-marked and losing their glue.

'What I usually do is give the client a tour of the treatment room, get them to read over the health questionnaire and consent form, and then we work up some designs together. Gie's two secs to finish the autoclave check and we can get on to it. Don't let anyone else in.' Rob locked the front door. Before he disappeared through the back, he gawked at her again. 'I swear I know you. Those cheekbones. Unmistakable. You could chib someone.'

Tuesday chucked the folder back on to the trunk. There was something majorly warped, she reckoned – something your mother probably would have warned you against if she hadn't been a junkie waste of space with not a drop of maternal instinct – about being locked in a shop full of poison with a guy six foot four and built like a brick shit-house. But if anyone was crapping it, it certainly wasn't her.

While Rob sorted whatever it was he had to do through the back, Tuesday decided to make herself comfy. The choice of seating was laid out in front of her like the kind of cheap personality test they were keen on at the clinic. The window seat padded with charcoal velvet cushions was obviously the easy option. Beside that, there was an antique oak and leather study chair which had the air of being the boss's and which she reckoned it would be sensible to avoid if Rob was the one inflicting the pain later, or an old-fashioned wicker and wooden invalid's chair with foldable foot rests and a stick to steer it. She chose the wheelchair. No contest.

Rob came back a few minutes later with his desk diary. 'Okay, what are we looking at? See anything you like?'

Tuesday flattened a scrap of paper she'd pulled from her coat pocket and handed it over. Rob studied it.

'Ah, the midge. Diminutive scourge of the Highlands and unwitting accomplice of the nationalists. The few foolhardy tourists who brave the badlands rarely repeat their mistake. Nectar running in their English blood, I reckon. Unlike the acerbic locals.'

Tuesday rolled her eyes. 'You're a freak, doll. D'you know that?'

'All your own work?'

'What gave it away?' She'd torn it from a textbook in the nature section in the library.

'Only I usually—'

'You gonnae do it or what?'

'The thing is . . . okay, maybe this once, but don't let on to the masses. Where d'you want it?'

Tuesday scrabbled to pull off her coat and pushed up the sleeve of her sweatshirt. 'Here.'

Livid tracks radiated up her arm from the scarred veins at the crook of her elbow. She stared at him, daring him to challenge her. To her surprise, he didn't flinch.

He opened the diary. 'What about next week? Early Monday?'

'Listen, doll,' she said, 'I'm no being funny, but I'm here now.'

Rob stroked his chin. 'True enough. Still an hour or two to torture before beer time.' He pulled out a printed sheet from the back of the binder and passed it to her. 'Is there anything I should know?'

The whole time she studied the form – following the words with her fingertip, mouthing them silently – she could feel Rob's eyes on her. When she reached the bottom of the page, she flung it back to him. 'I'm no HIV, if that's what you're on about.'

'Fair enough. Sign here.'

She scribbled her signature. He twisted his neck to read it upside down.

'Tuesday. Tuesday McLaughlin.' He was grinning, laughing, rubbing the back of his shaved head in surprise. 'I was right. I do know you. It's me. Rob Stevenson. I . . . we . . . were in your class at primary. Jed – Gerrard – my brother. Twins. Remember? Athletics club in secondary. We used to pal around together. Bloody hell. I cannae believe it. Tuesday McLaughlin.'

It was pretty astounding how quickly a perfectly reasonable idea could take on a hideous new shape. 'You know what?' Tuesday said, scrambling to her feet. 'Something came up.' The consent form fluttered to the floor.

'Hey, hey. You're no going, are you? Don't go. Hey. Come on.'

But there was no way she was hanging about. She snatched up her coat and hurdled the travelling trunk.

'I wouldna've had you down for bottling it.'

'Fuck off,' Tuesday said, jiggling the key in the lock. 'I'm no bottling it.'

'If you say so.'

'Aye, I fucking say so.' She was pissed off now.

Rob unlocked the door and stepped outside. He was chuckling to himself.

'What's so funny?' Tuesday could smell fireworks and burning Catholics on the winter air.

'I was terrified of you when I was a nipper.'

'So you should've been. You and your brother? Soft as.' Even in primary, Tuesday was harder than the twins. And wilder. By the time they were teenagers, she was already pretty much a legend, her name earnt by the inability ever to make it to school on the first day of the week. While Rob and his brother and their mates spent their Saturday nights innocently getting bevved on Tennent's lager (and leching over the less-than-appetising Lager Lovelies that decorated the tins in those medieval times), Tuesday was moving in altogether different circles, getting spannered on acid and vodka in weekend binges that lasted beyond Sunday and put to shame even the Jimmy-Choo-and-fake-tan brigade that hung out those days at the Arches and had slag fights in the street overlooked by police who'd been advised not to intervene unless they were wearing stab vests.

Rob grinned at her. 'What do you say? Mates' rates?'

She shrugged and went back in, making out like she was doing him a favour. He offered her whisky from his special stock through the back, but she went for tea, loading it with sugar from sachets that had come from the café up the road and, as there was no sign of a spoon, stirred it with the top end of the Biro she'd used to sign the form. Once she was settled back in the wheelchair, she blew on her tea, watching Rob over the top of the mug. He was peeling an apple with an army knife. The peel unravelled in a single spiral.

'Are you some kinda weirdo health freak, by the way?'

'Aye,' Rob said mildly, dangling the peel into his mouth.

'Still into all that fitness malarkey?'

'Aye.' He cut slices from the apple. Ate them off the knife blade. 'Yourself?'

'Don't be fucking stupid.'

The running club was probably the last place they had seen each other. Tuesday's one and only attempt at a legitimate extra-curricular activity. In the winter, they'd run the laughably named cross-country through the schemes round Knightswood and the Drum, getting abuse from the local kids who were after their Adidas three stripes and cagoules. And in the summer, endless laps round the playing field while Campbell Spence sat in his camping chair, feet up on his cold box, thumb on his stopwatch.

'Cannon Balls Spence, remember him?' Rob said, reading her mind. 'He had a thing for you.'

'Course he did. I was the talent.'

'Whatever happened to Tuesday McLaughlin?' he said, starting on a second apple. 'You left the party early, did you no?'

'Like anyone gave a fuck.'

Tuesday sipped her tea. Rob crunched on his apple slices. The wicker chair squeaked underneath her.

'Gie's a break,' Rob said eventually. 'Twenty years is a lifetime ago.'

'Eighteen,' Tuesday said. She'd been counting.

'Eighteen, eh? You've no changed.'

Tuesday bit the edge of her mug. The soft git probably meant it as a compliment. 'Cannae say the same about you, Slimster. What's the story? Anything new? Girlfriend? Boy-friend?'

Lister jiggled almost imperceptibly in the air current. Tuesday could feel the dust settling on the poison bottles, the calf brain decomposing in its tank. The baby gator gave a rictus grin.

'Nah, nothing to speak of,' Rob said sheepishly. 'So, are we gonnae do this thing or what?'

3

Mary Magdalen in Ecstasy

If Esme hadn't had other things on her mind, she would have been pleased to discover that Tuesday had had her tattoo done. It was part of a plan they had formulated at Tuesday's last outpatient visit and which was designed to distract Tuesday from any crisis where she might be tempted to sabotage her recovery. As it was, though, Esme was experiencing a crisis of her own. Since she'd started her consultant job a few months earlier, such crises had become part of her daily routine and, although she was at least getting used to expecting them, she didn't feel she had particularly improved the way she handled them.

That Monday morning, while two of her three sons were eating breakfast – ostensibly being supervised by their father – Esme stood at the sink, examining her eczematous hands and considering whether she was prepared to lose the battle to wash the previous evening's dinner dishes for the sake of a clean house and her own sanity. She had turned on the hot tap and was squirting washing-up liquid into the bowl when a squeal from Charlie made her turn round.

'Stop. Paddy. Stop.' Esme dropped the bottle of washing-up liquid and lunged towards the breakfast table. 'It'll end up . . . Fuck.' The word slipped out before she could stop it. She did a quick check of her middle son to see if it had registered but fortunately found him preoccupied with his thwarted attempt to feed his younger brother.

'Hey, mister, what are you playing at?' Dermot said, without glancing up from his phone.

'Oops.' Gingerly, Paddy placed Charlie's cereal bowl back down on the table. Charlie grinned and splashed his chubby hands in the milky slick creeping towards his lap.

'Yes, oops,' Esme said. 'I don't have time for this. Has any of it gone on you?'

Paddy shook his head, making his dark freckles trip across his nose.

'Good,' she said. 'Then eat your toast and leave your brother alone.' She soaked up the worst of the mess with a tea towel and flung it towards the sink. It landed with a slap on the draining board.

Dermot pushed his empty muesli bowl aside. 'Do you want me to see to him?'

'No, it's fine,' Esme said. 'You just sit there.' But her sarcasm was wasted on Dermot who went straight back to his phone. To make matters worse, when she lifted Charlie out of his high chair, soggy cereal dripped on to her work trousers and blobs of chocolate milk spread across the wool like bird droppings. She sighed. It didn't make much difference to her appearance. Her trousers were already a not-so-fetching shade of shitty brown. One of these days, she thought, it would be nice to arrive at work looking like the professional she was supposed to be. Looking more presentable than the poor souls relying on her for help.

While Esme attended to Charlie, Paddy spread his slice of toast with jam and conscientiously replaced the lid of the jar. She regretted how irritated she got with him. At times, it was easy to forget he was still only six. He was so resolutely independent. Not like her baby. She pulled off Charlie's wet jeans and her heart flipped at the sight of his piglet-pink bare legs and stocky thighs. She couldn't resist giving them a gentle pinch. He was so different to his skinny brothers. A fact that hadn't gone unnoticed.

Somehow in those few peaceful seconds, Paddy dropped the jam knife and scarred his sleeve with a gash of sticky raspberry.

'Oh, for heaven's sake,' Esme said. 'How many times have I told you to roll up your sleeves?'

'I don't know, Mummy.' Paddy looked at her, completely perplexed. 'Twenty?'

Esme strained to keep a straight face. She knew how he reacted when she laughed out of turn.

'This is what we pay her for, sweetheart,' Dermot said, nodding upstairs without taking his eyes off his phone.

'Oh God, what time is it? Is she up?' Esme kissed Charlie and gathered up his dirty clothes. Sometimes having an au pair was like having a fourth child in the house. Fifth if you counted Dermot. On her way to wake Kassia, Esme dropped the damp jeans in Dermot's lap. 'There's a clean hoodie and combats on the maiden. He can just wear the same T-shirt.'

'Daddy,' she heard Paddy say as she left the kitchen, 'Mummy said *Fuck*.'

The hall was cushioned by winter darkness. It was still night beyond the glass panel in the front door. The clock chimed in Esme's ear. She took a deep breath and shouted up the stairs. 'Kassia, it's eight thirty. Time to get moving.'

'Mummy—' Paddy said, when Esme was back in the kitchen trying to rub the jam off his sleeve with a decomposing sponge.

'Pads, I haven't got time for this. Eat up.'

'But Mummy . . .' Paddy was swinging his legs, kicking his stockinged feet against the underside of the table, making his plate clatter with every thump. In the living room, the television was blaring.

'Paddy, please.' Esme's head was starting to throb. 'What's Frankie doing?' Her oldest son lived by his own rules.

'He's ready. He's watching the news,' Dermot said. He pulled the zip on Charlie's sweatshirt all the way up and blew a raspberry under his chin. Charlie giggled and toddled out of the kitchen in his clean clothes.

'Keep an eye on him, Dermot. You know what he's like on the stairs,' Esme said, putting the jam back in the fridge and spotting the remains of last night's takeaway in their foil carton.

Paddy gulped down what was left in his mouth and climbed down from the table. 'Finished.'

'Right. Shoes, coat, action.' She patted his backside, driving him out of the kitchen, and then picked up his dirty plate and added it to the pile beside the sink. 'We need to get the dishwasher fixed, Dermot,' she said. 'Look at the state of my hands.' She held up her raw, cracked palms to show him.

'I can borrow you some baby cream.' Kassia was standing in the doorway with Charlie in her arms, her pale skin shimmering under the kitchen spotlights, her dark hair almost gold where the light struck it. She was wearing a pair of Dermot's pyjama bottoms and a dove-grey camisole, and the pyjamas sat low on her hips, exposing a ribbon of teenage belly. Her toned young body, her mane of thick black hair, her high spirits that changed with a flick to a teenage strop – everything about her – reminded Esme of an unbroken filly. Beautiful, spoilt and unpredictable. Next to her, Esme felt ready for the glue factory.

'It is the very best thing for ugly skin.'

The cotton of the camisole was clinging to Kassia's breasts. She wasn't wearing a bra, that much was obvious. Esme knew she ought to have a word with her, tell her it wasn't suitable to go about like that in front of the boys, but she didn't want to plant the idea in Kassia's head that she was at all worried by what Dermot might see.

'Lend, you mean lend,' Esme said instead, wondering why she was correcting the girl on her grammar rather than her morals. The baby lotion was hers, after all. Not Kassia's.

'Yeah, whatever,' Kassia said, beaming. 'Good morning, Mr Cavanagh. Dermot. I lend your pyjamas this morning. I find them upstairs. You do not mind, no?'

'Oh, yeah, morning.'

Esme took Charlie from Kassia's arms. It was a comfort to know that when it came to borrowing or lending husbands, she could be reassured that Kassia was on a hiding to nowhere. Dermot was oblivious, far too involved in the games on his phone to pay attention to the ones Kassia was playing.

Unperturbed, Kassia headed into the kitchen and opened the fridge. The light washed her face in its wedge of white. She took out the milk and drank straight from the carton. 'I find Charlie on the stairs. This is very dangerous,' she said, wiping her mouth with the back of her hand.

'Yes, well, Dermot was meant to be watching him.' Esme pulled her son in close and shoogled him gently in her arms, dabbing kisses on his temple so wisps of his blond hair tickled her nose and his baby skin cooled her face.

Kassia replaced the milk and investigated the fridge for something to eat. She resurfaced with the takeaway carton of curry.

'You can't have curry for breakfast,' Esme said, taking the carton off her and putting it back in the fridge, telling herself she was doing it because she had a responsibility towards the girl's well-being, and not because she had her eye on it for her own lunch.

Kassia shrugged. 'Charlie tells me this morning his brother helps him drink his milk and eat his chocopops.'

For someone who didn't have English as their first language, Esme considered it nothing less than a small miracle that Kassia was able to translate Charlie's chuckles and gurgles into something comprehensible. The majority of the time, the rest of the family relied on Paddy to interpret. Though heaven knew how much of what Paddy told them was anywhere close to what Charlie intended to say.

'And look, he saves some for lunch.' Kassia tickled Charlie under the chin where two soggy Chocolate Crispies were seeking refuge. He gave her a big, toothy grin and sucked the globs off her finger. Esme felt like she'd been shot with a bolt gun.

While this exchange was taking place, Paddy had plonked himself down on the bottom stair in the darkened hallway and was busy pulling his school shoes on to the wrong feet. Next to him, Dermot was leaning against the banister, still playing on his phone. Overseeing, he would probably call it.

'Everyone's late, Kassia,' Esme said, her voice on an edge between hysteria and frustration. 'You need to get dressed and take the boys to school.'

'Today, this is not possible.'

Paddy paused, ears flapping.

'What do you mean, not possible?' Esme set Charlie down.

'No can do, Mrs Dr Blythe. I am as sick as a dog.'

'What's wrong?'

'I am puking during all the night. And now, I have explosions in my head. Bang, bang.'

'You're not sick, Kassia. You've got a hangover. I thought you and Anna were only going for coffee last night.'

Kassia laughed. 'The manager of the coffee place he fancies me. He wants that I work there. He takes me to a nightclub as bribe. I tell him, no, I have proper job with responsibilities.' She switched on the hall light and crouched down in front of Paddy. 'That is right, no, kiddies?' Paddy put his foot in Kassia's lap and while she sorted his shoes, Charlie tried to scale her back. In the mayhem, a camisole strap slipped from her shoulder.

'Number two foot, please.'

'Kaka cool,' Charlie said.

'Are you taking us to school today, Kassy?' Paddy asked.

On the way to fetch Frankie from the living room, Esme squeezed past Dermot. As she passed, she stole a glimpse of the girl's breast – the breast that was on display for her husband. Skin as pale as elderflower. A rose-hip blush to her nipple. It was exquisite.

'Perhaps we will not bother with school today. Perhaps we will skive. We can watch daytime TV. It is good for my English. *Let's make a paternity test.*' Kassia winked at Paddy and pulled the strap back on her shoulder.

'Okay, enough,' Esme snapped. 'I've had enough.' Right from day one, Kassia had thought it hilarious to insinuate that Charlie wasn't Dermot's – *he is golden boy, not like the dark husband* – but the joke had never been funny. 'Dermot, watch Charlie. Kassia, go and get dressed. Quickly. It's nearly quarter to. They are going to be late. Again.'

In the living room, Frankie was sitting on the sofa, his dark hair blow-dried across his face and plastered with gel, and the flicker of the television screen playing across his sullen face. Esme turned the TV off and signalled him to move. In silence, he followed her into the hall and took his headphones out of the carrier bag he was using for school since he'd lost the rucksack Esme had bought him at the beginning of term. Deliberately, he dangled them around his neck. They were a statement, Esme knew. They weren't connected to anything. Because she had refused to buy him a phone of high enough spec to meet his exacting require-ments, Frankie had refused to have any phone at all. On the upside, it meant Esme saved a bit of money. The downside, though, was that it left Frankie to tunnel even deeper into his own world, even further from her. She was desperate to find her eleven-year-old funny, to embrace his pummelling silence as proof he still cared enough to want to hurt her, but she was finding it hard. He made her feel like shit.

'You'll have to drop Charlie off,' Esme said to Dermot. 'I've got a clinic in fifteen minutes.'

'No can do, Mrs Dr Blythe.'

'You're so not funny,' she said.

'No, really. Implant at nine fifteen.' He gave her a lop-sided grin.

Esme rubbed her temples to gain control over the dread that was gripping her. A dread entangled with the panic that came with constantly being late. A dread that gripped her every morning and threatened that one day she might not make it through the front door. 'Right, I'll go now with Charlie. Kassia can sort out the other two. You'll need to wait for her, though. Make sure she really does take them.'

'What about our stuff?' Frankie said.

'What stuff?' Esme said.

'For the collection.'

'Frankie. What collection?'

'For charity. Paddy was supposed to tell you.' He turned to his brother. 'Imbecile.'

'Frankie!' The rifle flash of anger left an after-burn of nausea when Esme realised how much she'd wanted to slap her oldest son.

'I'm not an imbecile. Daddy, Frankie called me an imbecile.'

'Yes, I heard.' Dermot laughed.

'It's not funny,' Paddy whined. 'I tried to tell Mummy but she wouldn't listen.' His voice was cracking. Tears were just a wrong word away. Behind her, Esme heard Kassia come down the stairs. The footsteps stopped. She must have paused to listen. Esme crouched down in front of the two boys and summoned all the moderation she could muster.

'What do you need for the charity collection?'

'Food for the homeless,' Frankie said.

'Okay. No problem. Take something each from the cupboard. A tin of beans or a bag of pasta.' That's if there were any. As with the washing-up, it was Kassia's job to do the supermarket shopping.

Daylight was stealing through the stained glass in the front door, casting translucent patches of red and green across the carpet, signalling to Esme that it was time to leave. She stood up and put on her coat. Too late now to get her leftovers lunch.

'Right, Charlie and I are off,' she said, kissing Frankie and Paddy in turn. She nodded to Kassia and paused a moment before kissing her husband, bracing herself against the affection that could undo her. Then she picked up her handbag and her youngest son.

Once she had turned the key in the deadlock, she hesitated. 'We should talk later,' she said, her back to Dermot and Kassia. 'Things aren't really working as they are.'

When the door was open, Esme glanced round. Kassia was nodding enthusiastically. 'You are extremely true,' she said. 'I prefer to do less skivvying. I like to play more with the boys and practise my English.'

Whichever way it went, Esme realised, the conversation would be nearly impossible. Dermot was adamant she should have help, that it was the only way to manage both work and home, but Kassia was hardly what she'd class as help. But she couldn't say so. She didn't want to be reminded how difficult she was finding things.

In the kitchen, Frankie was shouting at his brother. 'Eff off,' Esme heard. 'I'm not taking alphabet spaghetti. I'm taking this.'

Oh God, she thought, I wonder what he's found.

Outside, the first slivers of November frost spiked her face. Dermot's BMW was safe from the cold in the garage but her old Mini was parked on the street. Esme buried her nose in Charlie's hair. Buttermilk with a trace of peach. She inhaled deeply, trying to brand the smell on her brain for later. Protection against her patients' calamitous lives. When they were both strapped in, she started the engine. The Mini coughed in the cold. She slid it into gear. It shuddered and pulled away.

4

Sick Bacchus

Halfway through her end-of-exam night out with her class-mates, Lizzi excused herself, claiming exam fatigue and nerves and prep to do for the clinical placement that was starting the next day. Her excuse wasn't entirely fabricated, but the reality was more that she was desperate to see Finn. Earlier she messaged him to see if he'd meet up with her crowd but wasn't at all surprised when he declined. Aside from the fact he claimed he owed Rob a drink, these days Finn wasn't exactly into increasing his social circle. On more than one occasion in the last couple of months, Lizzi had been tempted to say that if he expended half the amount of effort on his work as he did on avoiding her friends, his portfolio would be bursting at the seams.

Once she'd successfully negotiated the hazard of the dart-board hanging on the back of the pub door without losing an eye (thanks, she decided, to her lucky beads which appar-ently worked their magic on more than just exams), Lizzi skirted the crowd to look for Finn. As usual, the bar was packed with dedicated mid-week regulars caught up in ani-mated discussions about the state of the Union and the football scores. Rob was easy to spot, head and shoulders above all the other customers, but all she could see of Finn was his waving hands. Although Finn had his back to her, Rob's indulgent expression told Lizzi that Finn was engaged in another of his elaborate theses. Like the one that had come up a few weeks ago in a late night discussion where Finn had forced them to choose a rodent to be reincarnated as. Finn had chosen a rat. Lizzi had gone for a guinea pig because of their cute teeth (realising too late the symbolism of her decision). Rob's unlikely preference had been a gerbil, reckoning they had the most sex, until Finn pointed out that they were often forced to eat their own abundant offspring when resources were poor and overpopulation a threat, but finally both Rob and he decided there were, on balance, worse things to eat than baby gerbils.

Finn had Rob's undivided attention so Rob didn't notice the first time Lizzi waved. She pushed into the mass of warm bodies and waved a couple more times until eventually Rob spotted her and signalled to ask if she wanted a drink. She shook her head, figuring that at that stage of the evening to make her way across the swirling Axminster without having an enthusiastic pint spilt on her was definitely pushing her luck, beads or no beads. Smiling, she tapped her watch and put her hands under her head as a pillow. It was late. She wanted to go home. Rob gave her an exaggerated look of disappointment and startled Finn from his oration by belting him on his shoulder and making his pint slop over the top of its glass. Together, they came over to join her – the masses parting willingly for Rob while Finn followed in the slipstream whingeing as much about his spilt drink as about the walloping he'd received.

'Hey, babe.' Finn kissed Lizzi and pulled up his sleeve. 'What do you think?' Spidery left-handed letters inched up his forearm. *Segui il tuo corso e lascia dir le genti.* The tattoo was exactly as he'd told her. Discussions about the text had been going on at her house for the last few days, predominantly while she'd been trying to study. In Lizzi's opinion, there was a fundamental problem with the philosophy Finn had chosen. If you really were going to go your own way and not give a monkey's, you either had to be emotionally retarded or monumentally self-assured and, at the moment, she wouldn't particularly say Finn was either.

'I can't believe you let him do it,' she said to Rob, absent-mindedly fingering her beads. The erratic font was not one of Rob's calligraphy scripts. Finn had done the template himself so no one could copy.

Rob kissed Lizzi on the cheek. 'What the daft cunt doesnae realise is that while he may like to indulge his amateur doodlings, it is my reputation in the steakhouse.'

Finn ignored Rob's comment. 'Good news and good news. The Bingo photies were a success and this clown here has persuaded his bruv to give me space in the church hall. All I have to do is a bit of refurb here and there, and the odd sermonising session on a Sunday when Jed wants to put his feet up. Not bad, eh?'

Lizzi smiled. He was the brightest she'd seen him since he'd told her how he'd let the Art School know exactly where they could stick their studio space (although she doubted the conversation had actually unfolded with the level of profanity Finn had described). 'That's fab. Totally.' She turned to Rob. 'Did he say thanks?'

'What do you think?' Rob said. 'How did it go, by the way?'

'Not too bad,' she said, pretending to glower at Finn. 'Thanks for asking.'

'Oh, aye. Lucky beads. Your exam. How was it?'

'Bin him, Lizzi,' Rob said. 'Even I'd make better boyfriend material.'

'Fuck off, you chunky cunt.'

Lizzi laughed. 'Right, boys, much as I'd like to hang out, I don't want to get in the way of your love-in. The last bus is in five and this girl will be on it.'

'Give me a sec to grab my stuff and I'll see you to the bus,' Finn said, downing the last two-thirds of his pint in a oner and squeezing back into the crowd.

'He seems better,' Lizzi said.

'Aye, tonight he does.' There wasn't time to say more.

Rob stayed on for last orders with a guy he knew who worked at the funeral director's round the corner from his shop, and Lizzi and Finn left together. Outside, the rain was coming down steadily. Finn unlocked his bike from the railings and walked Lizzi to the bus shelter. While she sat squinting through the scratched Perspex to check for the bus, Finn did static wheelies on his bike using the give way sign at the bottom of Dougal Street as a prop.

'Look at this. Trick cyclist,' he said, laughing at his own joke.

'Hilarious.'

Finn let go of the signpost and stood on his pedals so he was balanced on the bike without moving. 'And this. Demands skill and agility. Which I have in shedloads, in case you hadn't noticed.'

'I'd noticed,' Lizzi said lightly.

'Good,' Finn said, setting off to do laps of the bus shelter. For a while, Lizzi watched him cycle through the rain until her attention was caught by a man staggering out of the Vaults. Illuminated by the beam of light from the open doorway, the man looked pale and sickly and had no protection from the weather. A shiver of sympathy ran through her. The rain had plastered his thin hair to his balding head and his shirt tails were hanging out between old-fashioned braces. For a couple of unsteady paces, he meandered near the pub door until eventually he veered off in the direction of Partick Cross.

The rain was heavy now. Finn would be getting soaked, she realised, peering into the street to look for him. Over the road, the drunk had stopped to pee in a tenement close between the bookie's and the rent-to-own electrical shop. She looked away.

'What a shame,' Lizzi said to Finn, once he had completed his lap. By now, the man had finished and was gazing around vacantly, disorientated by the jeers from a huddle of smokers who had braved the rain to light up.

Finn steadied himself against the bus shelter. Through the rain, they watched the man shuffle a few steps using the window of the electrical shop for support. For a moment, the smokers broke their huddle to glance at him too, their cigarette tips glowing like the standby lights on the high-definition TVs in the window display. The gaudy orange light from the shop sign gave the man's skin a jaundiced tinge.

'Shit, it's Mo. Maurice. My neighbour,' Finn said, dropping his bike at Lizzi's feet.

Dumbarton Road was thick with closing-time traffic. Finn hovered on the kerb, keeping his eyes fixed on the man he'd called Mo, watching him totter and slide down the shop window. Lizzi cringed for the poor guy. The smokers were ignoring him now, intent on keeping their cigarettes dry, resolutely committed to their habit despite the downpour.

Eventually, the traffic thinned and Finn dodged between the oncoming cars. On the other side of the street, Maurice was on his knees, hands grazing the pavement either side of him, barely managing to keep upright. The rain was falling in columns, bouncing off the tarmac in thick fingers. Finn shouted to Lizzi but his words were distorted by the downpour. She wheeled his bike across the road, watching Maurice wipe rain from his face with the back of his wrist. Finn ran the last few steps just as Maurice lost his equilibrium and rolled into a puddle on the pavement.

Lizzi leant the bike against the shopfront. 'He's not moving,' Finn shouted against the weather. His voice was agitated, panicky and he was prodding Maurice to rouse him. The bus passed opposite, its fat tyres swishing through the flooded street, windscreen wipers chuntering at full speed. It veered towards the bus stop but sped away when there was no one waiting. Finn tried patting his friend's face to bring him round, calling him Mo, Maurice, big man, and pleading with him to wake up. Lizzi crouched beside them. Maurice's eyes were shut and his arms were out in a cross as if he was playing dead. The rain had soaked through his thin shirt and his flies were undone.

'Sir, sir,' she said, shaking Maurice's shoulder gently. A steady patter of drops from the gutter of the tenement was dripping on her neck and down the back of her parka. She shook him a bit harder. It was difficult to tell if he was breathing. All around, swirls of wind were lashing the buildings. She felt for a pulse in his neck. Her wet hair was hanging in her eyes, catching at the angle of her mouth, sticking to her cheeks. 'Oi, mister,' she said more loudly.

Maurice woke with a start. 'What the . . . Are you trying to strangle me, hen?' Bewildered, he struggled to prop himself up on his elbows.

'Sorry,' Lizzi said. 'Just checking you were still alive.'

He looked at her, watery-eyed and shivering. 'Diabetic,' he said, collapsing back on to the pavement. 'Must be having a wee hypo.' From his prone position, he introduced himself. 'Maurice O'Donnell. Of O'Donnell and Son. Pleased to meet you, pet.'

Lizzi sat back on her heels, squeezed her dripping hair into a ponytail and flicked the water on to the pavement. The reek of alcohol was overpowering, but for the moment she decided to give him the benefit of the doubt regarding the diabetes.

'Come on,' she said. 'Let's sit you up for starters.'

'Mo, you bumshite,' Finn said. 'You had me scared out my wits there.' He was laughing but his laughter was flecked with fear.

'Finn, help us out here.'

Together, they hauled Maurice to a sitting position and propped him against the wall. The downpour was easing and the building provided a degree of shelter by virtue of its height.

Lizzi went to find something to eat. The only place that was open was the chippy next to the bus shelter over the road. A neon sign – *The Last Supper* – was fizzing in the window and, inside, a pale lad in a greasy overall was piling crisp packets into the wire baskets beside the counter, humming along to a tinny radio while his spotty skin was irradiated by the ultraviolet bulbs in the electric fly trap.

'We're frying a new batch,' he said when he spotted Lizzi. 'It'll be five minutes.'

The price list was hanging off-centre behind him. Plastic letters, yellowed with age, were stuck into a black panel gridded with holes. Some of the letters had fallen out and were dangling by their roots like loose teeth or were missing altogether.

'I'm not in for hips,' she said, reading the disfigured sign. Water dripped from her coat on to the floor tiles.

The boy gaped at her.

'Sorry,' she said, smiling and smearing the puddle with the sole of her boot. 'Hips. Your sign.'

Under his spots, the boy turned crimson.

'Forget it. I'll just take a Mars Bar.'

He didn't move.

'Thanks.' She put the money on the counter. She was practically out the door before she heard his reply.

'No worries,' he squeaked.

Lizzi slipped the chocolate in her coat pocket and hurried back across the road in the dying rain. The pub was locked up now and the smokers were gone. Finn was squatting beside Maurice, his lanky figure intermittently silhouetted in the sporadic flash of headlights. As she approached, Finn shoved something into Maurice's hand.

'Take it, pal. Honest. It's no big deal.'

'Finjay, son, you're a Good Samaritan. A total saint. Hey, doll,' Maurice said to Lizzi, 'your lad's a pure hero.' A twenty pound note was crushed in his fist.

Lizzi raised an eyebrow.

'Maurice lives next door to me,' Finn said. 'He could do with a taxi home.'

'I'd better find the missus first,' Maurice said. 'She's at the Bingo.'

'It's well finished, pal.'

'Nah, Finjay. She said she'd come for me.'

'Mo, the Bingo finished at nine. I was with her. Remember. She took the bus.'

'Ach, man. You're havering. She wouldna've left without me.'

Finn looked over to catch Lizzi's eye, asking for guidance, unsure how much to push the matter. 'Do you reckon you can make it home in one piece, pal?'

'I should get going, Finn,' Lizzi said. 'It's late.'

Finn helped Maurice to his feet. 'Give me two secs to flag a taxi.'

'I tell you what, Finjay. You can get up the road with me.'
Finn looked at Lizzi. She shrugged.

'It's okay, Mo,' he said. 'I need to see Lizzi back to hers first.'

Lizzi shoved her hands in her pockets. He'd made it sound like an obligation. Her fingers brushed the wrapper of the chocolate bar. When she offered it over, Maurice's clammy fingers closed around hers. She flinched. The night was getting colder. The fog was coming in.

Because she'd missed the last bus and they had no cash left between them for a taxi, Finn ended up giving Lizzi a backie the three miles through the deserted streets to Knightswood. He dropped her at the door down the side of her building. Hers was an upstairs flat, one of four in the block – old council houses known to everyone but Finn as cottage flats. He'd teased her when she'd first used the term. Told her that was how the housing association was managing to screw so much rent out of her, by making her believe the place was something it wasn't. But he was wrong. This had been her home for her entire life.

Lizzi asked him if he wanted to come in. He said no, that he'd head off and let her get some rest. A lurch of disappointment made her head spin.

'Do you not want to warm up a bit before you hit the road?' She spoke with her beads in her mouth, chewing on the necklace like a little girl, using all her effort not to plead.

Finn shrugged non-committally and followed her up the stairs. Once inside, Lizzi put the kettle on and asked if Finn wanted to dry his clothes on the radiator or take a shower.

'Trying to get me naked?'

Lizzi blushed from being caught out. She was mad at herself.

'Get over yourself, mister.'

But Finn was grinning, teasing her. Looking at her in that way of his, like he could see beneath her layers, like he was examining every square centimetre of her skin and could see how he made her body react in ways she didn't always want it to. Measuring her, exposing her, playing with her, wanting her. It thrilled her and disturbed her, this vulnerability, this awareness of being so physically desired.

'See you in there,' he said, and disappeared off to the bathroom.

She waited until the kettle had boiled to join him. By that time, Finn was already in the shower. He was leaning back with his eyes shut, his head tipped under the shower and a stream of water running over his face, his chest, his abdomen. His body looked like it had been chiselled from stone, lean, sinewy, not an ounce of fat to spare. Lizzi undressed slowly.

Finn opened one eye. 'Coming in?'

'No,' she said.

He laughed and unhooked the shower head and aimed it at her, soaking the floor and the bathmat in the process. The warm water drizzled over Lizzi's breasts and tummy and the droplets trickled down her skin. A thousand delicate fingers caressing her nipples, settling on her pubis, slipping between her thighs.

Finn hooked the shower back on to its holder and flicked his hair out of his face. Every cell of Lizzi's body was prickling to be touched by him. She climbed into the bath. They kissed under the spray of water, his tongue flicking round her mouth, her teeth nipping his lower lip. Before she could get closer, he put his hands on her shoulder and inched her away, arm's length from him. He was staring at her, doing that thing he did, silently turning her inside out. She wanted to do the same to him. To incapacitate him with desire.

'Wait,' she whispered, glancing behind her to see how much space she had in the narrow bath. She lowered herself to her knees and dabbed kisses at the angle of his groin, glancing upwards to see his reaction. Her eyes were blinking against the spray but Finn's head was tipped back so she couldn't see his face. Instead she saw herself, kneeling before her man, naked and sensuous. She was as turned on by the image of herself as the reality. With a feather touch, she circled his foreskin with her tongue. Licked the tip. Went further. The water raining on the back of her neck was turning tepid.

At some point, Finn leant down and kissed her, guided her so she was standing again. Her mouth tasted faintly of zinc and salt. He cupped his hand under her breast, let the water pool in his palm, spill down her body. It felt like she was standing on a cliff edge, the sea swirling below. Lizzi had never wanted someone so badly. Not just inside her, but completely. To have him, know him, completely. She kissed the top of his shoulder, the hollow above his collarbone, the base of his throat. The water was running cold. Finn put one hand around her waist, jammed the other up against the tiled wall. She lifted a foot on to the edge of the tub and wedged it against the tiles. Finn rammed her so hard her foot slipped. She giggled, scrabbled to regain her balance, knocked her shampoo bottle into the bath. He looked over her shoulder to see what it was and gave a half-laugh. She kissed him through the water running down her face. The image of Rob standing in the shadows watching them popped into her head. She dug her fingers into the muscles of Finn's back. She was grinning, showing off. Finn's eyes were tightly shut, his face contorted. They were both panting. Lizzi threw her head back, her breasts exposed, her nipples craving his tongue. In her head, Rob was filming them. She wanted to laugh. Wanted to watch. She was close. Really close. The water was freezing. Finn lowered his head to her breast and put his teeth around her nipple. Something inside her gave way. She moaned and buried her face into the crook of his neck. Her brain was being compressed in a vice, her eyes squeezed through a mangle. Finn groaned and the convulsions spread right through her.

'You can't half do some amazing tricks, missus,' Finn said, when he finally got his breath back.

5

Jupiter, Neptune and Pluto

By the time Finn had been installed in his new studio in the church hall for a fortnight, the novelty of helping out around the place had more than worn off. Not that he wasn't adept with a drill or a screwdriver, he would hasten to add. It was simply that the refurb felt far too much like DIY, and he'd always heard the expression as a question. In his opinion, it ranked alongside gardening as a way not to pass your time. As an act of charity, he'd decided to let Maurice help out, reckoning that it would be good for the man's self-esteem even if it wasn't good for his pocket.

So, working on the principle that if they got off to an early start, they'd get their obligations out of the way and he could get on with the Bingo pictures, Finn arranged to meet Maurice at daybreak. That particular morning, the plan was to start on the garden and move on to the inside job to be finished by lunchtime. It was apparent, however, that Maurice was a little indisposed at this time of a morning. An indisposition, Finn realised, that he should have accounted for.

Indisposition accounted for or not, Finn was impatient to get on with his paintings, so despite his own long-held aversion to early mornings (recently compounded by a run of restless nights which he couldn't even blame on the irritating plopping noise that Lizzi made with her sleeping lips as he'd been camping out alone at his own place since she'd started her clinical placement because she was up for work at the crack of) he was already hard at it, raking damp leaves and shovelling them on to a hissing bonfire. He'd set the bonfire beside the overgrown borders and, under the choking smoke, he could smell clay and slugs in the mulchy soil. Maurice, meanwhile, was sitting on the garden bench, unopened can of Irn-Bru balanced on the armrest at his elbow, eating a breakfast roll, and tossing helpful comments in Finn's direction while simultaneously straining his eyes to study the sports pages. It surprised Finn to discover that there were in fact some occasions when Maurice was capable of multitasking.

'You'll kill it, Finjay,' Maurice said, without taking his eyes from the betting odds. 'You're smothering the life out of it.'

Finn stopped and leant on his shovel. 'And you're the expert, is that what you're telling me?'

'Aye,' Maurice said. 'Pretty handy at the auld fire-setting, so I am. A wee touch of accelerant, plenty of air and Bob's your uncle.' He turned a couple of pages of the paper. 'That's your Boys' Brigade training for you. All those lessons in Christian manliness.'

'Boys' Brigade? I thought you were a Tim.'

'Aye, I liked the marching, but. Nothing in the rule book to say it was only for the Orange boys.'

'How about marching yourself over here, then,' Finn said, 'and giving us a hand?'

'I would, son,' Maurice said jovially, 'but I've got a touch of the collapsing legs for the minute.' He took a bite from his roll. Yolk dribbled between his fingers and on to his wrist. 'This isnae bad, by the way. Egg and tatty scone. I'd even go so far as to say second best breakfast roll this side of the Clyde. All that's missing is a smidge of red sauce.' He licked the trickle of yolk before it reached his sleeve.

In Finn's world, egg and ketchup should never be heard together on the same breath, never mind seen together on the same slice of bread, but when it came to a fried breakfast Maurice considered himself a connoisseur. He'd said as much to Finn on more than one occasion. The mornings after the nights he didn't make it home from the Vaults – nights caught short for his bus fare home, nights spent on the very bench he was parked on just now or another as near as identical, nights exactly like the one Finn had spared him from just the other week – on those mornings, Maurice would pop down to the chippy for his breakfast if his nephew was on the early shift and cadge a pound or two off the boy for the bus back up to Maryhill. Which is where Finn would usually bump into him as he lugged his bike down the fire stairs and Maurice loitered in the stairwell waiting for Leanne to leave for work. *She's gonnae kill you, pal*, Finn would say as a greeting. And Maurice would grimace in reply, *Son, you dinnae know the half of it.*

'Sure I cannae tempt you?' Maurice held out what was left of his roll to Finn. Strings of saliva stretched between the layers of bread and teeth marks cut through the coagulated egg. 'I could have a word with young Michael, if you like. Put in a regular order. You could do with feeding up. There's about as much to you as a slice of streaky bacon.'

'Nah, you're okay,' Finn said. It wasn't the soggy dough stuck between Maurice's grey teeth that was curbing Finn's appetite. He was off his food full stop. An ongoing affliction he had put down to the upheaval of moving from the Art School. Wearily, he piled the last heap of leaves on to the fire. The morning light was making his eyes throb, his brain pound. Sensations heightened by the concrete-hard sky and the pervading reek of stale egg.

'Thanks for your help, Mo, by the way.'

Maurice shifted on the bench, lifted his left buttock half an inch, and let out a bubbling fart. 'Always a pleasure, son.'

To get his own back, Finn grabbed the paper off Maurice and dramatically cleared his throat. The paper was open at the death notices. Maurice collected rhyming couplets for Leanne's poetry. He stopped chewing to listen.

'For Kev from your loving wife Dinah. *You were the love of my life, my heart, my rock, but what I'll miss most is your stupendous cock.*'

Maurice spluttered, spitting chewed potato and cold egg white into his lap. 'Honest?'

Finn rolled his eyes and handed him back the *Gazette*. 'Are you done? I want to get on.'

'Give me half a sec to finish up, let my breakfast settle. My sugar levels are all over the spot. You know what I'm like with the diabetes.'

While he waited, Finn prodded the embers with a broken stick. It was more than diabetes that had Maurice's blood sugar seesawing, he knew that much, but you couldn't judge the man for liking his drink. There was a seam of addiction running below the skin of most folk, if you looked for it. Take himself, for instance. Not that he'd ever been addicted, but you could see how it could easily have gone that way. His thing had been plant-based recreationals. For a while, he'd had quite a production going in his flat. The high electricity bills had been worth the savings he'd made by cutting out the middle men, but he'd ditched the farm and the habit to please Lizzi, and his gesture of abstention had paid in dividends when it came to her showing her appreciation elsewhere.

Alcohol had its own merits, as Maurice would be the first to attest, dulling as it did the pain of creaking joints and middle-aged failure, of social isolation and society's back-turning, and it was only to be expected that some people found the more therapeutic aspects of the bottle so pleasing. This was one subject area where Lizzi and Finn disagreed. She reckoned there was more to dependence than just the medicinal benefits of a dram or two, because some folk managed without the crutches of drugs or alcohol, prescription meds or hand-holding, but the simple fact was those were the ones who hadn't had the stuffing squeezed out of them by their ridiculously lousy life circumstances. Quite literally in Maurice's case if the look of him this morning was anything to go by. Absent-mindedly, Finn flattened a snail shell under his foot. If you asked him, addiction wasn't an illness. It was a symptom – a totally fucking understandable symptom like those of half the other sad fucks who ended up on the psychiatrist's couch. Depression, anxiety, self-harm? Symptoms of the shite life threw at you. Finn didn't believe in mental illness. It was life that was mental, not the poor buggers who suffered from it. He gave the embers another prod, pleased with his insight. He must remember to tell Lizzi.

A flurry of sparks flitted from the choking heap. One danced upwards on the smoke plume. 'Whoah. A fairy,' Finn said.

Maurice practically choked on the remains of his roll. 'Come again?'

'That's what my old man used to say. The sparks. Garden fairies. Keeping the plants alive.'

'Thought you were referring to my physical incapacities.' Maurice chuckled and pulled a grease-stained rag from his pocket to flick the muck off his boiler suit. 'Fairy. What are you like? Or rather, what is your faither like?' He positioned the fraying cloth over his finger and used it to excavate his nostril. After a brief inspection of the pickings, he stuck the cloth back in his pocket.

'Finished?'

Maurice nodded. 'Near enough. A wee quick skoosh of my drink.' He laid the last bite of his roll on the bench using the sports pages as a napkin and tweaked the ring pull on the can, two times, three times. Finn heard dry pecks of aluminium against aluminium until eventually there was a hiss of fizz.

'Jesus Johnny, that hit the spot,' Maurice said, after he'd downed half the can in a single gulp.

'I thought you weren't supposed to take sugary stuff.'

'Och, one wee can of ginger willnae do any harm. Dare say, it'll do me some benefit. Been feeling a touch on the poorly side lately.'

'A touch?' Finn said. 'If you don't mind me saying, pal, you look absolutely fucking awful.'

Maurice laughed. A gust of wind rattled the bare branches of the horse chestnut above them and the thick smoke from the bonfire twisted towards them in the breeze. Maurice started coughing. Finn could see the smoke scratching Maurice's windpipe, winding through his lungs, making his scarred airways clamp shut, forcing him to wheeze and choke and slaver. His whole body shuddered with the effort to catch his breath.

Once the spasm was over, Maurice spat, wiped his mouth with the back of his hand and smoothed wisps of his thin hair back over his crown. 'Should never've stopped smoking,' he said. 'Never had a day's complaint until I gave up those blinking cancer sticks.'

Finn looked at the liver spots, the tuberous nose, the tinge of jaundice round his friend's gills. 'Don't give up the bev, then, Mo. You'll end up with cirrhosis,' and, with a tenderness he wasn't aware of, held out his hand to help Maurice to his feet.

They began the work inside by tackling the heating system. While Maurice loosened the radiator in the back corridor – his anorak spread out to cushion his knees while he worked – Finn leant against the wall and read the *Gazette*. Maurice had been at it for about ten minutes when Finn tapped the cast iron with his knuckle. It gave a musical clang. 'What's occurring down there?'

Maurice unfastened the adjustable spanner from the radiator bolt and hooked his pinkie through the hole at the end of the handle. The metal jaws creaked on the steel thread as he swung it on his finger. Finn could taste each rusty creak.

'Well?' He turned the page of the *Gazette* and snapped the paper straight.

'Quite honestly, son, I'm of the opinion we'd be better off installing a whole new system rather than trying to coax life back into this one. Dodgy valves, years of crud blocking the circulation, and a pump that's about to give up the ghost. We should put the thing out its misery. Rip it out and sell the parts for scrap.'

'That's not going to happen, big man,' Finn said, glancing down. 'You heard the priest. The church is skint. Can you not just spray the joint with a bit of WD40 or something?' From what Finn knew of these things, WD40 was the plumber's equivalent of the football physio's magic sponge.

Maurice murmured something Finn didn't bother to listen to and shifted on his knees.

The paper was bursting with news of no interest. A story about a local primary school charity collection, another about students being hassled by the addict community that hung out near the uni. Nothing that piqued Finn's interest. The next page, however, more than piqued him. It smashed him in the teeth and proceeded to kick his brains out, more or less. Grinning at him from between the weather forecast and an advert for drink driving by Strathclyde Police was Rob.

Once Finn had recovered enough to swear out loud, he made sure he did so.

'For fuck's sake.' He waved the paper in front of Maurice's face. 'The Robster's got himself in the *Gazette*. Unbelievable. He never even told us. Scheming toerag.'

'Finjay, lad, I'm trying to get a job done here.' Maurice pushed the paper away and rummaged in the toolbox.

'It's a joke,' Finn said. 'It has to be. *This year it isn't only a new outfit you need to think about for the office party. With only a few weeks to go before the festivities, local businessman Rob Stevenson is preparing for a bumper Christmas.* Blah blah *customers looking for something special* blah.' The sycophantic tone was bloating Finn's gut in a most unpleasant way. He burped to relieve the pressure.

Meantime, Maurice had scattered the entire contents of the toolbox around the peripheries of his anorak in the hunt for the WD40. It was on the bottom layer next to an electric circuit detector missing the batteries and a shrivelled tube of wood glue.

Finn waved the newspaper in Maurice's face again. 'Look.'

'Finjay, gie's a chance,' Maurice said, picking at the edge of a piece of tape that was holding the red applicator straw to the side of the can.

Impatiently, Finn shoved the paper under his arm and

snatched the canister. He shook it viciously and the ball-bearing rattled. He slipped the applicator from its sticky belt and positioned it ready to use.

'Will I?'

'Gie it here, son,' Maurice said. 'It isnae my nature to bail on a job.'

Maurice sprayed the bolt with what was left of the WD40. A cloud of hydrocarbon mist filled the corridor, making a wet cough rattle in his lungs. Finn saw a thick gob of phlegm, as lumpy as scrambled egg, settle on Maurice's tonsils. He swallowed his own inclination to boak and carried on reading.

'Listen to this right. *Each tattoo is a work of art in its own right, says Rob.* Jesus Effing Christ. Get over yourself, you pumped-up wee nyaff.'

Maurice hauled himself to his feet and took the *Gazette* from Finn. He squinted at the page. 'You know what? It never ceases to amaze me that Robin and Gerrard are related.'

'Sharp as a sharp thing, as per, Mo.'

'What's up with you?'

'Art. He says it's art. Get tae fuck. It's pigeon shit, that's what it is.' Finn actually couldn't credit that Rob would be so conceited as to class his work in the same league as Finn's own. It was a fucking outrage. Although what Finn didn't want to face was the equally disturbing idea that behind the studio door his own shit paintings were laughing at him.

'Don't agitate yourself, son,' Maurice said. 'No ahbody has the same ideas about things like that. And just because you're no in the paper yet doesnae mean your pics are nae use.'

'Too fucking right, it doesn't.' Finn snatched the *Gazette* and flung it down the corridor. 'How can you even read that bollocks?' The paper skidded as far as the kitchen.

'For your information, Sunny Jim, I don't actually read the *Gazette*. I use it to wipe my arse. And I'll use you to wipe my arse if you don't gie's a hand.'

To move things along, Finn demanded that Maurice hand him over the spanner. Rather than adjust the jaws to size, he aimed it at the connector joint and whacked the bolt with the spanner head. The spanner slipped from his hand and ricocheted off the cast-iron radiator, knocking over the empty can of WD40 and leaving a dent in the outlet pipe.

'Steady on, son. These auld beasts are fragile things.'

A touch on the hysterical side now, Finn gave a weedy giggle. 'Don't diss yerself, Mo. You're no that auld.'

'No me, the—'

'Mo, Mo, Mo. You're worse than my missus.'

'Oh, I get it. Very droll.' Maurice crouched down to inspect the damaged pipe. From above, his smooth crown and wispy strands resembled Lister's skull covered with a smattering of cotton threads. In Finn's opinion, anyhow.

'Verdict?' he asked.

'A job for the flamethrower, if ever I saw one.'

'Are you sure?'

'Aye, heat it up a notch, hammer the dent out of it.'

'Would you not be better just to forget about this one?'

'Finjay, do I look like a man so easily defeated?'

Maurice sent Finn to fetch the propane from the out-house. In the garden, the embers of the bonfire were still grumbling and the odour of stale egg hung over the bench. Finn rolled himself a fag and lit it with the tip of a smouldering branch he pulled out from under the soggy leaves. He dragged slowly on his cigarette, and tossed the branch back on to the fire. For the few seconds that the branch was airborne, the tip glowed brightly and traced an arc against the shadowy trees. Nearby, a rhododendron bush rustled and the gate squeaked on its hinges. Finn glanced around half expecting to see someone, but there was no one there. He finished his cigarette and languidly rolled himself a second. The garden was suffocating. As if there wasn't enough air to go round, he thought. As if someone else was there and stealing it for themselves. He stowed the newly rolled fag in his shirt pocket and cast his eyes to the darkest corner where the garden shared a boundary with the church. Definitely no one. A couple of seconds later, he relieved his tension by kicking in the door of the outhouse.

Back inside, Finn dropped the propane bottle in front of Maurice with a clank and left him to attach the torch gun to the bottle while he picked out mud from underneath his fingernails. A lot of fiddling later and Maurice still hadn't succeeded with his task. Hysteria was fermenting in Finn's gut. He stuck his reserve cigarette between his lips.

'Gonnae gie's a light, big man,' he said, giggling and letting his fag dangle down his chin.

Maurice stopped messing with the torch. 'Och, son. Don't be so daft.'

Finn put the cigarette back in his pocket, still giggling stupidly.

'You could do with learning a thing or two,' Maurice said. 'Having a joke is all well and good, but messing with inflammables isnae the time or the place.'

Finn grinned at him. 'Apprentice me, then, Mo.'

'Aye. If you're up to it. I'm what you call a perfectionist, mind.' Maurice stood up and handed the torch to Finn. 'You can start with this.'

While Finn fitted the torch head to the propane cylinder, Maurice hung his anorak on the handle of the studio door and readied himself to guide Finn.

'Okay? Pull the trigger. The ignition should spark automatically.'

'Yes, boss.' Finn knelt down, pointed the torch upwards and pulled the trigger. The gas gushed from the nozzle and the flame took, blasting out blue and hot.

Maurice stepped back. 'Jings, sonny. Steady on.'

Finn aimed the flame at the bent pipe.

'Gently, lad. Gently. You can turn it down a notch.'

Finn adjusted the flame. Morsels of white paint blistered under the heat.

'There you go. That's what we're after.'

For a few minutes, Finn skimmed the flame over the pipe, until the paint disappeared and the pipe glowed orange. Maurice told him it needed a touch longer.

'You know what, Finjay?' Maurice said, watching Finn work. 'That's no a bad effort at all. To be honest, I wouldna've minded an apprentice like you. A fast learner and whatnot.'

For some inexplicable reason, Finn felt a surge of pride. He glanced up. A blush was creeping down Maurice's pasty cheeks. Astonished, Finn turned back to the job. In all the time he'd known him, he'd never seen Maurice embarrassed about anything. Probably because it took a level of self-respect to be embarrassed and, as far as Finn could see, most of Maurice's had gone AWOL around the time Leanne went back to work to subsidise his business.

'If you were my boy, I'd be happy to hand over the reins. Your faither must be awfie proud of you, is he no?'

There was a danger, Finn realised, what with Maurice being a bit on the soft-headed side, that he'd tip himself over with his sentimental nonsense, and who knew where that might lead. It was up to Finn to nip it in the bud. 'Aye, right,' he said carefully.

'What does that mean?'

'Nothing really,' Finn said, still skimming the flame torch. 'Total mentalist, my old man.'

Maurice tapped Finn's shoulder. 'I reckon that should do it.'

'Like we were saying earlier. Completely away with the fairies.' Finn let the flame go out.

'Heavens, Finjay. I didnae mean to speak out of turn.'

Finn turned round and grinned at him.

'Och, you nearly had me there, son,' Maurice said, taking the torch and passing Finn the hammer. Behind the relief and bleary eyes was a flurry of confusion. 'You're wicked to me, youngster. A wee devil, so you are.'

'Except this time, Mo, I wasn't actually kidding. The true definition of a headcase, my old man. Hard as anything. And mad with it.'

'I'd never've guessed it,' Maurice said, after a pause to sort out his bafflement. 'I always reckoned under the scruffy get-up and the foul language there was a laddie fae a good home.'

Although Finn knew Maurice didn't mean any harm by the words, it still rankled to hear it. Still, he didn't have to admit the man was right. 'Italian background, you see,' he said. 'Impossible to escape.' He walloped the pipe with a hammer.

'Steady on, son. Steady on.'

Finn tapped the pipe more gently. 'It wasn't only the building business he was in, if you get my meaning.'

'No, son, I don't.' Maurice was fiddling with the torch again, trying to take the head off the cylinder, but it kept sliding between his fingers.

A wit lost its razor sharpness when you had to blunt it with explanation, Finn always found. Nonetheless, on this occasion, he helped Maurice out.

'Protection racket.'

'What? Like a Mafia whatsit?'

'Exactly.'

'In Dunkeld?'

'Aye, well, if you're in the area, don't go digging under any conservatories, that's all I can say.'

Maurice's finger slipped on the propane trigger.

BOOM!

Finn's laughter was lost as the empty can of WD40 exploded.

The explosion echoed off the corridor walls. Maurice dropped the torch and shrank back from the burning can. Finn leapt out of the way, laughing so much he was practically wetting himself. Maurice shuffled back on his bum, legs flailing, trying to escape the molten aluminium, but his foot caught the propane cylinder and sent it crashing over. Finn bent down to get it, the odd squirt of laughter still escaping, but somehow he misjudged and the cylinder rolled towards the kitchen door. Fuel was leaking from the valve leaving a fuse trail along the floor. Maurice looked on in horror as the flames darted across the spilt propane. They were dancing on the floorboards, skimming the skirting, heading towards the discarded newspaper.

'Holy Moses,' Maurice said, kicking out at the fire. Flames licked his boiler suit.

'Get back, you daft bugger,' Finn shouted, grabbing Maurice by the collar and pulling him away from the burning fuel. The man was a pillock. He would go up in smoke if he wasn't careful, and how would Finn explain that to Leanne. In the kitchen doorway, the *Gazette* caught and Rob's face disappeared as it burnt. Frantically, Finn looked around for something to extinguish the fire, his own cheeks burning with the unexpected panic that his paintings might go up the same way.

Then, through the flames, Finn saw a figure outside the studio. Furiously, he yelled for help, but when he blinked the heat from his eyes, it was only Maurice's anorak hanging on the handle. Finn dashed for the jacket, snatched it, threw it over the flames and used it to trample out the fire, flattening the hillocks of navy polyester under his feet, the laces of his trainers switching like whip worms as the anorak coughed out billows of thick smoke, while Maurice slumped impotently against the corridor wall, fingering the rip under the collar of his boiler suit.

Once the flames were smothered and the smoke had thinned, Finn fetched the fire extinguisher from the kitchen and sprayed the smouldering remains. When he was done, he picked up Maurice's sodden anorak and helped him to his feet. Above the sweet odour of extinguisher foam and scorched paint chemicals, the whiff of singed cotton and seared flesh was just distinguishable. Maurice's boiler suit was charred around the ankle, his scorched beige sock soldered to his papery skin.

'Sorry, pal,' Finn said, handing the anorak over. Slops of white foam dripped on to the floor. The quilted lining had melted to treacle black.

Limply, Maurice took the coat and all at once Finn was assaulted by the image of Leanne coming home with the new coat in a huge white carrier that fastened with a plastic zip, and Maurice almost fainting with astonishment that his wife had bought him anything with her own money, and Leanne handing it over without a smile on her face, saying if Maurice didn't like it he could lump it.

6

The Calling of Saint Matthew

It took until they were practically into December before Finn finally agreed to let Lizzi take a look at his paintings from the Bingo series. After a fair amount of to-ing and fro-ing and some minor histrionics from Finn, they eventually settled on a Sunday night. There were conditions, of course, the prime one being that Lizzi had to promise not to give even a hint about the pictures to anyone else. And by anyone else, they both understood Finn actually only meant Rob.

For most of the day beforehand, Lizzi had been doing course work – a case study of one of the clients at the day centre – but she hadn't made much progress. She was relieved when evening came and she could set it aside to go and see Finn. But although she was excited about seeing his paintings, she found herself staring blankly out of the bus window the entire journey there. The newsagents and greasy spoons and charity shops of Partick were closed up and passed by without her noticing. The ubiquitous tenements faded into the background. Even her reflection and her drizzle-frizzed hair failed to grab her attention through the condensation on the inside of the bus window. She felt troubled, perturbed, and it muddied her view. She felt like she'd pushed Finn into letting her see his work against his will, and she couldn't see past the worry that he wasn't sure enough of her to have offered it up freely.

Lizzi rested her forehead on the glass and pretended to be absorbed by the sights of the passing city, and thought back to how different it was when they first met. On their second date Finn had tried the *Why don't you come up and take a look at my sketch books?* line. The words had barely fallen out of his mouth when the two of them had collapsed laughing. But of course she'd fallen for it, fallen for him, for his daft jokes and the line of his mouth and the tendons on the back of his hands and the broken lift and fourteen flights up to his flat. And even though for some reason the memory made her want to cry, she smiled to herself and wiped the steamed-up window with her sleeve.

The bus slowed for a pedestrian crossing and through the haze of memories Lizzi spotted the neon sign of the Last Supper. She jumped up and pressed the button and almost stumbled when the bus came to a precipitous halt. The second she got off the bus, the rain started again. Puddles of orange from the street lamps blotted the pavement up Dougal Street and she pulled up her hood and quickened her pace to a half-run.

She slowed as she neared the church. Sunday evening Mass was spilling on to the pavement, an umbrella or two mushrooming above the crowd, and Jed was standing in the doorway of the vestibule in his priestly robes, shaking hands and chatting with the congregation as they left. Without thinking, Lizzi gave him a friendly wave and then wondered if she had imagined the protective hostility of his flock. She was about to slip away into the darkness of the garden, regretting her intrusion into this public part of his life, when he smiled at her over the heads of his parishioners and waved back.

The church hall was separated from Our Lady of the Assumption by a low sandstone wall punctuated with ellipses of iron railings claimed for the war effort and a garden gate that was half open and hanging loosely on its hinges. Lizzi squeezed through and crunched up the gravel path. Rain was pinging off discarded Special Brew cans scattered among the weeds and a whiff of damp dog shit drifted up from the overgrown plot. At the top of the path, a heap of wet leaves and twisted brambles lay rotting beside the dead ashes of an old bonfire. A rush of affection for Finn and his friends and his half-done handiwork caught Lizzi by surprise.

Inside, the entrance porch smelt of damp and worn rubber. Lizzi hung her parka on the coat pegs next to a cork noticeboard and ran her hand over the cold radiator pipes, making a mental note to mention to Jed the red velvet curtains hanging across the fire doors. She realised they were there to keep out draughts, but they were breaking the fire regulations.

In the main hall, Rob was sitting on the edge of a makeshift stage drinking beer from a bottle, faded jeans covered in paint, but there was no sign of Finn.

'It smells like my primary school in here,' Lizzi said. Her voice echoed off the painted plaster and the polished floor. The parquet was thick with toffee varnish and scored with chipped badminton lines.

'Hiya, gorgeous.' Rob jumped down from the stage and kissed her cheek. 'Well? What d'you think?'

Lizzi stood for a second, taking in the room with its vaulted ceiling, cobwebs singeing on the fluorescent strip lights and dense windows gridded with reinforcing wire. The walls were covered in a smooth layer of white emulsion and a paint-spattered ladder was lying on its side in the middle of the hall. 'Looking good,' she said. 'Where's Finn?'

Rob swigged his beer and nodded vaguely towards a door

in the corner next to the stage. 'Drowning in his moral turpentine, I should imagine.'

'I take it he didn't help.'

'Nah, he successfully shirked the entire show. Beer?'

'No thanks. I'm fine. I should go and find him.'

In the back corridor, an old radiator was propped against the wall next to a bracket and a sealed-up heating pipe, and there was a strong smell of charred wood and melted paint. Fleetingly it registered that the renovations were not going smoothly, but before Lizzi allowed herself to dwell on it, she opened the door of the old stockroom that was serving as Finn's new studio and found him leaning on an old badminton post, examining a canvas that she couldn't see. He was lit by a single overhead bulb that was draining the light from the corners of the room and whose incandescence cast a pool of shadow in the hollows below his cheekbones. Sometimes when she caught sight of him like this, the intensity of it, the shock of how he made her feel, was like being impaled on a stake. She stepped over the net tangled round the base of the badminton post, wondering if the impaled feeling was a positive thing.

Finn turned when he heard her and kissed her with dry lips. His thin stubble had grown to an almost-beard. He wiped the brush he'd been using with a sheet of kitchen roll and told her to shut her eyes while he got the paintings ready. 'There's two I'm going to show you.'

Lizzi shut her eyes tightly and listened to him rearranging the canvases. She realised she was biting her lip.

'Right, you can look.'

Cautiously, she opened her eyes. The first of the two paintings was on the easel and was listing against the wooden struts as if it was overwhelmed by the weight of its subjects. Two women in high heels were tottering away from her, wearing strappy tops that revealed arms the texture of the inside of a pork pie, and jeans that clung to their legs like sausage skins. The flesh around their hips oozed out over the waistbands like a lardy soufflé.

Lizzi smiled, nodded, smiled some more. She leant in to study the picture more closely.

'*Two Fat Ladies*,' Finn said, with a half-laugh. 'One of them is Leanne, Mo's missus. And this one' – he showed her the painting leaning against the wall – 'is *Sweet Sixteen*. Who shouldn't have even been at the Bingo in the first place considering it's strictly over-eighteens, but she was there with her sister and her pals for a hen-do.' He paused.

Lizzi stopped nodding and took a breath to say something but the right words evaded her.

Finn carried on nervously. 'There's something utterly lamentable about going to the Bingo for your hen-night wouldn't you say, but those lassies weren't bothered. They were having a right laugh.'

His chatter was peppered with fake laughs and he was watching Lizzi intently. Like he was trying to anticipate what was going to come out of her mouth before she said the words. Like he would be able to read them on her breath before he heard them in his ears.

Forewarned, forearmed.

'Well?'

'They're good,' she said.

'What do you mean, good?' He sounded crushed.

'Good. Really good.' At Lizzi's feet, a papier mâché donkey was staring forlornly from a cushion of tinsel in a battered cardboard box.

'Lizzi, that doesn't tell me anything. What does *good* mean? That's basically saying they're crap.'

'No, it isn't,' she said urgently, aware that she'd mucked up. 'Not at all. I like them.'

'But?'

'No buts.' Lizzi was stressing now, incapable of saying anything that didn't sound false. 'Finn, I don't know what else to say. They're . . . I don't know . . . sharp, astute, realistic.'

'You don't think they're . . . you know . . . cheap, insincere, exploitative?'

She chose not to hear the tinge of sarcasm. 'No, Finn. They're excellent. Honestly. I'm not just saying that. Believe me.'

'That's just it. I can't. I wanted your instinctive reaction to them but you filtered it, I could see. You were trying not to offend me.' Lizzi started to protest but Finn spoke over her. 'You're right, of course, they are completely superficial. Soulless even. I haven't got under their skin at all.' He pulled his hair back off his face, shook his head.

Lizzi had a freeze of brain panic. She hadn't criticised the paintings. She hadn't said the things he thought he had heard.

Finn laughed bitterly. 'The more I try, the more I mess up. No joke. The second I lift a brush, I'm all over the place.

'You know what it feels like?' he said, when she didn't respond. 'It feels like someone is watching me, judging me, cringing at my woeful attempts to do justice to whatever talent I'm supposed to have. Imagine a football coach watching, splayed-fingered, while his new multimillion-pound signing misses a penalty. That's what's happening here.' He kicked the leg of the easel. 'Fuck.'

Lizzi grabbed the easel before it toppled over. 'Hey, hey. I didn't say any of those things,' she said, finally finding her voice. 'And what do I know about art?' She repositioned the painting. 'Anyway, babes, even if you aren't happy with these ones, it's all good practice. You haven't lost anything. It's as important to make mistakes as to do things perfectly straight off. That's how you learn, how you develop your technique.' She hesitated, suddenly realising he was going to take offence. 'Not that I'm saying you've made mistakes here.'

Finn shook his head again. His fringe fell in front of his eyes. 'Good practice? I don't need practice. The technical stuff I can do already. No, there is something fundamentally wrong.' He waved his hand in front of the canvases. 'Look. They are utter shite.' He was practically wailing.

'I completely disagree with you, babe,' Lizzi said, reaching for his hand, 'but if you feel that strongly maybe you should discuss it with someone at college.'

'If you reckon that's the answer, I may as well quit right now,' Finn said, snatching his hand away from her. 'My tutor is a halfwit. I've told you that. She doesn't rate me.'

'I'm sure that's not true, babes.'

'Forget penalties. How am I supposed to score when I can't even get on the pitch?'

Lizzi did her best to hide her giggle but it came out as a snort. For a minute or two Finn sulked in response, but couldn't keep it up and eventually grinned sheepishly.

'Not your tutor, then. Someone else,' Lizzi said gently, trying a different tack. 'Rob, maybe.'

'Get lost.' Finn turned serious again. 'What does that fat bastard know about art?'

That response, Lizzi knew, she ought to have predicted.

'Anyhow, it isn't about talking,' Finn said. 'It's about painting.'

'Come off it, mister. That's rubbish. Everyone needs someone to spark ideas off. And anyway, you're always

talking about art. We can't shut you up.' Finn was so articulate when he was discussing the hold some work had on
him, the way he could see in some paintings the artist's con-
flicts, anger, passion, ecstasy. It went a lot deeper than the
paint on the canvas, Lizzi knew that much. 'You're forever
going on about your man Caravaggio and the emotional . . .
psychological power of his work.' It was exactly this power
that Finn's paintings were missing. She couldn't put her
finger on precisely why, but it was like he was holding back.
Like he was too scared to reveal anything of himself. Like
the world might turn on its head if he did.

'Maybe it isn't about getting under the skin of the subjects exactly,' Lizzi said, thinking aloud. 'Maybe it's about
giving more of yourself.'

Startled, Finn gaped at her.

'It isn't their soul that's missing, Finn,' she said, seeing the
problem clearly for the first time. 'It's yours.'

He forced a laugh but the colour drained from his face.
'*Ogni pittore dipinge sè.* Every painter paints himself,' he
said weakly. 'Spot the psychologist-in-training.'

'It isn't about psychology. It's . . . you know . . .'

'What?'

'Spiritual.' Lizzi felt herself blush. That sort of comment
would normally have driven him nuts but, to her surprise,
rather than tease her, Finn wrapped her in his arms and
buried his face in her hair. His breath caught in his throat,
stuttered out of him on to her neck, and she could feel his
body trembling beneath their embrace. As if, she thought,
he was astounded by the truth of what she said. And in that
moment, Lizzi felt like she was looking at a picture and was
part of it too, seeing an image of the two of them spotlit by
the single bulb – his straggly light-brown curls against her
deep red hair, his restless paint-blotched hands flitting over

her back, his scruffy trainers toe to toe with her biker boots – entwined and irreversibly entangled. For once he hadn't joked. For once he had let her see how defenceless he was. For once he'd listened to her and let her help him. It was the most intimate thing he had ever done.

When Finn eventually spoke, his voice was muffled but the smirk in it was unmistakable. 'You're assuming, of course, that I have a soul.'

Back in the hall, Rob was shifting ladders. 'There you are, you lazy cunt,' he said. 'Gonnae help or are you still wallowing?'

'Fuck off, titwank,' Finn replied, grinning and aiming a slap on the back of Rob's head while he wasn't able to defend himself. 'It wasnae wallowing. It was soul-searching. A spiritual quest.'

'Bloody hell, Lizzi. What did you say to him?'

The three of them worked for a while, stacking the ladders in the outhouse, pulling the dust sheets off the untuned piano at the foot of the stage, washing pallets and rollers in the stainless-steel sink in the industrial kitchen out the back. When it was all done, Rob opened more beers and they sprawled on the parquet to inspect his handiwork.

'You haven't painted the ceiling,' Lizzi said after a while.

'Aye, well, I'm waiting for Michelangelo here to do it,' Rob said.

'Michelangelo?' Finn said, drinking Lizzi's beer. 'Fucking amateur.'

They stayed like that for ages, staring at the ceiling, Finn and Rob trying not to spill beer down their fronts when they lifted their heads to drink, none of them saying a word, bathing in the afterglow of laughter. The floor was cold and hard on Lizzi's back, the lights were branding white-hot blotches on her retinas and the paint fumes were making her dizzy. But it didn't matter. Once or twice in her life, she recognised events for what they were as they were happening – things that would stay with her for ever, etched in her mind, good things and bad, little and big. It wasn't true that you could only appreciate happiness in retrospect. She had the proof. As the evening rain tapped its hidden code on the roof slates above her, Lizzi wished things could always be like this.

A loud burp reverberated off the newly painted walls.

'I'm starving. Who's for chips?'

LEAD WHITE

7

Seven Works of Mercy

As she ran, the book started slipping out from under her puffer jacket. Behind her, the librarian was screeching – she was calling the police, she was on the phone right this minute, don't think she didn't know who she was. Tuesday skidded into the close next to the greengrocer's, trying to hike the book up, and slammed through the back door out into the drying yard. Panting, she scrambled up the wall next to the bin shelter and perched for a moment on the corrugated roof, her skinny knees folded up to her chest as jagged and sharp as arrowheads. Poised above the deserted lane separating the back courts of the tenement blocks, she listened for her pursuer. Only the distant rumble of shopping traffic reached her. She jumped down. The book fell out and landed with a thud in the wet grit at her feet. A breath of laughter escaped while she rummaged in her pockets to find her beanie hat. She pulled it on, and leant against the wall to catch her breath. She got nearly as much of a high from nicking stuff as she got – used to get – from shooting up. But Christ, was it bad for her health.

Tuesday picked up the book and wiped the dirt off the back with her sleeve. That was the best thing about library books. The protective plastic on the cover. Cleaned up, it looked practically as good as second-hand, as Rob would say. *A Combined Textbook of Anatomy and Medical Physiology.* It was massive – over a thousand pages – and weighed a ton. Amazing that she'd managed to run with it at all. When she'd nabbed it, in that second when she'd felt the weight and thought she'd overstretched herself, she'd been ready to chuck it at the librarian, take the old hag out. But she probably wouldn't have even got it over the desk. Running was Tuesday's thing. Not shot put. See if Rob didn't appreciate her effort, she'd be raging. He'd invited her to this Christmas party at his brother's church and she hadn't wanted to turn up empty-handed. Really, she hadn't wanted to turn up at all but he'd said he needed her help putting up the decorations and promised her a free lunch. Rob thought she was daft, so she was pretty certain he'd assumed she hadn't twigged that she was his charity case. Wrong. Still, if it made the stupid muppet feel better about himself, who was she to piss on his party? The original plan was to gift him a bottle of single malt from the offie but bottles could be problematic. There was always a risk of dropping them during the getaway and smashed glass could be a hazard in soft boots.

The pages of the book smelt sweet. The writing was small, dense, with diagrams of muscles and complicated charts. She flicked through. There were words in there that she couldn't even pronounce. Forget it. She couldn't manage stuff like that. Not that she was illiterate but she preferred her reading material without the need for explanatory notes. Rob would like it though. He'd always been a swot.

Tuesday wedged the book inside her coat to protect it from the drizzle. Keeping to the back lanes where she could, she drifted towards Dougal Street. The high from the robbing was wearing off. Being rubbed out by the anger that was with her all the time now. Dr Blythe kept telling her anger was a good thing, something she could channel. Anger meant she was finally working through the grief at the shitty hand life had dealt her. Anger would give her the motivation to keep searching for her son. Methadone and rage made a better cocktail than heroin and oblivion. Or so she said.

Aimlessly, Tuesday weaved among the side streets where the money was, past sweeping stairs and stone pillars and brass-plated entrances, overlooked by Christmas trees flickering from the bay windows of the huge flats above. As she trundled on – fine rain wicking through her boots – she glanced up and wondered what Christmas in one of those places would be like. The twinkling garlands blinked down at her and it felt like pity.

When she reached the main road, she veered towards the swing park. In the distance, the church clock chimed quarter past. If she went to the hall now she'd be early but she couldn't think where else to go. Rob's book was getting heavier inside her jacket and the damp was seeping into her piercings. She pulled her sleeves down over her hands, trying to ignore how brutal the cold was, thinking about the librarian and how she'd said Tuesday couldn't sign up for the library because the B&B didn't count as a permanent address. They both knew that was another way of saying *We don't want your type in here*. The library was a public facility. *Your type?* Homeless. Addict. Fucked up. Fucked. While she walked, Tuesday replayed the scene in her head. Only this time, she made sure that the shock of having one of her precious books stolen gave the librarian a stroke that left her dribbling and incontinent like what had happened to her nan that time her ma – in one of the few interventions she had ever made in Tuesday's childhood – gleefully let it out that Tuesday was pregnant. *And get this, she thinks she's keeping it.*

At the pedestrian crossing by the swing park, the crossing man was red. Tuesday pressed the button and sauntered out in front of the oncoming cars. By the time the man turned green and bleeps to cross sounded, she was already on the other side. Several cars pulled to a stop for the non-existent pedestrians, not one of them prepared to bust the lights. She turned to sneer at them. Queue-sitters, the whole lot.

A bit further down the road the monthly farmers' market was in full festive mode in the playground of her old primary school. The smell of seared meat drifted through the perimeter fence from a burger stand and mixed with the sweet smell of chestnuts roasting over a charcoal burner. Tuesday's stomach cramped with hunger. She decided to hold off heading to the church hall and check it out instead. See if she could find something she could eat straight away and not have to flog in the pub for peanuts.

She followed the fence round to the main entrance, sussing out the stalls on the way. Pickings should be easy, she decided, with the apron-wrapped stallholders trapped behind their counters and all their posh gear on display out front, but at the school gates she hesitated, not quite able to shake off the dread of the imposing Victorian building. It was years since the school had moved to a flash new place, but the upstairs windows were still decorated with finger paintings, practice alphabets and tissue-paper butterflies. None of which, she knew for sure, would do a thing to alleviate the anxiety any seven-year-old would feel pushing through the massive front door as the bell hammered for the start of class. Never mind one whose mother had just ended up in the jail.

To give time to pull herself together, Tuesday perched on a rubbish bin at the entrance. The kids who'd done the pictures were long gone, but her memories of being cuffed about the head or holding out her hands to be belted hadn't faded. In the girls' toilets on the second floor, carved with a compass which she later plunged into Jed Stevenson's thigh for saying her mum was a manky whore: *Mrs Spence is a Virgin.* It was the biggest insult for her teacher that she could think of when she was seven. Had she even known what it meant? Corporal punishment in schools was banned a year later, but there was still something about the place that made her want to piss herself with fright. And, really, how the fuck did Jed end up a priest?

The place was heaving. Hordes of Christmas shoppers were flowing through the gates around her. Tuesday stretched out her legs to dam the pavement and the crowd instinctively diverted, stepping out into the road, squeezing between the kerb and the row of parked cars. She picked out one guy who wasn't paying attention, who was playing on his phone as he walked, somehow avoiding the potholes and the mounds of dog shit. He was well turned-out, fairly good-looking. Sharp hair. Hipster beard. Expensive trainers.

'Spare some change for a cup of tea?'

He carried on walking. Ignorant bastard. Didn't even trip over her feet. By the time Tuesday had hacked up enough phlegm to gob at his back, he was just outside spitting distance. The slick of gob quivered like a jellyfish on the asphalt, topped by a layer of foam with the same consistency as the scum that thickened the sea and fed the fish by the sewage outlets on Saltcoats beach where Tuesday had once spent Christmas doing smack and downers in a caravan with her mother's latest bloke.

He turned round. 'Did you spit at me?' His accent had a trace of Irish.

Momentarily, she was dazzled by his teeth. 'Just clearing my throat,' she said when she recovered. 'Seems I didnae speak loud enough.'

'Eh?'

'Either that or I'm fucking invisible.'

He put his phone in his pocket and approached her.

'Leave it out, pal,' Tuesday said.

'Sorry. Level 187. Demands my full attention.' He unzipped his bomber jacket and rooted in the inside pocket for his wallet. Under the jacket, he had on the type of chunky granny-knit jumper only the super-trendy could get away with, but she'd say he just about pulled it off. From the looks of it, he was worth a bit. Jackets like that didn't come cheap. It cost good money to cram so many pockets on to one sleeve, pockets that were essential for all the electronic shite required to navigate the West End. Not for the first time Tuesday asked herself how all those over-groomed, label-wearing gayboys survived.

He handed her a fiver. She took it without saying anything.

'Er, that's all I've got. Is it not enough?' he said, flustered by her lack of appreciation. His hair grew wild in the seconds she baited him.

'Depends on how much the burgers are.'

'Oh, sure. We can check.'

They both looked towards the market stalls. The burger stand was the far side of the yard, practically hidden by the queue that had formed next to a blackboard advertising heritage-breed turkeys. Tuesday recognised one of the customers with a chubby toddler in her arms. Her shortbread-blonde hair was tied back in a scruffy knot as it always was. Dr Blythe.

'Kidding,' Tuesday said. 'Gotta go.' There was no way she was hanging around for a lecture from her psychiatrist on the malign effects of begging on the level of one's self-esteem. She nipped through the gate, planning to take the

long way round to the burgers, but stopped almost immediately next to a van unloading parsnips. She hadn't thanked
the man. Where were her manners? She turned round. He
was heading towards the turkey queue.

'Oi, pal,' she shouted. 'Forgot to say . . .' He looked at
her expectantly. She grinned. 'Can I tap you for a fag?'

He gave her a backward wave. 'You're welcome.'

Warmed by a cup of sugary tea and a burger – which turned
out to be venison and was less tasty than she'd have guessed
for the price – Tuesday felt revived enough to think about
her own Christmas shopping. Rob's present was safely
stowed in the fancy carrier she'd lifted from behind a cheese
stall while the cheesemonger was busy luring customers
with his cubes of samples offered on a piece of slate, and
she'd hooked the bag over her wrist which was easier than
having the book rammed under her armpit. There was time
for a quick trip to Boots before she headed over to the
church hall. She had her eye on some flamingo-pink nail
varnish which would be great for a party. It was a while
since she'd treated herself.

The security guard stepped in front of her at the shop
entrance on Dumbarton Road. 'Not today, love.'

'Fuck off,' Tuesday said. 'I'm on a substitution programme.' Which was true, even if it wasn't from this pharmacy.

The security guard had his walkie-talkie in his hand.

'Check, if you want to. Tuesday McLaughlin. My doc is
Dr Blythe. Esme Blythe. I'm on a hundred milligrams a day,
supervised.'

He hesitated.

'You're new, eh no?' Tuesday said, chancing it. 'That's
how you don't know me.'

'What's in the bag?'

'Library book.' She held the handles open so he could look. He nodded, paused, and then stepped aside.

The make-up display was just inside the door. Tuesday decided she should set herself up in business as some kind of shop layout adviser. It was like the management actually wanted to be robbed. The guard was watching her so she meandered over to the prescription counter, keeping an eye on him, dropping down the queue when she got too close to being served.

It didn't take long for her opportunity to come. Two boys in light-grey joggers and matching hoodies, and the giveaway spots of glue-sniffing round their mouths, started arguing with the security guard when he barred their way into the shop. Tuesday crossed over to the make-up, slipped the bottle of nail varnish into her carrier bag and sauntered out the door behind the guard. No alarms. No nothing. He didn't even glance in her direction. It was too easy.

Outside, the wind was picking up and the rain had turned heavy. At the corner of Dougal Street, Tuesday took cover in the bus shelter next to the chippy to paint her chewed nails. The smell of stale fat was carried on the rain and permeated around the gaps between the Perspex partitions. She was regretting that burger now, which she could taste each time she burped. A fish supper would've been easier on her acid gut. Too bad. She blew on her nails to dry the polish and stretched out her fingers to admire her work. Tops.

After a while, when the nail varnish was practically dry and she realised the weather wasn't about to improve, Tuesday set off up Dougal Street. She pulled her coat in close to her neck and ducked into the oncoming wind, practically head-butting the gale-force gusts. When she reached the church hall gate, she stalled. She was having second thoughts about the whole thing. Rob, she could cope with, but she wasn't sure she was ready to meet his saintly brother. In front of her, a sodden poster was flapping violently against the wooden slats of the gate. She fingered the dripping poster, considering whether to make a run for it.

'It is saying *Christmas Party, All Welcome.* We know because we are making them.'

In the squall, Tuesday hadn't noticed anyone approach. Two girls were waiting to pass her, squeezed under a single umbrella which was close to turning itself inside out. The black hair of the one who had spoken was whipping around them in the wind. She was wearing a skimpy jacket that skimmed the curve of her hips just below her waist, and skin-tight jeans that emphasised how long and slim her legs were, and shoes even less suitable for the weather than Tuesday's own fake sheepskin. She looked stunning. She made Tuesday feel rough and scabby, like a kid that hadn't grown up.

'You come with us. You must get dry.' The girl took Tuesday's arm in place of her friend's. 'I am Kassia. This is Anna. I do not take no. Come.'

A huge fir tree stood inside the door, filling the small entrance hall with its perfume, a mix of musty forest and astringent pine. While Tuesday unfastened her puffer jacket, trying not to chip her freshly painted nails and instinctively noting that the shiny new first-aid box screwed to the wall was worth further investigation as soon as she had a minute, the other two girls dropped their umbrella in the wooden stand under the noticeboard and pushed through the fire doors into the main hall. They might not have been from round there, Tuesday realised, but they were more at home than she was.

Cautiously, she followed them. The hall was laid out with a long trestle table covered with sheets in place of table-cloths. Rob was on the stage fixing up the speakers for the music system, playing blasts of Christmas carols to his brother who was signalling thumbs up or thumbs down depending on the optimal reflection of the sound waves. Kassia and Anna greeted the priest with kisses on both cheeks, waved to Rob and wandered off through the door to the kitchen corridor.

Rob's tattooed biceps were bulging from his tight T-shirt. There was a six-pack under there, Tuesday was sure. He couldn't look more different to his angelic brother in his dog-collar shirt and ill-fitting trousers but they clearly had a similar warped way of thinking.

'You pair have lost it. Your average granny isnae gonnae notice the sound quality.'

Rob laughed. 'If a job's worth doing, it's worth doing it to death.' He jumped down from the stage, pulled off Tuesday's beanie hat and ruffled her damp hair. 'Good to see you. Hang your coat over a radiator. You know Jed, right?'

'Aye, well, depends what you mean by know,' Tuesday said, snatching her hat back out of Rob's hands.

The priest laughed. 'Listen, I'm going to see what those two troublemakers are up to. They need to be kept occu-pied. Make yourself at home. It won't be long before the food comes out.'

Tuesday shoved the hat back on. 'You could've spared the intro. Total beamer.' She scrabbled in the plastic bag to take out her nail varnish.

'Ach, there's no reason to be embarrassed. He gets it all the time,' Rob said.

'Aye, but, you know . . .'

'Don't stress. It's in his contract no to blab.'

'Oh, what? Does that mean you've telt him?'

'Told him what?'

'Fuck off, Rob. Have you telt him or no?'

'Calm yourself, missus. All I said was you'd had a hard time over the last few years.'

Tuesday scowled at him and held out the carrier. 'Christmas present.'

Rob put his hand in the bag.

'Don't take it out,' she said.

He grinned and peered into the bag. 'Understood.'

'See if you've got it already, I can easy take it back and change it,' Tuesday said. Rob glanced at her, uncertain for a second. She started laughing. He was such an easy wind-up.

'You're fucked up,' he said. 'Do you know that?'

As payback, Rob sent Tuesday to hunt for tinsel. He told her to track down Finn and Maurice in a storeroom off the back corridor. When she passed the kitchen where Kassia and Anna were making soup, the two girls waved to her, big friendly smiles on their faces. Tuesday reckoned they were either a bit dim or the fact that they weren't from round there meant they couldn't read the signs. Charity shop clothes, unwashed hair, teeth she was ashamed of. She stuck her finger in her mouth. Teeth that were giving her gyp.

Eventually, she found the storeroom and barged in without knocking. An older man in a manky boiler suit was sitting on a chair with a red curtain across his lap, invalid blanket style, and a toolbox balanced on his knee. His left foot poked out from under the curtain and was resting on a cardboard box. Beside him, a younger guy was slouching on the floor, mousy hair dangling in strands in front of his eyes. He was picking at loose threads round a hole in his jeans with fingers stained with paint, and tapping his scruffy trainers off the foot of an easel. He seemed wired and jumpy, pent-up like a pre-race greyhound. The canvas on the easel wobbled slightly with each knock.

'Are youse two Finn and Maurice?'

'Aye, hen. Maurice O'Donnell. Pleased to meet you. Call me Mo.'

By force of habit, Tuesday did a quick once-over of the storeroom. Apart from a couple of other canvases leaning against the wall under the only window and a racing bike propped up in the corner, the rest of the stuff was junk.

'Okay there, hen?'

'Nice,' she said, indicating the painting on the easel. It was a pair of legs in thick tan stockings seen from under a table, with two orthopaedic shoes kicked off and lying on a patterned carpet like beached fish gasping for air. The swollen knees looked like loaves of bread. The thighs were doughy, indented by a flesh-coloured suspender belt.

'No, it's not. It's shite.'

'Don't mind Finjay, lassie. He's all het up about his work. Cannae see how good it is.'

'Anyone I know?'

'*Legs Eleven*,' Finn grunted.

'Selfie?' Tuesday asked.

Maurice spluttered.

'Can I help you?' Finn said.

She didn't like his tone. 'Lighten up. Rob sent me for tinsel.'

Finn looked at Maurice as if he was about to say something. Tuesday flung him her dirtiest look. She wasn't waiting to be slagged off.

'Is it in here, or what?' she said.

'No idea.'

'Aye, Finjay son. This must be the one.' Maurice placed

his toolbox carefully on the floor and took his foot down off its resting place. The curtains slipped to the floor. When he tried to lift the cardboard box, a sheen of sweat glistened on his waxy forehead.

'I'll get it,' Tuesday said.

'A wee sparrow like you?' he said, puffing. 'It's twice your size, hen.'

'Sit yourself down, Mo. I'll do it,' Finn said. 'Where do you want it?'

'Entrance hall.' Tuesday followed him out and along the corridor. A packet of tobacco was poking out from the back pocket of his jeans. As they passed the kitchen, Finn spied the two girls and let out a low wolf-whistle.

'For fuck's sake, *Finjay*. What century are you fae?' Tuesday said.

'Get lost. Just because no one does it to you.'

Tuesday considered her flat chest and narrow hips. He had a point, but that didn't mean he wasn't a tosser.

In the hall, Rob was shifting boxes from one of the trestle tables. Finn took a detour to look at the contents.

'These are for deserving causes, Garvie, and you're no one,' Rob said.

'Is this the West End or what? Which Class A imbetard thought this was a good way of feeding the homeless? Excuse me, my good man, would you care for a drop of finest *olio al tartufo* to go with your Gregg's bridie and your bottle of Buckfast?'

'You're a total dick, by the way,' Tuesday said.

Rob laughed. 'She's got you sussed already.'

Finn shrugged without smiling. 'All I can say is you're lucky I have my hands full or that bottle would be coming home with me.'

After she'd finished decorating the tree, Tuesday spent

the rest of the party smoking roll-ups in the doorway and watching the rain batter the berry-laden holly tree. The guests inside were mainly congregation regulars, but there were one or two lost souls amid the crowd. She'd watched them standing rigidly clutching paper plates, hesitant about sitting or making themselves comfortable, and melting with relief when Jed went over to chat. Losers, the whole fucking bunch.

By four thirty, the place was starting to clear. Tuesday grabbed her coat off the radiator and went to find Rob. He was in the kitchen with his brother, finishing off a bowl of soup.

'I'm away, doll,' she said. 'Thanks and all that.'

Rob put the bowl down. 'I'll see you out.'

Tuesday nodded to Jed. 'Merry Christmas . . .' She couldn't bring herself to call him Father.

'Merry Christmas, yourself.'

'Do you think he remembers?' Tuesday asked Rob when they were out in the hall.

'Remembers what?'

'What a fucking dobber he was at school.'

'He's still a dobber,' Rob said. 'It's just that now he's a dobber who chooses to wear a frock of a Sunday.'

Tuesday sniggered. She stopped beside the trestle table. Tossed Finn's empty tobacco pouch on it. 'Listen, Rob. I need a favour.' He didn't say anything. Fuck knows what he was expecting her to come out with. 'Hey,' she said. 'You owe me. I busted a gut for your pressie.'

'The thing about presents, slapper, is that you're meant to give them without expecting something in return.'

'What's the point in that?'

Rob rubbed the back of his scalp. 'No my territory,' he said, frowning. 'You're gonnae have to ask Jed.'

Tuesday gawked at him. Like she was really going to ask Jed for a lesson in the morals of give and take.

'Outstanding,' Rob said, cracking up. 'You should see your face.'

He was such a comedian. 'No, honest, Rob. I need your help.'

'Go on.'

'Will you teach me computers?'

'What about computers?'

'How to find stuff out. Internet and all that. I was gonnae do it at the library, only I seem to have got myself barred.' She'd promised Dr Blythe. She couldn't put it off much longer. Apparently there were charities that could help her with her search, who could look into the adoption records and all that. Dr Blythe had already helped her put her name down somewhere to tell the people in charge she was wanting to be found so that if her boy contacted them, he'd be able to find her. If he wanted. Now he was old enough. Now that she was sorting out her shit.

'It depends.'

'On what?'

'On how dodgy it is.'

'Swear tae God . . .' Her voice trailed out. For the first time since she was a kid, she remembered what it felt like to need to cry. Rob looked horrified. She smiled weakly at him. He fidgeted. He patted her shoulder. Any second now, he was going to hug her. 'Fuck off,' she said. 'We're non-touching friends.'

'Aye, right enough,' he said, relieved. 'Call in the shop after the New Year. I'll see what I can do.'

'You're a doll. Now piss off back to your brother.'

Tuesday made it to the fire doors without losing it but she felt like she was walking through treacle to get there. Her throat was aching with the effort required to keep the tears back. She wiped her nose with the sleeve of her coat. Under the tree she'd decorated, the boxes for the homeless were piled up ready for Jed and Rob to make their Christmas Eve deliveries. By rights, she should be entitled to one. She flicked open the flaps of the box on top. In among the tins and bags of pasta was the fancy bottle that Finn had been eyeing up. She fished it out. Truffle oil. Product of Italy. For a moment, she considered taking it, to lift her mood, to spite the arrogant tosser. But what would she do with it? It wasn't like she'd be able to sell it down the pub. The only person she knew who would go for something like that was Dr Blythe. You weren't allowed to give doctors presents any more and she couldn't exactly ask the woman to pay for it. She put the bottle back in the box. She'd be better off taking something for her tea. A tin of alphabet spaghetti. That would do.

8

Adoration of the Shepherds

The stainless-steel kitchen was making Finn's teeth wince. A gigantic filling being teased by a scrap of foil he couldn't spit out. Too bright. Too keen. The white light, razor sharp. He pulled open the cutlery drawer to take out a teaspoon and the jangle sliced straight through him.

Once the charity bods had left the party and he'd snatched a curry from the Bengal Tiger and an emergency packet of Silk Cut from the convenience store when Rob finally let him off the hook with the clearing up, Finn had crashed on the floor of his studio, too knackered to cycle back up the road. All night he'd been agitated and restless – rendered insomniac by a massive lump of clay solidifying in his gut – blaming the veg pakora and chicken saag aloo that he'd hardly touched while knowing in reality it was the horror of spending the approaching forty-eight hours with his folks. He'd played and replayed scenarios in his head, scenarios where he bombed them out without jeopardising his monthly allowance, scenarios where they called to tell him Great-Uncle Norris had arrived from Timbukfucking-nowhere and needed his room and they were terribly sorry but could he make other arrangements and what could they do to make it up to him (well, he wouldn't complain if they cared to top up his bank balance), but finally he'd had to face it. It wasn't going to happen. To Finn's knowledge, there was only one long-lost kinsman hiding in the branches of the family tree, and it wasn't Great-Uncle Norris. For him, there was no escaping the curse of being an only child. No option but to suffer the clipped manners, invented traditions and stultifying bonhomie his mother insisted on. It was at times like these Finn envied Lizzi her loneliness.

The kitchen clock was tapping out seconds with mechanical clicks, each one firing fractures through Finn's already fatigue-splintered bones, and his retinas – cauterised by photons spat from the cathode tubes – were swimming with unseeing amoebae. He squinted past them at the clock. There was an hour or so before his train but he had still to get a present for his old doll. If he was expecting to survive the next two days with his manhood intact, it was a situation that had to be remedied. As soon as. But he was fucked if he was trailing round the city centre on Christmas Eve. He was too fragile, too friable, too fucking delicate in his current state to be capable of standing up to the marauding multitudes battling over bargains in the pre-Christmas sales.

Since when had that been a thing? Finn asked himself, taking the coffee machine in its frayed box out of the cupboard (first priority, coffee and a smoke or the day wouldn't be worth a rat's arse; after that, time allowing, he might make a quick dash to Princes Square, buy something – anything – from one of the overheated, over-scented shops his primped-up mother adored). Sales before Christmas had even fucking started? He untangled the electric cable, lifted the machine from the box, set it on the worktop with a clatter of righteous indignation. What about all the poor organised bastards who (unlike him) had bought their presents early, at full fare, before they were discounted? Who'd paid up their Christmas club week by week but who would have been better stashing their hard-come-by savings in their mattress where it would at least have kept them comfortable while their goods were devalued? Or for that matter, all those unfortunate buggers who got shite for presents and, in place of real currency when they took them back to Debenhams on Boxing Day, got credit-note-sale-price refunds because Auntie Betty hadn't included the receipt under the gift wrapping? Another corporate conspiracy to punish the decent poor. The devalued have-nots. The discounted majority.

Praising the foresight he'd had the previous day when he'd hidden his bag of premium Italian coffee in the innards of the piano and out of the clutches of the charity cases at the party, and despite his current near-terminal exhaustion, Finn managed to assemble the coffee maker and root out filter papers from the back of a cupboard behind a solidified jar of instant and a Viennese cake stand.

The machine was a filter contraption he'd exhumed from the vaults of the church larder the day he'd moved in and stashed in the cupboard out of sight of the holy twins who couldn't be trusted not to flog it at a jumble sale. It was a relic from the decade of shagpile carpets and lava lamps and that grotesque chair that Lizzi had insisted on disinterring from the skip outside her house and foisting on him. Design classic it may well have been, but it didn't stop the chair being an offence to his aesthetic sensibilities. Sadly, Lizzi's aim was always off when it came to these things. You couldn't fault her effort, he had to admit, but somehow her arrow always got stuck in the hay bale. Finn bit his bottom lip and clicked the teaspoon against his teeth. It was a harsh but tragic truth.

He filled the water container from the tap, yawning as fatigue threatened to overwhelm him. He squeezed his eyes shut – judging the quantity of water in the receptacle from its increasing weight and the sharpening pitch of the gurgle

– but couldn't keep the kitchen lights from pricking through his eyelids. Pre-caffeine persecution. He gave in, blinked against the fluorescent needles, clicked the full container into place and chucked a pile of coffee grounds into the filter without, in the end, using the teaspoon.

'All right, youngster?' Maurice popped his head round the kitchen door, disappeared again before Finn had the chance to reply. The heating system was up and running but Maurice had invented a couple of odd jobs around the place to keep himself occupied. Happily doing them *gratis*, he'd told Finn, counting on getting his rewards in heaven and all that shite, but Finn knew Maurice wasn't that much of a God man. It was part of the indispensable-handyman charade he'd assumed for the benefit of Leanne. Presumably he hadn't told her he was working for free.

Finn rinsed the glass jug, shoved the plug in the socket, flicked the switch. The hotplate fizzed into life, burning off residues of spilt coffee, and the water bumped and rattled as it heated. Its perkiness irritated Finn, made him even more aware of how badly he was flagging, how much he was dreading going back to his folks. What would he sacrifice to stay? A finger? A testicle (no, not that, he didn't want to end up as emasculated as his old man)? A toenail, perhaps, ripped off at the bed to ensure maximum pain, maximum gain? A bodily sacrifice to allow him to spend Christmas Day with Lizzi. Or work. Work. He needed to work. It was getting desperate.

Thoughts of his paintings – substandard, sub-his-actual-capabilities, sub-the-masterworks-they-were-supposed-to-be – hovered around him as the coffee dripped through the filter paper. Not that he was particularly ready to admit it but, in truth, he found Lizzi's platitudes a touch hard going. The way she kept telling him how great they were. The paintings were shite. Unquestionably shite. It didn't help to have people pretend otherwise, however well-intentioned. Finn was weary of the burden of his own half-utilised talent, of his terrible ambition, of the unvoiced expectations that haunted his waking hours and the few hours of sleep he cheated from his insomnia.

The coffee splashed into the jug and he squinted through the caramel drops. One by one, they diffracted the glare from the strip lights, refracted the surroundings, warped the rigid lines of the kitchen units and inverted the reflection of the double-paned window. In the far corner by the transposed fridge, a dark shape formed through the drops – stretched and twisted to an hourglass – but the image was too tiny, too contorted, too ill-defined to distinguish the details properly in such overbearing brightness. What was it? A mirage? A distortion of his own figure? Something in between, whatever that amounted to? His brain was too minced to consider the physics. Meanwhile, an interminable, indeterminable wait for the coffee to finish. This drip-drip nonsense was torture for a man with his Italian blood.

Coffee apart, a smoke was the only thing now that could settle his jarring nerves. Finn patted the breast pocket of his slept-in, unbuttoned shirt – a shirt that drooped lifelessly over Joey Ramone's lank hair and which, even with the addition of the newly unhung fire curtains, had proved too weedy to keep the night chill at bay – and pulled out his emergency cigarettes. Yesterday's tobacco he'd retrieved from a demobbed trestle when the party was over. As near as empty. Some robbing scumbag had raided it for roll-ups. It had piled on the torment of the party. How he had survived the fairy lights and festive tunes and Fenian faithful with only supermarket cola to lubricate the small talk, he had no idea. At least the scrawny lassie with the piercings that Rob knew from school had had a bit of bite to her chat. He could probably have whiled away a minute or two with her if he'd been a little more receptive. It would have beaten being mentally coshed by a conversation with an anonymous parishioner who, among the many charitable deeds she enumerated for Finn, ran the church folk group on Thursday nights, played the organ at Saturday morning Mass, and was treasurer of the Homeless Organising Committee (Finn had pictured a jakey home-guard-type operation), which is what occurred before he'd been able to escape back to the safety of his studio.

If the party had been hard work, he couldn't imagine how he was going to survive his parents' place. Everything about it was protracted torture. And it pained him greatly that, in the battle of wills, his old doll was always the winner because – regarding the monthly allowance situation – she was the giver and Finn the receiver. So he was obliged to keep quiet about how much he loathed the whole set-up: the family house, the single bed he was supposed to sleep in, his old doll's haircut and the way she said *supper* and lengthened her vowels when her pals were round. In the poky downstairs spare living room, which she insisted on calling the library, there was a gallery of old school photos that she paraded him past whenever the opportunity presented itself (and other times besides) to remind him of the advantages of the expensive education which he'd done his best to waste.

Advantages? Strict uniform, astronomical fees and top results, where the only acceptable follow-through was law or medicine. All of which meant – if you didn't want your balls crushed in a vice – sticking to the rules, doing your homework and having only the thoughts you were instructed to have. It was the type of place where short socks and short trousers were obligatory until you turned thirteen, which in Finn's book – in anyone's book, surely – constituted some kind of child abuse. The type of place where you learnt to assimilate or die the thousand deaths of a social pariah, particularly if your old man was social class C1 and drove a 1993 Fiat Panda, so you were never picked to be a prefect, never wangled invites to the right parties, never even got beyond the garden gate of the houses belonging to any of the fit girls. That was until you sourced a supply of coke and hash, which you were reduced to selling at a pitiful profit solely to get into the knickers of the stuck-up bitches. An enterprise that, had she known of it, his mother would have found perfectly acceptable – desirable even – greedy as she was for an entrepreneurial spirit in her only child that he didn't actually possess and a high-class daughter-in-law to disguise her son's shortcomings (whose sole *raison d'être*, she believed, was to deliberately malign her own social standing). Aspirations compounded, no doubt, by the fact that she'd always considered she had married beneath herself.

Those days were long gone, Finn thought thankfully, although he could do with a spliff or two for this trip. Enough to last him the two days of head-nipping he would be subjected to by his mother and the additional anaesthetic requirement engendered by having to hold some sort of conversation with his old man. But these days he didn't have a regular dealer. In an emergency, he still had the details of his old suppliers on the Dunkeld Silk Road, though they didn't produce anything of the quality to which he'd become accustomed. The effort of recall scraped the membranes surrounding his brain and he screwed his face against the pain as he tried to remember if the Dunkeld wholesalers were, or were not, in the practice of working public holidays.

'See you after, Finjay,' Maurice called from the corridor. 'Salutations to you and your lassie. Merry Crimbo and all that business.'

The greeting provoked a spike of anxiety in Finn, a flicker of extra worry, because he realised he couldn't quite remember what arrangements he'd made with Lizzi for the day. 'Aye, mate. Have a good one,' he shouted back, listening to Maurice limp away, the uneven click of his soles across the floorboards, the slam of the corridor door. Finally, the last drops of coffee splashed into the glass jug and Finn's blood pressure settled in anticipation. He poured himself a mugful and, before he nipped outside for a fag, went to grab his phone from the studio.

There was no signal in the vaults of the building. Thoughts of Lizzi wafted among the cobwebs as Finn drifted along the darkened corridor, unlit cigarette dangling from his lips, coffee cup in one hand, the other attempting to resuscitate his dying phone. Lizzi was spending Christmas with Jed and Rob, going to Jed's for dinner once he'd finished his priestly duties. It would be the first for years where she hadn't had an M&S meal for one in front of a bad film while her dad partied in a Santa hat and combat shorts between drilling shifts in the middle of the South Pacific. And she was ludicrously grateful to Finn for arranging it. To be honest, his entire contribution to the plan had amounted to agreeing when Rob made the suggestion (a suggestion that had caused him a moment or two of disquiet, he had to admit) although he was, of course, more than willing to accept the credit.

The light from the phone screen made no impact in the dark corridor. Resigned to losing his recently but deceitfully acquired brownie points, Finn slipped the phone into his back pocket, planning to phone Lizzi as soon as he got outside, and reached for the door to the main hall.

His hand flailed uselessly in the void.

Finn paused, unsure what had made him misjudge his surroundings. Cautiously, he groped ahead. Tapped along the corridor wall. Tried to suss the distance he'd come. Felt for the radiator. Something was wrong. Majorly wrong. Nothing was where it was meant to be.

Warily, he shuffled into the pit of darkness. Ears sharp, nose tuned, eyes turned up full. Gradually the darkness congealed and a subtle scent began to infiltrate his senses. It was eerie. Intense. A bit close up, like someone else was there. He called out, groped further ahead. Slowly, distinctly, the smell got stronger. The heady, chemical high of naphthalene and turps and, underneath, the musty fetor of stale breath and dried sweat. He shuffled forward, paused, listened. There was someone there. There must be. The seconds passed and the smell enveloped the passageway. The top notes stripped the lining of Finn's sinuses and made his eyes nip. The bass notes were lumpish and sickly. It was the smell of another century. Pungent and anachronistic and physically barring the way.

Someone. He was sure. Absolutely sure.

'Who's there?' Finn pushed his voice out into the emptiness and listened. His nerves were making leaps and connections in all directions to decipher the olfactory clues to the intruder. There was not enough semi-digested ethanol in the mix for it to be Maurice who anyhow would be out the door by now, even at his lamentable pace. Finn sniffed again. Overbearingly masculine with hints of mothballs and solvent. Linseed and oil paint. Putrid drains. And time.

'Is someone there?' He was much less panicked than he considered he ought to be. There was something reassuring in the stench of decay. It was comforting, loaded with promise, like the vinegar must of mildew in a second-hand bookshop.

'Come on. I won't let on to anyone else.' It might be one of Maurice's jakey pals hiding out, or a leftover from the charity do.

A shadow flitted across the darkness. A clang of steel against iron.

Finn's heart jittered and he took a tentative step forward, straining his eyes to see in the dark, but there was nothing and nobody concrete, the noise being only the newly flushed heating system clanking with the effort required to circulate water through its elderly pipes. A vague weight of disappointment settled on him.

His disappointment, though, was short-lived. Before he had the chance to fully revel in what might have been, Finn found the corridor door exactly where it belonged and, on opening it, was winded by the power of the vision that he beheld. In the hall below the stage, the contents of several cardboard boxes were strewn across the parquet. Tinsel, streamers, nativity outfits spilt from the cartons, and the dark-haired girl – the one he had seen at the party making soup with her blonde pal, the pair of them achingly familiar and yet utterly foreign – was there, with her shoes kicked off and her feet bare and the Virgin's blue cloak pulled around her shoulders, sifting through the objects and hum-ming Christmas carols to herself. Finn willed himself not to breathe, terrified she was another apparition who might disappear before he could make sense of her. Telling himself he might startle her, she might freak and chib herself with the kitchen scissors she was using to hack at the parcel tape sealing the boxes. But it was more than that. Much more. It was as if by not breathing he could prolong this moment, counterforce the spin of the earth, stop time trampling over this ecstatic vision, and he found himself praying she wouldn't look up, that she wouldn't notice how he had frozen into an effigy of himself, petrified by her astonishing beauty, or worse, that inside his organs were wriggling and play-fighting like newly hatched maggots.

The girl yanked more boxes from their storage under the stage, ripped off the tape, and tipped the contents on to the floor. Something snagged in Finn's heart at this confusion of innocence and slovenliness. Her humming ebbed and flowed, swirling into song, dipping into murmurs, depending on the force required to yank the boxes out. For the first time in Finn's life, it dawned on him that probability and genetics and Darwin and all those other religions he'd sub-scribed to over the years (logic, common sense, realism) couldn't adequately account for the power of the girl's beauty or the force of her presence, and that the only rational, sensible, logical explanation for an image so exquisite, so heavenly, so utterly fucking perfect, was the intervention of the big man upstairs. Finn grabbed the doorframe to stop his knees giving way, light-headed from this unnerving epiphany and a lack of oxygen. He took a breath and checked his mug of coffee. When the God thoughts started coming, you had to question your stimulants.

'I am looking for Jesus and his ass,' the girl said, when Finn eventually shook himself up enough to wander over.

'Sorry?' he sniggered. The image he was picturing seemed particularly blasphemous for the season. His newly found religion dissolved as rapidly as it had materialised.

'Baby Jesus and the donkey. The nice old man helps me find already sheeps and kings and Mary and Joseph. I am making nativity scene on church altar for Christmas Day. Good idea, no?'

'Aye. Deffo. Great idea.'

'Hello, I am Kassia.' She held out her hand for Finn to shake.

At the touch of her fingers, Finn's brain liquefied. 'Delighted to meet you,' he said ridiculously, while his ego – shrivelling with embarrassment at this ludicrous formality – tried to redeem the situation. 'Kassia? That's a cool name.'

'In Polish it is meaning *pure*.' She grinned coyly. 'And you?'

'No, not pure. Finn James Garvie. Finn. In English, it is meaning . . .' He put his hand up to shark-fin but thought better of it. His joke suddenly seemed utterly inane. Kassia was nodding politely. Pityingly. Finn felt his face burn up. He nodded too. 'Aye, you're right. Not worth it.'

'Ah, Mr Finn,' she said, brushing over his embarrassment with a practised air. 'You are here yesterday also. I am noticing your friend with the pierced eye and sharp yellow hair who doesn't like that you whistle to me.'

'Yesterday. Today. Tomorrow. I'm here all the time. To be clear, but, the skinny lassie? She's not my friend.' Although he reckoned she was spot on with the lassie's hair, the way the tips of her home-bleached bob had stuck out from her hat like the blades of a Stanley knife.

'No, no, you have a wrong,' Kassia said.

Her laugh, when it came, made Finn's spleen shiver. Goat-bells on a dusk-flecked mountainside, he decided, or other nonsense along those lines. Lit by the Star of David or some such seasonal wonder, he might have added, and perhaps would have said out loud if he hadn't thought Kassia would skim over his poetic aspirations as politely, as crushingly – as crushingly politely – as she had his earlier embarrassment.

'I tell,' she carried on. 'With her you flirt dirty like with your boyfriend.'

'Sorry, what?' Finn had missed something somewhere.

'The priest's brother,' she said.

He laughed. There was a certain logic, he had to admit. Flawed logic but logic nonetheless. He had to get both ideas out of her head pronto. 'I saw the donkey in the box with the tree decorations. In the porch.'

They found Baby Jesus cowled with a thin plastic bag, hanging from the top of the tree by a tinsel noose (he was, by the looks of it, a transgender Tiny Tears, identifiable as the Baby Jesus only by the brand-new crepe bandage wrapped around his lower half which Finn, remembering his childhood nativity plays, presumed to be swaddling clothes). On the branches nearby, the donkey – whose balls had grown to the size of two large red baubles fastened between its hind legs with a safety pin – was apparently humping a miniature penguin. Finn was regretting even more he hadn't had the chance to chat to the lassie who had decorated the tree.

'You reach Baby Jesus for me, please. This situation is not for a tree. Some people are too ignorant.'

Finn took the strangled Jesus and the randy donkey off the tree and gave them to Kassia. The doll was several times larger than the donkey. He wondered at what distance you'd have to view the altar to get a decent perspective on the nativity scene if the two were to share a stage, but he wasn't going to spoil the heroic rescue with irrelevant tech-nicalities. Kassia removed the cowl and unravelled the tinsel noose from the doll's neck, unpinned the baubles from the stuffed toy and placed Baby Jesus next to the donkey on the umbrella stand to recuperate.

Outside, the weather was inoffensively nondescript, neither cold enough to be wintry nor wet enough to be miserable. Finn lit his fag and leant against the door jamb, watching the layers of sallow cloud blister off the underside of the sky like syphilitic chancres. This world he inhabited was, at times, utterly magnificent. He took a long drag on his cigarette hoping that Kassia was watching through the open door. An ash worm dangled precariously from the tip. Without flicking, he took a second drag, attempting a record, but it crumbled mid-inhale and spilt down his front.

'Why is someone doing that?' Kassia said, joining him a few minutes later. She had changed out of the cloak and into her shoes. 'Really, this person has problems with their head.'

Finn laughed. 'Smoke?'

'Why not.'

Finn tapped a second cigarette out of his packet and lit it for her, hoping the taste of his lips would be more intoxicating than the taste of the nicotine. Kassia took a short puff and held the smoke in her mouth for a couple of seconds, before it spilt from her lips in white ribbons. After the first puff, she held the cigarette at arm's length for a while, letting it burn rather than smoking it. It was the sort of irreverence that would have normally deranged Finn, but instead he gazed placidly at her, aware of the idiotic grin on his face.

Kassia stared back at him, straight into his eyes, unfazed by his adoration. 'I know I do not inhale like professional. I learn. Rather, I pretend to be glamorous film star.'

'Works for me,' was the best Finn could manage in the state he was in. He could have happily gazed on her for eternity. But time was doing its thing, stomping on the blissed-out morning. He should get his act together, call in with Lizzi, head off to town. But he somehow wasn't able.

A rustling in the holly bush next to the porch distracted him and he broke Kassia's gaze to check it out, momentarily convinced that whoever had been lurking in the corridor was hiding there now. When there was nothing to be seen, he picked up a gravel chip and fired it into the bush. A blackbird fluttered out, hopped along the path a metre or two. It could fuck right off staring at him like that, Finn thought. It absolutely, totally, one hundred per cent did not count as any type of unfaithfulness to share a smoke with an attractive lassie. Not at all. Not one bit. Not when their relationship was purely nicotine based. Not that he would ever, ever, *ever* let on to Lizzi.

Even in heaven, though, the Christmas Eve public transport arrangements were shite.

'I'm gonnae have to head in a sec. Got a train to catch.'

'You will go at home for Christmas?'

'Unfortunately, yes.'

'Why you are saying *unfortunately.* To have your family at Christmas is the most important.'

'You think? You've clearly never met my old doll.'

Kassia knitted her brow. 'It is terrible that you think this way. To have parents who wait at home for you is very valuable. My parents, they do not expect me at home.'

'Count yourself lucky. I'd be delighted if my mother didn't want me there. Between the indigestible food and all the religious nonsense, it kills me. The old doll is a total Christmas Nazi. She takes it literally. I mean literally. Can you believe it? She honestly thinks baby J was born on December 25th and the date is nothing to do with pagan celebrations or the winter solstice or centuries and centuries of prehistory. How fucking stupid is that? I've told her, if that is the case, if the wee guy really was born in December, it doesn't leave a hell of a lot of time between sleeping in the cow trough and the old cross action in April.'

Somewhere in the middle of Finn's rhetoric (which, if he was honest, was more than a slight elaboration of the facts; these were things he'd only ever fantasised about saying to his mother), Kassia's face changed. 'If I understand what you are saying, you are misled. Jesus lives for thirty years,' she said.

'I was kidding,' Finn said. 'But I tell you, I'd swap you for parents that didn't give a shit any day of the week.'

Kassia handed Finn her smouldering cigarette. 'It is not that they do not give a shit,' she said simply, and disappeared back into the church hall.

For ages, Finn stared after her, hoping she might reappear, until the swinging fire doors squeaked to a halt and he knew she wasn't coming. Something had gone very, very wrong. How could he have misjudged it so badly? It wasn't simply that he'd offended her, he had a sense that he had let something slip through his fingers, let something disappear before it had taken shape. He knew the feeling exactly. He'd had it before when he'd processed a roll of film only to find a swathe of each precious negative blank and the images faint and swirly because he'd skimped on developer. Morosely, he sucked hard on the remainder of his cigarette and stubbed it out against the sandstone. Kassia's he extinguished carefully and gently laid it back in the packet. Then, with his head down, shoulders round his ears, hair drooping over his face in an effort to make himself invisible behind his mortification, he skulked back into the hall. By then, Kassia was nowhere to be seen.

In the studio, Finn stacked *Legs Eleven* against the wall next to the *Two Fat Ladies* and *Sweet Sixteen*, while metaphorically – and even from time to time literally – kicking himself. How was it possible for his life to be such a spectacular fuck-up? Whoever the hell was spying on him must be laughing themselves stupid. It was all of it. Work, relationships, the whole fucking scene. His Bingo paintings were shite, and he'd run out of numbers before he'd got a single line, never mind a full house. His girlfriend treated him like one of her patients, and his best mate had a superiority complex. And as for Kassia, he wasn't exactly sure what had happened there, but whatever it was, it was shit.

Listlessly, he gathered up a few belongings and wheeled his bike along to the kitchen. Without turning on the light, he balanced the bike against the counter and searched for his leftovers in the fridge, thinking they would do for the journey home. Cold curry. A reliable cure-all on a par with Maurice's Irn-Bru. The industrial fridge, however, was empty even of the milk that Finn bought from time to time and left to go sour, and he found the dirty carry-out container in the bin and a spinach plate leaking bile in the sink and maggots of rice blocking the plug hole. He had no energy to rail against the culprit. The only certainty on which he could hang was that Maurice hadn't eaten his food. For all he was fond of his oriental cousins, Maurice stayed away from the spicy stuff because, as he liked to stress (giving too much information for Finn's delicate constitution), it went straight through him.

With an ear out for the chimes to tell him how little time he had left to catch his train, and a deadly depression cadging a lift on his shoulders, Finn dragged himself and his bike out of the kitchen. Finally, even the Christmas tree conspired against him, hindering his exit with its heavy branches which snagged his bike frame as he shoved past. In the garden, he wheeled his bike down the path, past the superstitious heather bushes and Neanderthal ferns and, on reaching the gate, noticed a black BMW parked illegally at the bottom of the church steps, half on the kerb, hazards blinking. A spark of offence told him that, contrary to his own impression, there was, after all, a residue of life left in him, and he spat to rid himself of the bad taste provoked by the type of arrogance that deemed it acceptable to break rules that lesser folk had to abide by.

But the bad taste was nothing compared to the assault on his senses that followed. Kassia was standing by the car, smiling serenely at the chubby toddler in her arms, while the driver chatted to her, white teeth gleaming, elbow resting on his open window, and his glance lingering where his fingers were itching to go. It was an unbearable image. Finn dropped his bike into the flower beds and sank to his knees on the gravel, feigning trainer lace retying while in truth grinding gravel chips between his fingers and doing everything in his power to save his eyes from a vision he knew could destroy him.

9

Annunciation

For about the tenth time in the space of as many seconds, Lizzi checked her phone. Nothing. Finally, she sat down on the station steps and fired off another message. *Where are you? #gettingpissedoff.* Around her, Christmas shoppers were barging up and down the steps. She wished for once Finn would show some of the same urgency. Under normal circumstances, she wouldn't bother getting wound up. The one thing she could rely on ten zillion per cent was that Finn would be late. Especially when he was working, when time didn't tick by regularly, but leapt around in fits and starts and always seemed to take him by surprise. Or so he said. There was a possibility, she supposed, that he was in town attempting last-minute Christmas shopping, rendered incapable by the crowds and the crippling choice, failing to notice the time pressing on. That, she could understand. But these weren't normal circumstances. Far from it. Nothing would ever be normal again. It was her own fault though. She should have arranged to meet earlier. She was desperate for him to get there so they could have the conversation they needed to have before he disappeared for the holiday. So she could make sure he was the first to know, before Rob suspected when she avoided wine with her Christmas meal or she sneaked away to chuck up in Jed's bathroom. But mainly so she could stop worrying about how he might react and maybe – maybe – even celebrate a little.

But there wasn't enough time. It wasn't something she could spit out in two seconds.

Pregnant.

Pregnant. One of those simple words whose real meaning far outweighed its literal definition. A string of letters blindly innocent of the upheaval they spelt out. Like cancer, redundancy or death, Lizzi thought, and then immediately scolded herself for her ridiculous negativity. It wasn't that bad. It might even be good. Either way, though, the repercussions would stay with her for ever. Trite to say life-changing but that was the inescapable truth. She shifted the shopping bags off her knee and put the two biggest on the step beside her. When she glanced between the ribbon handles and the glossy stiffened paper of the smallest, her stomach fluttered at the sight of the leather-effect box inside, worried that she'd spent too much, that it might seem desperate, freak him out. And then she laughed gently at her own foolishness. It was a bit late to worry about appearing too keen.

Diesel fumes coughing from the taxis queuing in the mêlée on Queen Street drifted over her. They settled below the metal handrail, sank into the angles, the cracks in the stone. Sitting there was like being in a different world. An underworld. A subculture. It smelt, sounded, looked different to normal life. The tang of damp concrete from the structure looming behind her and the squeamish swirl of junk food from the station Burger King mingled with the exhaust fumes. Lizzi leant against the wall and pulled the hood of her parka over her head, letting herself sink into its warmth, and tried to concentrate on something other than her own nausea and apprehension.

The view was legs. Legs in jeans or woollen tights, in trackies or leggings, skirts or suit trousers. Hurrying or dawdling. Purposeful or aimless. Teenage feet dragged indifferently along the pavement. Well-to-do ladies clipping along at a pace. Workies finishing up early for the holidays and stomping up the steps, two at a time. Old men doddering along with walking frames. Scuffed leather, faded canvas, steel toecaps. Straps and laces and children's Velcro. High heels stepping over the dregs of fizzy drinks spilt from paper cups. Paper-thin soles grinding cigarette butts at the pelican crossing below. Globs of chewing gum splattered like bird shit on the pavement in front.

The whole of humanity represented by their feet.

What she noticed, though, was that when she peered out from her fur-lined hood, not a single person attached to those feet was prepared to catch her eye. People took the steps past her – up or down – without a flicker of acknowledgement, gaze fixed straight ahead hoping she would cease to exist if they ignored her. What must it be like to encounter that every day of your life? Lizzi wondered. It must eat you, this blind indifference. It must ravage your soul. She had shopping bags, winter boots with thick tread, a decent coat, a handbag. And a tub of fruit salad from Marks and Spencer that she'd bought for her lunch. She wasn't drunk. She wasn't homeless. She wasn't invisible. But if she sat there much longer, she could easily be convinced that she might disappear.

She pulled her stripy scarf up over her nose and mouth and shifted position slightly to stop the numbness that was creeping through her limbs. The wool over her face made her feel like a child hiding a guilty secret. Like the time when she was nine and she'd smashed her bedroom window with a glass paperweight she'd been using to practise her netball skills way after her official bedtime. The paperweight had crashed through the window and she'd dived under her bedcovers waiting for her parents to show, pretending to sleep, concocting an alternative story, aware of every breath she was taking, feeling each one damp against the blanket thrown over her downie, hearing how unnatural and ragged they sounded. That's how it felt now. Her breath ragged and damp against her scarf, pretending everything was fine, concocting a story for Finn, a version of the truth where she wouldn't have to work out why she'd messed up her contraception so badly.

Nine-year-old Lizzi had tried fake surprise and claimed it was a burglar (breaking out rather than in, it appeared, but no one had pointed that out). Of course, her mum saw straight through her but had played along and pretended to call the police, saying it was probably one of the boys who were always in the street outside, boys who hung out on their scooters and skateboards doing stunts that Lizzi copied when no one was watching, hoping that when she perfected them they might permit her to loiter around their edges. Boys slightly older than she was, boys she envied for their late nights and lack of homework. The police would catch whoever did it, her mum said, and the offender would be prosecuted. Which in itself would have been bad enough, but Lizzi understood the word as *executed* (having recently learnt of the unfortunate plight of Mary Queen of Scots) and had confessed in a hailstorm of fright.

This time there was no fake surprise and certainly no imaginary burglars to blame. She told herself she'd got mixed up from exam stress, and been caught out that night by the trap of desire or love or happiness. But what troubled her most was the thought that she had subconsciously sensed Finn was drifting and deliberately messed up her pills for the month. Because he was. Drifting. And she didn't know how to stop him. But the idea she could have been that deceitful, that manipulative, was too horrendous to contemplate, and she prayed it wouldn't count as a deliberate act if the deceit had been subconscious.

If her mum had been there, she'd have been able to tell her.

Time was pressing on and Lizzi's panic was rising. In George Square, the Christmas fairground was in full swing and the thumping bass notes carried across the square and she felt them under her skin rather than heard them. They mixed with the whine of indecipherable railway announcements wheedling down from the platforms and set her completely on edge. At this rate, there would barely be time to say their goodbyes.

A couple of minutes later, Finn pulled to a screeching halt in front of her.

'You're late,' she said, shoving the scarf away from her mouth. 'You didn't answer my messages.'

He dismounted, pulled her to her feet, kissed her. 'Sorry, babes. Lost track.' He was unshaven, hair unwashed, wearing only his flimsy Harrington jacket and a crumpled shirt over his T-shirt.

'Finn, you look a state. Have you even got a change of clothes?'

'Stop fussing, wifey.'

'You can't go home for Christmas without a change of clothes.' Lizzi was well aware that the whole look was purposely to wind up his mother but she still thought it was daft. 'What if the weather turns? You'll freeze.'

He smiled. Impassively.

It wasn't worth making a fuss about. If Finn wanted to freeze and annoy his mother, it was his choice. There were more pressing concerns. Like he had to actually get there in order to annoy her. Lizzi checked the time on her phone.

'You have approximately five and a half minutes to catch the train.' The idea that they would be able to have a serious talk was rapidly slipping away.

'D'you reckon that's enough time to get a present for the old doll?'

'Finn, you're joking. I thought that's what you were doing.' Lizzi was mad at him now, mad at him for not getting there on time, mad at him for not reading her mind, for not knowing her momentous news. There were options to discuss, choices to be made. This was where the road to the future took a massive and unexpected fork and, between them, they had to decide which path to take. It was crucial they got it right. There was no trial run, no second chance, no way to see if the untaken path led to a better or worse place. For Lizzi that was the scariest part. How could you ever know if you'd chosen correctly?

Oblivious to Lizzi's dilemma, Finn was messing with a brake cable. 'Had to take a last-minute detour so I could approach from the George Square side. Probably what held me up.'

'Honestly?'

'Yep.' He looked up, gazing at her as if he was seeing her for the first time.

Could he see what had changed? Was it obvious? To Lizzi, it was blindingly, glaringly spotlit.

'The desperate manoeuvre of a condemned man,' he said, lifting his gaze, standing up. 'A magnificent plan to stoke the Christmas cheer, except it slowed me up because my tyres stuck to the tarmac from the reek of candy floss coming from the fair.' He grabbed his bike by the saddle and bumped it easily up the station steps. Lizzi followed him, only half listening, her thoughts occupied by how – if she couldn't tell Finn before he left – she was going to hide her state from Rob and Jed over the coming days.

At the top of the steps, Finn tipped his bike on its back wheel and whirled the front wheel, making the spokes fuse to a spinning disc. 'You should've seen the wee lassies skating,' he said, applying the brakes so the front wheel squealed. He was talking fast, staccato, superficially excited, but his tone was flat and unfamiliar.

'That ice rink, right. No bigger than an Empire biscuit. And all the girls giving it laldy with their dance routines. Consequence: collision city. All these tinsy divas battering fuck out of each other because they had their dance routines dis-choreographed.' He took a breath. 'Do you think that's a word? It's probably not a word, eh? Sounds like it should be though. Dis-choreographed. Although, maybe it would mean choreography for discos rather than dance routine disruption. Whatever. What was I was saying? Aye, the lassies. Head-to-toe pink and white every last princess among them. They scared the absolute shit out of me.'

'Can you not get the next one?' Lizzi said. The noticeboard was flashing platform 7. *Passengers please note: doors close thirty seconds before departure.* He had less than four minutes.

'God, no. You know what she's like.'

Finn stood his bike back on two wheels. 'The wee boys weren't quite so scary. They were doing this thing on the carousel, standing on the saddles of the painted horses or whatever, while the poor miscreants manning it were trying to get them to sit down . . .' He set off roughly in the direction of the ticket office. 'They were like: *just fucking sit, you wee tossers* – but the kids couldn't've given a rat's arse. When I was a nipper, everybody knew those gippo guys on the switches weren't folk to mess with. Not if you didn't desire a doing. But see those kids. Unbelievable. The whole place was mental. Totally fucking mental.'

'Finn, you'll miss it.'

'I'm telling you, though, it was worth it. Feel totally invigorated. Give me screaming weans and muscled-up travelling folk, canned top twenty hits and sick-making confectionery over nativity scenes and churchy singing, stodgy meals and teaspoon-on-the-glass toasts any day.'

Lizzi wasn't convinced. Although Finn had the right words, he wasn't doing a great job of hiding the fact his newly invigorated Christmas cheer was totally fake. 'Come on, Finn. You've still to get her something.'

'Station flowers and a box of chocolates. It's the thought that counts.'

'Go. Hurry. I'll sort your ticket.' She left him heading towards the stationer's while she went to the ticket office. A couple of minutes later, they met up at the barrier. Finn was clutching a *Gazette*, a limp bouquet of carnations and a box of the cheapest chocolates.

'Two minutes twenty and counting,' Lizzi said, checking the board. He leant his bike against the ticket barrier and shoved the purchases into his bag and hugged her, pulling her so close her tub of fruit salad got crushed between their hips. She took it out of her pocket.

'I'll miss you, babes,' Finn said quietly, suddenly flagging completely. 'Will you be okay? You could come. Come. Please come. Keep me company.'

'Above and beyond, Mr Garvie,' Lizzi said. It would be a nightmare. They would never be able to have their conversation because they would never get a moment's privacy, and his interfering mother would probably suss her condition long before Finn did. Even under normal circumstances, two days trapped in rain-slashed Dunkeld playing

Monopoly and watching Finn resort to being a moody teenager was not Lizzi's idea of a great time. She'd only been to his parents' place once and she hadn't really hit it off with his mother. Beforehand, she'd expected to come away with a deeper understanding of Finn's family, but all she'd discovered was an emptiness she couldn't explain.

'Anyway, I've got plans,' she said, smiling weakly. 'Rob's picking me up tomorrow after Mass.' She played with Finn's fingers, trying her best not to give in to the tears that were never far away these days. Tears wouldn't change much. He might miss the train if she cried, but it would be a cheap victory, a victory worthy of his manipulative mother. So rather, with a brightness she didn't feel, she said, 'Thanks, babe. Did I say? You know. For sorting it out with Rob and Jed for me.'

'You said.' Finn ruffled her hair. 'You sure? It's not too late.'

But it was too late. Lizzi gave him his ticket. Finn grabbed his bike. In the last hurried seconds before he pushed through the gates, she handed him the present she'd bought.

'Merry Christmas,' she said. 'It isn't wrapped properly. Shop wrapping. Sorry.' She saw him glance at her other bags. Fleeces she'd bought for the others from the factory outlet. Finn wouldn't like them. They weren't technical enough for him. 'Rob and Jed.'

'How come the holy twins get bigger presents than me?' Finn said, shoving the gift bag into the front pocket of his messenger bag without even looking at it. He caught Lizzi's look of dejection. 'I'm kidding, you silly mare. I haven't got yours yet. I didn't want to get the first thing I saw. Plus, I was skint. I'll get you something nice. When I'm flush.'

'Where are you off to, son?' the guard said.

'Dunkeld.'

The guard opened the barrier.

'I don't want you spending loads of money on me, Finn,' Lizzi said, playing with the tub of fruit salad. 'I'd have been happy with something you'd done yourself. You know, a sketch, a photo. Anything. A bit of you.'

He laughed. 'I'm not that cheap.'

'Come on, son,' the guard said.

Lizzi gave Finn an upside down smile. 'Go. Go on. I'm not taking responsibility for you missing the train.' Without noticing, she nibbled the edge of the lid on the tub.

'You gonnae eat the fruit or only the plastic?'

She chucked it over. He caught it with one hand.

'Thanks, pal,' Finn said to the guard as he flashed his ticket. 'Merry Christmas, by the way.'

'Dunkeld's a nice spot,' the guard said as they watched Finn hare along the platform with his bike – shoving the fruit salad into his pocket, the cheap carnations drooping from the mouth of his messenger bag – and bound on to the train just as the pips for the doors sounded.

'Yes,' Lizzi said, remembering. The only good part about the trip had been the rainbow. A circular rainbow. Finn and she had gone for a walk up to the Hermitage. They'd been standing on the limestone turret, watching the swollen river tumble into the peaty depths, listening to the drum of the white water and feeling the spray coating their faces, when the mist had fragmented the sunlight. A rainbow halo floated above the haze and rocks at the waterfall's edge, spectral and exquisite. A glory.

10

Still Life with Flowers and Fruit

The first thing Finn did once he'd stowed his bike and found a window seat near enough to keep an eye on it was take out the present Lizzi had given him and set it on the grey plastic table put there to divide the forward facers (himself) from the perverted minority who actually chose to travel backwards (in his opinion, an acceptable mode of displacement if, and only if, the carriage was chocker, which this afternoon it wasn't). He'd bagged a *first-to-be-surrendered-in-the-event-of-an-oldie-or-a-cripple-showing-up* seat right before the luggage rack and had a whole four to himself. If he staked it right, it might stay that way. He stretched his legs under the table to discourage any unwelcome intrusions, stuck his messenger bag strategically on to the aisle seat beside him, and sank into the rigid embrace of ScotRail's finest upholstery. The screech of the guard's whistle set them on their way. Destination: holiday hell.

The train chugged out of the station, skimming the daylight slipping between the sidings. Finn zipped his Harrington jacket right up to the neck. Lizzi was right. When it came to it, he was cold and ill-equipped and unprotected for the journey. With his zip tag trapped between his teeth, he leant his cheek against the juddering window and let the hum of the tracks knead the space beneath his sternum until his guts turned numb.

What was going on in his life? He'd been totally thrown by the morning's events. All the stuff that had happened with Kassia. One minute happily being eviscerated by her quite phenomenal beauty, the next being rather rudely (in his opinion) excommunicated. But when insomnia and hopelessness and a feeling of constantly being watched formed the backbone of his existence, it was small wonder he'd cocked up on the conversation front. It hadn't been his intention to wind her up. Not at all. He'd been confused by the force of his reaction and misled by the uncanny familiarity of her appearance – the dark hair, the milky skin and the glint of insolence in her eyes – which he couldn't quite place.

And now Lizzi. Today, he had seen something different in her – something amiss, something vulnerable – but he had been too messed up by his own problems to be able to take her on. It was pretty impressive how deftly he'd blanked her signals considering how much his head was mashed, although it was a shame to score so badly in the boyfriend stakes. What was it she'd said? That she wanted a bit of him? Of course, he knew fine well she hadn't meant it literally, but the way he was feeling just now, he was having second thoughts about sacrificing even the toenail he'd been willing to forgo that morning. Nothing against Lizzi. Not at all. But the thing was, he was on a brink. It was nothing tangible, nothing he could swear an oath on, but he was clearly teetering. Below him, a chasm, a crevasse, a massive fuck-off gaping crater and all he could hear was Lizzi – kind, thoughtful, responsible Lizzi – telling him to step away from the edge. He had no way to explain. It was utterly without sense. But the only thing he actually wanted to do was to jump. And one thing was certain. If he was going to be fit enough to go there, fit enough to survive the leap, he had need of every single one of his body parts.

On the table, the ribbon handles of Lizzi's gift bag trembled in time with the vibrating engine. He had to go for it. He certainly couldn't wait until he got to his folks' place to open it. No way was he opening a gift from Lizzi with his mother lingering over him like a cloud of phosphine, sanitising the moment with her toxic interest, and gleefully underestimating the life expectancy of Finn and Lizzi's relationship by the magnitude of Finn's allergy to whatever it was. Privacy was essential. These things were personal, unpredictable and, if not perfectly judged – impossible without previous consultation between donor and recipient – liable to incite a rash of disappointment. As his old doll well knew.

When it came down to it, he wasn't that happy about opening it in front of an entire bunch of strangers either. Cautiously, he checked out the rest of the carriage. In the seats behind, a lifeless bunch of shop workers and hairdresser types were plugged into screens, tap tapping, swiping, wiping, obsessed – possessed – by the importance of posting the essential *I'm-on-the-train* hashtagselfieupdate. Further down, some five o'clock execs perturbed by the early finish were swearing full volume acronyms into their phones, a couple of bland parents shouting at their bland children to keep the noise down, and the usual wellmade-up, middle-aged ladies queuing for the toilet. Everyone preoccupied. All of them engrossed in their own misery. Unobserved, Finn picked up the glossy bag.

He wanted to like the gift. It wasn't like he'd pre-decided. He honestly wanted to fill his kecks with the pleasure of it and shower Lizzi with his unfettered enthusiasm, so to speak. He got no joy from their aesthetic divide. But when he peered inside the bag, the small white faux-leather box embossed with gold letters screamed at him its wasted extravagance, and all he wanted to do was muffle the shame of it.

Embarrassed, Finn opened the box quickly and set the contents on the table in front of him. A watch. Pretty flash. And not too cheap by the sight of it. Probably not four figure silly money but deffo not cheap cheap. Not much change from a half grand if his valuation was anywhere near accurate. Sitting there on its black velveteen cardboard cushion, round its fake plastic wrist, the thing was practically tossing itself off. How could a timepiece be that fucking pleased with itself? Finn took a deep breath and eased it from the box, weighing it in his palm, assessing the quality of the chunky steel links and examining its chronographic tachymetric sophistication. Solar powered, multiple dials, dive-proof to 100 metres. And – except for the kiddy-size numerals – wouldn't have looked out of place on the wrist of one of the secret agents in the vintage comics that Jed kept stashed behind the wine stock in the cupboard in the vestry.

But the shame was, Finn would never use it. Like, when did he ever go diving? Or have to count the fractions of milliseconds that splintered his hours between worry and work? Poor Lizzi. There was nothing worse than coughing up megabucks for a gift that wasn't appreciated. It was a shame. A crime. A crying shame. But she should know he didn't wear a watch. It was his thing. One of his things. The tyranny of punctuality and all that shite. He got his time cues from church steeples and libraries. From lazy cops and smart-arsed traffic wardens. From the news stream on the telly in the Vaults and the green combi time-temp sign outside the pharmacy (which incidentally was entirely fucked when it came to measuring the cold, because unless Dougal Street was on the edge of a blazing inferno that Finn was unaware of, there was no way even on a summer scorcher that it genuinely reached twenty degrees of heat, never mind the thirty-five the flashing dots were wont to claim). Sometimes for a laugh and if they could afford the thirty-something pence it cost them, Maurice and him would call the speaking clock from a public phone, wetting themselves if they timed it well enough to get a 'precisely'. *On the third beep, the time will be 3 a.m. precisely.* And there were even occasions, if he could face the sulky reproach of missed calls and unread messages and the irritating frivolity of useless apps that did nothing to enhance his life, when Finn had been known to check the time on his own phone. But he had never, ever, ever worn a watch. It was the ASBO-less equivalent of an electronic tag. Without any of the street cred.

Finn hooked the clunky strap back around its plastic support without trying it for fit, bundled the lot back into the gift bag and stowed it away. He'd have to work out how to play this. Another complication to his life. On the plus side, he told himself, it was common knowledge that there was a direct correlation between the measure of the worth of your nearest and dearest and the price tag on the pressie (multiplied by an income coefficient to take into account the donor's earning power). So, considering Lizzi's measly NHS post-grad clinical psychology student salary, Finn must be worth a fortune in her eyes. Which was deeply gratifying. In the same vein, the mottled carnations spilling from his bag looked magnificently cheap and nasty. He'd like to think that his old doll would appreciate the message, but the joke was these sickly sweet flowers cost a lot more than their lamentable appearance suggested.

If it had only been Lizzi who was this out of kilter, Finn would have put it down to misfortune. But the thing was, whoever he encountered these days was firing crossed purposes at him. Rob and his ridiculous delusions of art, Kassia taking his harmless jest as an affront, the lassie with the cheekbones having him down as a sexist maniac. Even Maurice was a bit unwilling to take him on which was rich considering all that Finn had done for him. It was a joke. A travesty. The entire living universe this side of Partick intent on misunderstanding him.

The train rattled on. Finn took the tub of fruit salad out of his jacket pocket, chucked it on the seat and curled against the window too frazzled to sleep. He stared at the scenery as it hurtled past: the twin blades of the dual carriageway slicing through the landscape; the river, hard and white from the reflection of the featureless sky; high-tech, mirror-blind offices miles from civilisation. On and on it went. Eventually, the train retched to a halt, jolting the passengers who were dragging bags down from the overhead shelf or lugging suitcases out from the between-seat storage. Through the greasy window of his carriage, Finn watched them hurry along the platform and wondered if they were aware in their precipitous getaway that the intricate wrought-iron roof struts above them had recently been repainted.

There were still countless stops to go. Still more than an hour before the train would reach Dunkeld. Time enough to work out where his next Bingo number was coming from, whether he could face another photo-reportage trip with Leanne, whether any of it – any of anything – was worthwhile. Instinctively, he took his cigarette packet from his shirt pocket, unconsciously aware that a fag would give him some relief from his jitters even if he wasn't supposed to light up. But when he opened the pack, Kassia's half-smoked cigarette was nestling between the rest of the untouched fags, and the faintly damp paper of the filter tip was teasing him, tempting him, seducing him. Slowly, carefully, guiltily, he pulled the cigarette from between its unsmoked neighbours, and held it delicately between his forefinger and thumb, lifting it up to the light to better examine the charred threads of gold, and then to his nose to sniff the fragrant burnt incense, and then to his lips to taste the oily perfume of the lipstick traces. It was too much. Just too fucking much. It was only adding torment to his torture. All he wanted was some peace. Finn shoved the cigarette back in the box and roughly folded the *Gazette* under his head as a pillow and shut his eyes and slowed his breathing to trick his body into thinking it was resting. But it didn't work. Rather than the withdrawal from the world he craved, he was more alert than ever. He could feel the carriage getting colder. The air turning sour. The unwelcome presence of his fellow passengers. He twitched an eye open, thinking some fucker had crashed his space but, as usual, there was no one there.

It was insane. This feeling that there was always someone there, hanging about like a literal bad smell. It was paranoia. Paranoia brought on by fatigue and going-home-sickness and who knew what else. If sleep was unwilling to humour him, a distraction to keep his mind busy was urgently required. Anything to keep this ridiculous rumination at bay. Idly, Finn pulled his phone from his jacket pocket. Two unread messages. The first from his old doll, the second from Lizzi. He didn't have to read them to know what they said. His old doll would be nagging, nipping, haranguing him about an unfathomable triviality that he would never be able to accomplish, and Lizzi would be making sure he was okay, seeing if the journey was fine and generally acting the adult to his hopeless adolescent. He deleted them both without reading and dragged his art book out of his bag, breaking the stems of a couple of carnations in the process.

Finn laid the book on the between-seat table and turned the front cover, letting the heavy pages fan of their own

free will. With a riffle and a sigh, they fell open at *Death of the Virgin*. Finn sighed with them. It was hard to rank Caravaggio's major masterpieces but this one did something to him that the others didn't. It wasn't the subject matter per se, nor the sacrilegious iconography, nor the scandalous depiction of grim poverty. It wasn't even that the Virgin had likely been modelled by a courtesan (old news with the big man by the time this painting was finished) or whatever else had caused the hypocritical bare-footed Carmelites to reject the masterpiece they had commissioned. It was more the stark truths of the painting. How separate we are in grief and in death. And, but for a certain pallor to the skin and a touch of rigor mortis, how little there was between the two. The apostles crowded round the dead Virgin should have been united in their loss and yet each one was stranded on an island of private suffering. Old men with nothing left to hope for but their own end. And Mary Magdalene, withdrawn now from the rest, alone in her despair.

When Caravaggio painted *Death of the Virgin*, it was pretty out there. If Finn remembered correctly from his study of the great man's life, the unofficial dogma of the Catholic Church at the time was that Mary Mother of God had transcended to heaven in full health. Well and truly alive. Well, and truly alive. Not even a little bit dead. No pain, no ablutions, no messy excretions or need of the copper pail Caravaggio had painted at her feet. Who would believe a simple bucket could cause such offence? But the painting bordered on blasphemy in its realism. Small wonder the priests had got their cassocks in a twist. In comparison, Finn's Bingo pictures were hardly going to break down the social order. Part of the problem nowadays was that it was nearly impossible to affect folk the same way. Everyone had seen too much and believed in too little. Poverty and realism were unremarkable and seeped into your bones if you were on the losing side. The rich didn't care and the poor were crippled by a collective lethargy. Righteous indignation was so much harder to provoke if folk had already lost the lot. So, unless you went for religions that were not your own to mock, or the one or two taboos that muckied the borders of taste and mainly involved children or bodily excretions, you quickly discovered that your average Jock and Sadie were effectively unshockable.

Not that Finn believed Caravaggio had painted this way to shock for shock's sake. It was more that the man was incapable of painting any other way. When Finn had seen the picture hanging in the Louvre on the first of his bike trips with Rob, he'd been unhinged by it and had hidden his real response with an intellectual one, gibbering on to Rob about how struck he was by the emptiness of Mary's body in death, and flippantly commenting on the futility of mourning if even the Heavenly Mother was reduced to a slab of meat. To reassure him, Rob had pointed out the halo, the divine light on the Virgin's ageless face, the swirl of fabric suggesting her soul had already ascended, thinking Finn had missed the subtle iconography. But it wasn't the fate of the Virgin that had unsettled Finn. In the figure of the distraught Mary Magdalene, the painting had unearthed a deeply buried lack in his own life: a terrible desire – an unfulfilled yearning – to lose someone who could render him that perfectly stricken.

The trip was before he'd met Lizzi and he hadn't tested himself to see if her passing would do it for him. He'd done some trial runs on his old doll of course, but even the most maudlin music and sentimental poetry at the imagined funeral couldn't provoke in him the smallest hiccup of regret. Obviously, he hadn't even bothered imagining his old man's end. Which was, when you thought about it, a fucking pitiful commentary on his filial bond.

Finn ran his fingers over the page, feeling the energy of the painting even in the shiny reproduction. When it came down to it, he reckoned, to do a piece of work that stark, you'd have to go about with your emotions stripped raw and your psyche practically flayed. No wonder the big man had got himself into so much shit back in the day. Finn closed the book and smoothed his hand across the loose jacket, suddenly ashamed of his own lack of ambition. His Bingo pictures were nothing when you compared them to this. He'd intellectualised the idea, externalised his sense of injustice, and was living vicariously through his subjects. It hadn't always been like that. In the old days, his works had been born spontaneously, from unconscious inherent talent. Each of them natural, unforced, organic. Incapable of doing wrong. Works of immaculate conception, so to speak.

Finn leant his elbows on the table and rammed his eye sockets against the backs of his hands. The pale flesh filled his vision until the whiteness and the unseeing nothingness became indistinguishable. He should be doing what Caravaggio had done. Addressing the big questions without holding back. But he was terrified. Life, love, death? Fucking impossible to bear if you did any of them properly.

He sat like that for ages. The train stopped at a few more stations and emptied out more passengers. The wheels clattered over the tracks. The journey was slipping by before he could prepare himself for the destination. Finally, he closed his eyes again and dozed fitfully, fighting for the sleep that had evaded him for the last few nights. Dreams mixed with memories mixed with terrible premonitions. The pleasure of idolatry vied with the inadequacy of his own attempts at immortality.

Was that it? Was that what it was all about? Was art simply a surrogate or metaphor or rehearsal for death? He could see how it might be. Could it be that the only way to truly understand the point of this existence was to plunge head first into death or its nearest approximate? It made sense. If something, anything – a painting, a poem, a piece of music – stabbed you through the neck, tore vents in your gut, made you scream to gouge out your own eyes and rip open your chest to stop your beating heart and the agony of the ecstasy, only then could you say you had ever been alive.

Finn leant back in his seat, his head lolling dangerously as the track curved eastward on towards Perth. His mind was swirling in his half-sleep, thoughts testing one track after another, until it came to him why he had been so unsettled by Kassia. The reaction he'd had to the vision of her was almost indistinguishable from the reaction he'd had that day in the Louvre. But Kassia had stropped with him in the way a painting never would and now he felt cheated. Upset with her for being pissed off with him. Let down by her unexceptional behaviour. Angry at her for being human.

It was bugging that her presence wouldn't let him be. She had conjured herself into his mind and fixed herself there. Finn could see without trying her black hair that trapped the light and shone as if it was gilded, her lips plump with blood, her delicate feet vulnerable in their nakedness. To rid himself of the vision, he switched dream channels to Lizzi. Pictured her in his studio, clothed as Caravaggio's Virgin, approaching him, offering herself with her russet hair lifted so he could unfasten the buttons of her dress, buttons that traced a line from the nape of her neck down her spine to the hollow of her back. Finn felt his dick stirring but, in his reeling dream, he realised to his mortification that the woman he was caressing was not Lizzi but Kassia. In his half-sleep, he was conscious enough to consider the cost of betrayal in a fantasy and weigh it against his own worry of who might feature in Lizzi's dreams. But even as he was telling himself to respect Lizzi, resist Kassia, he was fumbling with the silk-covered buttons of Kassia's scarlet dress, completely entranced and knowing that, in the living world, his studio would never be quite the same again. The train lurched around a steep bend and Finn's cheek lolled against the bristles of the seat fabric. Unfastened, the dress slipped from Kassia's shoulders and fell in folds around her bare feet, and she stepped out of it and turned to face him. Her skin was flushed with passion. She was biting her bottom lip and her teeth were glistening and her dark, wide pupils were sucking him in. Her breasts were perfect hemispheres cupped in a calico bodice. Slowly, she unlaced the bodice. Now, she was tugging at the ribbon tie of her petticoat, the tip of her tongue teasing her upper lip, her cheeks inflamed. Finn's dick hardened. Kassia's petticoat slipped down. Underneath she was naked, her skin luminescent but for a slip of pure black that drew him down to the promise between her thighs. His head was spinning. He could see every curve of her body, her breasts, her hips, the dreamscape allowing him to see her from every angle. He shifted in his seat. He was standing behind her, kissing her collarbones, letting his fingers tease her hair that was falling in loops across her shoulders, and he paused a moment more before he unbuttoned his flies and let her sighs dally beneath his skin. He kissed the nape of her neck and the unknown space between her shoulder blades. His erection was bursting, painful, but he was grinning stupidly. She was groaning, reaching behind for him with one hand, the other steadying herself on the back of the chair. His cock was rammed against the cold skin of her naked buttocks. Her breasts were quivering, her nipples hard as pebble shot, her legs lips eyelids parting and he was nudging, probing, pushing.

The train screeched to a halt.

CUT.

Half-conscious, Finn crossed his legs and scrunched himself into the corner of the seat. He was awake enough to know that to have her, even in a post-Renaissance-themed porn-dream, would be a temporary pleasure (not to mention a messy affair on public transport unless he took himself off to the toilets, but train toilets, he knew from experience, were not conducive to a satisfying finish).

'Congrat-fuck-ulations. A masterly performance, if you don't mind me saying.'

A voice thick with halitosis and stale curry choked Finn from the remnants of his fantasy and his dick sagged. Refusing to be so rudely awakened, he curled further into the armrest as the train pulled out of the station, pissed off that his space had been invaded while he was too asleep to protest.

'I lie, of course. If it prognosticates your general aptitude to rise to the occasion, we are, alas, completely fucked.'

Finn let his eyelids lift a millimetre, wondering who the unfortunate degenerate was that his unwelcome companion was addressing. Furtively, he peered between his lashes and it surprised him to discern, from his half-eyed evaluation, that the trespasser appeared to be talking to him.

'I assume you *do* possess testicles? Perhaps you keep them in your handbag. Is that the problem? Yes, you. Master Faggot in the corner.'

Reluctantly, Finn opened his eyes fully. The last of the afternoon daylight was strobing between the industrial units lining the rail tracks, the trackside nettles jabbing directly through his irises. 'Are you talking to me?' he said, dry-throated from his restless dream.

'Are there any other faggots in this carriage? Of course I am talking to you.'

The rest of the coach was silent. Finn screwed up his eyes to compensate for the extremes of the strobing light but his vision wouldn't adapt. Each flash of daylight forced him to blink before he had time to get a decent measure of the intruder. It was out of order for someone, anyone, to gate-crash his private moment like that and chuck insults around like they were already well acquainted. And even Maurice, unenlightened old fogey though he was, wouldn't go round calling folk faggots. Which Finn decided he would point out, the second he could see to say it.

The train moved steadily through the outskirts of town and bit by bit the gaps between the buildings lengthened and the out-of-town showrooms dried up and the shocks lessened and the muddy farmland stretched to the dirty horizon and Finn was eventually able keep his eyes open without blinking. As his dazzled retinas recovered, a figure took shape against the window. A broad, hunched figure with a swathe of black wool cloaked around his shoulders.

'At what precisely are you gawping?'

The train hooted its warning signal and passed into a tunnel. The relative darkness was soft on Finn's eyes and gradually he distinguished a feature or two on the stranger's face. Ugly lips and wild hair. Eyes hooded by a thunderous brow. A bristling black beard. Features that were murkily familiar. Features that carried the threat of an unwelcome acquaintance, a previous life. A teacher who persecuted him? A tyrannical classmate? A bullying uncle? He knew but didn't know. Didn't want to know. But before the train plunged back into daylight, Finn caught a fat worm of a scar ploughing through the swarthy skin of the man's right cheek.

He started. He couldn't believe it. It wasn't possible.

He clamped his eyes tight and looked inside his head.

'Do you not converse? Are you some kind of dumb mute?'

Terrified, Finn forced his eyes open, his rational mind not willing to take in what he was seeing. Wildly, he looked around the empty train, taking sideswipe glances at his companion while he compelled his panic to settle. There were only the two of them left in the carriage. No one to verify what was staring in front of his eyes. What he was seeing wasn't possible. It wasn't possible. Not possible.

There was no mistaking who the uninvited guest was.

It made no sense. No fucking sense at all.

And yet it made perfect sense.

'Or are you simply too rude to introduce yourself?' Flouncy sleeves drooped around the intruder's wrists as he pared a wart on his pinkie with a dagger.

Finn held out a trembling hand. 'Finn James Garvie. Pleased to meet you.' His voice wobbled as he stuttered his name.

'Yeah, yeah, I know. Same. Scudded.' The stranger didn't take Finn's hand.

'Really?' Finn's gut lurched at the unexpected pleasure of being pleased to be met.

'Well, frankly, no. To be honest, this whole thing, being here, talking to you, sucks worse than a nun with false teeth.'

'Oh,' Finn said, his voice wavering even on the one syllable. 'But it's you, isn't it? It is. It has to be.' He could hear the shrillness in his tone. He was almost crying with anxiety, anticipation, confusion. It was unbelievable, incredible and all those other words that meant the same thing, and at the same time, completely, utterly and exactly as it should be.

The bloke rolled his eyes, held out his free hand. Finn clutched it. It was limp and damp and stubby.

'Michelangelo Merisi da Caravaggio.'

And Finn burst into tears.

By the time he recovered the use of his senses, Finn realised he was still clasping the clammy hand. He dropped it and the man-who-called-himself-Caravaggio shook it out and inspected his crushed fingers.

'Sorry,' Finn said. 'It's just . . .' He wiped his nose with the back of his hand, grinned through his drying tears, tried to laugh. Believing. Not believing. 'Oh my God. Oh my absolute literal God. Is it really you? I can't tell you how . . . I knew it. I totally fucking knew it. You've been around for ages, eh no? No wonder . . . It is totally amazing to meet you. Sorry, sorry. It all makes . . . You know we're related, right? Great-great-great-something . . . Of course you do. Honestly, I don't want to seem like an entire fucking lunatic, but I really am your number one fan. Your work . . . it's exactly . . .' Finn was choking up with fandom, not even cringing at *number one fan*. There were some things that had to be said, no matter how much of a saddo you came across as. Some things that . . . 'I honestly, totally, can't tell you how—'

'Jesus, stop snivelling. It is making me vomitous.' The self-proclaimed Caravaggio leant across the dividing table and prodded Lizzi's tub of fruit salad with the tip of his dagger. 'May I?'

Bewildered, Finn nodded and peeled off the lid. 'Aye. On you go. Help yourself. Maybe cache the weapon, though?'

'Death makes me ravishing.' Caravaggio shoved the dagger under his cloak and stuck his stubby, wart-riddled fingers straight into the tub. He pulled out an orange segment, which he flopped around until it resembled a goldfish, and guzzled in one. As table manners went, they were verging towards the revolting, but Finn was incapable of looking away. Everything matched what he already knew of the man. In a certain cast of shadow, with a certain sideways scowl, Caravaggio was utterly recognisable. His moth-eaten cloak, his filthy chemise, his uneven teeth coated with a film of yellow scum. Yet, still . . .

'I think you'll find the word is ravenous.'

'I think not,' Caravaggio said, opening Finn's book with his sticky fingers. Finn watched him turn the pages, nod with satisfaction at his own paintings, all the while picking pieces of fruit from the fruit salad. After a while, he stopped reading to suck the last of the juice from the plastic tub. When he tipped his head back, Finn caught sight of thick nasal hair and black pellets of dried snot in his nostrils.

'Superlative,' Caravaggio said, dropping the empty tub on the table.

'I know them all,' Finn said, unsure if Caravaggio was referring to his own work or to the fruit. His ability to think in straight lines had been scuppered by a critical dose of hero-worship and the whole inconceivable notion. If it was him, *if* it was him, there was so much more Finn wanted to say. He wanted to tell Caravaggio how much his work had defined him. How he looked for answers in it when he was lost, and what a huge influence it had been on his own work, and how he wished his wee granny was still alive because she'd have been beside herself to meet him. But he couldn't find the words.

'Anything else of an edible nature?' Caravaggio slammed the cover of the book shut. The train clattered over a set of points in the rails and the tub slid off the table.

'Chocolate,' Finn said, bending under the table to pick up the tub and getting an unwelcome eyeful of Caravaggio's lumpy crotch bulging in his threadbare black breeches. He noted also the sword rammed down beside the armrest of his seat.

'That'll do,' Caravaggio said.

Finn scrabbled through his bag for the chocolates he'd bought for his mother, scratching his memory for colonial history. 'You know what chocolate is, right?' Easier to concentrate on trivialities than on the questions he didn't dare to ask.

Caravaggio sneered. 'Correct me if I am erroneous but you appear to be insinuating that I possess the intellectual incapacity of a gnat's bollock.' His hand wafted vaguely over the secreted sword. 'I encourage you to reconsider.'

Given the size of the clandestine blade, Finn decided it was prudent to keep silent rather than risk offending Caravaggio further. He handed over the cellophane-wrapped chocolates.

'Fucking bollocky scum shite,' Caravaggio said, when he couldn't get his stubby fingers to break the cellophane wrapper.

Before the dagger made a reappearance, Finn snatched the box and hastily unpeeled the cellophane. He opened it up and showed Caravaggio the selection card.

'Much gratitude, I'm sure.' Caravaggio took a coconut cream. For some reason, the choice surprised Finn.

However grateful Caravaggio was for the edible confectionery, Finn realised he risked humiliation if he told this Caravaggio of his own pitiful confections. At this juncture, there was no way he could claim to be an artist. Not yet. Not when confronted by a genius of Caravaggio's calibre. Not when Caravaggio had a mouth on him like this bloke. All he – Finn – was doing, he realised, was painting copies of photographs, which was frankly no more real art (inverted commas loud and clear) than Rob and his ridiculous tattoos. A day earlier and an insight so explosive would have shattered Finn to smithereens but, at that particular moment, on that particular journey, with a man he was praying really was Caravaggio sitting opposite him (albeit guzzling chocolates in a manner that was physically repellent) it didn't. For the first time in as long as Finn could remember, the road ahead wasn't a highway to oblivion, tarmacked and tedious and taking him somewhere he hadn't chosen to go. Far from it. It was as potholed and perilous and full of possibilities as a prowl through the backstreets of a medieval *cittadella*. And who better than this mad fucker to show him the way.

The train rattled on through the Perthshire countryside while Caravaggio chomped his way noisily through the box of chocolates and, with each moment that passed, Finn allowed a little more of himself to believe that Caravaggio really was there, that, however bizarre and inexplicable his appearance, there was no refuting the slathers of saliva spattering the table, the chocolate-shaped holes in the crinkly tray, the empty fruit salad tub rolling one way and another across the table, until he, Finn, was convinced enough to dare to take his eyes away. He glanced out of the window, glimpsing hedgerows and flooded fields and ploughed mud and tree-scarred hillsides. Cloud was descending, dark and pleasantly melancholic, preparing for the end of daylight, which was not far away. The train trundled onwards until the approach of the journey's end was signalled by the outskirts of the town and its sandstone villas scattered in the gaping dusk. Finn yawned deeply and then, unable to do otherwise, closed his eyes and, to the accompaniment of Caravaggio's slurps and gurgles, for the first time in ages fell into a deep and dreamless sleep.

11

Martha and Mary

Christmas Day in the Cavanagh/Blythe household was turning into an unexpectedly formal affair, mainly because everybody (with the exception of Kassia's friend Anna, who was squeezed on the sofa between Paddy and Charlie, smiling pleasantly if a little uncomfortably) was in a bad mood with somebody. Mostly with Esme or so it seemed to her, as she scratched her itching palms and struggled to retain the last of the Christmas spirit that had been gradually oozing out of her since she'd popped into the ward to drop off her contribution to the Christmas party. The activity coordinator had the patients lined up and singing 'In the Bleak Midwinter' when she arrived, so even the souls who weren't depressed beforehand were in need of a citalopram or two by the time the carols were over.

The wintry light outside the bay window set the Christmas tree in relief and the tinsel was shivering and the baubles twisting slowly on their hangers from the draughts sneaking through the window sashes. Even Paddy – who had been at bursting point when he woke and found his stocking full of cheap plastic – was subdued because Dermot had decided the boys should wait to open their proper presents until Kassia and Anna arrived back from church. It was asking too much of them but Esme was too fed up to argue. And then, in a move that more or less finished Paddy off, Dermot, in his wisdom, insisted on serving the drinks before present opening. By the time the cork was finally popped, Esme decided the only hope left for her was to put her faith entirely in the champagne. She perched herself on the armrest of the easy chair next to the fire and resigned herself to getting drunk.

'You want fizzy, Mrs Blythe?' Kassia asked, selecting the smallest of the mishmash of crystal glasses she'd discovered behind dusty bottles of Cognac and Drambuie in the Arts and Crafts dresser, having designated herself as Dermot's helper. The minute she'd arrived back from Mass she'd rushed upstairs to change into her Christmas outfit, leaving Esme to take Anna's coat and make polite, forced conversation, and had reappeared a good half-hour later with her hair pinned up loosely, piled in dark curls, some of which had now escaped and were trailing ink-black flourishes on the milky vellum of her neck. She held the glass for Dermot to pour and handed it to Esme without smiling.

Esme took the drink, only mildly regretting the premeditated snideness that had made her put a pack of Happy Families in the bottom of Kassia's Christmas stocking. So what if Kassia was in a mood? Of course, Esme had meant it as a joke, but perhaps she shouldn't have assumed Kassia wouldn't understand, or that Paddy wouldn't cheerfully volunteer to teach Kassia how to play. *I try to learn the rules*, she said, *but it is not always easy.*

An hour or so earlier, not long after the girls had arrived back from church, Esme had met Dermot at the bottom of the stairs when she was hanging Anna's coat in the cloakroom, taking care not to let her cracked skin leak on to the cashmere. 'Madam got her friend to buy the cream,' she said. Cream for the trifle that Esme had asked Kassia to fetch on her way home. There was only loose change in her purse to reimburse Anna, which didn't make sense because she'd withdrawn cash only a day or two earlier. When Esme mentioned it, Dermot raised his eyebrows without comment, and she wondered (yet again) how many times they would let these things pass. In the end, he offered to say something if it bothered her that much, but she thought they shouldn't make accusations without direct proof. Especially not on Christmas Day. Not in front of the boys. Not in front of Kassia's friend. Strangely, it wasn't anger Esme felt. More disillusionment, cold disappointment, which was ironic considering how low her expectations of Kassia were. It was as if the girl had no boundaries, or at least had decided she was exempt from those that restrained everyone else. As far as Esme could see, whatever Kassia might claim, it didn't appear that she was trying *that* hard to learn the rules.

At the far side of the fireplace, Frankie was leaning against the oak surround, staring into the abyss of his glass of sparkling pear juice and ignoring everyone with the degree of intent only possible from someone who was, in reality, acutely aware of every breath being taken in the room. He was wearing a Christmas outfit of his own choosing – his boy band trousers, a school shirt and the jacket from his confirmation suit which was too small for him now – and had even put on Dermot's knitted tie and knotted it himself. It was disproportionately wide on him and the squared-off end hung down below his belt.

Esme felt a tug of pity for her son. 'You look nice, Frankie,' she said.

He waved away her compliment and a fug of aftershave Esme recognised as Dermot's wafted towards her. Where Esme was concerned Frankie's foul moods were hardly breaking news, but when she'd arrived home from the hospital earlier in the day she had compounded her usual crimes by asking if he wanted help wrapping the present he had been hunched over and attempting to hide since she'd left. In response, Frankie had outdone himself with his pre-pubescent vitriol and scrunched up another length of sellotape.

'Dermot? You want?' Kassia smiled at Dermot and adjusted the bodice of her party dress. Frankie twitched in reflex. Kassia's dress was a mauve, strapless thing, staying up by an act of faith rather than good tailoring, Esme felt, and for a moment considered telling her to stay clear of the flames because the cheap viscose was surely a fire hazard. But she thought better of it and took a sip of her champagne.

'Visitors first,' Dermot said, pouring a glass for Anna.

Kassia took a glass of champagne for herself and plonked herself in the other armchair. The skirt of her dress rode up to show a little of the tulle petticoat underneath, and she folded her legs beneath her so her spiky heels pointed directly at Esme. It was such a provocative gesture that Esme wanted to laugh. Despite the attitude, though, and the cheap dress and the precipitous heels, Kassia looked beautiful. No other description was adequate. Esme wondered briefly whether it was too late to rethink her own outfit, loosen her own scraped-back hair.

'Thank you for inviting me, Dr Blythe. It is very kind of you.' Anna held her glass aloft to prevent Charlie from drinking it. Her nails were immaculately manicured in an understated shimmering gold, and a tiny diamond on her ring finger glinted in the flicker from the fire.

'It's nothing,' Esme said, thinking how odd it was that Kassia hadn't mentioned that Anna was engaged. 'Thank Kassia. It was her idea. Or my husband. He's doing the cooking. Except the trifle which was all me.' She giggled nervously, aware that her voice was trilling, unsure why she was feeling so discomposed. Anna was very different to Kassia. Poised, pretty, almost blonde. Not as arresting as her friend but more adult somehow. Her high-neck chiffon blouse and tight black trousers cut an expensive contrast to Kassia's get-up.

Esme's unexpected nerves calmed a little when Dermot sat down beside her in his chair. He'd barely had the chance to make himself comfortable when Kassia stood up in a flurry.

'Before we go further, I have something to say. To all of you, I say thank you for sharing your Christmas Day with me. It is important to pass Christmas among friends and family.'

'Wow, Kass. Nice sentiment.' Dermot raised his glass. 'How about it, boys? Happy to share your Christmas with Kassia and Anna?'

In response, Paddy giggled and Frankie reddened under his curtain of fringe. Charlie chose that moment to bite Paddy's ear and the two boys scuffled on the sofa, giddy and silly for a moment, until Anna pulled Charlie on to her knee and kissed him. A fleeting look passed from Kassia to Anna, but to Esme's surprise Kassia merely smiled. It was as if she was physically restraining her natural response, Esme thought, and decided maybe it was time to curb her own natural cynicism towards the girl. Improbable though it was, Kassia genuinely seemed happy to be sharing their Christmas. Either that or the champagne was working its magic on them all.

'Has everyone a drink? Frankie? Paddy? So now I say a clink clink toast.' Kassia beamed and raised her glass. 'Cheese.'

The last trace of Esme's hostility shattered into a thousand pieces of crystal. 'It's *cheers*,' she spluttered, swiping her wrist under her nose to catch the bubbles of champagne and snot that had sprayed from her nostrils.'

Kassia's hand leapt to her mouth. She searched Esme's face. 'Honest?'

Esme nodded.

'Cheers? OMG.' Kassia started giggling. 'I am imbecile. I have been saying this every time.' Her words were squashed between her gasps of laughter. She turned to Frankie, who was rigid against the fire surround, and clutched his arm to hold herself up. 'I was thinking it is cheese. Like, you know, cheese and wine party.' She raised her hand to give Frankie a high five. He managed to respond but the effort involved made it look like he had melted.

Esme's good mood lasted through the rest of the champagne and supermarket nibbles, through the giving of presents and the frenzied unwrapping by Paddy and Charlie. It even lasted long enough for her to keep her thoughts to herself when Frankie presented Kassia with a pair of pearl earrings he had absolutely no way of being able to afford.

By the time the turkey was cooked and the crackers were pulled, it was dark outside and beginning to freeze. The dining room, by contrast, was warm and beautifully lit. In the corner, the parlour palm was draped with fairy lights. Three candles burnt from a silver candlestick on top of the piano and another in the centre of the table surrounded by a tinsel and pine cone garland that Paddy had made in class. The day before the end of term, Esme had been called into school by the teacher to be told that Paddy had graffitied a penis on the toilet door with the silver spray they had been using to decorate the pine cones. They discussed it calmly at home that evening, and Paddy was devastated by the unfavourable evaluation of his work. 'It was a Christmas tree,' he wailed, but Dermot chose not to believe him. And completely failed to hide how proud he was of this idea of his son. For once, Esme was glad Dermot hadn't attended the school meeting.

Only Esme and the boys were wearing their paper hats. Dermot was at the head of the table, sharpening the carving knife against a flint and with each screech of blade across stone, the candle at the centre of the table stuttered. Paddy was trying to make himself heard over the noise, reading out everyone's jokes in his after-school drama club voice and, at the other end, Esme was playing with the casing of an empty cracker to distract Charlie from the flickering lure of the candle flame. From time to time, she glanced at Dermot enquiringly. They were waiting for the turkey to make its entrance.

'She said she wanted to do it,' he said finally.

'Should I see if she wants some help?' Anna said.

'No, I'll go,' Dermot said, just as Kassia kicked open the dining room door.

'Ready, ready, I come now,' she said.

Dermot held the door while Kassia brought in the turkey on a large white serving dish. Esme couldn't believe quite how ugly the bird was, its basted breast bulging out like a grotesque forehead, plump thighs protruding from the sides like bulbous ears, and the stuffing-filled cavity gaping like the mouth of someone howling in pain. Kassia leant over the table to put the plate down and the candlelight scattered across her collarbones, her bare shoulders, the ivory skin of her long neck, leaving one side of her face in shadow.

'Move the potatoes, please, Frankie. Quick. Quick. I drop.'

It was left to Esme to move the bowl. Frankie didn't budge. He couldn't. He was absolutely transfixed. Since Kassia had unwrapped his gift, he had hardly said a word, although his silence was less tortured than his usual. As soon as the ribbon was off, the paper torn open, Kassia had taken out her gaudy hoops and put in Frankie's earrings. They were intricate and fussy – deeply untrendy – with tiny black bows tied above the pearl drops, but she had beamed as if they were real treasures.

Remarkably, the main course passed off uneventfully, although Esme hardly touched the turkey and drank more red wine than she knew she ought to. The older boys argued over ownership of the trinkets from the crackers and Charlie fell asleep in his high chair.

When it was finished, Anna offered to clear the table.

'Good idea,' Kassia said, pouring herself another glass of wine. 'But me, I prefer to rest as I have been already working.'

Anna said something in Polish under her breath as she scraped gravy and turkey bones from the dirty plates. Kassia sipped from her glass, watching Anna over the rim, her dark eyes as liquid as the ruby wine. It was difficult to interpret their relationship, Esme thought. Hard to imagine how they had become friends.

'She tells me I am lazy and that I should be more respectful. In fact, I think it most important to keep the host happy.' Kassia smiled coyly, biting her bottom lip so the tips of her white teeth gleamed in the candlelight. 'Dermot, you want?' she said, offering him the bottle.

'Come on, Anna. I'll help you,' Esme said. She glanced in the mirror in the hall as she passed. Blue teeth. Her own personal red wine curse.

'I am sorry about my friend,' Anna said when they were in the kitchen. 'She has drunk a little too much, I think.'

'You don't have to apologise for her, Anna. We know

what she's like. We don't always get along, but the boys worship her.'

Anna rinsed a couple of dirty plates under the tap and handed them to Esme. 'She loves them, you know. Believe it or not, they are the most important thing to her. I guess she misses her own family.' She scraped some food into the bin. 'She isn't always like she pretends to be, you know. All this joking and flirting. I think maybe she is scared to show her more vulnerable side.'

'It's hard to imagine Kassia with a vulnerable side,' Esme said, stacking plates in the new dishwasher.

Anna handed Esme the last one. 'Sometimes, you know, I think she is ready to be different.'

Esme laughed and the plate slipped in her fingers and clipped the edge of the granite work surface. She caught it before it smashed on the floor. There was a tiny chip on the rim and a hairline crack that ran to the middle. She shoved it in the dishwasher with the rest.

When Anna and Esme returned to the dining room, Frankie was twisting in his seat, pulling his fringe in front of his eyes, looking more upset than Esme had seen him in a long time. Kassia's face was ugly with rage.

'What's up?' Esme mouthed to Dermot. He shrugged.

Paddy said, 'Kassy is upset because Daddy was rude about Church or God or something.'

Esme opened another bottle of wine. She couldn't be bothered to mediate. Dermot wore his atheism like a badge of honour, with the type of fierce energy only a lapsed Catholic could muster. Kassia, on the other hand, was a regular at the Dougal Street church, although Esme had assumed it was simply because the new priest was quite cute.

'I wasn't rude,' Dermot said. 'We were discussing the scandalous cover-up of child abuse in the Catholic Church, that's all.'

'In my world,' Kassia said, 'that is rude.'

They ate dessert in silence, the thick smoke of Kassia's mood choking the conversation. Even the boys were quiet. Eventually, Esme pushed her trifle aside and with a brittle cheeriness asked the girls how long they had known each other.

All their lives, Anna told her, because their parents were friends.

'Ah, I see,' Esme said. Now it made sense why Anna would tolerate Kassia's sniping and the petty attempts to undermine her. It was the sign of an unbreakable bond, an inescapable friendship. A friendship that may have been altered by time but had left them bound by a loyalty for something they used to have. That was Esme's theory anyway, although it didn't look like Kassia was affected in quite the same way. 'Did you come across here together then? To do your au-pairing?'

Kassia sniggered. Anna blushed. 'I'm not an au pair, Dr Blythe.'

'Oh, I just assumed. Assumed you worked with children. You have a flair for it.' Esme knew it was the wine talking. 'I wouldn't mind an au pair like you.'

'You think she is better than me, no?' Kassia said, her face darkening.

Esme felt Frankie's eyes on her. 'Don't be daft,' she said, not able to stretch to a smile. She was punishing Kassia but she wasn't entirely sure why. 'You have a special relationship with the boys.'

Kassia glowered at her. 'I understand *special relationship*. That is to say you think I am crap.'

'No, Kassia. It isn't that at all. I was just wondering what Anna worked as, that's all.' Esme glanced at Anna. Her eyes were lowered and her hands were folded in her lap. Penitent. Like she was praying.

Kassia tossed her head. A single dark curl fell over her face. 'You want to know what Anna does for work? You want to know?' The strand caught in her mouth. She spat it out. 'I tell you, shall I?'

'Don't, Kassia,' Anna whispered.

'You want to know?' Kassia was practically shouting. 'Really?' She was laughing now. Strident and desperate laughs. 'You think she is au pair. Ridiculous. She is prostitute.'

Kassia looked around wildly, between Dermot and Esme, at Anna, at the boys. Frankie and Paddy were frozen in their seats as if someone had stopped the music. 'And you know what?' Kassia said, spitting the words between Esme and Dermot. 'Her parents think this is good way to make money.'

Anna was twisting her napkin in her lap.

Unbelievably, Esme managed to stay calm. 'Okay, girls, let's drop it.'

'You are kidding with me, no?'

'What's prostitute, Mummy?' Paddy asked.

'A prostitute is a person who is paid for doing someone a favour,' Anna said quietly.

Paddy nodded vigorously. Frankie seemed on the point of disputing Anna's words, but she glanced at him and he changed his mind.

'See, she is so holy but she refuses even to be ashamed,' Kassia said. Anna said something softly in Polish. Kassia laughed. Mocking her friend.

Esme picked Charlie out of the high chair and buried her face into his peachy hair. 'I'm going to put him to bed, Dermot,' she said.

'Fair enough. I think we're done here anyway,' Dermot said. 'Boys, do me a favour please and clear the table while the grown-ups have a chat.'

Esme flinched at the word caught on Dermot's tongue.

'Can I get paid?' Paddy beamed. 'Can I get paid for doing Daddy a favour? Can I be a prostitute?'

'No way,' Frankie said, bursting out laughing. Kassia sniggered.

'No,' Esme said, almost under her breath. 'I'm not having it.' She clutched Charlie closer to her. There was no air left in the room. A candle burnt out with a sputter of wax. Dermot told the boys to go to the living room and play with their presents. Paddy climbed down from his seat and waited at the dining room door for his brother. Frankie looked around desperately, not wanting to go.

'Now!' Dermot shouted.

Charlie twitched in Esme's arms.

Frankie got up from his chair and made for the door. He passed behind Kassia's seat, and she reached out to touch him, her fingers trailing off the sleeve of his jacket.

Anna picked up her handbag. 'I'm so sorry—'

Dermot interrupted her. 'It isn't your fault, Anna.' He turned to Kassia. 'You went too far, Kass. Too far.'

'Too far? It is not me that makes the wrong life. All I try to do is make a nice time for your children.'

Esme pushed her chair under the table with her foot, carried Charlie towards the door.

'No,' Dermot said. He looked at Esme. Turned back to Kassia. 'You fill their heads with garbage. With stuff that is irresponsible and too old for them. They are too young for all your carry-on, your bad language, the stuff you let them watch on television.'

'Frankie isn't too young.'

'Kassia, he's eleven.'

'You do not know how to have a life. You think you are trendy cool. But no. You are stuck in mud together with her.' Kassia gestured towards Esme.

'Come off it,' Dermot said.

Esme paused in the doorway, caught between the dining room and the foot of the stairs. Dermot was trying to catch her eye. Trying to get out of it.

Eventually, he said, 'I think you should go.'

'You can't fire me for making fun.'

'We can, Kassia. It isn't only these things. It's the lies, the deceit, the stealing.' Dermot sighed. 'Go and pack your things,' he said quietly. 'We don't want you in our house.'

Kassia gasped. 'No. This is not fair. You do not appreciate me. What am I going to do now for job? You make me homeless on Christmas Day? You are disgusting.' When she got no response from Dermot, she turned to Esme. 'You know this is not right.' Her voice was splintering. Her eyes were brimming with tears. Until that point, her anger had been goading her, but now she seemed defeated. 'You make your husband do this to me.'

Anna laid her hand on Kassia's arm and said something to her in Polish. Kassia shook her head, tears flowing down her face now. Esme squeezed Charlie more strongly than she meant to. The stairs creaked. Frankie was standing on the half-landing eyeing his mother with cool hatred. Esme's blood pooled in her veins.

Anna said, 'It is okay. She can come with me.'

Kassia smoothed out the ruffles in her dress. On her way out of the dining room, she pushed past Esme and kissed Charlie on his plump forearm. 'With you I know it is jealousy,' she whispered to Esme. 'You do not like that your son gives me this present that costs so much.'

Half an hour later, Esme watched from the doorstep as the two girls left. The cold had sunk into the crevices between the neighbouring houses and the city had the stillness that accompanies the rare nights when the whole world is resting. In the distance, night lights twinkled and the frost hardened. As the girls walked down the path away from Esme, they were caught in the glare of the security light: Anna with her hand on Kassia's shoulder, pulling her friend's suitcase over the flagstones; Kassia viciously wiping away tears with one hand and, in the other, carrying the rucksack Esme had bought Frankie at the start of term. Given to her. Not stolen.

12

Rest on the Flight into Egypt

The time between Christmas and New Year was way more tedious than Tuesday expected. Way more than way more. The hours stretched out for ever, getting longer and thinner but never actually ending. In much the same way, she reckoned, that spat-out chewing gum stuck to the sole of your shoe.

For the best part of three days she hadn't bothered to get out of bed. She'd passed her time shoving folds of her quilt between herself and the clammy wallpaper to stop her bare skin touching it, and counting down the days till Rob would let her loose on his computer. Last time she'd seen outside light was at the party the day before Christmas Eve. And, if you didn't include the torture that was the Sally Army communal Christmas lunch, which all the residents (except the lucky-bastard refugees) had taken in the breakfast room, and a couple of trips downstairs to get her home-supply methadone from the locked fridge in the staff quarters (her wee holiday treat from the Health Board, gifted to her for good behaviour and the fact that the chemist didn't trust anyone else to take over for the holidays), in all that time, she had barely crossed another living soul.

She'd heard them though. The beige wallpaper – skid-marked with a brown leaf arrangement – was practically all there was between her and the banging and crashing and thumping of the other residents' comings and goings.

Tuesday pulled her quilt over her head and sank into the fusty mattress. She didn't want to hear the soundtrack to their chaotic existence or be sucked into their pathetic misery.

Fortunately, today she was off out and about. The holiday meds were done and a pharmacy trip was due. With a burst of effort, she threw back the quilt, and for a minute or two lay sprawled in her knickers on top of the thin sheet, considering whether it was worth a slight deviation on the way to the pharmacy to take in the day centre and prostitute a made-up version of her life story to Elizabeth-the-trainee-psychologist in return for a cuppy and a shortbread biscuit. Deciding on balance it was probably worth the temporary humiliation, Tuesday dangled her legs over the mattress and forced herself upright. While her body adjusted to the vertical, she sat on the edge of the bed, watching her knees knock and measuring the finger thickness of the gap between her mottled thighs.

It made her light-headed and vaguely sick to stand up. She hadn't eaten much since the Christmas lunch and it wasn't as if that had been a feast. Turkey so tough she hadn't taken the risk to her teeth, and a lukewarm slime-fest that one of the bonnet-wearers had oathed was Brussels sprouts. And on Boxing Day, her tin of alphabet spaghetti. Cold from the can with a spoon, shivering on the edge of the bed with her lank quilt wrapped round her, feeling queasy and almost sentimental for the times she'd dine in herself as a kid.

This hunger thing was rubbish. When she'd been using, it had never troubled her. Those days, she must have eaten something, but she honestly couldn't say what. She had a vague recollection of a bunch of them scavenging in the bin lanes behind the restaurants on Gibson Street. All of them living together under the bridge like a proper community. Looking out for the wasters who were so totally fucked or inexperienced they were bound to OD, allegedly out of neighbourliness but really so they'd get a head start on their stuff if one of them copped it. It was out of order to pounce if someone still had a pulse, and with some of the hard core it could be difficult to tell if they were alive or dead even when you were chatting with them, but once the rigor mortis set in, it was a free-for-all. It was surprising what even the most expert junkies considered more important than their next hit, things they would never pawn or trade, things they guarded with the remains of their life or kept stashed in various orifices. Tuesday had acquired a charm bracelet and a Celtic key ring by that means and, briefly, a fluffy toy rabbit, until one of her companions mistook it for a rat and lobbed it in the river to drown.

In the corner of the bedroom there was an old-fashioned hand basin and a wall heater that never came on. Jelly-legged, Tuesday went over and loaded her toothbrush with toothpaste. She didn't have the money for tokens for the washing machine, so she laundered her stuff in the sink with a shrinking square of soap that stank of petrol and draped her washing over the defective heater. Now her clothes had that smell to them, that hum of dog pee and raw onions that she thought she'd left behind when she'd finally been given accommodation with water that ran out of a tap, rather than down the walls.

Because of that, because these days she was actually conscious enough to give a toss, because she couldn't stand any more to stink like a urinal, she'd landed herself in trouble. After she'd abandoned the dinner on Christmas Day (on religious grounds, she told the Army ladies – hair covered with a headscarf she'd found hanging in the porch –

claiming that she was off to join the jihadis up the stairs) she'd borrowed an electric fan heater from behind the unmanned reception desk to blast some warmth into her bones and dry off her laundry while the day staff had a piss-up in the boiler room. But some fucker had grassed her to the management and now she was on an eviction warning for frauding the electric and theft of council property.

From now on, she'd have to watch her step. The B&B was bad but the alternative was not doing it for her. It would be too hard to sleep rough without the comfort of using. She was getting soft, getting used to her lumpy bed and the taste of a clean mouth, even if most of her teeth were too far gone to rescue. Warily, she poked around her mouth. They were turning green from the methadone and she couldn't be sure the manky one at the front didn't have a wobble to it. When she tested, though, it was hard to tell if the tooth was moving or just her finger underneath.

She rinsed and spat and checked herself out in the mirror above the sink. If she was planning to head to the centre, it was important to look the part – which basically meant as sorted and undeserving as possible and with an attitude to match – to keep all the emotional incontinents who worked there from drowning her with pity. Only if they saw what she could see, she was stuffed. Somewhere along the way, her face had had even the white sucked out of it. Her hair was filthy and the roots were coming in and under her pierced eyebrows, in the space where her eyes were meant to be, all she could see were ugly craters ringed by slashes of black eyeliner (an eyeliner Dr Blythe had said she could keep one day when it fell out of her handbag at a clinic session, but which annoyingly had turned out to be waterproof and wouldn't come off with soap and water). Pancakes for tits, collarbones like razors, corrugated ribs.

Tuesday twisted round to see her backside. The knickers that she'd slept in for the last three days – age twelve and several years too big for her – were drooping off her bum in granny buttock folds. It was pitiful. Even Tuesday McLaughlin at her most intolerant would feel sorry for that skanky bitch.

There wasn't a lot she could do to improve things. She shoved her hands under the cold water and combed her fingers through her hair. Wet them again and wiped the backs under her pits. Did the same under her fanny. Sniffed. A bit fishy but it was too Baltic to do an extensive wipe down. Finally, she got dressed. Her clothes were still damp and the sole of one boot was coming off, flapping at the toe like the death gasps of a landed haddock. As a temporary measure, she lined it with a paper napkin she'd guarded from the Christmas lunch.

When she was ready, she headed downstairs, all set to duck past reception if one of the power-crazies was on. With certain staff, the harassment was constant. An interrogation every time she went in or out. Said they were obliged to check for drugs or other criminal behaviour, making out there were standards to maintain, tapping the notice taped to the glass partition to prove it, as if they were forced to single her out, forced to frisk her and question her and empty out her pockets, when the simple fact was they were gutless bullies. Second-rate thugs who weren't mental enough to get employed as prison guards.

Happily for her, it was the waste-of-space duty manager on reception. He was sitting with his feet up, drinking coffee and chatting on his mobile. She rapped on the glass partition and he glanced over and carried on his conversation without shifting. Tuesday swore through her throbbing teeth. What she loved most about this accommodation was the five-star personal service. High standards that had worked their way down from the bandit who owned the premises. A gangster the council was perfectly happy to fellate *and* pay for the privilege, on the promise that him and his missus took the dosser-scum-scroungers off their hands. From what the other residents told her, their housing benefit went direct to the pair – to mono-block their four-car driveway, heat their indoor swimming pool, upgrade their home cinema system. Sports car and beautician's bills for her. Golf club fees and tennis lessons for him. Last time they showed up at the B&B on some sort of deal to fiddle an insurance claim, the wife was sporting a boob job her man had bought her for her birthday. Class.

Tuesday rapped again and shoved her face right up against the glass partition but the duty manager swivelled his chair round so he wouldn't have to look at her. She rapped again, harder. What cracked her up most was the pretence that the place was anything other than a dosshouse. There were stickers in the front window behind the twisted venetian blinds which rattled every time the main door opened; stickers from the tourist board or guidebooks that had stopped existing twenty years before, stickers whose reds had bleached to pigskin pink and blues to fag-ash grey. Outside, there was one of those *Vacancies/No Vacancies* signs hanging from the hook on the porch beam which told a different lie each time the wind changed. From time to time, some unsuspecting tourist or beaten-up housewife or trashed student who'd lost his pals and his sense of direction showed up asking about rooms, like it was a real B&B, like ones you got at the seaside, with clean sheets and a price list and breakfast included.

The tosser gave her no alternative. Tuesday dragged the front door wide open and let the storm in. It swirled into the foyer, bringing dead leaves and horizontal rain with it. She didn't have to wait long.

The manager swivelled round and stretched to open the sliding panel, his phone still stuck to his ear. 'What do you want, McLaughlin?'

'Have I got any letters?'

'For fuck's sake,' he said, shutting the panel and returning to his phone call. Tuesday gave him the Vs and left the door open on her way out.

The storm was wild. Tuesday tanked it up Great Western Road in the shelter of the high wall running beside the Botanics. Further up, at the fancy terraces with decoration chipped into the sandstone blocks that reckoned it was ancient Greek but even to someone as untravelled as Tuesday was blatantly some chancing Glaswegian's idea of the exotic, there were private roads parallel to the main road, with individual parking bays and 4x4s and the topless sports cars essential in a climate as balmy as Glasgow's. She took those private roads because the shelter was better, even though the dripping money turned her stomach. Before the entrance to the psychiatric hospital, Tuesday crossed back over the main road, but she didn't hang about. Six months had passed since she'd ended up there after an escapade with a duff batch that had more or less killed her. Her uninvited escape had brought her to the attention of the medical profession who'd shunted her over to Dr Blythe the second she could breathe on her own. At their first encounter, she was still too weak in the legs and in the head from the effects of being half poisoned to put up a fight. By the time she was well enough to scarper, it was too late. Spellbound already by Dr Blythe's witchcraft. And a court order.

The business hotel next door was even bleaker than the hospital. Tuesday carried on, battling the storm, admiring the hotel's artificial pond that backed on to the hospital car park. She'd love to shake the hand of whoever was responsible for that particular bit of urban planning. Congratulate them on achieving such an immense piece of dross. The pond was supposed to be a nature reserve but there was more wildlife living in her mattress. If it hadn't been for the two swans swimming in the slimy water – caressing each other among the pondweed and bobbing lager tins – she would have been the only thing in this wasteland that actually had a heartbeat.

A notion that Tuesday didn't feel was in any way contradicted when she spotted an acquaintance from her former life sitting on a bench on the concrete bank, tattooed bare arm around his blank girlfriend and the other lifting a can of Special Brew to his lips, happily unperturbed by the rain pissing down on him and the wind thrashing through his thin T-shirt. She went over to say hello.

'Long time, no see, sunshine,' he drawled.

Tuesday pulled her arm out of her coat sleeve and showed him her tattoo. From what she could tell, he approved.

'What you up to?' Her shouts were carried off towards the swans.

'Ach, you ken. This and that.' He squeezed his leg. 'Had a wee mishap but they managed to save it.'

'Ya chancer.' Tuesday had only advanced as far as her feet when Dr Blythe had worked her magic. Big veins were risky. Femorals especially had a habit of misfiring. A last resort when all the others were fucked. There was a whole army of hopalongs in the city living with the after-effects of arterial emboli and high leg amputations. Not that anyone should waste their time feeling sorry for them. When it came to footwear, they'd hit the jackpot. All those single shoes displayed outside shoe shops, racked up and asking to be nicked. Perfect if you'd had the right – correct – leg chopped and were speedy on the getaway crutches.

'Got a place in here until they shift me to the rehab unit.' He winked. 'Or they kick me out.'

Tuesday pulled a face. 'Rather you than me.'

'Och, I dunno. Free scran, your own room, and if you arenae on a section, you get to come and go when you want. We even had a Christmas do. With crackers, presents, the lot. For which we got ourselves a decent return.' He smiled sappily at his girlfriend. The girl's eyelids twitched. 'Anyways, we were just away to partake of the proceedings. Care to join us?'

'No me, doll. I'm reformed.'

'Aye, aye. So you are, hen.'

'Couldnae tap us a fag, but?'

'For you, sweetheart, certainly.'

Tuesday took the cigarette and the shaky light. Left the pair to their canoodling and carried on up the road. She finished the cigarette in the petrol station, crouching behind a petrol pump to hide from the CCTV and the weather.

The day centre was in one of the massive houses with stone animals on the gate posts and sweeping front lawns and a servants' entrance round the side. Except that in the case of the day centre, the grass had been turned over to tarmac and the gate posts were hidden by a Health Board notice that had North Glasgow Psychiatric Services branded all over it. It was properly touching, the consideration they'd given over to patient confidentiality. A sign that size ensured every passing school kid clocked you for a nutter.

Tuesday buzzed the buzzer and waited to identify herself through the intercom. When no one replied, she waved at the security camera. Nothing. She shoogled the door handle and rattled the brass letterbox. It was only when she was on her way round the back to find another way in and her practised eye spotted the blink of red from the burglar alarms that she realised the place was shut up. There was a notice taped to the window of the day room, informing her that they were closed until 3rd January. She swore and about-turned. At the pond, the lovebirds and the swans had gone.

To get to the pharmacy, Tuesday cut through Hyndland. Passed a parade of shops with a deli, a florist, an offie without bars across the counter. Jed and Rob and some other kids from her class at primary were from this neck of the woods. Once, when she was six, she'd been invited to play at Lauren Gray's house behind the cricket ground and they'd given her Barbie a Mohican for a laugh and Lauren had made out like she wasn't really crying. When you were little like that, the differences weren't so big. Everybody looked cute in infants, even if your school shirt was a charity hand-out and your socks were washed-in grey, and your knickers had no elastic and were held up with a safety pin. It was only by primary three or four that you could see the kids who were heading for trouble. The ones with bags of sleep deprivation under their eyes, or patterns shaved into their skinheads, or who knew the exact meaning of all the sex words graffitied in the public toilets. By that stage, it was too late. Outlived their chance to turn out different. Tuesday thought back. Had she had the chance to turn out different? Not fucking likely.

At the next corner, where a fancy hairdresser's was offering *Champagne and Shellac*, neither of which was really Tuesday's thing, she dived into the call box to shelter from the rain. The tinsel-decorated bottles of lotion in the window of the shut-up hairdresser's cost more than she got on the social for a week. Lauren and her Barbie girl pals probably grew up thinking that was normal. But then, who was to say they weren't right?

To cheer herself up, Tuesday tried calling Rob. She wanted to see what he was up to, see if she could maybe start early on her computer course, maybe make some arrangements for New Year because she couldn't face another festivity by herself, but the operator told her you couldn't reverse charge a mobile. Tuesday got her to look up the shop number and call that instead, but it went straight to answerphone. Before she had a chance to leave a message, the operator cut the call. Raging, Tuesday slammed the receiver down. It didn't make her feel any better, so she lifted it again and yanked the cable out at its root.

Her plan for the day had only gone as far as the pharmacy. She exchanged a bit of banter with the chemist, turned down the offer of the hand drier in the toilet out back to dry off a bit (there was no way she was doing that in close proximity to someone she actually had some respect for, not to mention whose drugs she relied on; the second her kit warmed up it would stink the place out and she might not get invited back) and then dawdled aimlessly back up Dougal Street, ignoring the thunder rumbling overhead and the gusts of wind threatening to lift her off her feet.

The play park was deserted. The swings were swaying in the wind and the seesaw was creaking on its hinges. For lack of anything better to do, Tuesday wiped a swing with her coat sleeve and swung for a while, scuffing the flapping sole of her boot along the ground while the wind birled through the bars of the climbing frame and the roundabout twisted of its own accord. After a bit, she turned her face up to the driving rain and tried to keep her eyes from flinching.

She used to meet her ma there sometimes after school – those times when the hackit bitch hadn't buggered off somewhere or got herself locked up – and Tuesday would fight for a place on the swings, hoping she'd get a push from her old doll like any other wean. But her ma was always at it, always scamming something or other, giving it: *Where d'you get to, you wee tinker?* like she never even knew Tuesday had school to go to. She'd set her robbing sanitary towels or condoms or painkillers or whatever other adult stuff she had need of, reckoning nobody would suspect a wee one, not even one as scabby as Tuesday.

Tuesday picked off a solid piece of gum from under the swing and chewed it, swinging until her clothes were drenched and goosebumps had pock-marked every square centimetre of her skin. The church bells chimed three. There were still hours before it was acceptable to hole back up in bed. The only way she would manage to stay longer, to overcome the shitty weather, was to use a trick she'd learnt when she lived rough. The skill was not to fight the cold. To relax every muscle in your body so they couldn't shiver, your teeth couldn't chatter. That way, when you died of hypothermia, at least you went quietly.

After a while, she got sick of her own thoughts. She spat the gum into her hand and kneaded it to a putty. It was the major problem she'd found with staying off the gear. Hideous hours of emptiness filled with all this reminiscing crap. If anything was going to finish her off it was that. Tuesday stuck the flapping sole back on to her boot with the gum and jumped from the swing. She landed with a splash on the spongy surface. She had to find somewhere more lively.

Despite the gale-force winds, she made a decent speed through the streets. Halfway to the lights and shops and bustle of Byres Road, she spotted someone leaving one of the mansion blocks ahead of her. Even through the weather, she recognised him. It was the guy from the farmers' market, the one with the wanky jacket. She sprinted to catch him, thinking he might be worth another tap, that he might be good for a few more quid, but he was already locking the storm door, springing down the stone steps, climbing into his flash car parked outside. Before she could shout on him, he slammed the car door and started the engine. The head-lights flashed on and wipers swished the heavy rain from the windscreen. There was enough time before he pulled away for Tuesday to get a clear view of the passengers. Dr Blythe and her boys. The picture of a perfect family.

Out of sheer nosiness and because she knew it was always useful to arm yourself with info about your health care practitioners – (Tuesday knew all the terms. She'd picked them up from the leaflets they handed out at the clinic; leaf-lets that spouted phrases like best practice and fit for pur-pose, service providers and end-users, all of which translated, as far as she could tell, into the patients getting fucked over time and again; she hadn't even got her head round being a client when she'd been upgraded to an end-user. Whichever fuckwit had decided on that terminology obviously hadn't thought about the connotations for the smackheads) – she climbed the six or so steps to check out the brass plaque screwed to the stone portico. DERMOT CAVANAGH *Member of the British Society for Aesthetic Dentistry* followed by a whole string of random letters that were clearly there to big himself up. Tuesday peered through the window. Not like any dentist place she'd ever seen. Designer chairs and flashy magazines and a plasma screen that blinked adverts for teeth whitening and state-of-the-art dental implants. No sign of the posters telling you bills must be settled immediately and the management would exercise their right to pursue non-payment, and to please inform reception if you thought you might be infected with one of the following. No wonder she never went.

Thunder cracked directly overhead, and the rain came down in girders. Tuesday headed off again. A ferocious wind howled between the mansion blocks and lashed around her legs. She stopped at the first café she came to.

It was warm inside and smelt of milk and sugar. She was on her way to dry off when the manager stopped her.

'The facilities are for customers only.'

'I am a customer.'

'I'm not even going to dignify that by taking your order. Beat it.'

Tuesday didn't have a full enough stomach to argue. Instead she loitered in the doorway considering her options. The café was in a converted cinema and the doorway was a good old-fashioned dossers' doorway, covered and wide enough to take a sleeping bag at full stretch. The conversion had obviously been done before the council bods got on their crusade to install anti-jakey measures all over the shop. Bus shelter seats that pivot. Park benches made of metal too cold to sit for long, armrests slap in the middle to stop you lying down. Spikes on the top of park walls, under bridges, on shop window sills. Bright lights in underpasses. There was no place to rest any more. Defensive architecture, they called it. Like anyone would need defending from her vagrant pals who didn't eat, didn't sleep and didn't have the cash to take a shit in a paying establishment. Tuesday wrung her sopping coat out over the mosaic tiles and leant against the wall taking bets on which one of the customers who could afford to use the facilities would be the first to slip on the wet tiles and break their neck.

By the time the manager decided he was coming out to have a word, Tuesday had had one or two near successes, a twisted ankle but no actual fractured bones. She recognised the girl with the manager. Kassia or whatever her name was, from the church party. That was the thing about this part of town. It was so fucking small. You couldn't fart in the West End without your granny smelling it.

'Oi, you can't stay here.'

'Fuck off,' Tuesday said. 'It's a free country.'

'Not here, it isn't. Not when you're bothering my clientele.'

'I'm no bothering your clientele.'

'Wrong. Now, piss off or I'll call the police.' He grabbed Tuesday's arm and dragged her away from the wall.

'Get your hands off of me, ya fucking rapist,' Tuesday said, 'or it'll be me calling the polis.' She snatched her arm in.

'I do not think this is the nicest way to ask,' Kassia said. 'Perhaps you give her cup of coffee and some tasty biscuit and then she is pleased to leave.' She winked at Tuesday. The manager grunted.

'Like the lassie says,' Tuesday agreed, 'I'd be mair than happy to leave, if you make it worth my while.'

The manager couldn't bring himself to look at Tuesday. 'Don't tell me this is the way it is going to be from now on,' he said. 'Don't make me regret taking you on, Kass.'

'No regretting,' Kassia said. 'This girl, she is friend of mine.'

'Okay, coffee and a biscuit. But she isn't coming in.' On his way back in, his pointy shoes slipped on the wet tiles.

'Milk and four sugars,' Tuesday yelled after him, pissed off that he hadn't actually landed on his arse.

'He will not do it for you. Give me a short time. I will help you out with hot drink and loose change.'

'Don't get yourself into trouble on my account,' Tuesday said.

'It is no problem. This guy he owes me.' Kassia turned to go back inside.

'He's a fucking wankmerchant, by the way,' Tuesday said, because Kassia looked like she needed protecting. 'Just to be clear.'

Kassia smiled. 'Wankmerchant?' she said. 'This is not a word I know already. I add it to my dictionary. I am so happy to improve my English.'

Tuesday grinned and a flash of lightning split the sky.

13

Judith and Holofernes

Hogmanay was a bit of a mix for Lizzi. All the usual crowd came round to her house. Rob was on good form, playing up to the neighbours with his scary tattooed man act and making sure everyone's glass was topped up. Finn, on the other hand, was a total pain. For most of the night, he wouldn't join in and then was horrible to Rob about his tattoos in front of everyone (going on about how the whole Celtic Book of Kells thing was totally passé and unoriginal). Then, for some unknown reason, after the bells and once most of the neighbours had left, he decided to hit the Baileys, even though there was still plenty of wine and beer and whisky left. God knows how he'd discovered the bottle hidden in the back of the TV cabinet. It wasn't something Lizzi drank. Must have been duty free her dad had got in on one of his trips home, thinking it would impress his lady friends. It seemed to impress Finn, anyway.

Once Finn had drunk most of the bottle and was sprawled out on the carpet hogging the heat from the gas fire in the living room, complaining about how unfair it was that he had to buy his own Christmas presents, and his mother didn't give a single thought to him from one day to the next and she hadn't even reimbursed him for the funds he'd dispensed, and how nobody gave a shit about him and how he might as well have spent Christmas by himself, drunkenly deaf to Lizzi's sarcastic request for the time, it took all of her effort (and Rob's too) not to stamp on his stupid face.

At three, she left him to it and went to bed, hoping that Rob wouldn't bother to send him through to join her. In a troubled sleep, Lizzi dreamt of New Years gone by, when the neighbours were the same and the countdown of the outgoing year was the same and the bagpipes and drums and fireworks at the castle were the same, but everything else was different. She woke when a shiver of cold air ran across her naked arm.

Finn was sitting on the window sill, wearing only his jeans, with one hand out of the open window. The sky was glowing from the false light of the city and the heavy clouds looked radioactive.

'What time is it?' she croaked.

'Not sure. About four?'

She reached over the edge of the bed. Felt for the pyjama top she slept in when she was alone. 'Finn, it's freezing.'

He pulled his hand in and drew on his cigarette. The window thumped shut. He pushed it open again, flicked the dog end outside, secured the latch.

'Come to bed.'

Finn lay on top of the covers next to her, his hands behind his neck, staring at the ceiling. Lizzi was too sleepy to maintain her mood. For a while, she lay with her head on his chest, feeling the bones of his ribs under her ear, listening to his heartbeat, hearing his breaths go in and out of his lungs. It felt like she was clinging to him. She *was* clinging to him. Sometimes she wondered what her mother would say if she could see her like this.

After a little while, Lizzi raised her head from Finn's chest and looked at him in the half-light. He was still staring at the ceiling.

'Finn, what's wrong?'

He didn't react. Too tired to force the matter, she snuggled back into him, her body tingling from the half-forgotten ache of intimacy and the knowledge of the baby growing inside her. They hadn't spoken properly since he'd come back from his mum's, swept along as they were by the obligation of enjoying themselves. She missed him. She wanted *her* Finn back. The Finn who cracked her up with his stupid jokes, the Finn who noticed her and did weirdly seductive things – like the time he filled an entire sketch book with pictures of her feet – the Finn who when they first met said that the two of them were kindred spirits. Both virtual, if not actual, orphans.

Sleep dragged Lizzi back to her dreams. She saw her mother watching over her as usual, but this time it was different. It was as if her mother was struggling to understand her, trying to make sense of Lizzi's new life, trying to square it with the past. A past that had unfurled in this room – the room that had been her parents' – where rather than squeezing her mother's hand or stroking her face, ten-year-old Lizzi had sulked in the corner refusing to cry. Lizzi tossed in her sleep and at the rustle of the bedclothes, her ten-year-old self sneaked her head around the door desperate to find her mother there, but found in her place only this impostor and the restless young man beside her.

Finn shifted off the bed. Reluctantly, Lizzi flickered her eyes open. He was grappling with the shirt he'd left buttoned when he'd taken it off earlier.

'You're not—'

'Shh. Go back to sleep.' He leant over the bed and kissed her.

'Finn, it's late, it's freezing—'

'I'll be fine. I'll text you. Go back to sleep.'

The front door slammed shut. A moment later, she heard

his footsteps racing down the stairs and the bottom door banging. Lizzi wrapped the quilt around her and hobbled across to the window with her feet tangling in its edges. Forlornly, she peered out across the patch of garden and watched Finn drag his bike between the parked cars and straddle the frame and spin the pedals to gain a footing. And as he sped off down the deserted street, the first few snow-flakes started to fall.

It was mid-morning before Lizzi dragged herself out of bed again. She padded around her bedroom, the sound of her movements muffled by the snow that had carpeted the rooftops and streets and cars. She found Rob in the living room filling black bin bags and putting out the empties for recycling, sleep-deprived after an uncomfortable half-night on the sofa. For a while she helped him fill more bags, and for the rest of the morning they ate toast and drank pots of tea, and neither of them mentioned Finn.

Eventually Rob decided to head home. Lizzi hugged him hard when he left, trying her best to ignore the depression that had sunk over both of them. All afternoon she mes-saged and called Finn, but it was nearly five by the time she got hold of him. His battery had been flat, apparently. He trumped her chance to rant at him with the news that his paintings were ruined.

'What happened?'

'A flood. Leak from frozen pipes. Aided and abetted by Maurice's top-notch repair job.'

'Oh, Finn . . .'

'It's not like it's the end of the world.'

Lizzi's heart sank. He was pretending for her benefit. She asked if she could come round.

'If you want,' he said. 'If you can get here.'

An extortionate New Year taxi took Lizzi through the

slushy streets to Maryhill. As usual, the lift in Finn's block was out of order. She took the fire stairs to climb the fourteen flights, examining the warts in the paintwork and the fissures in the concrete as she made her way up. The more she saw of these blocks, the less she understood why Finn chose to live there. The bleak surroundings couldn't be good for his state of mind, for anyone's state of mind.

Lizzi paused on a landing to catch her breath. The flats were under continual threat of demolition, but they always got a last-minute reprieve when the housing authorities realised there was nowhere else to put people. But she reckoned their days were numbered. They were so different to how they had been imagined when they were first built, when the slums were cleared and people left their old communities to move to these strange dovecots on the promise of an urban Utopia. She'd seen the adverts from the 1960s: celestial living, Formica kitchens and inside toilets. It had turned out to be an empty promise. It didn't take that long for the flats to become as bad as the slums they'd left behind, when the lifts were vandalised and pissed in, the stairwells grafittied and the windows barred over. There was no community when people were piled on top of one another like this.

At last Lizzi reached the fourteenth floor. She leant on the railing outside Finn's flat for a moment to recuperate. Over the sound of her own hard puffs, she heard a kerfuffle in the flat next door. When she got her breath back, she listened more carefully. Banging and thumping. And a scream. Followed by the crash of furniture being overturned.

In a panic, Lizzi rang Finn's bell, rapped on the door. Finn opened it a crack, looking blue-gilled and drowsy. When he saw it was her, he unhooked the chain.

'Something's going on next door.'

As a welcome, Finn groaned and disappeared down the poky hallway.

'Finn?' The neighbours were shouting at each other now.

'How did you not stop me? I don't even like Baileys. Rank on the way down, worse on the way up.' He burped and disappeared into the living room.

'Finn! Someone could be getting hurt,' Lizzi shouted after him, hesitating in the hallway, unsure whether to follow or go and intervene next door. The yelling was making the plasterboard walls between the flats vibrate.

'We have to do something,' she said. 'We can't just do nothing.'

In the living room, the last of the snow-tinged daylight filled the curtainless window. The place was a tip. Absently, Lizzi picked up an overflowing ashtray and emptied it into a box with a half-eaten pizza. The cigarette stubs were so crumpled, so thoroughly mangled, they could have been chewed.

'Finn?'

'It isn't anything to fuss about,' Finn said. 'It's only Mo and Leanne, welcoming in the New Year.'

'What?' Lizzi almost dropped the pizza box. 'Maurice? It sounds like he's killing her.'

'Nah, it's just a wee domestic to warm themselves up.' Finn shrugged.

'Finn!'

'Don't get your knickers in a twist. Leanne's mad at him for bringing home one of my drowned paintings, that's all.'

'What?'

'Final straw. She's threatening to leave him. Well, that's part of it, anyhow.'

'Part of what?' Lizzi couldn't believe how unfazed Finn

was, how totally blasé. And she completely failed to see how Finn's painting could have anything to do with what was going on next door.

'Part of why she's so pissed off at him. But mainly, it's because he hit the bev too hard last night and she's been on at him for ever to give it up before it kills him.'

Suddenly, it dawned on Lizzi. 'So are you telling me that it's *her* that beats *him* up?'

'Aye, that's what I said.'

'Does that mean . . .?'

'Fret not,' Finn said. 'Mo will be round here the sec Leanne chucks him out. Or sooner, if he values his crockery.'

The drawer was jammed with freezer snow. Lizzi yanked it but it wouldn't budge. She crouched down to look, to see if she could work out where it was getting caught.

'Finn,' she yelled. There was no reply. She stood up, fished a bread knife from the cutlery drawer, and crouched back down, poking at the ice round the lip of the plastic drawer. A lump the size of a potato fell to the floor. She rattled the drawer. It was a bit looser. She prodded the mouth of the shelf with the knife and some more chunks fell away. Another yank and the drawer gave way, scraping across the frozen shelf. Inside was a tray of ice cubes, opaque with age and covered with frost.

She took the tray out and slammed it on the work surface. Three blocks popped out. That should do, if she added in the lumps of snow. She chucked the tray back in the freezer and jiggled the drawer until it juddered back into place. The drawer below was frozen shut too and, from what she could see, was as lacking in food as the one she had forced open.

The fridge wasn't any better. The glass shelves were

ringed with bottle stains, and the rubber seal was speckled with black mould. As for food, there was a rind of Parmesan wrapped in clingfilm that had lost its cling, a withered bunch of basil, and a papery onion. Nothing more.

Lizzi shoved the fridge door shut. When she first started coming here, Finn used to make a real effort. He liked showing off his Italian heritage. One time he gave her Martini Rosso with orange slices as an ironic aperitif, and made spaghetti puttanesca just to laugh at its name, and he bought a bottle of Chianti that had cost him more than a tenner, because he wanted her to see that it could be good, that it was a misunderstood wine. Now, she'd be lucky if she could get a bowl of stale cornflakes or a slice of toast without penicillin mould.

A steady patter of water drops on the lino brought Lizzi's attention back to her task. The ice cubes were melting, dripping off the Formica. She opened the cupboard under the sink and pulled out a screwed-up Asda bag from the dwindling supply Finn used for the rubbish. She put all the ice into the bag, tied a knot in the top and searched through the drawers and cupboards for something to hit it with. She settled for a frying pan.

After five hefty bashes, the ice was crushed to gravel shots. She tested out the bag on her forehead. Perfect.

'Here, Maurice, try this,' she said, when she was back in the living room.

'Aw, hen, cheers.' Maurice took the ice-pack from her and wedged it up against his swollen eye. The glass of his watch face was splintered.

'Man, that's gonnae be a corker.' Finn laughed.

'Aye, tell me about it. She was really going for it the day.'

Maurice was sitting on the only chair in the living room. Lizzi called it the Star Trek chair but Finn got offended whenever she said it: *It's a Robin Day seventies design classic . . .* He'd found it in a skip outside her house a few months ago and recognised it for what it was straight away. Made from white moulded plastic with sulphurous orange cushions, it revolved on a spindle coming from a single, saucer-like foot and had armrests in which she expected to see key pads that could beam them to another age, another planet. Maurice certainly looked like he'd come from another planet, sitting there in his sagging vest and suit trousers, his pale, thinning hair slicked back over his crown and temples in a style bordering on a comb-over. He'd taken off his shirt at the door of the flat when he'd come in. It was covered with blood where he'd pulled it out of his pants and used the tail to stem the flow pouring from his nose. Lizzi wasn't sure if pity was a noble sentiment or not. There didn't seem anything noble about wanting to weep for this pathetic, shaky man, with hairless, freckled skin and nostrils crusted in dried gore and snot.

'You know what they call those vests in America?' Finn said.

Maurice shook his head, grimacing.

'Wife-beaters.' Finn laughed at his own joke. Lizzi winced but Maurice was grinning.

'Aw, son, don't make me laugh.' He rearranged the ice-pack on his cheek. Lizzi saw a bruise blossoming beneath the liver spots and thread veins.

'Can I get you something, Maurice? A cup of tea? Coffee?' She wanted to escape the strange smell permeating the living room.

Maurice looked at Finn before he answered. When he did, he spoke slowly, enunciating his words as if he thought Lizzi wouldn't understand. 'Nah, you're all right, hen. I'm fine as I am.' And then to Finn, 'She's awfie well spoken, your lassie. And bonny. For a ginger.'

For the sake of politeness, Lizzi forced a smile. 'I heard you had a bit of a to-do at the church hall.'

'Och, hen. Your man's paintings. What a terrible shame. He says they cannae be rescued. If it was me, I'd gie it a go. But then what do I know about things like that?'

'Mo, they were shit. The lot of them,' Finn said. 'No disrespect to your lovely wife but, honestly, they weren't worth rescuing.'

'Finjay, laddie. They were worth rescuing. They were so.' And then to Lizzi, 'He let me take one. Did he say?'

'Hang on a sec,' Finn interrupted. 'I want to show you something.' He disappeared to his room to fetch his book. In the ensuing silence, Lizzi and Maurice smiled awkwardly at each other.

When Finn returned, he spread the book open on Maurice's knee and stood at his shoulder, leaning over the chair and pointing out a picture. 'This is what I should be doing. Not the Bingo shite.'

Maurice nodded sagely.

'This one, I first saw when I was a nipper and my wee granny took me on a trip to Rome. Even though I was only knee high to a grasshopper, I knew as soon as I saw it that this was what I was born to do. My granny said it was in my blood . . .' Finn hesitated when Lizzi came and stood next to him. She knew why. She had never bought into that particular family myth.

'Which one is it?' she asked, peering over Maurice's shoulder.

'*Judith and Holofernes,*' Finn said.

'Poor sod is getting his heid chopped aff,' Maurice

explained helpfully. 'And the wee lassie doesnae want to get blood on her dress.'

Lizzi nodded. On the surface, that wasn't a bad summary. The beautiful Judith – forehead puckered in concentration and mild distaste – was sawing through the head of the tyrant general, wielding her scimitar at arm's length.

'See the girl,' Finn said. 'She was a prostitute. In real life, I mean. Not in the picture.'

'I'd gie her one,' Maurice said, grinning. 'I'd pay, but. Nae funny business.'

'She turns up in a few of the big man's pictures,' Finn said. 'You can recognise her by her crooked finger. You can't see it here, though, because of the way she's holding his hair . . .'

He faltered. He suddenly looked wrung out.

'And Holofernes?' Lizzi asked, to encourage him. 'He looks swarthy enough to be your man.'

He didn't say anything. Just glanced at her.

'Finn?'

'Aye,' he said, regaining the flow. 'You know Caravaggio was probably the girl's pimp in real life? Definitely her lover.'

'That ugly bugger?' Maurice said.

'Yeah, ironic, isn't it. Not what you'd expect. But then, there wasn't much about the big man that you could take for granted. And we're not just talking his life. His entire body of work is full of irony, of inversions, of orthodoxies turned on their head. You can see it in the way he painted this scene. For all the other lads working at the time, Judith represented humility, justice and chastity. Shorthand for the virtuous woman. A prefiguration of the Virgin Mary.'

'This one doesn't look particularly chaste or humble,'

Lizzi said. Something about the girl's erect nipples suggested there was more than an element of pleasure in her actions.

'Exactly. And you wouldn't expect anything else from the big man. What you've got here is a parable of the triumph of the biblical underdog. A female David with her own Goliath.'

Although she nodded again, Lizzi wasn't really convinced. For her, the painting told a different story. It didn't seem like chance that Caravaggio's Judith was a whore. Poor old Holofernes looked like a client caught with his trousers down. In Lizzi's opinion, this young temptress was no lucky winner outmanoeuvring a more powerful opponent. Under those soft curves was a core of flint. Judith was never going to lose. The painting read like a confession of the weakness of the flesh: the artist, slave to his lust, seeking absolution in the ultimate penalty.

'Magnificent, eh no?' Finn's words came out as barely a whisper but they crept under Lizzi's skin. Even though she didn't agree with his interpretation, she could perfectly understand the power of the painting in its erotic beauty and violence. A surge of desire made her shiver.

'Anyhow, you have to admit,' Finn said, suddenly cheerful, 'the Bingo pics are pretty pale by comparison.'

'Well, I reckon you do yerself an injustice, sonny. But good on you for trying, that's all I can say,' Maurice said. 'More rewarding than being a plumber, I'd imagine.'

Finn laughed. 'I was away to say you never see a skint plumber. Except you're the exception that proves the rule.'

Lizzi tightened. Finn could target people's vulnerabilities with a surgical precision, but Maurice wasn't worried. He laughed and trails of spittle caught at the angles of his mouth. All at once, a wave of nausea rushed over her. She steadied herself against the back of the chair. She wasn't sure if it was her condition or Maurice's spittle or the flecks of dandruff sticking to his slicked-over hair and the coarse gingery hairs sneaking out from his ears, but she was feeling distinctly off-colour. 'I could do with some fresh air,' she said.

'I'll be heading, then . . .' Maurice folded the book shut and lifted it off his knee.

Finn took it from him. 'Don't let us chase you away.'

'Och, the missus should've settled down by now,' Maurice said, standing and passing the ice-pack to Lizzi. She took it from him wordlessly, finding herself compelled to stare at his bruises, fascinated and shocked that a woman could injure him like this. He wasn't Holofernes, that was certain, but surely he had done something to genuinely provoke his wife. Was it alcohol that made him so defenceless? Or some kind of misjudged chivalry? The whole situation was pitiful. Maurice was pitiful. The lax skin around his eye was pitiful – livid and globular, as if the blood had collected under its folds. If she stuck a needle in, would rusty tears trickle down his cheek? Lizzi looked down, ashamed of herself, and noticed the leaking bandage tied around his slippered foot.

The coffee bar was heaving, filled with escapees from the house arrest imposed by the festive season and partygoers giving their livers a rest before the drinking started again in the evening. People were crowded into booths with folding down cinema chairs, lit with table lamps. The subdued evening lights took the edge off the bustle. The staff were wandering around in their black T-shirts and trousers, collecting empty cups and wiping tables as if they had all the time in the world. Lizzi stood in the queue while Finn sorted out somewhere to sit. He was fussing, distracted, unable to make up his mind. Finally, he found a spot at the end of the counter and dragged two high stools over. Meanwhile, the queue was budging slowly. In spite of its length, there was only one person actually serving. Lizzi felt sorry for the guy. It was too big a job for one person.

A little further down the counter, a girl who should probably have been helping was arguing instead with the manager. At least, Lizzi assumed he was the manager because he wasn't wearing the regulation STAFF T-shirt. The pair of them were lit by the recessed spotlights above the till, and from time to time there were flashes of gold or silver or polished stone as the light glanced off the girl's jewellery and her angry gestures. Even though the manager had his back to Lizzi, she could tell he was reprimanding the girl. He was pointing at columns on his clipboard sheet as if he expected her to explain them. Whatever she said in reply incensed him further and he jabbed at his clipboard so furiously that Lizzi was convinced his finger would go through. The girl, though, was no longer paying any attention. She gazed past him with a smirk playing on her lips and pulled her thick dark hair into a ponytail. Whatever the impatience felt by those in the queue, it was alleviated to some extent by her performance. When the manager finished and turned away to calculate the week's takings or whatever it was, Lizzi expected the audience to applaud, the girl to bow. Instead, she pulled out a black apron from underneath the counter and looped the long cords round her waist to tie it at the front.

'You want what?'

Lizzi ordered two double espressos and a peppermint slice. She handed over a twenty.

'No.'

'Sorry?'

'No can do. You must give exact money.'

'I don't have any change.'

'Too bad.'

Lizzi stood there holding out the note. The girl shrugged, unconcerned.

'But . . .'

The manager approached. 'Is there a problem?'

'She wants to pay with that.' The girl pointed to the twenty pound note as if it was pestilent. 'I say no. It is not good for me to do the math.'

The manager took Lizzi's note and opened the till to give her the change. Lizzi nodded her thanks, still looking at the girl, and moved along the counter to wait for the coffees. While she waited, she poured a couple of glasses of water for herself and Finn, not really watching what she was doing but listening instead to the low thunder in the manager's voice.

The girl's voice rang out clearly over her boss's. 'You say this because I do not fuck you.'

'What was all that about?'

'Not sure. I don't think she could subtract in English.'

'Ha, mental arithmetic in a second language. Impossible. The one thing I can't do in Italian.' Finn took his coffee. 'I know her.'

'Really?' Lizzi sipped her espresso. 'Well, maybe advise her on customer relations then.' The coffee tasted too strong for her this evening, coating her palate and the back of her tongue in creosote bitterness. Finn drained his cup in a oner. She pushed hers over to him and nibbled the peppermint slice. The chocolate coating was thick and dark, and there was a luminous green stripe of fondant above the biscuit base that smelt of toothpaste and was claggy and tooth-achingly sweet. She swallowed the mouthful in a lump and slid the plate towards Finn.

'You'd be the same if you had to deal with the shite you get in a place like this every day.'

Compared to what she got dealt every time she had a clinical session, Lizzi would have thought serving in a West End coffee shop would be a doddle. 'Why does Maurice stay with Leanne?' she said, changing the subject. 'If she treats him so badly?'

'Love is very peculiar.'

Lizzi held up her glass of water. It was murky, yellowish, with bits that looked like small snotters floating in it. A blast of nausea filled her mouth with acid.

'It's only lemon,' Finn said.

She got down from her stool. 'You want anything else?'

'Nah, you're all right.'

'Mineral water, please. Sparkling,' Lizzi ordered when her time came. The young guy was still serving. The girl appeared to have been promoted to making the coffee. Or perhaps it was a demotion to keep her away from custom-ers. In any case, it was clear that she wasn't happy. Hidden in the darkest corner behind the counter, she was banging spent grounds into the bin and violently flattening the hill-ocks of fresh stuff in the filter. Lizzi grinned at the lad as she handed over her money. He raised his eyebrows.

'Fucking stupid machine.' The girl was flicking the switch of the coffee grinder on and off.

'Wassup, Kass?' the serving guy said.

'Motherfucker will not work.'

He glanced over while he was giving Lizzi her receipt. 'Out of beans. You'll need to open a tin.' He nodded towards the shelf above the grinder. Five huge drums of beans, three or four kilos each, were towering above the girl. She tutted and dragged a kick stool over, glaring at Lizzi as she stepped on to it. Lizzi picked up her bottle and glass and went back to Finn.

'He could get help,' she said, stepping on the foot rail of the stool as she clambered back up. 'For his drinking.'

'Och, I'd say that was the least of his problems. Mo likes a drink but so do half the population of this city and you wouldn't classify them all as alkies.'

Lizzi twisted the cap of her bottle. The gas eased itself out. She poured some water. The needle tips of escaping bubbles stung her hand. 'Why? Is it his diabetes?'

'Diabetes, emphysema, arthritis. You name it. Leanne wants him to go on the sick.'

'Why doesn't he? Especially if he isn't making a good living.'

'Pride, I reckon. For him, it isn't about the money. The business was started by his old man. He's the *Son* in *O'Donnell and Son.*' Finn was watching the girl lift down the drum of beans.

Lizzi gulped a mouthful of the prickly water. Finn licked his fingertip and pressed it on to the crumbs from the peppermint slice. 'Yum. Don't know how you didn't want it.'

She smiled weakly.

'Leanne's lucky,' Finn said. 'He'd do anything for her. Give her anything if he could. There aren't many lassies that can say that about their man.' He laughed, but he wasn't looking at Lizzi while he spoke. He was watching the girl open the coffee tin. There was something in the way Finn was staring at her, something that Lizzi had never seen before, that made her heart leap to her throat and her stomach churn with the dreadful apprehension that one day, not too far from now, whether he knew it himself or not, Finn was going to leave her.

'He'd certainly never bugger off. Too scared and too pissed most of the time to have the wherewithal.'

'Not much of an endorsement,' Lizzi managed to mumble. Her head was swirling. Her pulse was thumping in her temple and she badly wanted to cry. She had to tell Finn that she was pregnant and she had to tell him now. It was the right thing to do and not for her own sake. If he was planning to leave, he had the right to know exactly what it was that he was leaving. Lizzi swallowed and tried to keep it together. 'Can you call that love?' she said. 'That lack of inner strength that keeps you bound to someone when you know you should leave?'

'Och, I'm not sure it is that straightforward. Leanne's a cracking woman. It's the strength of her personality that has kept them together all these years. Maurice is a good lad but he's a bit flaky. And a bit dodgy with the welding—'

His words were cut short by cries of pain coming from behind the counter. Muted yelps of genuine agony. Lizzi glanced up. The girl was standing beside the coffee machine, clutching her left hand. She was pallid-cheeked and chalky-lipped. Blood was seeping through her fingers, pattering on to the boards at her feet, and she was staring at her lacerated hand in disbelief. In the void, the espresso machine squealed, forcing steam through an empty filter. For one long second, nobody moved.

Finn was the first to react. He jumped from his stool and clambered over the counter. The serving lad rushed towards the injured girl. Someone was asking if anyone knew first aid. A customer lifted up the bar hatch. Someone else dragged a chair across the floorboards, sat her down, poured her a glass of water. Parents were telling their kids not to look, shielding their eyes, gathering coats. The manager started ranting about safety valves, how they were fitted on the tins to prevent accidents, how what she'd done wasn't possible, she must have been messing around and, all the while, blood was pooling on the girl's apron in a thick, tarry glue.

Lizzi stood up. She could hear Finn calling her name, telling the others about his girlfriend's St Andrews qualification. She could hear the lad who served her asking the injured girl if she was okay, calling her Kass, telling people to give the poor lassie some breathing space. And the girl, animated again, screaming at the manager to stick his fucking-crappy-shitty job up his frigid-tight arsehole, and a customer saying to Finn, 'Your girlfriend looks like she's away to faint.'

And then she did.

14

Narcissus

At Lizzi's insistence, Finn let her take a taxi home herself. She said she'd be fine, said she'd been overdoing it and that she'd sleep it off once she got home, but when he saw her into the car, when he kissed her goodbye, when he still thought he was doing what she wanted, she came over all mad at him and he couldn't decipher why. She'd said she didn't want him there, fussing over her, keeping her awake when she needed to rest, but he didn't realise until too late that her words were encrypted. Apparently, though, she was under the impression she had spelt out what she hadn't said. On an illuminated manuscript with two-inch letters inlaid with gold leaf, if the force of the slammed door was anything to go by. Even the taxi driver glowered at Finn like he, Finn, was conniving some heinous plot.

Once Lizzi had gone home and he was forced into the predicament of being able to offend at leisure, Finn decided to check up on Kassia. He was not so emotionally derelict as to think it was a particularly wise move, especially if Lizzi were to find out, but he couldn't actually help himself. Compelled, he'd say, if he were forced to confess. Impelled by a will greater than his own, but not for the reasons you'd have thought. So he found himself in A&E, sneaking past reception and passing himself off as a lost family member when he stuck his head around the curtain of the wrong cubicle, until he eventually spotted Kassia being wheeled on a trolley towards the porters' lift looking luminous and glittery-eyed with painkillers. Her hand was wrapped in a fresh dressing and supported on a splint, and her hair was a shock of gilded black against her bland hospital gown. Finn attempted to inveigle himself into the lift but the porter said trolleys only, the patient was going straight to surgery, she could have visitors on the ward after the operation. And Kassia all the while drugged and drowsily protesting. What operation, Finn wanted to know, but the porter said he wasn't an expert in matters medical, although he was an ace at manoeuvring trolleys into tight spaces. As the young man could surely see.

It was well past midnight by the time Finn left the hospital. He had no means of transport because he'd left his bike at the church hall after the clean-up campaign earlier in the day. At this time of night, Finn reckoned, there was no point going back to his flat simply to toss and turn in an empty bed. The most convenient and sensible thing he could do would be to head straight for the studio. Aim for a bit of kip and if he didn't succeed, at least he would be surrounded by paints and brushes and turpentine, which by their mere presence – or at least by the fumes they emitted – might ease his troubled spirit or make him light-headed enough not to care.

It was bollocks, of course. This talk of convenience and sense. Finn didn't know who he was trying to kid. There was more to his need to go to the studio than the draw of his painting materials or to recuperate his bike. He could pretend all he liked, hide his real thoughts from whoever he imagined was reading them, but he had to face it. He was haunted. Haunted by a ridiculous notion that had had him bolting from Lizzi's at 4 a.m. A ridiculous, illogical, absurd notion that would not leave him be. An idiotic idea that made no sense if you questioned it too deeply, but all the same had its own, perfect, irreproachable logic.

Quite simply, Finn *had* to check in at the studio. Where else would Caravaggio go if he was planning to show his face again? Where else but the studio where for weeks Finn had been spied upon and had his work scrutinised by someone who skulked in the shadows and smoked his tobacco and scoffed his leftovers? It was the single morsel of reassurance on which Finn had survived since he'd been rudely awoken by the train guard and lobbed off the train at Dunkeld on Christmas Eve, when he'd stumbled from the carriage confused and disorientated and mortified by his mother yodelling to him from the far end of the platform (did she not realise he would make his way back to the family pad on his own two wheels?) and he'd searched in vain and increasing panic for the slightest trace of Caravaggio. No, Finn could not return to the flat. Because, while ordinarily you might think the chance of Caravaggio turning up in Partick was about as likely as the pope getting it on with his old doll, the fact was, Caravaggio was evidently already well acquainted with the church hall. And as far as Finn knew, the man didn't have his Maryhill address.

Beyond the hospital doors, the night air was granite hard. Finn put his head down and charged into it. He knew how crazy he sounded. Honestly, he did. Even sleep-deprived and mind-bended after the hideous few days at his mother's, he wasn't so daft as to honestly, truly, genuinely believe that he had actually met Caravaggio on the train. Or that the man had conversed and enjoyed a coconut cream. Or that, even if he had, he would actually manage to find his way back from wherever he'd got off the train to Dougal Street. And, frankly, who had ever heard of a seventeenth-century, moth-eaten artist with a liking for second-day pakora?

The thing was, however outrageous it sounded, it was the only thing that made any sense in Finn's life. Which was undoubtedly either a reflection of the general level of shite he was having to contend with, or the fact that he was fatigued to his bones. An affliction that was exacerbated the moment he turned into Dougal Street and climbed the hill. The closer he came to the church, the steeper the slope. He was a cretin, a moron, an absolute fucking tool, if he actually believed any of this was more than a hope-fired illusion.

A flickering light in the tiny stained-glass window at the north end of the church tugged Finn's attention away from his self-flagellation. Rather than have to face the unwelcome reality of an empty studio, he trudged up the church steps and creaked open the heavy door of Our Lady's. There, in liquid darkness, kneeling on the stone step of a side chapel surrounded by votive candles, was Jed. His black clothes merged with the darkness, save for the flash of his clerical collar, and candlelight brushed the side of his face and his clasped hands, so they floated lambent against the shadowy chapel. He was too deep in prayer to notice Finn's intrusion.

Finn sat at the end of a pew and silently observed his friend. He had known Jed almost as long as he had known Rob. He remembered the story Rob told him about his brother's conversion. Apparently, when they were kids there was a witch who lived in the toilets in the play park next to their primary school. For the price of a few ciggies, she'd dole out hand jobs to any passing punter (which put her more desperate whore than witch in Finn's book but it wasn't his story to tell). Anyhow, one day when Jed was skiving school assembly, she cornered him and dragged him into a pox-ridden cubicle. Where, Rob claimed, she'd rammed Jed's kiddy fist into her knickers and rubbed it against her slimy cunt, and told him that for the right price she'd show him what all the grown-up carry-on was about. To which Jed's reply was to scream like a girl, so she punched him in the gullet and nicked his lunch money. According to Rob, the whole sordid experience was what turned him. Refuge in the celibate embrace of the Catholic priesthood.

In all religious ideologies, Finn and Jed disagreed as a matter of principle. Many times they had argued long into the small hours about the origin of the universe and other such trivialities and, on the same evidence, drawn contradictory conclusions. But Finn didn't despise the priest for getting it wrong. Not in the same way he despised the unthinking flock. Jed's wasn't a blind faith. His was a faith that fought a daily battle with reason. A faith that he struggled to reconcile with his own common sense. A faith that had deserted him before he took his orders and which he had had to overturn boulders to find again. From the back of the church, his muttered words weren't audible, but the beseeching tone was clear. Finn sighed. You had to pity the man.

Bolstered by the vision of someone else's suffering, Finn slipped out of the church without disturbing the priest. In the hall, the back corridor still smelt of rusty water and sodden embers and, inside the studio, the remaining warped canvases were propped against the wall where Maurice and he had stacked them that morning. His bike was sitting under the window where he'd left it, along with his present to himself from his old doll still in its original packaging.

Finn slumped on the floor behind the empty easel and pulled the fire curtains around him. In the end, however much he wanted his Caravaggio to be real, it wasn't going to make him real. Common sense conquered irrational yearning. Finn knew his history. Knew all the question marks over the events surrounding Caravaggio's death. Knew every one of the conspiracy theories and – although he would have given anything to prove them correct – he was more than aware that it would have had to have been some stupendously major conspiracy for the man still to be alive after four hundred years. Finn sniggered at what a tool he had become, hoping to embarrass his urge to weep.

For a couple of hours, he tossed and turned and dreamt of Caravaggio. When dawn began to break through the high window, Finn pulled himself out of the pile of curtains and attempted to pull himself together. In the clear light of day, however, things didn't look any better. At seven, he made himself a coffee. At half past, when he couldn't stand his own company any longer, he kitted himself out in his newly gifted threads and when he was ready phoned Rob.

'On your bike, cunt-tard. We're going out.'

Fifteen minutes later, in his new cycling kit and on his recently pimped bike, Finn hurtled through the gates of the Botanic Gardens. Mounds of dirty snow lay along the edges of the muddy flower beds. He scooted past the warder's cottage and the wooden noticeboard without altering his cadence for the wildlife scattering around his wheels. With his brakes screeching louder than a mating fox, he made the turn on to the bottom footpath. Along the flat into the shadowy corner at the disused railway station, and then right, back into daylight at the vegetable plot. He was flying. Ahead, the path climbed. He flicked down a gear, stood on the pedals, took the hill. A full-on push to the top, eyes, lungs, legs burning in the frozen air. The gradient steepened. The strain intensified. Each pedal stroke, each turn of his wheels, each chain link coupling to the gear teeth, kept him focused, on track, kept his mind on the job and away from the nonsense that was doing his head in. He was dancing on the pedals now, the bike's narrow tyres skating easily up the icy road. He raced past the glasshouses – iron frames creaking as the tropical heating system slammed against the creeping cold, window panes blinded by cataracts of condensation – and took the final ascent. As he mounted the crest – cheering crowds of rhododendron bushes lining the road – he spotted his name on the tarmac among the ice-trails and frost-cracks. The incline was easing, the finish only metres away. Back in the saddle, head down, muscles pumping, heart spurting, breath slipping in and out of his airways like lubricated latex.

Sensational.

Finn sat up in his seat, took his hands off the handlebars and shook his arms loose at his sides. Too modest for a full-on salute, he placed his hand on his heart. To onlookers, no doubt, an effortless performance. Physically, he was on form, at his peak, at the peak. Only the faintest seep of sweat at the angle of his nostrils betrayed any exertion.

Rob was waiting for him underneath a monkey puzzle opposite the Japanese garden. He was wearing old trackie bottoms and a hoodie pulled up over his woollen hat. Finn drew up beside him and steadied himself against the tree trunk to avoid slipping his cleats. He pulled off his cycling gloves and shook Rob's hand.

'Outstanding. This idea of yours.' Rob's breath condensed as it hit cold air. One hundred per cent proof. They could distil it, Finn thought, and sell it to the park-bench jakeys. 'Every twat knows today is recovery day.'

Ace, Finn thought. There was going to be tension. Although he had to concede Rob did have a point. The 2nd of January was Scotland's exclusive holiday. A bonus for her hardworking, hard-drinking citizens. A day for watching shite on the TV and medicating your hangover with a greasy fry-up, full-fat Irn-Bru and a low to moderate intake of Whyte and Mackay's. Still, Finn hadn't forced him to come.

'I didn't force you to come.'

'You know me, pal. Cannae say no to any cunt.' Rob spun a pedal to orientate the toe clip. 'What's with the fancy gear? You look like a frog in a Muppet costume.'

'Fuck off. This is proper kit,' Finn said, putting his gloves back on. 'You should get some yourself.'

'Having a laugh? You wouldnae catch me red-handed in those tights.' Rob took a swig of water from his bottle, rinsed it round his mouth and spat.

Finn let out a silent fart of relief. He didn't know why he'd been concerned. With Rob Stevenson, there was one thing on which you could always depend: it was banter all the way. 'These are cycling legs as used by professionals. Christmas present fae the old doll. Along with wheels, pedals and shoes.' He pulled the elasticated material out from his thigh. 'No bad, eh? Note the technical fabric that allows breathability while at the same time providing warmth and compression.'

'Tights,' Rob said, slaloming between some pine cones on the path.

'With a bib.'

Rob braced himself against a rubbish bin. 'You big wuss. Gie's a look.'

Using one hand to prop himself against the monkey puzzle, Finn unzipped the top of his green jersey. Two straps held up his leggings.

Rob started laughing. 'Magnificent.'

'Too right,' Finn said. 'It's no every day you get to see a body like this.'

'Thank fuck. Why are your ribs covered in uncooked pastry, by the way? Cover them up. Even your nipples are embarrassed.' Rob pushed away from the bin and attempted a wheelie. His front wheel lifted less than a centimetre. 'What's the plan, then, Kermit?'

'Over the canal at the lock gate, up Maryhill Road to Bearsden, west along the Stockiemuir Road,' Finn said, zipping himself back into his clothes. 'We can loop back via Balloch if you want, but I'm not taking the cycle route. Main roads only. These tyres are too high quality to wreck on some shitty tourist path.'

Rob set off towards the main exit. From the side gate, a forest path descended to an iron bridge spanning the Kelvin. The river was swollen with winter rain.

'Last one to the iron bridge is a geriatric scrote,' Finn shouted.

'Oi, you cheating cunt,' Rob said, circling back up the hill, crunching on the pedals to overcome inertia and a high gear. 'You said main roads only.'

The hefty git was too unwieldy for this sport, Finn reckoned, and altruistically decided to put him out of his misery. He waited at the gate until Rob drew alongside him, and then reached out and nudged him. Already unsteady, Rob toppled over into a bramble bush, unable to free his battered trainers from the toe clips in time to save himself.

Finn laughed manically and set off into the forest, his road tyres bouncing hard down the dirt track. The woods smelt of fungus and rotting leaves. Gloriousness of the highest order. Exactly what was required to settle his nerves. At the bridge, he braked hard, tossing up gravel chips with his back wheel, and skidded to a halt in a melt-water puddle. Daylight had barely made it into the gully. Rob was still at the gate, untangling himself from the briars. For the moment, Finn lingered on the bridge, leaning on the metal railing, sucking in the aroma of compost and dripping lichen. But just as he was sinking into its putrescent caress, his sight was unwittingly dragged into the foaming water. The spume was artificially white and powerful and it stung behind his eyes and frothed his brain and threatened to undo the good work of the gently rotting forest.

Finn unclipped his shoes from their cleats. The unspeakable dismay he'd felt the moment he awoke to the empty train carriage was beginning to resurface, but he wasn't ready to confront it. He poked his toe at a long stick lying under the bike frame. A casualty of the winter storms snapped from a silver birch. While he waited for Rob, he peeled off some of the psoriatic bark. Shallow breath, shallow pulse, he noted. Keeping his thoughts equally shallow, he stripped the stick down to raw flesh, and clattered it along the railings. The metallic clangs echoed through the gully.

Caravaggio was skimming the surface but he was only part of Finn's torment. Finn had no idea what was going on with Lizzi. She had withdrawn from him and he felt guilty for reasons he couldn't discern. And underneath it all swirled unsolicited, unnerving thoughts of Kassia. It wasn't how it seemed. It wasn't a relationship he wanted. Lizzi was the person he was meant to be with even if she didn't realise it. But something else was going on with Kassia, an idea he couldn't even formulate, a notion too overwhelming to consider. In the hurtling river, a broken reflection flailed in the water, unable even to catch Finn's eye.

On impulse, Finn hurled the stick into the current. As it hit the water, a surge of fear washed over him. Below, the stick was tossed and battered by the icy water. It was dashed against the rigid pillars of the bridge, slipping on and off the muddy bank, dragged from the moss-covered boulders and pulled from the slimy fingers of river weed by the lather.

Finn grabbed the railing to steady himself. Upstream, an oak tree on a flooded island stood solid and unmoving as the torrent swept around its twisted roots. With his hand welded to the iron railing, he tried to fix his stare on the knotted roots, but each time his gaze drifted within reach of their shelter, it was swept downstream again.

Finn shook his head to free his gaze from the foaming river. Rob was almost on him and he had to escape. He spun his pedals, clipped his cleats, sped off. Took the track along the river bank, against the flow of the churning water, flying again but this time without pleasure. He was pedalling for his life, trying to out-sprint the panic that was nipping at his heels.

Park bench memorials to dead dog walkers, broken bottles and rinks of rimy vomit, a vandalised junction box and its danger of death registered only in a preconscious part of his brain. Likewise, he had only the dimmest awareness that Rob was calling him, shouting on him to slow down, wait up, stop being such a competitive cunt. Instead, it was Finn's body that told him what his mind was trying not to think: sickness nestling in the pit of his stomach, anxiety clawing at his skin, acid stinging his throat. Frost bit his face and the frozen air swirled into vortices as he blasted through it at speeds that he hoped would leave his thoughts behind.

'Oi, Eddy Merckx. You could've waited,' Rob said, twenty miles later, when he eventually found Finn sitting beside his bike on the verge, having a smoke.

'I did.'

'Going off for an hour, then stopping for a gasper, isnae waiting,' Rob said, lobbing his bike towards the undergrowth and plonking himself down beside Finn.

Finn shrugged and sucked the last smoke from his roll-up and flicked the stub into the nettles. There was a burger van in the lay-by opposite. He nodded towards it. 'D'you want something?'

The smell of bacon frying on the griddle against a backdrop of damp grass reminded Finn of a Cub Scout camp when he was eight where he'd wet his camp bed and been made to sleep in the same tent as Akela to stop the rest of the pack tearing him apart. Even when he was a nipper, his old doll wasn't backward in coming forward if there was a chance of someone taking him off her hands. She made him go again the following year.

He ordered two bacon rolls. They came in brown paper bags with plastic sachets of tomato ketchup.

'Who the fuck puts salad in a bacon roll?' he said, after he handed one to Rob. He picked out the lettuce and lobbed it into the brambles.

'BLT, you fucking salad thrower,' Rob said. 'Bacon, lettuce, tomato. The clue is in the name.'

Finn grunted and bit into his. After one bite, he put it aside.

'So, are you gonnae tell me,' Rob said, with his mouth full, 'or am I gonnae have to divine it?'

Finn was silent. What could he say? Banter aside, things had changed between him and Rob. He lay back on the damp grass and stared at the curdled sky that stretched beyond the bristling hedgerow and was punctured in the distance by barbs of migrating geese too remote to hear, and let the porridgy cloud massage him and the melancholy light seep into him.

'Want to know how I spent yesterday?' he said eventually.

'Only if it offends my sensibilities.'

Finn lifted his head an inch. 'You're sick, by the way.' He let his head flop back. 'Mopping up a flood in the church hall.'

'What?'

'Mo up-fucked the welding, so to speak. Burst pipe.' Finn laughed without smiling. 'Gonnae not mention it to your brother. Don't want to get the daft sod into trouble. Plus, it's all sorted. Only collateral was my paintings.'

'You stupid cunt, how did you no say? Your paintings? Are they okay?'

'Nah.' Finn glanced at Rob. 'All of them floundering in a watery grave.'

'Fuck, man, that's shite. Proper shite.' Rob was shaking his head, rubbing the back of his bald scalp, his mouth turned down. It surprised Finn to see that Rob genuinely appeared to be upset.

Finn stretched and yawned and swallowed a mouthful of the lumpy sky. 'Aye, but you've got it wrong. This is a good thing.'

'Why?'

'They were average in the extreme.'

'Fuck off, you twat. You don't mean a word of it.'

Finn sat up and rolled another cigarette. 'No offence and all that, but you don't know shit.' He cupped his hand around his lighter, shielded the flame and sucked hard on his skinny cigarette. 'Lizzi fainted yesterday, by the way.'

When he looked up again, Rob was staring at him. 'What's going on, Finn?'

'Thought you might be able to tell me.' Finn blew a smoke ring. It quivered and thinned and faded into the grey sky.

'I take it that means Lizzi is fine,' Rob said calmly. Slowly, he climbed to his feet. 'Well, I cannae sit here all day chewing the breeze. I appear to be developing scrotal hypothermia. Move it.'

'She'd never go out with you. You know that, right? She reckons you're gay.'

Rob lugged his bike out of the nettles. 'Wake up to yourself, man.' When Finn didn't shift, Rob carried on. 'You're one fucking deluded cunt, Finn Garvie.'

Finn lay back down and closed his eyes again. The black trails of his retinal capillaries meandered across the white burn of the inverted sky. Rob's silhouette loomed black at the periphery. He wasn't deluded. Things were never the way they first appeared. Likewise, you could never say for certain what was real and what was unreal. Even with his eyes tight shut, he could quite clearly see Rob's outline, so who was to say that Rob was any more real or unreal than Caravaggio.

'Come on, Finn. Move your arse.'

Same with the priest, if you thought about it. Jed was a man not so different to himself. Another man unable to sleep and haunted by the irrational. Another man who doubted his own convictions but, nonetheless, was prepared to sacrifice this life for the next, better one. Obviously, Finn wouldn't go quite that far, but he knew for sure he wasn't taking instruction from some mass-market lightweight who drew cartoons for a living.

'Get the fuck up, Finn. I've had enough.'

Finn stubbed out his fag and flicked the butt towards Rob. It hit him on the shoulder. He didn't flinch. Only stared.

Lazily, Finn got to his feet and pulled on his helmet. As he fastened it under his chin, he caught his straggly beard in the clip. 'You absolute cunting cunt,' he said, smirking at Rob while he detached the bristles from the strap.

But Rob didn't rise to it. He just stood there. Holding his bike and staring at Finn like he was hurt or disappointed or something. What a fucking sap he was at times. Did he not realise that puppy-dog eyes didn't work when you carried that much bulk?

Finn climbed astride his bike, slipped his shoes back into his cleats, stood on his pedals, balanced effortlessly without moving. Rob kept watching. Finn shifted his weight. Pulled on the handlebars. Did a spectacular wheelie.

A phone started ringing. Finn's front wheel thudded on to the tarmac. He smirked again. Rob reached down and took the water bottle from his bike frame, glugged back some water, wiped his mouth with the back of his hand, keeping his eyes on Finn. Like he was waiting for a reply to a question that hadn't been asked.

Finn circled Rob and his bike. Rob didn't move.

The phone was insistent. Finn zigzagged the lay-by. Rob stared after him. Eventually, the ringing stopped.

The phone rang again. Rob took another drink. Finn slalomed the puddles. Rob put the bottle back in its frame. The phone stopped.

The phone rang for the third time.

Finn skidded to a stop. 'Answer the fucking thing.'

Rob pressed the screen. 'Aye.'

Finn listened in. The tinny voice at the other end was just about audible.

'Hold on, hold on, hold on. I didnae mean literally the day after New Year, you daft bint.' Rob checked his watch. 'I can be there in an hour and a bit. Can you wait?'

The metallic voice whined back at him.

'Find somewhere that's open. Get a coffee or something. I'll pick up the tab.' He hung up.

'You chickening out?'

Rob sucked air through his teeth before he answered. 'Aye. Slight misunderstanding on the arrangements front.

Promised someone I'd help them out.' He climbed on his bike, set off, spoke without looking back. 'Coming?'

Finn shook his head. Cowardly fuck. Not that he was bothered. That battle would keep for later.

LEAD TIN YELLOW

15

Boy Bitten by a Lizard

When Tuesday arrived at the pharmacy for her prescription one morning a couple of weeks into February, there was no sign of her usual pharmacist. Done a runner from the taxman or dead, she decided, knowing how grudging he was to let anyone else behind his counter. Instead she was confronted with a locum. A locum who didn't know her from Adam. A locum who didn't seem to know the meaning of pleasantries and who, after five minutes of heated argument, slammed his fist on the counter and refused to give her her meds on the grounds she couldn't prove she was who she said she was and for all he knew the prescription she was attempting to pass off was forged.

Tuesday grabbed the counter. 'You've gotta be fucking kidding me.'

The peal of the over-door bell signalled another customer entering the shop and the locum handed back the ragged paper. 'Madam, I am not in the business of kidding my customers. As I said, I need some form of identification.' He had a round face and slack lips that spurted fountains of spit when he spoke.

Tuesday wiped her face with the sleeve of her puffer. Madam? No one had ever called her madam. It rated close on the worst insult of her entire life. 'Listen, rubber-lips. You've gotta gie me it. You're legally obliged.' She was starting to feel as rattled as the change in the cash till. She jabbed her finger towards the door. 'That's what the sign says. *Dispensing Chemist*. It means you are supposed to fucking dispense.'

'I cannot administer this prescription without some kind of photographic identification. Passport, driving licence, suchlike.' He was already looking over her shoulder, past her, through her.

'Why the fuck would I have a passport?' Tuesday said. 'Do I honestly look like I'm going some place?' Behind her, she could feel the next customer invading her territory, breathing her air, listening to her secrets. The pharmacist reached over to serve whoever it was. In desperation, she grabbed his arm. 'I'm no being funny, pal, but I come here every day.' The sleeve of her jacket brushed a rainbow display of throat pastilles, spilling the cardboard boxes on to the floor. Each clatter shot holes in her bones, in her teeth, in her brain and, through the polyester white coat, she felt the hairs on the pharmacist's arm bristling.

'Take your hand off me immediately or I will call the police.'

Tuesday lifted her hand away, held it up, submitted. The mention of the police always had the same effect on her. Like being bashed over the head with a hit of naloxone. 'I have a CPP agreement,' she said, trying to soften her voice, hoping he couldn't tell she wanted to break his nose and his fake NHS glasses and ram his fat face down the pan. 'Look it up. The folders are behind you.' Even a locum from Sticksville should know how these things worked.

'I can vouch for her, mate.'

Startled, Tuesday swung round. Rob's pal – Finn, Finjay, whatever he was called, the prick from the Christmas party – was standing there playing with a box of Nytol, spinning it on the base of his thumb so the writing made kaleidoscope circles. He was smirking at her. What a condescending dick. He couldn't vouch for shit.

The pharmacist took a Lever Arch file down from the shelf behind the counter. 'Well, we could have saved ourselves this whole rigmarole if you had thought to mention that at the beginning.'

'Sorry, pal,' Finn said, tossing the box into the air like he was flicking a coin. He caught it between his index finger and thumb.

Tuesday sneered. The stupid knob thought the pharmacist was talking to him.

The pharmacist flicked through the file. 'Name?'

'Finn Garvie.'

'Not you.'

If she hadn't felt so wired, Tuesday might have laughed. As it was, she was calculating which of the two she was going to deck first. 'Tuesday McLaughlin,' she said through gritted teeth.

'Tuesday McLaughlin,' Finn repeated as he rooted through his wallet. He put his driving licence on the counter and then, as if he couldn't believe what he had said, '*Tuesday*?'

The dickhead had just made her decision for her. Tuesday stepped up – right into Finn's face so all she could see was his scrappy beard and thin lips – and ignoring the fact that he towered over her, jabbed her finger into his shoulder. 'Hey, pal,' she said. 'Gonnae mind your own fucking business.'

'Whoah, missus. Only trying to help.' Finn held his hands up in defence but quickly crumbled.

A total demolition job on Tuesday's part. For a second, she almost felt sorry for him, but quickly thought better of it. While the pharmacist poured her methadone into a measuring cylinder, Finn picked up his licence from the counter and replaced it with loose change for the box of Nytol. The bell gave a feeble clink as he left the shop. The pharmacist transferred the contents of the measuring cylinder into a disposable cup and handed it over.

'Cheers.' Tuesday downed the methadone and smacked her lips. On her way out, she picked up a couple of the boxes of throat lozenges, tossed them on to the counter. The pharmacist lined them up ready to rebuild his display.

'See you tomorrow, pal,' she said.

Finn was waiting for her outside, leaning against the wall, with his lank hair hanging in front of his face and his filthy jeans falling off him. He was chewing his fingernails and intermittently flicking his fingers as if they were being bitten by some unseen beastie he couldn't shake off.

'What's up with you?' Tuesday said. The methadone was working its way through her system, creeping through the lining of her stomach, sloshing round her organs, crawling under the hairs of her skin. It was a shame really. He was woeful.

'You should be grateful to me.'

'Privacy. Patient confidentiality. These things mean nothing to you?' Tuesday took a box of throat lozenges from her pocket, punched one out and put it in her mouth. Why had she even bothered feeling sorry for the stupid wanker?

'Like I said, I was trying to help.'

'Next time, pal, keep your help to yerself.' She pulled the sleeves of her coat over her hands – the red nylon had turned to a manky bruise colour at the cuffs – and set off down Dougal Street.

'Hold up,' Finn shouted. 'You can't claim the confidentiality clause. For starters, you're not my patient-stroke-client.'

Tuesday cut across the street and through the square of wasteland in front of the funeral director's. She wasn't in the mood any more. She wanted to go to Rob's, have another look at the computer. She'd found one of those sites where you could slag off your teachers and she wanted to see if she could track down Campbell Spence. At least find out what city he worked in. If he was still teaching, that was.

'I have no obligation towards you. I have no privileged information to disclose to a third party.' Finn's words were flies buzzing around her head. Why could he not take the hint, piss off, leave her alone to work out her plan?

Cannon Balls Spence. It freaked her to admit it but there was a part of her hoping they might get it back on. She still got shivers of teenage angst – shivers that went straight from her lips to her clit – when she thought about how he used to let her give him blow jobs in the sports pavilion on training nights while Rob and the rest of the team waited outside. In the end though, to stop him getting done, they'd split. He'd made out like she'd been spared, like she wouldn't want to be with an old git like him, that she should be with someone her own age, but she hadn't fallen for it. She knew he was as gutted as she was. It had broken her heart at the time. Tuesday McLaughlin, the skanky bitch everyone thought was made of stone, demolished by a broken heart. Totally fucking lame. If she could turn the clock, she'd have been stronger. Not listened to her old doll when she told Tuesday she was a fucking disgrace – which was rich coming from someone who had spent most of her adult life in some kind of restricted facility or another – or when she said there was no way another grubbing, grasping wean was sponging off of her. She called Campbell a paedo, a perv, a sicko, said he'd better sort something quicktime or he'd find himself on a list, and laughed at Tuesday when she said it was love.

But the bitch had probably been lying dead in a gutter for the last fifteen years, Tuesday reckoned, so things had a way of working themselves out. And, if she ever tracked Campbell down, she always had blackmail as a back-up if he'd got fat and bald or didn't want to know her.

Tuesday walked as fast as she could. Behind her, Finn was still at it, still churning it out, still spewing words over the crumbling tarmac until they merged into a garbled slick under her feet. 'For main course, it isn't my fault if the shop is so small you can hear everybody's business, and for dessert, I see you every day anyhow, so it's apodictic.' He was panting slightly.

Tuesday stopped. 'Apodickhead. Is that a fancy way of saying you're stalking me?'

'Fuck off. It isn't stalking. I see you, that's all.'

'And now you know all about me?' There was something not right about him, Tuesday reckoned, something weird, like he really could see everything and had sussed out more about her than she was happy to let on. She was so used to being invisible, it spooked her. 'You know what, pal . . .' She shook her head. It was too much effort.

Finn gave her a smile, weak, washed out. 'Come on, I'll buy you a coffee.'

'Get lost.'

'A cup of tea. An iced bun? A Tunnock's Teacake. Surely you can't turn down a Tunnock's Teacake.'

Tuesday's stomach clenched in anticipation.

'Help me out here,' Finn begged. 'I'm trying to make amends.'

'Chips. You can buy us a bag of chips. And then you can piss off.'

There was only one seat inside the chip shop, a high bar-stool with a slashed vinyl seat. Foam stuffing was bulging from the gaping wound. Tuesday flung her coat over it.

'Chips and water. And channy.'

Finn looked at her blankly.

'Chewing gum.'

'Why didn't you say so?'

'Knob.'

Once Finn had bought her stuff, Tuesday placed her chips on the window ledge and went outside with the bottle of water. She took a gulp, swirled it round her mouth and spat it in the gutter. She took a second gulp and put her finger in her mouth to rub her teeth clean before she spat. They were dissolving, she was sure of it. She'd spent hours calculating how – with the info trade she had going down with Dr Blythe – she could get the doc's dentist bloke to check them out. So far they'd only traded mundanities, like which supermarket Dr Blythe shopped in and where her boys went to school, and in return Tuesday fed her some harmless crap about her ma's prison stints. The trouble was, if the money flashing around her man's private practice was anything to go by, any treatment was bound to be pricy. And if that was the case, the stakes would go up, and Tuesday wasn't prepared to give anything away that her psychiatrist might actually want to hear. So she'd dismissed the whole idea, thinking that, all in all, it would be cheaper and less painful to have her teeth pulled and buy a replacement set from the wee shop on the corner.

She did one last rinse. Behind the blinking neon sign of the chip shop, Finn was chatting away to the boy at the counter. In sync, they turned to stare, gawking at her like she was one of the specimens on display in Rob's jars – grotesque, transparent, jelly organs rotting slowly in the thick liquid. She spat and gave them the Vs.

'Can I help you?' she said to the kid when she went back

inside. He blushed the colour of the squeezy ketchup bottle on the counter next to the malt vinegar and, for a second, the red disguised his mustard spots of acne.

'Leave him alone,' Finn said. 'He's a good one, this one. Mo's nephew. You met my pal Maurice, right?'

Tuesday climbed on to the stool and stabbed a chip with a wooden fork. It was hot, salty, soft inside, but the fork was dry and splintered on her lips. 'Yum, yum,' she said mockingly.

The boy gave a drippy smile and went back to filling the hot counter with battered sausages.

While Tuesday ate, Finn leant against the wall, sipping coffee. She offered him a chip, holding the greasy paper out towards him, but he shook his head.

'No appetite,' he said. Instead, he opened the box of Nytol and read out the instructions. 'Take one tablet twenty minutes before going to bed. Do not drive or operate machinery. Do not drink alcohol.' He spluttered. 'Fuck that for a game of soldiers.'

Tuesday carried on eating her chips.

'Listen to this, right,' Finn said. 'The most common side effects are tiredness and drowsiness. Is it just me, or is that not the whole fucking point?'

'I don't know why the fuck you're bothering with that herbal crap. Waste of time.'

'Right. One of your areas of expertise, is it?'

Tuesday shrugged.

'So, do you reckon you could get me some quality shit then? To help me sleep.'

'Fuck off. Go to your GP.'

'I haven't got one. Not here anyhow. Never quite got round to signing up.' He gave Tuesday what she imagined he thought was a winning smile. 'Come on, you know you can.'

'What makes you think that?' she said.

'Och, I don't know. Let's think. Oh, yeah. Maybe because you're a tinkie-junkie-addict.'

'Fuck off, arsehole.' Tuesday glanced around to see if the boy was listening. 'Keep your offensive speculations to yerself. For your information – no that it is any of your fucking business – I'm clean.'

'Aye, for the moment.'

It was pretty obvious to Tuesday that Finn reckoned he was smart, and in a way she supposed that what he'd said was fair enough. You could try to hide who you really were but the traces were always there. But what Finn didn't get was that it worked both ways. Behind the fake scruffiness, the unwashed T-shirt, the bloodshot eyes and twitchy hands, there was a nice middle-class boy waiting to be taken advantage of. You could tell from his clear skin and his fine bone structure.

'I suppose I might be able to help you out,' Tuesday said, screwing up the chip paper. Considering the third degree she got each time she went through the doors of the B&B, it was a dangerous game. But there were ways and means without resorting to anything overly illegal, especially now that she had a good idea where to find Dr Blythe most days of the week.

'It'll cost you, but,' she said, just to be clear.

'Didn't expect anything else.'

Tuesday chucked the wrapper towards the bin. 'So, what's the story?'

'Can't sleep.'

'You don't say.' Apparently the tosser thought she was retarded as well as a junkie loser. 'How no?'

'Dunno. Stuff. Work and stuff. My paintings.'

'You're having me on, eh no? I thought fae the state of you, it was something serious.'

Finn dragged a hand through his hair, pulling it back off his face and gripping it like he was going to tear it out by the roots. When he let go, it sprang back in front of his eyes. 'It is fucking serious,' he said, shredding the polystyrene cup. White nodules of foam were sticking to his fingers like warts.

'Yeah?'

'I'm doing a Masters in Fine Art. I know, I know, fucking art students. I'm a post-grad, but.'

'What's that got to do with the price of haddock?'

'I'm telling you why I can't sleep. You asked.'

'I didnae ask for your fucking life story.' Although, if he was a student or whatever, it went without saying his parents had more money than social obligation. A slice of that cash might come in handy if Campbell Spence lived the other end of the country. Travel expenses and all that.

'Do you want to know or not?'

'Go on, then,' she said. 'But skip the detail.'

'I'm supposed to have a portfolio of work by the end of May. For my degree show. Only, I haven't got a single painting.'

'What about that lovely pair of legs I saw?'

'Trashed. That one and the others. Heating system flooded in the hall. After the renovations.'

'Pisser.' Tuesday could feel a sarcastic smile twitching at the angles of her mouth.

'Aye, well, not exactly. They weren't that great. Gave me an excuse to start again. But the trouble is, I've done fuck all. I'm stuck. The painterly equivalent of writer's block. A couple of months ago, this artist kind-of-distant-relation of mine showed up and I thought maybe he'd help me out a

bit, you know, maybe give me a few pointers, bit of reassurance or whatever. Only he buggered off without warning.'

'And?'

'Well, that's it, really.'

Tuesday sniggered to herself. Finn actually looked like he
was away to cry.

'So, basically,' she said, 'if I'm hearing right – because your
wee cuz isnae here to hold your hand or give you stickers for
your star chart – you cannae work and you cannae sleep.'

'Aye, that about covers it. Except he's not my cousin.'

'I feel for you, doll,' she said. 'I really do. It must be a
total fucking nightmare no to know where your next painting is coming fae. A real bastard. No wonder you cannae
sleep.'

Finn flicked a nodule of polystyrene at her and pulled an
upside-down grin. 'I'm glad you find my predicament
amusing, bitch.'

'Just paint anything. Anybody. It's no fucking life or
death.'

After a pause, when Finn's eyes went glittery and his
mouth did an imitation of one of the fish on the wall chart
behind the wire baskets of crisps, he said there was a girl.

'Oh aye? Should've known.'

'No, nothing like that. I'd paint *her* if I could. Deffo.'

'Well, fucking do it and stop your whingeing. It's gieing
me a migraine,' Tuesday said.

Finn seemed to think she was kidding. 'It's not that simple.'

'Course it isnae.' She was getting bored now.

'This girl, right. She's different, special. She's . . . I don't
know . . . exceptional. Plus, she doesn't like me.'

'Bummer.'

'Fuck off. I didn't expect you to get it. I've got – had –
this girlfriend, right. I say had but I don't know for sure—'

'You're a half-wit, I take it.'

'Sorry?'

'Or deaf?'

'I'm not—'

'What did I say? Skip the fucking detail.'

'Oh. Right. Okay. Summary. Girlfriend – moon: beautiful, luminous etc. etc., but delicate, pale, kind of fragile. The other lassie: dazzling, fierce, fucking solar storms and burning rays. It hurts my eyes to look on her but, like they say – or even if they don't – the more intense the light, the deeper the shadows.'

'Jesus fuck. Your poor girlfriend.'

'Aye, well, it isn't like that. And anyhow, like I said, I think she dumped me.'

'Nae fucking wonder.'

'Nah, you've got it wrong. The other lassie. I don't want to go out with her. But if I could paint her . . .' Finn shook his head. 'Nah. Not possible. She's so intense, so fucking alive. I'd never do her justice.'

Tuesday laughed. 'You know what your problem is, pal. You're one of thae uptight perfectionist kinda peeps. You know the sort. Cannae even take a shite in case they mess it up. You've gotta chill, relax, start with someone with a little less life in them.'

'Like who?'

'How the fuck should I know? It's your picture. What about your pal, Maurice? When I saw him, he looked more than ready to pop his clogs.'

Without warning, Finn chucked the remains of his polystyrene cup on to the window sill and grabbed Tuesday by the shoulders. Automatically, she flinched. Then, to her amazement, he roared – properly roared, like a pure maniac – and planted a massive smacker on her forehead.

'Fuck off, dickhead,' she said, rubbing the kiss off with the heel of her hand.

Finn let her go and leapt around the shop, crying that she was a genius, a *total fucking* genius no less, at the top of his voice.

The boy behind the counter was watching the two of them.

'The lassie's a genius, Michael. Did I tell you?'

Tuesday unwrapped a stick of chewing gum and shoved it in her mouth. 'I could've telt you that without the snog.'

'It wasnae a snog. It was a mark of my eternal and unbounded gratitude.'

'Well, next time keep your unbounded gratitude to yerself, thanks very much.' Tuesday picked out the old piece of gum from her loose sole and replaced it with the newly chewed piece.

'Nifty,' Finn said.

'Condescending twat.' She got up to leave.

'You'll no forget my stuff.'

'What stuff?'

'Come on. When can you sort me out?' He had fixed a grin on his face, not sure whether she was winding him up. It was pitiful.

'Gie's a couple of days or so. Take the plant pills if you have to. I'll find you.'

Finn picked up her coat, held it out for her to put on. 'You're a star, by the way. An absolute total stellarific star. Even if you do have a stupid name.'

Tuesday snatched her coat from Finn's hand. 'Tosser,' she said. The chip shop boy was gawking at her again.

As she shrugged on her coat, Finn ducked past her and barred the door. He was grinning like an idiot.

'Okay, Michael, answer me this,' he said. Behind the

counter, the boy started dripping chip grease from his pores. 'Don't stress. It isnae a trick.'

The boy, Michael, nodded slowly.

'Gen up,' Finn said.

Tuesday and the boy looked at Finn.

'A simple question. Think you can answer it?'

Michael cleared his throat and squeaked his reply. 'Depends . . .'

'Do you, perchance, happen to know what day it is today?'

'Seventeenth. February 17th. Pancake Day.'

'Not date, you cret. Day. Of the week.'

'You've lost it, you know that.' Tuesday punched Finn's arm out of the way.

'Tuesday,' the boy said.

Laughing, Finn clutched his arm, and Tuesday barged out of the chip shop. She could see him through the neon sign, creased over, bumping his forehead on the gashed seat, rubbing his dead arm, slamming his hand on the window ledge next to him. Tuesday hammered on the window as she passed. He was totally ending himself, the stupid twat. She watched the boy tap him on the back and hand him a glass of water. Finn took it, wiping tears from his eyes, and practically choked on his laughter when he tried to drink. What an absolute fucking tool. Tuesday pulled her sleeves over her hands, hugged her arms across her body. She'd put the price up for the pills if he was going to take the piss like that. She set off, grinning to herself, because whether she wanted to admit it or not, there was something majorly warped about the cocky prick that she actually found quite attractive.

16

Cardsharps

'Hey, miss. Miss. Dr Blythe.'

Esme looked over. Tuesday McLaughlin was sitting on the railing next to the supermarket entrance waving to her.

'Oh hi, Tuesday.' After nearly ten years of living in Glasgow, Esme was finally getting used to these unexpected encounters. In London, she'd lived happily in the comfort of anonymity, but there was something to be said for the small town feel of this city, if only that she could be more intimately involved in her patients' lives. The drawback was that usually she left her professional mask at work so meetings like this caught her exposed and unprepared.

She kicked the wheel of the shopping trolley to manoeuvre it over a speed bump in the car park. The trolley was cumbersome, irrational, taking a different route of its own accord, and it wasn't made easier with Charlie rammed in the baby seat squirming to get free. The trolley failed the speed bump, so she reversed and had another go, acutely aware that Tuesday was watching her. At the same moment, Paddy cut between Esme and the trolley, and attempted to lift his brother down.

'Paddy! Will you give it a rest? How many times do I have to tell you?'

Paddy's face crumpled. 'I'm helping.'

'You are not helping, Paddy.'

'Everything okay there, miss?'

'Yes, fine,' Esme said curtly. She cringed when she heard her clipped reply. It had been a long day and she was dropping on her feet. What she really wanted to do was turn her back on the supermarket, go home, get Dermot to put the boys to bed, pour herself a glass of wine and watch some rubbish on the TV that didn't involve any mental or emotional involvement. Nevertheless – as her mother-in-law liked to remind her whenever she came to visit – manners cost nothing.

'Sorry, small boys. Very distracting. How are you?'

'Could be worse, I guess.'

'Very good.' A hefty shove and the trolley juddered on to the pavement.

'What about yerself, miss? You look kinda peaky.'

'I'm fine thanks, Tuesday. Paddy, where's your brother?'

'He's gone to look at the games,' Paddy said.

Tuesday jumped down from the rail. 'I've been taking your advice, by the way.'

'Good, glad to hear it,' Esme said. 'Sorry, Tuesday. I need to get on.' Charlie was gurning in the trolley, tugging at his shoes, demanding with his blurry consonants to get down.

'Aye, course you do, miss. On you go.' Tuesday climbed back on to her perch.

They had barely reached the ramp up to the entrance when Charlie finally succeeded in ripping open the fastening of his shoe and throwing it out of the trolley. Esme bashed her head on the handlebar when she bent down to get it.

'I could gie youse a hand,' Tuesday said. 'If you want. Only it looks like you've got your hands full there and I reckon the wee man wants down.'

It wouldn't hurt, Esme thought, rubbing the bump on her head. Charlie was on the point of having a meltdown.

'Okay, then,' she said. 'How's your driving? Do you think you could steer this thing while I fill it?'

'Aye. Easy-peasy.' Tuesday took the handle of the shopping trolley and pushed it through the entrance. Esme lifted Charlie down and followed on, hoping Tuesday wouldn't mention the snippets she knew about the boys. It was only trivialities Esme had given away, but Frankie in particular didn't appreciate her telling even his grandmother the tiniest detail about his life.

'Pads, hold your brother's hand.'

'You're a big fella,' Tuesday said to Charlie. 'What's your name?'

'His name is Charlie and my name is Paddy and my other brother Frankie is over there looking at the console games.' The words poured out of Paddy's mouth like spilt sugar.

'Nice to meet you, Paddy. I'm Tuesday.'

'Is Mummy your doctor?'

'Pads, what did I say about that?'

'It's okay, miss. I'm no bothered.'

'Mummy helps people with mental health issues. Do you have mental health issues?'

Tuesday laughed. 'That's awfie grown-up words for a wee guy like you.'

'Mummy doesn't like it when Daddy calls them nutters.'

'Nutters isnae so bad. You should see some of the crazies your ma has to deal with. I can think of way worse things to call them.'

'Like what?' Paddy said.

'Okay, enough.' Esme dropped a bag of potatoes into the trolley, remarking to herself how similar, in many respects, Tuesday was to Paddy. Both of them cheeky, funny, vulnerable. But Tuesday was thirty-two not six and, although her build and mannerisms were that of a child – her growth

unmistakably stunted by a diet deficient in almost everything except sugar and hard drugs – her face was pinched
and her skin as colourless as the straggly ends of her
bleached hair. She looked like she was about to skip adult-
hood altogether and sink straight into old age. A hazard
of addiction that was uncomfortably familiar to Esme.
Tuesday, at once as dependent as a child and as haggard as
someone four times her age.

While Paddy and Tuesday giggled conspiratorially, Esme
found herself staring at the pallets of vegetables desperately
planning what she could cook for the week ahead. By force
of habit, she selected onions, sweet peppers, a couple of
aubergines, knowing most would be met with protest. Then,
with no real plan, she picked the least hard of the unripe
tomatoes, a head of broccoli, a bag of apples, a bunch of
bananas. Even as she was piling them up in the trolley, she
pictured half of them rotting in the bottom of the fridge,
uneaten. Perhaps she should miss out the fridge stage
altogether, give some of it straight to Tuesday, force-feed her
some nutrients. It was hard to believe a piece of fruit had
crossed the girl's lips in decades. It was a wonder she didn't
have scurvy.

'Moving on,' Esme said, with effort.

'Don't forget lemons, Mummy,' Paddy said. 'We have
lemon on our pancakes. It makes me go like this.' He sucked
in his cheeks and opened his eyes wide to show Tuesday his
sour face.

Charlie imitated his brother. Tuesday pulled the same face
back.

Paddy giggled. 'Are you having pancakes tonight?' he
asked.

Tuesday shook her head.

'You and Charlie choose two lemons then, Pads,' Esme said. 'Nice ones, mind. Then we'll get eggs and milk. Daft isn't it, coming shopping to buy the things for Pancake Day.'

From the blank look Tuesday gave her, Esme guessed the thought hadn't crossed her mind. She felt a tiny bit ridiculous for imagining Tuesday would have supplies in her cupboard to use up.

Paddy led the way towards the chiller cabinets, dragging his brother along, with Tuesday pushing the trolley at their heels. At the fridges, after milk, butter and eggs were piled in, Esme added two packets of smoked salmon.

'Sea-ham,' Paddy said. 'Do you want some? I can get some for you. Mummy, shall I get another packet for the lady?'

'Nah, you're all right, doll,' Tuesday said. 'I prefer my scran cooked.'

'It's very good for you,' Paddy said. Esme had never persuaded any of the boys to eat fish that wasn't reconstituted and coated in breadcrumbs, but since Kassia had christened it sea-ham, salmon had become a staple. Hard though it was to admit it, Kassia was proving tricky to replace. Which meant Frankie and Paddy were spending long days in afterschool club, and Esme was stretching the limits of the child-minder's good nature.

'Okay,' she said at last. 'I think we are done here.'

Paddy chose the route to the checkout that passed the shelves prematurely stacked high with foil-wrapped Easter eggs. He and Charlie stopped to admire the different possibilities. Tuesday pulled to a halt behind them.

'We're not allowed. We're giving up sweets for Lent.' Paddy's voice was hushed with reverence. 'Are you giving up anything for Lent?'

'Aye, you could say that,' Tuesday replied, catching Esme's eye.

'Do you want anything, Tuesday?' Esme asked, waving her hand towards the chocolate bars and neatly stacked packets of biscuits. She was certain Tuesday hadn't helped her out of charity. In the clinic their interactions were exclusively based on a tit-for-tat basis, but on this occasion Esme had still to work out exactly what Tuesday was after.

'Nah, you're okay, miss. Bad for your teeth, all this.'

At the till, the rhythmic beep of the bar codes lulled Esme into a brief trance which was broken after a minute or two by Tuesday's nattering.

'Talking of teeth. I reckon mines are all away to fall out. You wouldnae believe the agony, doc.' Tuesday was packing the shopping into carriers, stowing the carriers in the trolley. Paddy was listening intently, still holding his brother's hand.

'I'm wrecked, miss, if you cannae tell,' she said. 'Cannae sleep. Total insomniac. Need my kip and always have done. You've nae idea what a nightmare it is, staring at the stained patch on the ceiling of my manky bedsit every night, wanting to sleep and all that, but my teeth throbbing like a . . . aye, whatever.'

Tuesday grinned at Frankie who had joined them at the checkout. He acknowledged her with a half-nod, skirting the edges of politeness.

'See the stained patch, by the way, it's fae when the auld dosser upstairs copped it and naebody found him for three weeks. It was the flies that gave it away. That's social services for you. I'm telling you, what with rotting neighbours, no sleeping and my fu . . . effing teeth ('scuse my French, boys), it's taking everything I've got no to . . . well, you know what I'm saying.' She pulled back her lip to show Esme her teeth.

'Do you know anything about teeth, miss? Do they teach you that at doctoring school? I think it's all the sugar in the green stuff, eh? You couldnae prescribe me something, could you?'

'You should be getting sugar-free methadone,' Esme said, punching in the code for her credit card, hoping the cashier wasn't listening. She was beginning to get the feeling that she was being played. 'I'll check the prescription when I'm at work tomorrow. The other things aren't really my territory, Tuesday. You should see your own GP or go to the dentist.'

'I've no got a GP, but. Cannae get on a list. You know what it's like. Naebody wants me because I cost them too much.' Tuesday hesitated, looked at the boys, played her trump. 'Your man's a dentist, is he no? Mebbe he could sort me.'

'I'm not sure, Tuesday. He's very busy.' It was something of a relief to Esme that a dentist was all Tuesday was after, although she was puzzled how she had found out that particular piece of information. Esme had been very careful not to mention Dermot in their little exchanges. His opinion on that aspect of her consultation technique was forthright to say the least, but then he didn't encounter people with the type of issues she faced every day. Sometimes she had to use whatever technique would work. Besides, whatever Tuesday thought she knew, she obviously hadn't realised that these days Dermot was exclusively private.

'I tell you what I can do,' Esme said. 'I can organise for you to see the community dentist at the hospital. You might have a bit of a wait though. I can't prescribe you painkillers. At least, nothing stronger than paracetamol. You know why, don't you? It goes against everything we've been trying to do.'

'See if I could get some kip, but . . .'

'Okay, okay,' Esme said, as they finished packing. 'I'll

write a prescription for something to help you sleep. I'll leave it behind the desk at the day centre. Come up and get it when you can.'

Tuesday stood aside to let Esme take the trolley handle. They walked together to the exit. 'You know I need double dose, right? Otherwise it'll no touch me. And can you make it mebbe enough for a few weeks?'

'We'll see,' Esme said, waiting at the kerb. 'When's your next outpatient appointment? Boys, cars. Hold the trolley.'

'Dunno. Three weeks or something.'

'Right. I'll write you up for two weeks and I'll bring the appointment forward. We can review it then.' A surge of unexpected confidence energised Esme. She was pleased with her solution, pleased to have exerted her authority, not to have been completely outmanoeuvred by Tuesday. She basked for a moment in Frankie's astonished gaze of admiration.

Once the shopping was crammed into the boot of the Mini, Tuesday wheeled the trolley back to the stand and recovered the pound coin. Paddy watched her jiggle the coin in her palm on her way back towards them. 'Mummy, the lady called me *Doll*.'

Esme smiled. For once, he seemed to have missed the swearing.

'Right, that's me,' Tuesday said cheerfully.' Here's your squid, by the way.'

'Keep it,' Esme said. 'Thanks for your help.' And, in that instant, for that short moment, she meant it sincerely.

'No, thank *you*,' Tuesday said, grinning. The tip of her discoloured tooth showed under the edge of her chapped lip and Esme's spirit faltered as she realised she hadn't won at all. With a cheerful wave, Tuesday skipped off in the direction of Dumbarton Road, leaving Esme staring after her, trying to elucidate exactly what kind of elaborate hoax it was that she'd just fallen victim to.

17

Medusa

Thursday evening a week or so later, Lizzi was in the library slogging away at the case study that had been assigned to her at the beginning of her clinical placement. It was her last study day before her clinical sessions were increased for the remaining few weeks of term and she'd basically wasted it. She was supposed to be writing a discussion of the psychological approaches she'd taken in the case and whether the interventions she'd made had been worthwhile. As the course handbook stressed, there were objectives to be achieved, methods to be evaluated, outcomes to be assessed, both for the end-user and in terms of her own training, but the way things stood at the moment, objectives, methods and outcomes amounted to precisely zilch because her particular end-user had refused to give anything away. Not a thing. Not the slightest scrap of information. Not the smallest shred of her life which, with a bit of imagination and a large amount of the desperation Lizzi already possessed, could easily have been elaborated into a 5,000-word essay. Talking therapies were the staple of clinical psychology, but when the therapee refused to open her mouth, there wasn't a lot of help the therapist could offer.

The library was so quiet it was impossible to concentrate. Lizzi rubbed her eyes and focused on her laptop, staring hopelessly at the white page of the screen below the couple of lines of perfunctory text that was all she'd managed. It was completely pointless. She pushed her computer aside and leafed through the pages of the handbook on the pretext of checking the content of the next term's module. It was a form of active procrastination, she was aware of that – almost on a level with Finn lining up his brushes in preparation for a painting he hadn't even planned – but at least it was a distraction. *Module 5: Service Based Evaluation 1*, she read. Which was essentially an audit, she discovered – or more accurately the outline of how to put an audit into practice – with some relevance to clinical psychology. She bowed over her notebook, jotting ideas that morphed into doodles, and prayed for an idea to bob to the surface of the chaos in her head.

Of course, Lizzi knew perfectly well it wasn't the silence of the library, or her constant headache, or even her unco-operative client that was stopping her working. It was all the other stuff. Sooner or later, she had to face the mess she was in. Sort out what to say to her supervisors, find out if she would have to repeat any of the year, think about how she was going to manage financially if the NHS part of her contract didn't entitle her to maternity leave. Although given the fiasco of her placement and the fact she'd have to stop before the end of the summer term, they would probably kick her off the course anyway.

It wasn't fair. Other people had their parents to turn to when things got tricky, but Mike had devolved himself of all paternal and financial responsibility when he'd signed the tenancy over to her. The emotional support had ended long before that. She shouldn't complain, roof over her head etc., etc., but it wouldn't have been like this if her mum was still around. All these years later and she still missed her every single day. Like today. Like most of the afternoon, before she finally dragged herself out of the house, when she'd sat at the kitchen window, staring at the Japanese maple her mum had planted, whose leaves were beginning to bud in eruptions of scarlet needles, and the circle of pale green on the back lawn where the grass had never properly recovered from the shadow of her trampoline. In the months following her mum's funeral, Lizzi would find herself there sometimes, cross-legged in the middle of it – sheltered from real life by the veil of the safety net and the curtain of evergreens beyond the flimsy fence – letting rain pour down her cheeks and soak through her clothes, trying to trap her memories so they couldn't escape, and knowing, even then, that each moment of recall fixed the past into something less real, less painful, into something artificially beautiful but essentially fake. Like tropical butterflies pinned for display.

A tear dripped on to her handbook and made the page dimple. Lizzi put her forehead on the desk and covered her head with her arms. Soon she was properly crying. Sobbing, trying to muffle her gasps and snivels so the other students wouldn't hear, too embarrassed to show her face. It was all coming out and she couldn't stop it. All the grief about Finn, and him not knowing, not being with her, and how useless she was at the course she had worked so hard to get on to. In the midst of it all, out of the blue, an idea for her next module popped into her head. Access to clinical psychology in bereaved children. Or its effectiveness in early intervention. Along those lines anyway. Christ, she was nuts, she thought, working all this out while she bawled into her course book and a Biro she hadn't moved dug into her forehead, while her fingers went numb from pins and needles.

She moved the pen without lifting her head and wiggled her fingers to revive them. It was difficult to imagine how she would have reacted to a psychologist when she was a bereaved child. Would it have helped her to manage her grief better? The whole concept of managing grief well was an idiotic notion in itself. What did it mean? That you cried appropriately and had your spell of denial and anger and bargaining, and then sank into a depression until everyone around you was fed up and you finally went off and played football with the rest of the kids?

That wasn't how it had happened for her.

She'd sat for hours this afternoon at the kitchen window, dwelling on every negative aspect of her life that she could possibly dredge up, watching the February sun flit in and out of lime-washed clouds and bleach the back lawn until the dying patch of grass could no longer be distinguished. At a certain angle, the rays of sunshine diffracted through the tears trapped in her eyelids and, light-blinded for an instant, she had glimpsed the slow-motion silhouette of her mother and herself, bouncing on the trampoline, the sun catching their red hair in arcs of molten lava, and her dad looking at them both with a flickering smile on his face like he knew already he was watching a memory.

The silence of the library was broken only by the click of keyboards and the rustle of occasional pages. Lizzi kept her head down on the desk and shut her eyes tight. The trampoline had been her refuge long after she stopped playing on it. Mike had taken it down one day when she was at school. She'd gone crazy at him, told him he had no right, that he was a heartless traitor. But he had said it was time, she had to let go. A few months later, only weeks after she'd finished her Highers, he'd taken the job in Jakarta. She was so angry with him that she refused to kiss him goodbye at the airport. Angry not so much for leaving her as for not clinging to the grief that had bound them together after her mother's death. A shared grief that had saved her, kept her afloat. His moving on was a betrayal, of her and of her mum. But what she was struggling to admit was that she was guilty too. Guilty of letting the past fade. Guilty of letting the pain heal. Guilty of daring to let happiness into her life. And now she was paying for it.

Eventually, Lizzi lifted her head and opened her eyes and jammed her fingers up against her lower lids. Her tears dammed briefly and then spilt over. She gathered her belongings quickly, ashamed of her ridiculous behaviour, desperate to hide herself away.

And then, in the lift on the way to the ground floor, something happened that almost took her legs out from under her. For the first time, she felt her baby move. Its pale flutters juddered through her like distant earth tremors, and her pulse skipped a beat, and her throat tightened, and her stomach leapt to her mouth and she couldn't tell if it was terror or joy. For a moment, she thought she would fall to the floor, and she put her hand against the mirrored wall to steady herself. Her lonely, terrified reflection stared back at her. And she knew she had to find a way to let Finn in.

By some means or another, she summoned the courage to go to his place. Climbing the fire escape, panting up each concrete stair, she felt sure she wouldn't make it. Each gasp expanded her lungs more until she thought she would float to the ceiling, bloated-fish style. When she rang the doorbell – insides churning, head frothing, heart pounding – she braced her knees to stop them giving way. But even then, part of her was praying it would all work out okay, that Finn would kiss her and scoop her up in his arms.

It was Maurice, not Finn, who answered the door. In pee-stained pyjamas, with his lanky hair clinging to his temples like tendrils of seaweed and his dead mackerel eyes trying to focus on her to work out who it was who'd come calling at that time of night. Checking the time on the watch that she had given Finn for Christmas. Telling her that he was living there now and Finn was staying at the studio. The slurred words and the spit rained down on her like pumice, and for the rest of that night – dazed, bruised, desolate – she wandered the streets until, at daybreak, she eventually found herself home.

18

Saint Jerome Writing

Dougal Street was special. A type of no-man's-land that marked the boundary between Partick and the rest of the world. That was what Finn realised as Friday afternoon drew to a close and he stood on the porch step, smoking a roll-up and watching the street lamps stutter to life. Around him a faint drizzle dampened the birdsong and softened the leather backs of hidden woodlice. Maybe the place itself would be draw enough to bring Caravaggio back. If it wasn't, he was done for. Because in the last two months, he hadn't got anywhere by simply willing it.

Nervily, Finn sucked the last breath from his cigarette and ground the stub into the step. In the garden beds, between the heathers and the bracken, the first daffodils had forced their way through the freshly turned soil. Their flowers glowed artificially bright in the dusk. He loathed the things. Gaudy and self-satisfied. The season's golden boys, trumpeting for attention. In a different mood, he would boot their heads in. Instead, he flicked the stub at the nearest one and headed back inside, where Maurice was waiting for him on the set he had staged for the first of his new paintings.

'All right, big man?' Finn said.

Maurice was enthroned at the table with the red velvet fire curtains draped around his boiler-suited midriff, casually quaffing a cup of tea and perusing the *Gazette* in the poor light as if, in Finn's assessment, he was ensconced in a drawing room of palatial splendour and not on the set of Finn's first stark and unflinching masterpiece.

'Indeed. Ready when you are, laddie.'

Finn squeezed fresh oils from aluminium tubes on to a new wooden palette and let their heady fumes swirl around him. He was apprehensive without photos to work from. Nervous about making a hash of it. But this process wasn't new to him. Years ago – before he'd been fettered by the chains of accomplishment and had had to stop trying to slacken them in case they accidentally came apart in his hands – he had always painted straight up without photos or preliminaries to work from, with no sketched outlines to trace, no smoke and mirrors to illusify his audience.

It was time, at last, to go back there. But it had to be said: he was shite-ing himself.

'In position then, Mo.'

'Like this?' Maurice sat up from his paper and struck what he clearly considered to be an artistic pose.

'For fuck's sake, man. Not at all like that.' Finn dabbed at the paint blobs with the rounded bristles of an unsullied brush. 'We've been through this.'

'This?' The whiff of stained bandages billowed out from underneath the curtains as Maurice pulled the velvet drapes flamboyantly around his shoulder. He glanced coyly at Finn with his forefinger pressed into the dimple on his chin.

'Come off it, you pillock.' Maurice's antics were beginning to get on Finn's nerves. However, a quick re-evaluation told him that it wasn't just his model's antics that were uncalled for. 'Come to think of it,' he said, 'you're gonnae have to take your kit off. Otherwise it looks ridiculous.'

'You're having a laugh, Finjay, are you no?' said Maurice, abandoning his deviant attempt to look saintly. 'Who wants to look on my naked bits?' He flapped over a page of the *Gazette* which was spreadeagled across Finn's art book and squinted in the semi-darkness at the latest death notices.

Finn wanted to get on, make that first mark on the prepped canvas, lose himself in the painting of it. The longer they procrastinated, the more the jagged edge of poor sleep (which, incidentally, as Tuesday had predicted, had not been aided by the Nytol) rasped against his vexations – aggravation over Rob, fears about Lizzi, his uninvited obsession with Kassia, and crowned, of course, by the haunting absence of Caravaggio – raspings that were liable, if he wasn't careful, to saw straight through his newly rediscovered motivation.

'Come on, big man,' Finn said eventually when Maurice didn't shift. 'I want this done tonight. Not a week on fucking Friday.'

'Aye, I'm warming up, but.' Maurice lifted up his chipped mug in demonstration. 'What with the cold and all that. It shrivels a man's assets.'

The milky tea slopped over the brim and on to the pages of the *Gazette* and Maurice smoothed out the drops on the paper with his sleeve. Finn was on the point of bawling him out for real when the studio door brushed open and Tuesday McLaughlin appeared. For a breathtaking moment, she was silhouetted in the doorway by the consumptive light of the corridor. It was, for Finn, a vision nothing short of divine.

'Why are you boys hiding in the dark?' Tuesday said, clicking the light switch on. The overhead bulb ploughed a furrow through the dusty atmosphere.

Finn rubbed his stinging eyes. 'I'm trying to get St Jerome here to undress for the part. What he doesnae seem to realise is that he's modelling for a painting. A work of art.' He turned to Maurice. 'Not a fucking porn film. Naebody's asking you to get your wanger out.'

'Jings, sonny,' Maurice said, pouting like a pilchard. 'If you'd have said so at the start, most likely I wouldna've signed up.' His lips were wet and wobbly and stained with emphysema.

A colour, Finn reckoned, midway between the glisten of an earthworm and the spilt guts of an eviscerated rat. Repellence at its most magnificent and he was dying (almost literally he believed, given the way his heart was battering against the bars of his ribcage) to transfer it to canvas. But Maurice was off again with his posing routine, playing to his audience, popping open the press studs of his torn boiler suit and slipping it down his shoulder to expose the anaemic polyester of his short-sleeved shirt.

Tuesday laughed.

'Don't laugh, McLaughlin. He's about as seductive as a dose of genital warts and it profits no one to encourage him. And for the record, Mo, you didnae sign up. You owed me.'

Piqued, Maurice pulled his boiler suit back up over his shoulders and refastened the press studs. He could sulk if he liked, Finn thought, but there was no way he was apologising for pointing out a few harsh truths. Up to now, neither of them had explicitly apportioned blame for the trashed paintings. Up to now, Finn hadn't deemed it necessary.

'Talking of owing . . .' Tuesday rattled the contents of the pharmacy bag she was holding. 'Should keep you going for a month or two if you take it like you're meant to.'

'You are an angel of deliverance,' Finn said. 'Literally. My actual salvation.'

Tuesday backed away. 'If you snog me again, I'll deck you.'

'Given the presence of the young lady,' Maurice said, sliding his chair away from the table, 'I shall disrobe in the lavatory, if you do not mind.' He staggered to his feet and the bulk of the curtain fabric tipped the chair backwards. It toppled with a thud. 'I shall be back when I return.' He yanked the curtains free of the upturned chair and limped out of the studio with swathes of crimson velvet trailing behind him.

Finn rifled through his jacket pocket to find his wallet. The way Maurice was behaving it was as if, until that very moment, he had been spectacularly insensible to the notion that Finn might hold him in any way responsible for the heating catastrophe. Holding a clutch of notes, Finn waved his hands in a gesture of wonder.

'I've decided it's a gift he was born with. His ability to slide between the hours of the day without making any connection with reality.'

When Tuesday worked out what and who Finn was talking about, she said she thought it was a shame to pick on the old man like that, but Finn said that actually Maurice was younger than he looked. He handed Tuesday the money and she flicked the notes to do a rough count and slipped them under the elastic of her knickers. She caught Finn watching. 'Safest place, if you get what I'm saying.'

Squeezing the pill packs into his shirt pocket next to his emergency fags, Finn contemplated the sad truth that he could in all honesty say Tuesday McLaughlin was one of the few lassies whose knickers he had never considered getting into. He did, however, realise it probably would offend to say as much, so he offered her a cup of tea instead.

'Won't say no.' Tuesday took off her coat and hung it on the back strut of the easel. She rapped the canvas with her knuckle. 'What's it gonnae be, then?'

Finn flapped the *Gazette* off the table, showed Tuesday the colour plate on the open page of his book. He explained how necessity had forced a few minor adjustments because he was somewhat lacking on the authenticity front when it came to props and suchlike.

'In that regard, where we should have *Saint Jerome Writing*,' he said, 'we will in fact have *Saint Jerome Reading the Partick Gazette*.'

'Underwhelmed.'

While Finn tended to agree with Tuesday's assessment, he pointed out that it was an irrefutable drawback of working with a model as temperamental as Maurice, who had outright stipulated the requirement of having the headlines to scan while he sat for the painting. But even before the sun had fully set, Maurice had been struggling to read. His stipulations would shortly be completely scuppered when Finn cut the extraneous illumination.

'I'll be maxing out on the old chiaroscuro effect,' Finn told Tuesday.

'Whatever you say, doll.' Idly, Tuesday turned a page of the book and peered more closely at a picture. 'Does it no get tiring? Talking shite all the time.' She pushed up the sleeves of her sweatshirt and continued turning the pages, careful to touch the book with only the very tips of her fingers as if she was afraid she might contaminate it. Every now and then, she paused over a painting, unconsciously rubbing at the tattoo in the crook of her elbow. Finn stroked his scrappy beard. Whatever, *whoever*, the midge was supposed to represent, the creature was clearly the talisman keeping her off the gear.

'Did your cousin turn up?' Tuesday said after a while. 'The one who was gonnae help you?'

'Nope. Reckon he's as underwhelmed as you.'

Tuesday turned back to the original plate and tapped the page. 'If you're gonnae dae it, you should dae it right.'

'Sorry?'

'Lister. For the skull.'

Sometimes, Finn realised, the simplest ideas were the most genius.

Tuesday held up her fingers in a crucifix. 'I'm warning you. Keep away fae me.'

Finn grabbed her. She squirmed like a weasel in his embrace.

When he let her go, he asked her about her tattoo.

'Mind your own business, knob-end. Get my tea.'

In the kitchen, Finn searched for a clean cup and Tuesday sat at the table and questioned him. She wanted to know how he would go about finding someone if all he knew about that person was which city they lived in but had no idea of their address. Once Finn had established he wasn't being interviewed for a position in MI5, he wanted to know if it was a hit job.

'If it is, they'll do the finding for you. Milk and sugar?' He didn't know how he knew that, but he did.

'Don't be fucking stupid. Both. Three sugars.'

Finn sniffed the milk carton from the fridge. It smelt of fresh vomit. He put it back. 'Wouldn't advise it,' he said.

'Sugar then. You don't know, do you?'

'Aye, I know. Phone directory.'

Tuesday took a bit of persuading that the phone directory in its entirety was available on the internet. Even for folk from Edinburgh.

'Unless he's ex-directory, of course.'

'I never said it was a bloke.'

'You didn't have to, hen.'

On their way back to the studio, Finn and Tuesday bumped into Maurice staggering along the corridor under the weight of the velvet curtains. He held them clasped under his chin and from his other hand, tapeworms of crepe bandages fell in dirty tangles.

'Tah-dah.' Maurice gave something approximating a twirl. The curtains slipped slightly. Under the loosely wrapped curtains, he was naked apart from his old man's underpants. Underpants that Finn decided it would be wise not to investigate too closely.

'You look ace, big man. Exactly how I wanted.' Where Maurice's shoulder socket joined his collarbone, his bare skin was stretched almost transparent over the knobbly joint. The rest of his skin fell in fine wrinkles over his ribs and pot belly.

'My dressing came aff with my socks. You couldnae gie me a wee hand with it, could you, son?'

'Mo, that's months you've had that now. Is it not about time you had it looked at?'

'Stop fussing, laddie.' Maurice turned to Tuesday. 'Finjay knows I make it a rule to avoid the medical profession whenever possible. All the docs ever want is to stick you in the infirmary to rot. Seems to me, the only sure way to avoid pegging your last in a hospital bed is no to go in there in the first place.'

'Quite right,' Tuesday said.

Finn held the studio door open for Maurice to limp through. He was about to follow him when the corridor door crashed open and Kassia whirled through. When she saw Finn, she froze. After a second, she spoke to Tuesday.

'Hello again, my friend. What are you doing with this wankmerchant?'

Tuesday laughed and said to Finn, 'I taught her that.'

Finn pulled his lips across his teeth in an attempt to smile. His cheeks tightened, his jaw locked, he was sure he was dribbling. Kassia was gawping at him.

'Are you sick?'

He didn't like to picture what kind of gargoyle she was seeing.

'Yes. No, no. Not at all. Sorry. I mean . . . What do I mean? I mean, how is your finger?'

Kassia pushed her hair behind her ears. A pearl earring – an earring Finn was sure he knew – quivered on her lobe. She held up her left hand to show her finger. It was bent from severed tendons. Finn flinched. His skin shrank. His ears popped. His vision closed to a pinpoint. He steadied himself against the wall. All he could sense was the smell of Maurice shuffling around the studio. What the fuck was wrong with him?

'The doctor tells me I am lucky, nevertheless. If I cut more deep, I cut also the nerves.'

'Nasty,' Tuesday said.

Kassia told them that she was there to pick daffodils to decorate the church. She was on her way to find scissors.

'Aye, great idea. Daffodils, fucking beautiful. The best,' Finn croaked. And then, with difficulty, added, 'But it's dark out.'

'This is not a problem.'

'If you say so,' he conceded, and volunteered to fetch the scissors from the kitchen. There, he fumbled in his pocket for his pills. It wasn't only sleep he was after now. Inside, he was a swarming hive of agitation, a veritable nest of slithering vipers, and it didn't exactly feel pleasant. He knocked back two tablets but they lodged in his throat. To rinse them down, he drank straight from the tap.

There was an energy in the surge of sleepiness that followed. A palpable energy that engulfed him and sucked his breath and made his pulse slow, like the first and best drag on a spliff. An energy that turned his arms to spider's webs and liquidised his skin and hollowed out his chest so it felt as wasted and empty as a coffin. A glorious energy that put the romance into necromance, he told himself with a giggle, and that made images of Kassia dance in front of his corneas and to which he succumbed without struggling.

He sank against the worktop and scarcely noticed when the real Kassia came into the kitchen and took the scissors from the cutlery drawer. She left again without comment.

'You pox-ridden dildo. You should have informed me of her visit.'

The words jolted Finn rudely awake. Caravaggio was leaning against the door jamb, backlit by the insipid haze leaking from the corridor, his bent elbow propping him at a jaunty angle to the frame, one squat leg crossed over the other. His cloak was pushed aside and his right hand was resting on his hip. A single narrow plume swooped from his cloth hat and was echoed in the silhouette of his sword sheathed in a wooden scabbard hanging from his waist, which reached below his bulbous knees.

'What the—' Finn wanted to laugh. Wanted to cry. Wanted to melt in a puddle on the kitchen floor. He rushed over to greet Caravaggio, his drugged legs a little unsteady beneath him.

'Two months. Two in-fucking-terminable months I've been trapped in this cesspit of a city with no decent company, and all that time I could have been cavorting with Fillide.'

Finn clasped Caravaggio's warty hand with both of his, vaguely aware Caravaggio's fist had been clenched around the pommel of his sword rather than resting on his hip as he'd initially assumed. Subconsciously, he suspected Caravaggio was planning to chib him, but dismissed the threat before it registered completely.

'Honest, man, didn't realise . . .' He was being eaten from the inside by moths. 'Cavorting? With who? Kassia? I don't think she cavorts.'

'Of course she does.'

'Where have you been?' Finn croaked. His thoughts were wispy and unconnected. 'I thought you'd given up on me.'

'I've been waiting for you to restitute me, you gonorrhoeal pustule.'

Through the moth-picked holes in Finn's brain, Caravaggio's recount made only the flimsiest type of sense. From what he could gather, Caravaggio was blaming him for his no-show. Said he'd been hanging out in the dives and clubs of the city centre, that Finn had deliberately chosen to prolongate his purgatory. Finn clung to the threads of the conversation, endeavouring to grasp exactly what it was he was responsible for, while the absurdity of the situation tugged at the loose ends.

And then he couldn't help himself. 'Prolongate your what? Sounds like a surgical procedure.' He slapped Caravaggio affectionately on the back of his head (a move that he instantaneously regretted; with a baldy bastard like Rob, you could be sure of a clean swipe; with a bloke who'd been hanging around God knows where for God knows how long, it was altogether a different prospect; Finn was left with a greasy residue on his hand and a niggling worry of lice).

'You are more irritating than a scrofulous testicle,' Caravaggio said, smoothing down his wayward locks as if it might improve his appearance.

Finn grinned. Up close, he noticed, Caravaggio smelt of mould and bad drains. In a manner he hoped would pass for discreet, Finn held his breath until the stink drifted from his nostrils and he had moved far enough away to be spared. He told Caravaggio there were a couple of people he'd like him to meet and chose to interpret his reluctance as reticence rather than rudeness.

In the studio, Tuesday was crouching down tying bandages back on Maurice's infected foot. Maurice had his back to Finn and Caravaggio. Before he made the introductions, Finn explained to Maurice that the painting had been postponed.

'Until we procure young Lister's assistance.'

'The skeleton?' Maurice said, while Tuesday secured the end of the bandage under one of its loops.

'Aye. Well, just his baldy bonce. If we're gonnae dae this, Mo lad, we should dae it right. Plus, we've got an important visitor to impress.'

Even when all you could see of him was his tortoise neck and his shiny pate, Maurice wasn't one for hiding his feelings, Finn realised. At the initial disappointment, his shoulders slumped but, at the mention of a visitor, he rallied.

'I'll leave you boys to it,' Tuesday said. Caravaggio stood aside with a flourish. 'Creep,' she said.

'The lassie with the attitude is Tuesday McLaughlin,' Finn said to her disappearing back.

Tuesday gave Finn the Vs and stomped along the corridor.

Maurice poked at his weeping sore under the bandages Tuesday had expertly tied.

'So, Mo, I'd like you to meet one of the greatest artists of all time and my . . . what did we decide you were? Great-great-something?'

Maurice twisted round awkwardly. Caravaggio bowed from his waist and his scabbard clunked off the floor.

'Let's just say *cugino*. Cousin.' There was no sign of the genealogy police, so Finn settled for ease at the expense of accuracy.

Maurice gaped in astonishment. 'Finjay?'

'I know, I know. Can you believe it? Totally crazy, eh no?' Finn slammed his palm on the pages of his art book on the table. 'How is it possible that this fucking ugly brute of an ugly fucker is *a:* related to me and *b:* the hand behind works of such magnificence?' He jabbed his finger on the image of St Jerome. 'Who would credit it?'

'Sonny, I know what you're like. You're joking with me, are you no? Tell me.' Maurice's gaze flitted between Finn and Caravaggio.

'This time, Mo, I absolutely absolutely swear.' There was a manic tinge to Finn's giggle.

'I fail to comprehend what is amusing,' Caravaggio grunted.

'Is this for real?'

'Totally.'

Maurice struggled to his feet and wiped his sweaty palm on the velvet nap of the curtains. 'Can I say hello?'

'Go for it, big man.'

In what Finn took to be disbelief at his own stupidity (although why he should be so disbelieving when the evidence was incontrovertible, Finn wasn't really sure), Maurice shook his head and strands of wispy hair slipped from his bald patch. 'And here's me thinking your man was a dead guy. What a numpty. Good tae meet you, pal.' He held out his hand. Caravaggio took the proffered hand unenthusiastically.

'Aye, indeed, indeed.' Maurice was still marvelling. 'Any kin of Finjay is as good as kin to me. Excepting his mother, I should say. Very pleased to make your acquaintance, sir.

Maurice O'Donnell. Of O'Donnell and Sons.' He paused. 'You can call me Mo.'

Caravaggio cleared his throat. 'Michelangelo Merisi da Caravaggio,' he said snootily.

Finn gave Maurice an *I-told-you-so* look.

'Say again?' Maurice said. 'The auld drums are no what they ought to be.'

Deaf, Finn gesticulated to Caravaggio by way of explanation. Maurice was smiling innocently – kind of vacantly Finn would go so far as to say – with his hand behind his ear, and a snigger bubbling from his festering wound. He winked at Finn. Finn bit his cheek to hide his grin. He knew what was coming. The two of them were poised, ready – literally in Maurice's case – to absolutely piss themselves.

For a second time, Caravaggio cleared his throat. 'Michelangelo Merisi da Caravaggio,' he repeated pompously. He too paused. And then, 'You can call me Vadge.'

19

Fortune Teller

The phone directory idea was the best lead Tuesday had had since she started her search. From the church hall, she headed straight to Rob's to use his computer, but when she got to the shop the sign was turned in the window. *Gone home to ink my gun*, it said, in a poncy Commie style that had the Robster written all over it. The metal shutter wasn't down, so she knew the sign was lying.

'Is that no against the law?' Tuesday said, when Rob eventually let her in. He was giving Lister a full-body wipe down with a damp cloth. He said she'd got it wrong. Lister was a handsome man, but he preferred his conquests with a bit more meat on their bones.

'Like me, you mean?'

'In your dreams, tart. The computer's on. Help yourself.'

'Tops,' she said. 'I'll no be long.'

Tuesday perched herself on the stool behind the counter and prodded the sleeping computer awake with her two-fingered typing. There was a taste in her mouth that she didn't recognise but for once wasn't coming from the pain in her teeth. It was watering out from under the edges of her tongue – kind of intense and steely, like the aftertaste of strong coffee – and her heart was tripping like she really had downed a mug or two.

A couple of clicks and she found her way to Directory Enquiries. The search page came up. *Surname (e.g. Smith);*

Location (e.g. St Albans or AL1). She'd expected there would be much more to it. It was nothing like the carry-on she went through each time she called the operator. It didn't help that by now the operator either recognised the phone box number or recognised her voice. Either way, these days the calls never ended in success.

Before she gave herself time to crap out of it, Tuesday typed in the entries: *spence edinburgh*. Four pages of results came up before she had even refocused. A, B, C.

C Spence.

On the first page there were five. Five.

'Okay there?' Rob asked, putting Lister back in his corner.

'Aye, fine,' Tuesday said. She might have been ready enough to use Rob's hardware, but there was no chance she was letting him in on her latest scheme. Considering the way the world regarded him, she would've expected him to have had a more degenerate outlook on life, but he always went for the strait-laced option. If he knew she was going after Cannon Balls Spence, he'd find some reason – twenty reasons – why it was a bad idea.

Tuesday read the list of addresses, nibbling the raw skin at the edge of her thumbnail. How was she supposed to tell which one was Campbell? For all Finn was full of bright ideas, he'd failed to mention the minor detail that the results came up initials only. What was she supposed to do now? She stared at the screen. Maybe if she stared at the names long enough, one of them would grass themselves up and confess to being the Cannon Balls Spence she knew. But of course that wasn't going to happen. She thumped the desk, mad at herself for getting so high on a stupid daydream. She was such an idiot. Hope was toxic. That lesson she'd learnt years ago. There was a reason for always looking on the worst side.

In the meantime, Rob had moved on to wiping down the poison bottles on the shelf. His fingers were sausaged in a pair of pink Marigolds. He asked her again if she was okay.

'Fuck off asking me that.'

He shrugged, and after a while said he was away through the back. 'Don't let anyone in.'

Whatever Rob was up to in the treatment room Tuesday reckoned he was deliberately making a drama of it. The rattle of the surgical instruments in the steel cabinet bored straight through her teeth. She turned back to the computer and clicked the links to the maps for each address. They were scattered around the city. How the fuck was she meant to get to all of them?

Using her recently acquired IT skills to distract herself from her downer, she took a photo on the web cam and changed Rob's screen saver (which before she replaced it with her own grinning face had been an olden-days, black and white photo of the funeral director's round the corner; apart from the colour it had nowadays, it basically hadn't changed). After that, she made some edits to the appoint- ment diary with a Biro, swapped the contents of Rob's in-tray and out-tray. It wasn't really helping her mood so she wandered over to the travelling trunk and picked at the latest issue of *SkInk*. A female model clad in micro-knick- ers, arms folded across her paps in a cleavage-enhancing pose, which accidentally didn't actually hide her nips, was poking her studded tongue out from the cover of the maga- zine. Both her arms were completely covered in tats – vines, fruit and all that biblical stuff – and a snake was winding its way from one side of her abs, round her back, so its head came out at the other aiming straight for her snatch.

Tuesday yawned. Some prick probably thought it was clever.

She Biro-ed in a moustache, some underarm hair and some bushy pubes, and then for good measure added a huge knob. When that was done, she sat back at the desk and stared vacantly round the shop, kicking her heels off the bottom of the chair. She hadn't expected to reach the end of the line so quickly. Absent-mindedly, she shifted a few more things around Rob's desk, picked up the Bakelite telephone to check the underside for make and age (a valuation habit that hadn't been dulled by the methadone), and then practically laughed out loud. She'd been searching a phone directory. A fucking phone directory. As in telephone. Sometimes, she was as slow on the uptake as people gave her credit for.

Tuesday dialled each of the numbers in turn. The first two answered with hello and she was forced to ask for Campbell by name. *Sorry love, wrong number.*

The third one was different. No greeting. Straight in there. *Isobel Spence. How can I help?*

Astounded, Tuesday slammed down the receiver and the phone gave a tinkle of protest. *How can I help?* Of course you can't fucking help, you fucking hackit-faced hag. Of all the scenarios she'd run through where the whole carry-on turned to shit, this one she hadn't even considered. That his missus would answer. That he would still be with the ugly heifer.

The walls were closing in. Tuesday ran her tongue around her dry mouth. How could they have stayed together? He couldn't stand her. He'd told her as much. Over and over. It can't have been by choice. Every possible explanation for why Campbell was still with his wife mashed around Tuesday's brain until she came up with the answer. Isobel

Spence had found out about the baby and had been holding Campbell hostage in their dried-up marriage for the last eighteen years. It was the only thing that made any sense.

A few minutes later, Tuesday was checking out train times, and there was a brisk rap at the window. 'Fuck off, can you no read?' she said, without taking her eyes off the screen. 'We're closed.'

Rob came through from the treatment room.

'Do you want me to see them off, doll?' Tuesday said, looking up. There was a massive, sappy grin on Rob's face. Made her want to boak. She glanced over and almost fell off the desk chair. It was Elizabeth from the day centre. Jesus fuck.

Rob unlocked the door and hugged Lizzi before he'd even said hello. The clinch lasted longer than was good manners.

Tuesday coughed and put her hand up in front of her eyes. 'Don't mind me.'

Lizzi let go of Rob in surprise. 'Oh, hi.'

Tuesday sniggered. Elizabeth's innocence act didn't convince anyone. Her coat was unfastened and under her top, her nips were sticking up like blister-wrapped tabs.

'Hi, doll.'

'You two know each other?' Rob asked.

Lizzi looked first at Rob and then at Tuesday. 'Sort of.'

'Sure we do. I'm one of the sad fucks that Elizabeth practises psychologising on. Is that no right, doll?' Tuesday smirked and carved Campbell's address on to the back of her hand with the Biro.

'That's the West End for you,' Rob said. 'Every cunt is some cunt's cousin.'

Lizzi frowned. 'I only popped in to say hello. I was on my way to the library.' She looked at Tuesday. 'Work to do.'

'I'm a pure nightmare for the lassie,' Tuesday said. 'Cannae tell her anything she wants to hear. Make it up, doll. Honest, I'm no bothered.'

'You can't spend a Friday night in the library,' Rob said, taking Lizzi's coat. 'Come on, I'll make you tea.'

'I'll do it,' Lizzi said, and disappeared through the back to put the kettle on.

'I'd no have had her down for your type,' Tuesday said, using the Biro case to chip away at the remains of her pink nail varnish. She'd sold the empty bottle to a wee laddie on her landing to sniff. Now she was deciding what colour to get for spring.

'Yeah? What's my type, then?'

Tuesday showed him the magazine. Rob laughed and told her he didn't get turned on by lassies with moustaches. The massive boner though was a different matter. They were still sniggering when Lizzi came back with two mugs of tea.

'Did you put sugar in mine, doll?' Tuesday said.

'Oh, I . . .'

Rob intervened. 'Ignore her, Lizzi. She's winding you up.'

Tuesday took the tea. Rob volunteered to go without.

Eventually, Lizzi got her coat. 'I think I'll head.' On her way out, she trailed the sleeve of her parka across the floor-boards.

'See you, doll.' Looking at the size of the lassie's tits and the way her hand flitted over her belly without her even realising, it suddenly dawned on Tuesday why Lizzi was there. And Rob – the stupid panty liner – didn't have the faintest. No wonder the lassie was getting pissed off.

Rob followed Lizzi out. Tuesday watched them through the window. Lizzi was kicking a flattened Irn-Bru can against the kerb. Rob's shoulders were hunched, his hands shoved in his pockets, his hoodie hanging unfastened. The muscles around his jaw were twitching. Tuesday chewed the dry skin on her lip. It wasn't Rob's fault if he had mince for brains. Things like this had to be spelt out for blokes.

Finally, Lizzi stopped kicking, said something, and then headed up the road. Rob stared after her for ages.

'Didnae mean to get you in trouble,' Tuesday said, when he came back inside. 'I'd've cleared off if you'd asked nicely.'

'I'm about to cash up,' Rob said. 'Are you done?'

Five minutes later, Rob punched in the code for the alarm, and the pounding of the buzzer filled the shop. He shouted something above the din. Tuesday shook her head. She couldn't hear. Once they were out, he pulled the security shutter down and the clamour stopped. 'Come on. I'll get you up the road for a pint.'

Tuesday tugged at her sleeve with her matchstick fingers. If she went, he'd be on her case the whole night to spill her guts to Elizabeth. There was no chance that was happening. Not when the lassie didn't play fair. 'Nah, you're okay. Things to dae.'

'Since when?' Rob said, turning his phone around in his hand. 'You never have things to do.'

Tuesday reached up, cupped his face in her hands and squeezed as violently as she could so his mouth ballooned into paunchy fish-lips. 'For God's sake, call her, you big petticoat-wearing lady-boy. It's like watching someone self-harm.'

On her way up the street, Tuesday weaved between the lamp-posts and the overflowing bins, and was halfway to the main road when she stopped.

'Hey, Rob, Rob. I forgot to say.' She stepped out into the road to see him more easily and stood with her legs apart and her knees slightly bent, leaning backwards under the imaginary weight of her own body and shaping the outline of a swollen belly with her hands. She didn't really know why she was giving him her blessing.

'Congratulations, by the way.'

And she was gone before she had the chance to regret it.

20

The Sacrifice of Isaac

The mission to procure Lister happened later that same evening. While unbeknown to Finn, Rob had actually taken Tuesday's advice and phoned Lizzi (although not for the reasons Tuesday believed) and the two of them were having a cosy tête-à-tête in Lizzi's kitchen, Finn was freezing his arse off waiting at the entrance to a close in a quiet side street at the corner of Partick Cross where Maurice was having a piss. Somewhere not far away, Caravaggio was ogling every shop window in the vicinity.

What had he done, Finn wondered, leaning against the shadows and sucking on the roll-up stuck to his lips, to be saddled with companions in possession of such an immense capacity to fanny around? By the time Maurice reappeared, zipping up his flies, Finn was on to his second fag.

'Gonnae get laughing boy while I finish my ciggie?' Finn said, on the in-breath. The drops of urine spattered on the tartan slippers Maurice had taken to wearing were giving off a powerful odour of honey-scented ammonia.

Maurice tugged his underpants through his suit trousers to rearrange his tackle. 'Mebbe it's too late,' he said. 'Mebbe we lost him.'

The way Maurice's face lit up at his own idea was, Finn reckoned, enough to light their way around the darkest of Partick's backstreets. But there was no way he was letting Caravaggio disappear off on his own again. Not without an escort. Not when he'd waited so long for him to reappear. 'Come on, Mo. He'll settle down. Once we get started.'

'Och, I'm sure you're right, Finjay. Only I wasnae of the expectation he would be so peevish by nature.'

It wasn't hard to see where Maurice was coming from. Caravaggio was still holding a grudge with them both for their response to his nickname. Like they explained (once they'd collected themselves and Maurice had dried off his trousers in the toilets), they were only trying to stop him sounding like a twat. But Caravaggio wasn't having it. So Vadge he was, and Vadge he would remain. It added a whole new meaning to *Ogni pittore dipinge sè*. On the other hand, it wasn't uncommon for great artists to be beset by personality afflictions from time to time, and it wouldn't take much to put Caravaggio's sensitivities down to a few minor issues of cultural and temporal adjustment so, for now, he'd give the man the benefit. And encourage Maurice to do the same. For the sake of a bit of peace.

Finn took a final drag on his cigarette. Partick was particularly magnificent on a night like this. The wind carried on it the smell of the river and the hoots of container ships, the ghostly clangs of the long-dead shipyards and the final rallying cries of coal and steel. He couldn't stop himself smiling.

'It's good to see you cheery again, son.' The stiff breeze stole Maurice's breath and he coughed hard and spat. 'Didnae like to say, but I wasnae such a fan of melancholy Finjay.'

'You know what, Mo?' Finn said, coming over all sentimental. 'It's really great of you to model for the paintings. It's changed things around for me. Honest to God.' He chucked his fag end in the gutter. 'See if there were a few more like you . . .'

'I'll ask young Michael for you, if you like,' Maurice said, ever helpful. Even standing still, he was panting slightly. 'You'd no have to pay him or anything. He'd do it as a favour for his auld uncle.'

A gust of wind blew grit into Finn's face and he wiped his watering eyes.

Among a rabble as peculiar and assorted as was found at ten thirty on a Friday night around the streets of Partick Cross, Caravaggio was not that easy to spot.

The place was teeming. More life on one square of pavement, Finn reckoned, than in the entire area at any other time of the week. All around the Cross, packs of lads were swarming from one oversized football screen to another while their female counterparts downed prosecco cocktails – or whatever the latest fad drink was – in single gulps (without, Finn noted admiringly, smudging their lipstick) and made sure they didn't let the boys out of their sight. What's more – with an aside to baulk at the outrageous appropriation of his name – Finn could see without looking the up-their-own-arse students poncing along past the hospital and the Art Gallery towards the hipster hangouts of up-and-came Finnieston. It was the few stray genuine drinkers that he felt sorry for. The poor buggers who had taken a wrong turn and ventured too close to this Hedonopia and who might never find their way back to the sanctuary of the dives of Partickland.

They tracked Caravaggio down to a shop selling false teeth where he was marvelling at the gleaming denticulation in the window. *Glamorous Geggies*, said the smiling sign. After a fake promise that they would come back for another look when the shop was open, the three of them continued on their way.

'How much frigging further?' Caravaggio whinged after less than a block. 'My feet are as blistered as a syphilitic cock.'

'Hear that, Mo? And you thought you had problems.'

Outside the tattoo parlour, while Maurice paused to tighten his bandages, Caravaggio took random stabs at a wheelie bin with his dagger. The security shutter was fastened with a padlock but Finn had the keys stashed in the inside pocket of his messenger bag. Back when they were best mates, Rob had given him a set in the event of an emergency. In many respects, this *was* an emergency. It merely depended on your outlook.

'What's the plan then, laddie?' Maurice said.

'To be honest, I've no idea.' Finn giggled, and said the first thing that sprang to mind – 'It's a three-man mission. Obviously. Because there are three of us' – and then giggled again, wondering if it was evident to onlookers that he was winging it. But when you considered the assembled troops – an almost blind and crippled alcoholic, and a chib-wielding nut-job who had theoretically breathed his last four hundred years previous – it wasn't as if either was in any position to question his leadership.

'Here's how it's going to pan. As soon as the security shutters open, the alarm will sound. I have two minutes precisely to unlock the inside door and enter the code. We want to be in and out as quick as, before anyone gets suspicious. No lights. No noise. No attention rousing.'

Maurice coughed. It took Finn a moment to realise he wished to interrupt.

'A wee thought, Finjay. A tad late in the day, I admit, but I'll put it out there notwithstanding. Would you no have been better just asking young Rob? He's very amenable.'

Finn shook his head in such a manner as to make it absolutely clear to Maurice how mistaken he was. 'It's a front, Mo. That nice guy image. A total front. The Robster and I are no longer friends.' To say the pair of them weren't getting along would – in Finn's consideration and not to put too fine a point on it – be to sugar-coat a massive unflushable jobbie. Putting aside Rob's delusions of his own artistic ability, their differences essentially amounted to everything else Finn could possibly think of. Mainly in connection with Lizzi. 'Plus, you should hear the things he says about your Leanne.' To be fair, there was no actual evidence for anything going on between Rob and Lizzi, but he'd heard they were spending an awful lot of time together, and Finn couldn't think why else Lizzi had stopped wanting to see him. And the worst he'd ever heard Rob say about Leanne was that he didn't know how she coped with Maurice sometimes, which even Finn had to admit as an insult was pretty understated.

At the alleged discourtesy to his wife, Maurice wilted. He perked up again when Finn gave him the job of lookout.

'Should the feds approach,' Finn instructed, 'shout. Vadge—'

Not having heard the punctuation, Maurice practised shouting *Vadge*.

Finn rolled his eyes. 'As I was saying: Vadge, while I disable the alarm, you will undertake the head-nap.'

'Are you out of your pox-riddled mind? There is no rationale in having a near-blind man as lookout.'

'Aye, aye there is,' Maurice said manfully. 'Leaves the heavy-mob free to do the dirty work.' He winked at Finn.

'Flattered,' Caravaggio said, and gave Maurice a scum-toothed smile of genuine amicability.

Surprised, Maurice blushed back.

Finn ignored them both. 'As you are aware, I have every right to be here. You boys, however, might take a bit of explaining.' He examined the backs of his hands to portray an aspect of gravitas. 'In the event of a shit-fan-hit situation arising, I suggest we split up and tank it back to the church. Every man for himself. Got it?'

'Loud and clear, Finjay, lad.'

'And you, smiler?'

'I do not require instruction of this nature, you half-witted eunuch. Do you take me for a novice?'

Rather than answer, Finn crouched down at the foot of the shutter and unlocked the padlock. He chucked it to Maurice, who predictably fumbled it. As quick as he was able, Maurice rescued it from the gutter and stood to attention. 'One, two . . .' Finn glanced at his men and spun the shutter up. The segments clattered as they rolled open. 'THREE.'

Immediately, the alarm began to squeal. Finn screwed up his ears against the din and unlocked the main door. The noise was blinding. It was hideous. Inside the darkened shop, he fumbled behind the coat stand for the central box. The code was . . .

Memorable.

Even.

With.

A.

Racket.

Like.

That.

Liquidising. His. Brains.

With a modest degree of panache, Finn punched in his birthday. Astonishingly, the screeching didn't stop. He double-took. Tried the date again. Still, the howling continued. A protracted, tortured wail, stretched on the rack, disembowelled and thumb-screwed. Bastard. A treachery so cowardly deserved a doing. Or if not a doing, some other less risky revenge.

With the alarm still screaming in his ears, Finn tried Rob's birthday. No success. Nearly didn't bother with Jed's given they were twins, but had a shot anyhow. Had a moment of fear that it might be Lizzi's and was almost relieved when it wasn't.

He had to get on. Closing his ears to the racket, Finn took stock. There were more props here than only Lister, but he had only limited carrying capacity. He settled on the mottled mirror, a large tome on anatomy and the jellied eel hiding in the jar behind the rotting brain. A touch over-eagerly, he snatched the brain tank from the shelf. It slipped from his hands and brains spilt all over the floorboards. There wasn't time to resurrect them, so he simply fished the eel out of its jar and shoved the slimy creature in his mes-senger bag along with the other pilferage. Briefly, he consid-ered the merits of poisoning Rob's stash of single malts with the contents of one of the many glass-stoppered bottles, but decided on balance it would be a waste of good liquor and purloined instead a couple of bottles of 1994 Glen Garioch (to be stored with his coffee outwith the reach of his delin-quent companions). Then he slopped through the carnage to the other side of the shop where Caravaggio was already off-task, flicking through the pages of Rob's folders, leering at the designs.

'These are mag-frigging-nificent,' Caravaggio yelled over the wailing.

Finn couldn't bring himself to acknowledge the com-ment.

'Have you seen them?' Caravaggio foisted the folder under Finn's nose and flicked past various porno-princesses. He stopped at a sultry seductress whose leather corset was bursting from the thrust of her unnaturally enhanced breasts while a pack of snarling jaguars strained at the leashes she was holding.

'Yes, I've fucking seen them.' Finn shoved the book out of his face and unhooked Lister from his scaffold. The skull was joined to the spinal column with thin twists of wire. His hands were still sweaty and shaking with excitement as he tugged at the wires to loosen them when Maurice stuck his head around the door.

'That'll be the rozzers.'

'What?'

'The rozzers. The pigs. The cops. Whatever it is you youngsters say. The polis.'

'For fuck's sake, Mo. Speak English.' Panicking, Finn lifted Lister as he was. The bones clattered against each other. He shoved his hands under Lister's bony oxters and dragged him towards the door, yelling at Caravaggio to grab the rest of the stash.

Caravaggio said something Finn didn't quite catch about a suppurating fistula in place of a brain and pushed him aside. Lister crashed to the floor. Caravaggio unsheathed his sword. With a single swipe, Lister's head rolled. Finn winced. The lifeless skeleton lay sprawled across the wooden boards next to the spilt brains. The violence had left Finn light-headed. He didn't want to imagine how Lister was feeling.

Caravaggio bundled the skull under his cloak and made for the exit. Maurice was wavering at the threshold. Finn grabbed the bounty bag and pushed past them to check the escape route.

'Jesus fuck, Mo. That's the Sally Army. Not the police.'

'Ha. I wondered why they had ribbons in their bunnets.'

Finn gaped at Maurice in wonder. Sometimes the man really outdid himself. As soon as the Christian Soldiers had marched onward to shake their money tins in the nearest pub, Finn and his men quit the tattoo parlour. The wailing petered out behind them, leaving the echo of tinnitus itching their eardrums.

21

Musicians

No matter what, no matter how much of a prat Finn had been, he had the right to know what was going on, was basically the gist of what Rob spent that same Friday evening at the end of February persuading Lizzi while they drank endless cups of tea in her kitchen (although had he known what was happening at the tattoo parlour in his absence he would have likely been less charitable). Lizzi wasn't sure she agreed, but what wasn't up for debate was that Finn *had* been a prat – breaking up without telling her, letting his phone go dead so she couldn't get hold of him, moving out of the flat, letting her find Maurice there in his place (not to mention the watch) – and that was enough to give her yet another night of tears and headaches and of generally beating herself up for how much of a wimp she was these days. So much so that by the time the sun came up, she'd decided it was time to get it over with once and for all. Which was how she found herself traipsing along Dumbarton Road so early on a Saturday morning.

Outside the Vaults, the brewery lorries were unloading their daily cargo. The crash of the cellar hatches and the clang of the steel barrels followed Lizzi up Dougal Street. The morning light was already too bright for her. Even before she reached the church hall gate her head was throbbing so badly she was tempted to forget the whole idea and go home. Gingerly, she squinted into the garden. Every dew-bent blade of grass, every spray of heather weighed with droplets, every rain-polished gravel chip added to the thousand tiny lenses that splintered the sunlight and sharpened the contours of the garden.

How long since she'd been here? she wondered. And yet not long at all. Was there any trace of the happiness she'd once felt, hiding under the glistening roof slates perhaps, or absorbed into the sandstone walls? She didn't want to believe it had all gone. A lifetime ago, someone – her dad, probably – told her that the past was a foreign country. As distant and unreachable as the remotest island. That it was pointless trying to return because, even if you did go back, no one there would know you any more. But it wasn't true. It was this present – this aching, blinding present – that was strange and unfamiliar. Everything, *everything* had changed. She could see it in the tended beds and the neatly clipped grass, in the carefully pruned shrubs and the freshly potted bay tree. Where was the tangle of weeds spreading over the gravel? Where were the empty beer cans and plastic bottles littering the undergrowth? Even the holly bush around the porch door had been cut back.

The well-cared-for garden was telling Lizzi something about Finn that she didn't want to hear. She had imagined him struggling and anxious, unable to work, pining, if not for her then at least for his lost paintings. It was the only way to make sense of his distance. She didn't want to know that she was wrong. The bristling light and ache of her anxiety were too much for her. To cool the pain, she rested her palms over her eyes and counted slowly, reluctantly – one, two, three – while she listened to the chirrups of finches splashing in the miniature puddles that had collected in the limestone hollows of the rockery and allowed herself a few moments of respite before she forced herself to face what she'd come to do. When at last she uncovered her eyes, she saw Jed float ghost-like in the distance past the gate and up the church steps, and she raised her hand in greeting but he didn't notice. For ages, she stayed like that, with her hand trapped in a hesitant wave, foolishly signalling to a presence that had already passed.

Eventually, Lizzi forced herself to move. When she went inside, a piano tune came tripping unexpectedly through the fire doors. Although it lacked the odd note in the lower register, the melody was delicate and unnervingly spritely for that time in the morning. To her surprise it was Maurice she saw at the piano when she went into the main hall. He was standing bent-kneed in his boiler suit, with his toolbox next to his slippered feet, tinkling away on the keys.

'Gosh, that was lovely,' Lizzi said, when Maurice finished his tune. The dirt-clogged windows had smoothed the edge off the daylight and it dripped across the waxy floor like honey. 'I used to play, but not like that.'

'Och, it's nothing, hen. I play by ear is all I do.' He saw her look of astonishment. 'No literally, you understand.' To clarify, he tugged his earlobe.

All at once a gush of nausea washed over Lizzi. It sucked its way into her nose, mouth, even her ears, rushing in like it was filling a vacuum. She clenched her throat, calculating whether she had time to dash to the Ladies, and flapped her hand at Maurice by way of an apology. He signalled that no offence had been taken and happily went back to his music. Before she could stop herself, she retched. Black speckles danced in front of her eyes and saliva flashed around her mouth. For a moment she went deaf. She retched again and the sting of vomit hit the back of her throat. She wouldn't make it to the loos. Instead – her whole body rushing with cold sweat, shallow breaths to stifle the urge to throw up –

she bolted for the kitchen, pulling her hair into a ponytail on the way.

At the sink, she caved. She vomited, and her throat and mouth and nose filled with acid. She vomited, and drops splashed up against the sink walls. She vomited, and lumps caught in the plug hole. She vomited and vomited, heaving and retching until her sick ran clear and her ribs ached, her sternum ached, her stomach muscles clenched in protest and she was too weak to bring up more. Then, clutching the draining board, she hunched over the sink and let her fore-head rest on the tap and her hair hang down the sides of her face, and dribbled ribbons of stained mucus between the cross-struts of the plug hole.

When she was able to move again without heaving, she rinsed her mouth with cold water and sprayed the cold tap around the sink. Vaguely aware of the mess in the kitchen, she grabbed the pole to prise open the old-fashioned window. After a couple of shaky attempts to hook the catch, the window tipped forward with a clunk and the bad air slunk out through the gap. Only when she'd gulped down the fresh stuff did she fully notice the chaos around her. Upturned chairs and the table strewn with dirty glasses and upturned empty wine bottles and a skull who on first glance she thought must be Lister, until she told herself not to be so stupid because how could you really tell one skull from another. Then, carefully, so as not to trigger another bout of vomiting, she picked up one of the overturned chairs and sat down to rest and let her queasiness settle. She folded her hands across her growing tummy and wondered what Finn would notice when he saw her, whether he would see their baby growing, see its peanut heart beating, see it shifting around inside her as restless and fidgety as its father.

When she was sure she had recovered, she decided it

wouldn't hurt to clear up a bit. She ran the hot water, squirted in the washing-up liquid. The rainbow bubbles trapped the morning sun on their surface. As she wiped a squeaky glass clean, she asked herself how it had come to this. This ridiculous state of affairs where she was too scared to speak to Finn, to wake him, to tell him what should be the most momentous news of his life. She had left it too long. They were nearly into March. It was months now since she'd fallen pregnant.

That expression. Fallen. Like it was an accident.

'Lizzi?'

She looked up from the sink. Finn was at the threshold of the kitchen, vacillating, hesitating, his greasy hair sleep-ruffled and his beard grown straggly and long. He was bare-chested and his jeans hung below the crest of his hip bones and every muscle in his arms as defined as the diagrams in Rob's anatomy book. Despite how gaunt he was, how drawn, how shocking his appearance, Lizzi felt terrible stabs of desire.

'I was clearing up. The kitchen, the sink. I puked.' She stared at his hollow chest. 'You've lost weight.'

Finn crossed to the sink, stood beside her, filled a glass with tap water. 'Huh?' The space between them was soft, pliable. Lizzi could hardly bear it. She wanted to touch him. Wanted to kiss him. Wanted to cry.

'Can we go somewhere?' she said, using all her effort to stop herself reaching out. 'Somewhere to talk?'

He gulped down the water and muttered something that could have been a yes. Lizzi dried her hands on a tea towel but her relief was shattered by the sound of someone rattling along the corridor. A couple of seconds later, Tuesday McLaughlin appeared in the doorway. She scowled at Lizzi without speaking.

'McLaughlin,' Finn said, grinning at her. 'You missed the party.'

'So I see.'

'Wasnae the same without you.'

'What's she doing here?'

Finn grinned stupidly and slid, TV-cop style, across the table. He laughed at Tuesday, teased her for being jealous, and he grabbed her to hug her. Tuesday pummelled his arms with her fists. The roots in the mat of bleached hair were dark against Finn's pale chest. His heart was pumping between his ribs. Lizzi was crumbling inside.

Eventually, Tuesday twisted free and kneed Finn in the balls.

He stooped over in pain, still laughing. 'Actually, Lizzi just got here.'

Tuesday seemed relieved. It didn't make sense. Lizzi refused to be taken in by what her eyes were telling her. But when Finn noticed the horror on her face, he tapped Tuesday's shoulder to show her and started giggling again. Slowly at first. Then stupidly. Idiotically.

'Me and her?' he said, pointing melodramatically between himself and Tuesday. 'Fuck off, Lizzi. You've got to be kidding.'

'Fuck off yerself, chubs,' Tuesday said. 'I only came to tell you that your bright idea actually worked.'

'Is that a thank you?' Finn said. 'You can thank me with more of your magnificent pills.'

Tuesday snorted and gave Finn the Vs, and all of a sudden it was clear.

'Are you mad?' Lizzi said. 'Drugs?' She'd always thought Finn's cannabis habit was more for effect than anything else. But drugs made some kind of perverted sense. It would explain why he'd become so withdrawn, chaotic. But why hadn't she seen? Why hadn't she noticed? 'Finn, I can help. Let me help.' She went up to him. Touched his bare arm. The skin was cold. The bones like stone.

'Nah, you've got it wrong.' Finn shrugged Lizzi's hand away.

'Come on, Finn. Don't do this. Don't let yourself end up like her.'

'See if you werenae up the duff, doll,' Tuesday said mildly, 'I'd deck you.'

'Eh?' Finn said. 'What are you on about?'

'Up the duff. As in preggers. You know, sproglet on the way. Or do they no teach you that at posh school?' Tuesday said. When Finn still didn't get it, she told him to get Rob to explain.

But Finn still looked confused. Lizzi told him not to listen to Tuesday, she didn't know what she was talking about, it was nothing to do with Rob and at first Finn looked uncertain as if he couldn't believe what was dawning on him, but then he gave her a look of such devastating contempt she thought her legs would give way.

'No, Finn. It isn't true. She's a pathological liar. Not right in the head.' This was awful. It wasn't how she wanted Finn to find out.

'Point of fact, Lizzi,' Finn said coldly, 'you know fuck all about Tuesday McLaughlin—'

'No, but I do—'

Tuesday snickered. 'Aye, course you do, doll.'

'I do. I know enough.'

'You reckon?'

'I know your mother was a sex worker. I know that the baby you had when you were fourteen was taken off you because you were an addict. I know that you've spent the last however many years shooting the remains of your life into your veins.'

Tuesday paled. 'Fuck off. I never telt you any of that.'

'You didn't need to. It was all in your notes.' Lizzi was hyperventilating.

'You fucking sneaky bitch.'

'You left me no choice,' Lizzi said, backing off, angry at herself because she was squealing. It was all going wrong. The pounding in her head wouldn't let up. She couldn't focus. Why wasn't Finn listening? Why couldn't he see what was happening? 'You wouldn't tell me anything. I had to know what I was dealing with.'

'I hadn't realised you were so childish, Lizzi,' Finn said.

'Yeah, right,' Lizzi said, blinking from the shock of sudden anger. 'That from a man who can't stand on his own two feet, whose mammy feeds him and clothes him and pays all his bills.' She turned to Tuesday. 'Did you know that about him?'

Tuesday grinned and shook Finn's hand. 'Congratulations, doll. If my auld doll was that flash with the cash, I'd be bragging about it fae the church steeple.'

Finn laughed.

Lizzi stared desperately between the two of them. They were smirking, colluding, sharing the joke. It was her they were laughing at. She was the joke.

'For God's sake,' she cried, with one last attempt to make Finn see reason. 'Look at her, Finn. She's a junkie. A junkie whore.'

Tuesday winked at Finn and mimed a blow job and they both cracked up laughing.

It was too late. Everything was lost.

Lizzi fled blindly and Tuesday's cheery words bounced

after her down the corridor in time with the jig Maurice was hammering out on the piano.

'You need help, by the way, Elizabeth. You're sick.'

22

The Lute Player

Isobel Spence was snoring. Lying on her back and grunting like a professional wrestler. Silently, Tuesday slid the sash window shut and pulled the curtains behind her. Only a sliver of moonlight escaped into the room. She pulled her hat down as far as it would go and fought through the knot of house plants to get a better look. Apart from the tits sagging into her armpits under her winceyette nightdress, Mrs Spence still looked like a man. Same home-hacked hair, same moustache bristles, same square jaw. She'd always been bigger than her husband, more stocky, more broad in the shoulders. And it was obvious even in the middle of the night that time had been a total bitch to her. Her cheeks were sunk into the two caverns made by her open mouth, and with each breath her jowls wobbled at the side of her chin. It was a fucking horrendous sight.

Campbell was lying on his side, back to his snoring wife. In the moonlight, he didn't seem so different. Still slim, fit-looking, hard-limbed and athletic. He'd done that thing that guys did when they started losing their hair – shaved his head to disguise the baldy bits – and it had made him look quite cool. Except, his skin was too big for him now and it folded into creases between his shoulder blades, like he needed ironing.

Faced with her ex-PE teacher and his snoring wife, Tuesday realised she didn't have a clue what to do next. Her head was all over the place. It was mental. All these years and he was only a train ride away. Not that she was planning to make the train a habit. When the guard had clocked her in first class he'd tried to chuck her off, convinced that she'd stolen her ticket. Once she showed him the receipt, they reached a compromise. She'd move quietly to second if he left her alone for the rest of the journey.

On the train, she'd convinced herself that she was bound to come across some trace of her son in his father's house if she looked hard enough. But what? Birth certificate? Adoption papers? Not likely. Maybe there'd be a photo some place but, if there was, it was bound to be hidden. Not even Cannon Balls Spence would have the brass neck to flaunt his dick in public that blatantly.

Apart from that, she hadn't made plans. Plans were not her thing. Plans were for losers, for uptight manual readers like Elizabeth. And to be honest, when you broke and entered, you had to be prepared to improvise. Things had a habit of turning out badly if you stuck too close to the programme.

Outside, a cloud slipped across the moon and turned everything in the room black. Tuesday waited for her eyes to re-accustom themselves, listening to the sounds of sleep. Isobel Spence had no right to rest so soundly. Her dreams should be tormented by the kids she bullied, by the girls she'd taken a ruler to, the boys she belted. By all the poor weans who went home every night with fingerprint bruises on their skinny arms after being dragged from class by her rugby player's hands.

A gust of wind rushed through the swaying fir trees in the front garden and the moon reappeared from behind the cloud. Isobel rolled on to her side. Her snoring changed to a damp snuffling and her tits flopped across her chest. The neckline of her nightie was low enough for Tuesday to see the rough skin and wrinkles of middle-aged cleavage. Payback hadn't even been on her list when she'd started out, but seeing Campbell sleeping next to that woman – tolerating that grotesque snorting without even a flinch – was too offensive not to do something about. Not that it was Tuesday's job to save the poor bastard from the bed he'd made, but she couldn't help but pity him. She wanted to smother Isobel Spence with her plump feather pillow, suffocate her until her breath stuck in her flabby nostrils and her slack throat, choke her until her gut spasmed and her orifices poured liquid shit. The problem was she might wake up and Tuesday hadn't quite got over her primary school fear of the bitch.

Instead, Tuesday crept round to Campbell's side of the bed and knelt down next to his bedside cabinet, her face level with his, working out if his features matched the half-remembered ones that used to visit without asking when she was off her face. It was surprising. He wasn't in bad nick. Pretty much exactly how she remembered. For the whole journey here, she'd been on at herself not to feel anything when she saw him again – except maybe some kind of misplaced nostalgia for her adolescence – but there was definitely something tingling in her knickers. The bloke was nearly sixty. Practically one of the bus pass brigade. There was something majorly wrong with her if she was even thinking of going there. What was the opposite of a paedo? O-A-Paedo. That's what she was. An O-A-Paedo. Gross.

Campbell stirred and coughed in his sleep. Tuesday slid into the angle between the bed and the floor, mucky sweatshirt and dark leggings merging with the shadow. She drew a breath and kept it in her lungs, waiting for him to wake and discover her. But nothing. He murmured and pulled the quilt closer to him. Still sleeping.

Choking back a snigger, Tuesday eased open the drawer of his bedside cabinet. It was filled with the kind of everyday shite that normal people kept – books, reading glasses, loose change. No papers. No photos. Nothing official-looking. She found a pen torch, hooked the shoelace strap around her wrist and worked her way through the drawers below. Underpants, thermal vests, cotton pyjamas. She scrabbled under a pile of walking socks. A box of Viagra and a tube of KY. Jesus fuck. It was too disgusting to think about. She slid the drawer shut, feeling sick. The porn pills were bad enough, but lube to grease his dried-up missus? Too fucking disgusting. But what was she expecting? They were married. They'd stayed together. Really, what the fuck was she expecting?

Before she left the bedroom, she reset the alarm clock for 4 a.m. It was all she could think of as revenge.

Downstairs, darkness filled the hall and pushed into the joints of the walnut panelling. Tuesday tapped her way along the wood until she found a door. She flicked the torch around the room. Two stiff-backed armchairs and a bow-legged table were outlined against a picture window in the formal sitting room. She glanced around, looking for anything that might help her. The beam of the torch caught the glass of a framed photo on the mantelpiece. She lifted the picture down and shone the torch into the eyes of the people smiling back at her.

She may as well have torn her heart out while it was still beating.

A family photo, a girl of twenty or so in graduation robes, her brother a year or two younger in his school uniform with his sister's mortar board on his head, and the parents beaming proudly. Sister and brother. They both had their old man's granite eyes and their mother's scarecrow hair. The girl looked like the kind of badge-wearer who would be friends with Elizabeth. The boy had teeth he hadn't grown into, flecks of a ginger moustache, and a square jaw that didn't suit him. Gangly in his school blazer, sleeves stopping halfway down his wrists, he was laughing, joking with whoever was behind the camera.

In the kitchen, Tuesday turned on the light, not bothered any more if she was discovered. It didn't matter a toss. None of them would want to get the police involved. She stared at the photo she couldn't let go of. Campbell had always told her there were no kids, didn't want them – at least not with his missus. Implied it would have had to have been a miraculous conception or whatever. But the parents in the picture didn't look too different to the sleeping beauties up the stairs, so the photo was recent enough. And the school uniform didn't hide the fact the boy looked old enough to be seventeen, eighteen. Tuesday slipped the photo out of the frame. It didn't take a genius to work it out. Campbell Spence was a lying bastard who already had a daughter when he started messing around with her. But what made it even more horrendous – totally offensive, made everything that had happened in her life since a total fucking joke – was that old vinegar-tits Spence must have been pregnant at near enough the same time as she was.

Tuesday sat down at the kitchen table and slowly tore the photograph into pieces. A silent howl engulfed her. Eighteen years. Eighteen years of fucking kidding herself.

Eighteen years ago, in the changing rooms after training, scabby knees on the concrete floor, giving him a blow job while he phoned his wife to tell her he was held up in traffic. Eighteen years ago, the rattle of stainless steel when he fucked her up against the lockers, her legs wrapped round his waist, padlocks digging into her ribs and back, his muscular arms easily holding her weight. Eighteen years ago, shivering with cold, grinding on his lap in nothing but her school skirt, watching his mouth twist with lust in the changing mirror while he fucked her from behind on the bench underneath the coat hooks. Hearing over and over how alive she made him feel, how she was the adrenalin rush he got when he was ice-climbing or paragliding, how she was his own personal extreme sport, his own wee headcase. His contorted face as he spurted on to her, into her, over her. Chucking her a tissue and telling her to take her time in the shower. Pulling tight the cord on his trackie bottoms and tossing her the key. Lock up when you leave.

Tuesday threw the pieces of torn photo into the air. They floated confetti-like to the floor. She dropped the glass from the frame and ground her heel into it. It didn't shatter.

It was mental how your past got distorted by time. Or maybe it was the other way around. Ignorance warped what you chose to remember. That pathetic fourteen-year-old, thinking she was something because the only fit teacher in the school was taking an interest in her, honestly believing that he saw more in her than a chance to show off his coaching skills and get his dick sucked. How he'd even given her a lift home once, told her ma how talented she was, how she was a natural and thanks for letting her spend all those evenings training. For once the daft tart had been stuck for something to say, speechless when she didn't have an audience who'd want to hear her slag off her daughter. Tuesday cringing when her old doll slimed over him, offered him a drink, touched his elbow with her lizard claws, never one to pass over the chance to ply her trade. It was the worst humiliation Tuesday could have imagined for herself – in those days there were still some things she was ashamed of – but Campbell had never mentioned it after.

Tuesday was seeing clearly now and she would do anything to unsee. All those wasted years grieving for a past that had never existed. All those years of trying to escape the tragedy of what she thought was love with a rusty spoon and a blunt needle, funding her habit with petty theft and minor misdemeanours. The only thing that had made any sense to her during those hideous years was that she was adamant – totally adamant – not to reduce herself to the life her old doll insisted she would inherit. Tuesday thought back to the running spikes from the lost property bin, the second-hand gym kit, the money for bus fares to race meetings. The sickening, sordid truth? Less than a needle scratch between her mother and herself. Elizabeth's words came back to her. *Junkie whore.* Exactly.

When Elizabeth had made her comedy exit earlier that morning, Tuesday had stayed on a few minutes to tell Finn of her plans for the day. A day like never before, her one and only time in the capital. A trip to the zoo to see the shagging pandas, a visit to the castle. But when she'd told him about Campbell, about how she was planning to track him down, Finn had properly laid into her. Not at all the soft lad who'd stuck up for her a few minutes previous. He asked her what she thought she was doing, what made her think that if she tracked down her bloke he would help her out. Eighteen years on and still with his wife, he was sure to have put it all behind him. A heroin addict girlfriend – ex or otherwise – was not the sort of person he'd want turning up on the doorstep. At the time, she assumed he was being a dick. Now she realised that he was trying to protect her from herself.

Upstairs, the alarm clock hammered. Tuesday slammed the front door behind her and looked up at the house from the road. Campbell was at the window in his underpants and Damart vest, silhouetted by the bedside light, blinking with confusion and peering out across the garden. Next to the tangle of house plants, he appeared smaller than she remembered. It didn't give her the slightest thrill of satisfaction.

23

The Betrayal of Christ

Even the first time round when they were all still high on the thrill of the successful head-napping of Lister, Finn had been dubious about the wisdom of stealing from Our Lady. In his party mood, he'd gone along with it and shown Caravaggio the sideboard in the vestry where Jed kept the Eucharist and his collection of vintage comics. They'd come away with a heap of votive candles for work and a couple of bottles of wine for the celebratory party (Finn had drawn the line at snaffling the communion wafers; even he knew that interfering with the body of Christ amounted to blasphemy and, while he wasn't worried for himself in his status of confirmed unbeliever, the Church was not likely to grant much indulgence to Caravaggio when he was already on such dodgy ground). Back in the kitchen, however, Finn had had an existential crisis. They had surely acquired themselves a one-way ticket to damnation. He'd gone so far as to consider returning the church supplies and breaking into the whisky that he'd stashed inside the piano. A bottle of wine and a sleeping pill later, though, and Finn had transubstantiated. Seen the bigger picture, so to speak, and settled down to enjoy the celebration of the successful acquisition of the skull and other accessories. Although to be truthful, Finn felt Lister looked a bit down in the mouth in his new environment. Evidently missing the more corporeal parts of his frame, he decided. No doubt keen to be recapitated or re-embodied or however you chose to regard it.

Shortly after the kitchen party, however, things had gone badly awry. For Finn, the hour of Lizzi's early morning visit was a shock in itself, not to mention the fact of her sudden reappearance. It had coincided with the first real day of painting, but her visit had messed with his head and been compounded by the racket coming from Maurice torturing the piano. Once Lizzi and her misfired accusations had left, and Tuesday had gone off on her jolly to the capital, Finn had been left confounded by the confusion of the morning's events and had only survived thanks to his well-practised distraction techniques.

But he had had to wait an eternity with his palette squirted, his brushes lined up and his nerves shredded for his sitter to costume-up. When Maurice had limped off to the bogs to prepare himself, Finn had burnt the candles near enough down their wicks before he'd finally resorted to going to the facilities to physically cajole him – as in haul him by the scruff of his saintly robes – back to the studio, whereupon he'd only just resisted the temptation to strangle him with his smelly bandages. It wasn't Maurice's fault if he was a tardy invalid but, astounded as he was by the revelation of Lizzi's unexpected expectancy, Finn knew his own temper to be uncharacteristically short. There were, he divined, some things in life that could make a man question his grip on reality. Some things that were inexplicable and light years beyond a rational explanation. In one short afternoon, he had said it a hundred million times, had asked himself until he was blue in the face and he could no longer bear to hear the words: How far-fetched was it that Lizzi was having Rob's baby?

Even Caravaggio thought it was out of order when Finn explained the situation over a pint in the Vaults later that evening, and no one would claim he was the most emotionally intelligent guy this side of the Clyde. He suggested going after Rob's bollocks, but Finn felt he should show more restraint given that that particular approach hadn't panned out at all successfully for Caravaggio in the past.

Happily, things settled somewhat during the course of the week. Aided in part by sleep in a plentiful sufficiency thanks to Tuesday's pharmaceuticals, Finn recovered his equilibrium. So passed the days. Maurice sat (not exactly still, to be brutal; the hopeless degenerate had a tremble on him to rival a poorly blancmange) and Finn painted (masterfully, soulfully, fervently) while Caravaggio did a fair imitation of the dead guy Maurice had mistaken him for at the start, with the odd resurrection to check out Finn's progress and accompany them to the pub in the evening.

The evening trip to the Vaults became a habit that Finn found strangely beguiling. True, the first had been a touch on the nail-biting side. Hooked by the ads on the TV in the electrical shop next door, Caravaggio had unwisely – given the locality – ordered a Baileys (*nectar from a virgin's quim*, his conclusion on tasting it) and in the tense moments that followed Finn had doubted the three of them would escape the Vaults alive. Thankfully for all involved, Maurice had heroically convinced the regulars that although, yes they were quite right, and yes Baileys was a girls' drink, in this exceptional case the cream therein was medicinally required to alleviate a gastric ulcer. After that, things had quietened down.

It wasn't only the Baileys that had caught Caravaggio's fancy. To say he had developed a taste for Tuesday's medicament would be understatement of the lowest degree. It was fortunate that the man was not already habituated to the stuff, so even a wee half was enough to ensure hours of unconsciousness. It meant that over the course of the week, Caravaggio did little more in daylight hours than pop the odd pill, fart and snore, and hog the velvet curtains for bedding (until Finn re-appropriated them after a struggle for St Maurice's get-up). To be fair, though, considering Caravaggio was catching up on several centuries of purgatorial insomnia (he'd never properly explained the extent of his eternal wanderings but, if his granny's testament was anything to go by, Finn was pretty sure there was more to it than simply a wrong turn on the way out of Naples), Finn couldn't really blame the man if his sleeping habits outslothed your average adolescent. In contrast, his own few hours of sleep he preferred to snatch on the bare floor, wrapped in one of the tablecloth sheets from the Christmas party.

In summary, the arrangement was working well. After barely a week, Finn was almost done with *Saint Jerome*. All that remained were the finishing touches – tarting the highlights, tarring the lowlights – and, while it had to be said that St Jerome had been a tad on the peely-wally side throughout the entire process, the painting wasn't far off the masterpiece Finn had been aiming for. Caravaggio, in the rare minutes between his drug-induced stupor and his Baileys'-derived semi-consciousness, had very little to say about the painting and Finn chose to take this taciturn approach as understated admiration.

Nevertheless, a minor problem arose when the candles finally burnt out completely. Finn had been ready to purchase them from the pound shop next to the funeral director's, but each time he ventured out he spotted Rob loitering in the vicinity. After an entire Monday afternoon of this,

Caravaggio suggested the second mission to the church, a suggestion that Finn was right to suspect was not entirely altruistic.

The temptation, of course, was to refuse. It was one thing to toy with damnation, Finn felt. Quite another to guarantee it. That said, as far as the painting was concerned, he had to admit that the stolen candles were the icing on the cake.

Hence, at sunrise on a Tuesday morning at the beginning of March, and totally against his better judgement, Finn accompanied Caravaggio for a second heist. In the light of early dawn, with the air as sharp and cold as a flick knife and puffs of spring clouds trotting across a bleeding sky, they stole together over the low wall to Our Lady's and slipped through the creaks of the barely open door to sneak into the church unnoticed and duck into a back-row pew.

Altar end, Jed was pottering around spring cleaning, checking the hymn books for torn covers, prayer cushions for moth holes. Crouching in the viscid darkness, trying to avoid the reek of Caravaggio's sour coffee cream hangover, Finn listened to the priest's rubber soles squeak back and forth across the ancient flags and considered how to reach the supplies unseen. Unfortunately Jed appeared in no hurry to leave. Finn was about to suggest abandoning, or at least postponing, when the front door flew open and daylight flooded the aisle and his unspoken words were carried off on the scent of the first blooms of cherry blossom and the randy calls of spring warblers that chased in behind.

'I come at wrong time I know. Have you time for confession?' It was Kassia. She paused by the chalice at the top of the aisle, twisting the end of her loosely plaited hair, only metres from where Finn and Caravaggio were hiding.

Jed's welcome echoed around the hollow church. Kassia smiled and dipped her finger in the holy water, and when she genuflected, Finn actually believed he would die. It was the most erotic thing he'd ever seen.

Kassia's heels clicked off the stone floor as she walked up the aisle and the unexpected sunshine sneaking through the rose window settled on her dark hair and surrounded her with a halo of scattered light. She greeted the priest with a kiss on each cheek.

In response to which, Caravaggio paroxysmed. Although it had to be said that even Finn, with his atheist morals, felt the priest had overstepped it somewhat. It wasn't exactly correct, he reckoned, to take a confession from a lassie when you'd just snogged her.

Kassia waited at the foot of the apse while Jed cleared the stack of damaged hymn books blocking the front of the confessional. The rose light poured between the grain of her blouse and a groan of painful ecstasy spurted from Caravaggio's lips.

'For fuck's sake,' Finn hissed.

'I can't help it. I'm overcome by her exquisiteness,' Caravaggio whispered, uselessly mopping at the crotch of his breeches with the yellowing sleeve of his chemise.

'Well, undercome yourself, pronto. We've got a job to do.'

Which they did as soon as Kassia and Jed took their places at confession.

It was to be several hours after Finn and Caravaggio got back to the studio with candles, wine, a prayer cushion and some bonus edition spy comics, before Maurice came for his evening sitting. In the intervening period, Caravaggio cured his habitual hangover with half a bottle of altar Cabernet Sauvignon, but it did little to relieve his humour.

'Take a chill pill, big man,' Finn said.

He did but reluctantly. Even on his kiddy dose, supplies were dwindling.

While Caravaggio snored, Finn contemplated how much life had turned on him recently. Nothing was the way he had hoped it would be. He refused to think about Rob and Lizzi, but mulled instead on how disappointingly base he was finding Caravaggio. That said, Caravaggio's reaction to Kassia may have been – was certainly – physically repellent, but it was only the lack of restraint that had made it different from his own. And it was wrong to judge a man because he didn't meet your expectations. Besides, while Caravaggio in person may have been a little different to what Finn had imagined, it didn't – at least at this point in time – detract from Finn's regard for his work. Or so he believed. Just to be sure, he checked out his book.

The pages opened at *The Betrayal of Christ*.

This was a picture that Finn had never properly understood. In its most simple terms, it was an image of Judas kissing Christ as the soldier came to take him. But it wasn't simple. It was full of mixed messages that Finn had always had trouble deciphering. Codes that were disguised by the light and the darkness, by the brightness and the shadows. What was blindingly obvious was that the light that illuminated the face of Christ came from outwith the scene, from a source that was hidden yet omniscient. Bizarrely that same extraneous light gleamed brightly on the soldier's black armour. Good and evil under the light of God? That could make sense, Finn thought. But what had always seemed odd to him was that Caravaggio had painted himself into the scene holding a lantern, and the glow from his lantern was feeble compared to the light falling on Christ. In the past, Finn had wondered if this was one of the few examples, perhaps the only example, of Caravaggio showing a modicum of humility – his guiding light not strong enough to compete with God's – but it didn't fit what he knew of either the artist or the man.

For a while, Finn studied the painting, trying to look at it with new eyes. For the first time it clicked that Caravaggio's face was picked out by the same light as Christ, as Judas, as the soldier, and the artist's face was as pale and unblemished as Christ's. Finn laughed to himself. It was so blatant now that he'd seen it. The message wasn't so subtle after all. The light picked out your team colours. Swarthy Judas and the soldier's black armour versus Christ and Caravaggio. Humility? Caravaggio? What was he thinking? The man had a big fat overgrown Messiah complex.

Corny as it sounded, if Finn hadn't actually met Caravaggio, he might have been tempted to agree with this self-assessment. It was a little difficult to reconcile the artist struggling with such fundamental tenets as good versus evil with the whingeing hypochondriac with no sense of decorum and a penchant for Irish Cream Liqueur. It shamed Finn to think they were related. But hypochondriac whingeing or otherwise, it didn't detract from the uniqueness of his style. You only had to take this picture to see how the contrast of the light and the shadows, the subtleties of composition and the conflicting themes could all add depth to a well-known narrative. There was so much Finn could take from it. He didn't want the feeble lantern of mediocrity to guide him. He wanted the glare of the light of life and death, of truth and lies, of loyalty and betrayal to shine from his work as it did from Caravaggio's.

By the time evening came and Maurice had finished his self-imposed chores around the place and was ready to sit for the finishing touches, Finn was feeling better. In contrast, Caravaggio's afternoon nap appeared not to have alleviated his mood. He was crashing around the studio, replacing the burnt-out candles with the freshly stolen ones, muttering a torrent of obscenities.

'What's up, buddy?' Maurice said, but Caravaggio didn't answer.

Finn replied for him. 'We saw Kassia.'

'Fillide.'

'And you should have seen the state he got himself into,' Finn sniggered.

Maurice nodded wisely. 'I'm no one to rub salt and all that, but is the lassie no meant to be a friend of yours?'

'He was her pimp.'

'Lover,' Caravaggio growled.

'Let's get started,' Finn said, handing Caravaggio the remains of the bottle of Cabernet. Caravaggio took it with a grunt and slouched against the back wall to watch Finn work.

Maurice shuffled into position. 'Don't get yerself worked up, maestro. You have to be patient. It's the same the world over. It's the lassies who call the shots.'

Caravaggio slugged back the wine. 'And precisely what do you know about ladyfolk?'

'Aye, fair enough,' Maurice said. 'Finjay wants to paint the lassie, did he tell you?'

'Rapture. The sooner he bestirs himself, the sooner I can escape this flea-ridden slumtown,' Caravaggio said. 'No offence to you, *amico*.'

'None taken.'

While Finn worked, Caravaggio went on to explain to Maurice the conditions of his purgatorial contract. Some shite about assisting with work that was an improvement on the ill-contrived amateurish crapulence that plagued him whenever he opened his eyes (whatever that was supposed to mean) and that it was no wonder they called it purgatory because how was he meant to achieve anything when he was expressly forbidden to influence the artist's journey of self-discovery. Maurice volunteered to pay for the fare for that particular journey if it would help in any way, but Finn would have to take the bus because his finances didn't stretch to the train. 'If that's all right with you, Finjay.'

But Finn wasn't listening. He was engrossed in his painting and his thoughts of where to go next. What his next picture would be, and the one after that. Of who he could get to model and where he could find the props. And in the corona of the candle flames, he caught shimmering visions of Kassia in the church and wondered how much longer he would have to prepare before he was ready to do her justice.

24

Toothpuller (Attributed)

At roughly the same time as Finn was re-evaluating *The Betrayal of Christ*, Esme was shoving papers around the desk in the day centre consulting room. Tuesday was there too, sitting at the window in a high-sided wingback armchair, which formed one tip of the horseshoe of assorted seating. The chairs were clustered around a low table and the arrangement was intended to bring some intimacy to the vast room, but even Esme found it authoritarian and condescending. Ever since she'd got this job, she'd been meaning to ask if there was a budget to do something about the decor. The institutional squalor of the tatty carpet and mismatched furniture was emphasised by the faded grandeur of the villa. In its heyday, before the house had been bought by the health authority or left by some well-meaning, well-to-do geriatric in their will, the first-floor consulting room would have been the drawing room or the master bedroom. There were still traces of its previous incarnation in the rope-thick sashes of the huge windows and the elaborate plaster cornice and wide chimney breast. These days, though, the window sashes were trapped behind secondary glazing and the cornice was severed by the partition wall that divided the consulting room from the treatment room next door. The only trace of the bricked-in fireplace was a couple of marble tiles from the old hearth which Esme had discovered one day when she'd pulled back the edges of the carpet.

'I've asked Elizabeth to join us.'

'Aw, miss. What did you do that for?' Tuesday said. Beneath the buttress of the armchair wings, in the bolster of its horsehair padding, she looked shrunken and shrivelled, Esme thought. Like the peat bog mummy in the museum that she'd seen with the boys at the weekend and which had freaked and fascinated them all.

'It would be best if we could resolve the situation for the benefit of everyone.'

To Esme's surprise, the clock above the door already had Lizzi ten minutes late. For the monthly multidisciplinary meetings, Lizzi was time-conscientious to the point of regularly shaming Esme.

'Would you like some water while we wait?' Esme scooped up her handbag. She had a terrible taste in her mouth.

'Whatever.'

The water cooler was on the landing next to a row of waiting room seats pressed against the wall. Some of last year's magazines were piled on the floor and in the background a radio was playing eighties pop to no one in particular. From the first-floor landing, the staircase swept down in an elegant arc giving a glimmer of the building's former splendour. The effect was spoilt, Esme thought as she filled two cups with water, by the years of gloss paint that had blurred the twists and curlicues of the wrought-iron banisters that lined it.

Tuesday looked worse than Esme had seen her since their first encounter, when she'd come to the clinic fresh from an overdose that Esme had never believed was entirely accidental. It didn't add up. Off hard drugs, she should be thriving. Her hair should be glossy, her skin clear, her eyes alive. And her teeth. Her teeth. Damn. Esme almost crushed the flimsy plastic cups in her hand. She'd forgotten to arrange an appointment with the community dentist. Mentally, she added it to the list of tasks that never seemed to get done.

She was battling with unyielding fire hinges on the door to her consulting room when Lizzi came rushing up the stairs. She had her coat over her arm and the handle of her bag gathered in her fist and a glaze of sweat glossed her upper lip.

'I'm so sorry, I'm late, Dr Blythe,' she said breathlessly. 'I . . .' She held open the door for Esme but offered no further explanation.

'Well, you're here now. Take a seat.' Esme dropped her handbag in front of the chair opposite Tuesday's and handed her a cup of water. She offered the second cup to Lizzi who took it gratefully and gulped it down. Esme kicked her handbag under her seat and sat down, the taste in her mouth still bitter. There was a line between generosity and being a pushover, she realised, and she appeared to have crossed it somewhere back on the landing.

Lizzi placed herself between Esme and Tuesday. Esme was still looking at the two women wondering where to start when Lizzi dragged a file from her bag and waved it around. 'My notes. I came prepared.'

'This is an informal meeting. Not a clinical consult,' Esme said. 'I thought I'd made that clear.'

'Are you Elizabeth's boss, miss?' Tuesday asked.

'Not exactly,' Esme said. 'I'm the director of the centre and Elizabeth is here on placement as part of her training. I'm not her line manager.'

'Question is, but: can you sack her?'

'What?' Lizzi exclaimed.

'Tuesday!'

'Get her struck off then?'

'Dr Blythe. This is mad.' Lizzi glowered at Tuesday. 'I don't know what this is about, but you're completely out of order.'

Tuesday shrugged and smirked.

'Tuesday, Lizzi is a student. This is part of her doctoral training. You know that.' Esme wasn't quite sure what was going on between the two of them, but there was obviously more to it than either of them were saying. 'We're here to reach a resolution, not deepen the divisions.'

'Can I say something first?'

'No, Lizzi. We should hear from Tuesday first. It was her, after all, who asked to see us.' Someone had put a pot of hyacinth bulbs on the window sill and the strong perfume of the budding flowers was nipping Esme's eyes. She felt the prickle of an approaching sneeze.

'You, miss. I asked to see *you*.'

While Esme searched her trouser pockets for a hanky, she gestured to Tuesday to continue. Lizzi passed her the box of tissues from the table – tissues that every office, every consulting room, every clinic in the place had on standby.

'I said already. I want Elizabeth off the case.'

'Yes, I know, Tuesday. But you haven't really explained why.'

'Because I cannae stand the stuck-up bitch.'

Esme blew her nose loudly. 'Let's avoid making personal attacks.'

'How should I? See if you don't take her off the case – if you *cannae* take her off the case – I'm gonnae make an official complaint.'

'This is ridiculous. I haven't done anything wrong. You can't complain about me.'

'Aye, I fucking can.'

'Hang on, hang on. This isn't getting us anywhere.' Esme

tried the tactics she used with the boys. 'Let's start from the beginning. Tuesday, you knew Elizabeth had to write up some case studies for her assessment and you agreed to be one of them. So what's going on?'

'I changed my mind.'

'Which you are perfectly entitled to do. But it would make things clearer if you could tell us why.'

'Dr Blythe, I need this case. If she changes her mind . . .'

'Oh, for God's sake, doll. I telt you. Make it up.'

Esme asked Lizzi if there was another client she could work with.

Lizzi shook her head. 'Not at this stage. I've almost finished my placement. I haven't got time.'

Tuesday put her feet on the coffee table. Her grimy boots kicked over an empty leaflet stand. She was grinning.

'I don't know why you think this is funny,' Lizzi said. 'I'm trying to do my job, that's all.'

'Fuck off. It isnae a job. You're no even qualified, ya silly cow—'

'Tuesday!'

'Dr Blythe.' Lizzi was pleading with Esme. 'If I don't have this case, I won't be able to finish the placement. I can't repeat . . .'

To be honest, Esme did feel some sympathy for Lizzi. She was a typical, high-strung overachiever, unable to distinguish the things that mattered from the things of no importance. Her whole, artificially constructed world was on the brink of collapse if she couldn't prop it up with her academic achievements. That kind of drive was a short cut to dissatisfaction, a quick route to unhappiness. Esme herself had always been more of a plodder when it came to academia, progressing step by step almost by accident. Surprising herself as much as other people by her achievements, rising way above other people's expectations and feeling obliged to continue when she had got so far. Which was how she accidentally took the consultant job without even considering that it didn't suit her personality and that she might rather stay home with Charlie. Perhaps then, in the end, all she'd done was take a slower route to unhappiness.

She came back to the situation in hand. 'Enough, both of you. Tuesday, you were told at the beginning Elizabeth was doing this as part of her training. You are perfectly within your rights to change your mind, but you are not entitled to be ill-mannered.' A girl like Lizzi was easy sport for someone with Tuesday's forked tongue.

Tuesday sniggered. Esme shoved the tissue up her sleeve.

'Can I still write it up?' Lizzi said. 'Even if she drops out? This case has taught me a lot. About the way some patients hide behind the label they are given, the way they lie to themselves, and what lies behind their lack of cooperation.'

'Get lost. You didnae even psychologise me. And whatever you think you know, you stole. You cannae write fuck all about me. End of.'

Esme stood up and gazed out the window. She was tempted to leave the two of them to it, but it wasn't really fair on Lizzi. It was a completely uneven match. The flat roof of the bay window below was lined with lead, and moss had gathered in the angles. Around the perimeter, a gutter full of leaves – rotted to mulch over winter – had sprays of delicate purple flowers growing from the leaf mould. Flowers that Esme couldn't put a name to. Pretty but opportunistic. No doubt she'd discover they were weeds.

'I'm no listening to any more of this shite.'

Esme turned round. Tuesday was on her feet, white with

rage. By the looks of things, they had both underestimated Lizzi.

'Sit down, Tuesday. Please.'

'How should I? How should I sit here and listen to this heap of crap? How should I have anything to do with a lassie who goes around shooting her mouth off about my private business and telling lies about me to my pals?'

'Lies? You're joking, right?' Lizzi was rubbing her temples, shaking her head, blinking hard. She turned to Esme. 'This is all an excuse. Tuesday doesn't want to succeed. She's deliberately ruining her own recovery.'

'See if this wasnae a medical facility, doll, I'd fucking have you.'

'Calm down, Tuesday. Calm down,' Esme said, realising she had let the situation get out of hand. 'You don't have to do anything you don't want to. We can sort this out.'

Lizzi rubbed her eyes. 'I guess she didn't mention she was dealing.'

The gasp of dismay that escaped Esme was involuntary. It was out before she could stop it. She tried to cover her mistake. 'Come on, let's—'

'Fuck the pair of youse, preaching to me, judging me. You think we're losers, Dr Blythe, the folk that come here to your hug-a-nutter sessions. That we're tragic no-hopers and we're lost and worthless. But we come here for you. Do you no see that? All us fucking wasters with nae life now that we've no got our addiction for company. We come to your stupid centre because we're trying to please you, trying to make you happy. How does that feel, eh? To be pitied by the fucking dregs of the dregs.' Tuesday laughed bitterly. 'I cannae dae it any more. Seriously. I've had it with your shitty centre and your drug replacement programme – which you know as well as me isnae ever gonnae break me free – and your false hope that you peddle like a pusher.'

The eczema on Esme's palms was burning.

'And as for the bloody Girl Guide there, I havenae even got the words left to slag her off.'

'Dr Blythe, I'm sorry, I'm feeling a bit off. I might have to . . .' Lizzi stood up, swaying unsteadily. She grabbed the back of the chair to steady herself.

Esme tipped her head back, wondering if the stress tears that were threatening might roll back in if she stayed like that long enough. In the corner above the desk the wall-paper was peeling where a downpipe had been leaking slowly over the decades.

'I'm sorry. I need a few minutes.' Lizzi was gathering up her belongings, shoving her file in her bag, picking up her coat.

'Jesus fuck, you attention-seeking—'

'Sorry, sorry, Dr Blythe. We'll have to finish this another time.'

'Hang on,' Esme said, but Tuesday was already on her way, barging past Lizzi, hissing something at her as she passed.

'I was trying to save you, Tuesday,' Lizzi said.

Esme flinched at the girl's self-righteousness.

Tuesday hauled open the heavy door. She looked at Esme with pity. 'You should've shown mair faith,' she said.

Esme's chance to defend herself was stolen when Lizzi bolted past her and vomited violently in the waste-paper basket. By the time Lizzi had recovered, it was too late. Tuesday had gone.

25

The Conversion of Saint Paul

If it wasn't for the fact that any of the basket-weaving mob could get one over on Dr Blythe, Tuesday would have had to admit a grudging admiration for Elizabeth's deviance. As it was, when she stormed out of the day centre she had no clue where she was heading and all that was going round in her head was how much she wished she'd never asked for that meeting. Dr Blythe was a waste of space. Well-meaning intentions were sweet and all that, but when it came to real life, you had to salute the woman's ineptitude.

Somewhere between leaving the centre and reaching the swan pond, though, Tuesday reached a decision. She would go and see Rob and warn him what he was getting into. Elizabeth was a conniving two-timing, two-faced bitch and he had to be told. Without her assistance, he wasn't capable of seeing the bad side of anybody. But she'd have to tank it if she was going to make it before he shut up shop. It was already heading towards five thirty.

More than one well-to-do granny clutched their handbag to their bosoms as Tuesday flew along the road, but she was in too much of a hurry to reassure them. This was speed for the sake of hurrying, not speed for the sake of law-dodging. By the time she'd run through Hyndland and cut across the play park, run down the hill past the funeral director's and the space where the fish van parked up on a Friday, she was sweating. And gutted to see the shutter was already pulled most of the way down over the shop door. A handwritten notice was sellotaped to the inside of the window. *Taking Stock*.

Tuesday hammered on the window.

'We're closed.'

'Open up, dickhead.' He knew fine well it was her. Did he not realise she was here to save him?

Rob opened the door and pulled up the metal shutter high enough for her to duck underneath. Which was up to his knees, give or take.

'For fuck's sake, McLaughlin,' he said, when she got inside. He was holding a clipboard and had a pen tucked behind his ear. 'Look at the state of you.'

'D'your ma never teach you that it's bad manners to make personal remarks?' Tuesday snatched an elastic band from the desk tidy and scraped back her hair, tying what she could into a scrawny ponytail. The elastic caught in the knots and ripped some hairs out at the roots. With the back of her hand, she wiped away the spiky tears that had sprung to her eyes, conscious that Rob was observing every move. Poised there with his clipboard at the ready, he was like one of those fake cheery charity collectors who harassed the general public on Sauchiehall Street – the ones who were so desperate to meet their targets that they would stop any sad fuck who caught their eye, including Tuesday if she felt like playing. All Rob needed to complete the look was an ill-fitting T-shirt in a primary colour with a logo designed by a five-year-old. But Tuesday felt shit. So shit she couldn't even be arsed to honour him with her insults.

'What's up with you?' he said, putting the clipboard on the counter and lifting a plastic storage crate on top of a couple already stacked against the back wall in the corner, next to where a collection of bones on the floor were all that remained of Lister.

Rather than using up energy to reply, Tuesday climbed on to the computer chair and fidgeted with the paper clips in the desk tidy. That meeting was a joke. What was the point of putting herself through the torture of recovery if everyone still treated her like junkie-scum?

'McLaughlin?'

'What? I'm fucking spangdangling. Couldnae be better.' Except even without eyes in the back of his baldy head Rob could have seen she was talking bollocks. The afternoon's events had wiped her. She barely had the energy to manage her shakes. Every bit of her ached. Her muscles, her bones, her nerves. She strung the last of the paper clips together and dangled them around the computer screen as a garland and moved on to the stapler, stapling together the pages of Rob's diary and whatever other random pieces of paper she could find.

Pain. That's what recovery was about. Nobody warned you. Nobody ever said that you'd never know suffering like it. The medics were in on it with those evangelical types who'd been through it and were intent on converting the rest of life's users, although they never advertised how crap it was or they wouldn't have got any takers. All that shite about pain making you realise you were alive or whatever? Only the certified brain-dead would get taken in by that. Pain made every second of your life never-ending and it made you ready to sell your soul and confess to crimes you hadn't committed. Or even those you had.

Tuesday looked at the pile of bones in the corner. The way she was feeling just now, even Lister's fate seemed appealing. With bottles of poison all over the joint, it was probably just as well it required motivation to do yourself in.

Rob dragged a crate packed with Betadine hand wash out from behind the counter. 'Hate to break it to you, doll, but this whole corpse-chic thing you've got going isnae your best look. Screams methadone dodger to me.'

'Get lost,' Tuesday said, without feeling. She spun listlessly round in the chair. This was her life now. Spinning nowhere. Snatching shots of other people's lives while they got on with whatever it was they did.

When he was done counting the bottles of hand wash, and checking the use-by dates, and noting the stats on his chart, Rob stacked the crate against the wall with the others and moved on to a packing box of vinyl gloves. Tuesday stopped spinning and watched him work. Not that it was any of his business, but what he'd said was true. She should be at the pharmacy now, taking her dose, battering fuck out of the methadone cold turkey that was giving her the jitters. But what was the point? For months she'd taken all the crap that Dr Blythe had prescribed, the methadone and basket weaving and all her other bright ideas, and dumbly swallowed them along with the dregs of her self-respect, and look how far that had got her.

After a while Rob got Tuesday to shift so he could enter his stocktaking on a spreadsheet. He said ten minutes and then she could have the computer. But she didn't want it. She was done with all that. Instead, she wandered aimlessly around the shop. Whatever wishful thinking her psychiatrist indulged in, Tuesday couldn't avoid the conclusion that hers was a treatment plan going nowhere. It wasn't like the methadone made her feel good. Or even much less bad. It didn't stop her dwelling on the crap in her life. Didn't stop the horrendous regrets that kept her awake at night. Or stop her debasing herself at reception every day asking for a letter from social services or the adoption charities. There was no letter. There never would be a letter. She knew that, and they knew that, and every day they laughed at her some more. Without even noticing, she'd turned into one of those deluded saddos she used to take the piss out of.

Meanwhile, Rob had upended another crate in the middle of the shop. A landslide of the kind of trappings Tuesday knew from the clinic slid across the floor. Individually wrapped gauze squares and cotton wool balls, cartons of alcohol wipes like the ones they'd used the few misguided times they'd gone for her blood, various shrink-wrapped disposable instruments of which she only recognised tweezers.

The thing was, if she didn't want to be lumped in with the rest of life's losers she had to up her game. She went over and fingered some of Rob's stuff. 'You could open a hospital with all this. Branch out. Vein cut-downs. Amputations. Backstreet abortions. I could use my connections, supply you with punters. We'd mint it.'

'There's a flaw in your business plan, McLaughlin. None of your dropout pals ever have any dosh.'

Eventually, when she had irritated him one time too often, Rob chucked her the key to the cabinet in the treatment room and told her to make herself useful. 'Ink. Unopened vials only.' He pulled one of his printed sheets from the clipboard to take with her.

The glass doors in the steel cabinet caught the last of the daylight and turned to mercury. Avoiding the blank eyes of her own reflection, Tuesday unlocked the doors and knelt on the cold tiles with her feet tucked underneath her. She counted out the vials of dye and tallied each on Rob's table, marvelling that he had trusted her to do the job properly. It was a shame, really, she thought. Rob was one of life's innocents. So trusting, so ignorantly blissful that she was beginning to wonder if she should keep her opinion of Elizabeth to herself. He might not be able to take it.

After several minutes of dye counting, Tuesday's knee-caps were burning and her hips hurt and her toes stung with pins and needles. She stood up to stretch just as Rob stuck his head around the door.

'Did you eat?'

'Nah.'

He waved a packet of tuna sandwiches and an apple and offered to go halfies.

In the front shop, Tuesday flung herself on to the window seat and pulled at a thread of cotton in the seam of one of the cushions Rob had sewn himself, while he was through the back boiling the kettle. No question, the sandwich and mug of sweet tea would help the clamminess and the shakes, but she didn't want to feel obliged. She knew she was meant to be grateful, but the way Rob carried on sometimes made it seem like he thought he had the right to have expectations of her. Like he was waiting for her to turn into the person he figured she was supposed to be. If that was the case, he was in for some wait.

The whole time they were eating, Rob sat in his poncy chair, giving her the lowdown on the robbery and how he'd had to fake a break-in because he wouldn't get anything on the insurance if they knew he'd given someone the key. Hence the stock-take, for their records.

'Would it no be easier to go round and ask for your stuff back?'

He didn't answer. He sat in his chair tossing the apple from hand to hand.

'Have it,' he said, when he saw her watching. He chucked it to her before she had the chance to tell him where to go.

Tuesday polished the apple on the front of her dirty

sweatshirt and bit into the crisp green skin. It flooded her taste buds with cold acid and metal, and a trickle of juice dribbled from the corner of her mouth. Roughly, she gulped down her half-chewed mouthful and licked the juice away. She was about to take another bite when she hesitated. Rob was gawping at her.

'What?'

He shook his head, turned away. Tuesday glanced down at the apple in her hand. The white flesh was stained crimson.

'No,' she said weakly, her hand flitting to her mouth. 'Aw no.'

She looked up at him. Just looked at him. With her hand across her mouth. Silently pleading with him to tell her it was okay.

Rob laughed nervously. 'Fuck, McLaughlin.' His cheeks were twitching in panic.

'Is it bad?' she said, checking the blood-stained saliva on her fingers. Rob handed her a tissue. She held it to her gum. Prodded the space with her tongue. Checked the tissue for blood.

When the bleeding eased up, she took her hand away. 'Can you tell?'

'Aye. Pretty much.'

Tuesday gulped to hold back her tears. 'You could've pretended.'

'There's a massive great hole staring at me straight from the middle of your face, you diddy. How could I no tell?'

'Mirror?' she asked, getting to her feet.

He shook his head. She pushed past him, ran into the treatment room to check her reflection in the glass of the medical cabinet, but the daylight had gone and the glass was no longer stained with mercury. Even so, Tuesday knelt down in front of it, trying to see, trying not to see. A moment later, Rob came up behind her. His bulk filled the doorway and blocked out the light from the shop and turned the glass doors black. Tuesday bared her teeth and saw the dark space of the missing tooth pushing against its neighbours.

She tried to speak, but her words were mashed by gasps and hiccups.

'McLaughlin. Cut it out.' Rob hesitated, came over, patted her shoulder, put out his hand to help her to her feet. 'It's no use crying over milk teeth.'

Tuesday battered his hand away. 'It wasnae a milk tooth.'

'A figment of speech, you daft bint. You know that.'

Tuesday hauled herself up. She wanted to spit at him.

Next thing, Rob was on his hands and knees in the shop, scrabbling around the travelling trunk for the missing tooth, his light denim jeans tight against his wide backside.

'Forget it,' Tuesday said, climbing into the wheelchair. 'I must've swallowed it.'

She put her feet on the leather seat, stuck her knees under her chin, wrapped her skinny arms around her legs. She was tragic. So fucking tragic, Rob couldn't even look at her. She ran her frayed thumbnail across the tan leather next to her feet but didn't manage to leave even the faintest scratch. Dejected, she let her feet slip off the seat, her arms flop over the armrests, her head loll over the back of the chair. She shut her eyes and waited for the end.

A few moments later, Rob's phone rang. Tuesday opened one eye, raised her head an inch.

'Hey.'

Elizabeth.

By the time Rob hung up, Tuesday had opened her other eye and was sitting up straight.

'What happened? What did you do?'

'Forget it, doll. She's just being a princess.'

'Tell me what happened.'

'How? You've already got the version you're gonnae believe.'

Rob picked up the empty mugs and took them through the back.

'Don't be stupid,' Tuesday shouted after him. 'She's cheating on you, ya fucking bimbo.'

'Do you know what?' Rob said, when he came back in. 'I've about had it with your shite.'

'Wake up, Rob. You think she's Miss Fucking Perfect but she's a lying bitch. Ten grand says she's shagging your pal Finn behind your back.'

'No my pal. No behind my back.'

Tuesday gave a vicious, toothless laugh. She couldn't believe he actually knew. He knew and he hadn't done anything about it. Elizabeth was walking all over him and there wasn't a thing Tuesday could do to save him. He was even more of doormat than she thought.

Rob brushed his hand over his shaved head. 'You're twisted, McLaughlin, do you know that? You're sad and desperate and you cannae stand to see anyone make something of themselves.'

'Fuck off—' Tuesday started, but Rob wouldn't let her speak.

He cut through her, laid into her, coming out with all this crap about how she thought she had the right to behave how she wanted because she'd been given a label by a mug psychiatrist. How there was nothing wrong with her except that she'd chosen the easiest way through life. All this stuff came out, resentful and violent, as if he'd been saving it up for the moment she let him down.

Tuesday shut her eyes, put her hands over her ears. In her head, she chanted nursery rhymes, the alphabet, the months of the year. Old habits she could rely on. Any way to escape from it. Any way.

For the first time in months, Tuesday let herself remember. Other old habits, other escape routes. Heroin. The rush after shooting up. How it made you walk on clouds and how your feet sank into the spongy cushions and sunshine streamed straight into your brain cells. How the heat of it made your blood bubble and the light of it sharpened your eyes so that you could see everything in high definition – the antennae whiskers of a cockroach, the mosaic eye of a bluebottle, the scaly back of a woodlouse. And a silence so sharp, so intense, that you could hear the hairs on your body sighing. Euphoria was what they called it. But not the kind that made you go whooping about the place, telling everyone you loved them, mad with fake energy. It was still and it came from deep inside you and gave you the answers to all questions you never even knew you were supposed to ask.

Finally, she opened her eyes. Rob had stopped. He looked spent.

'If you're done with the computer,' he muttered, 'you've no really got a reason to keep coming here, do you?'

'Don't do this to me, Rob,' Tuesday whispered. She used her last drop of dignity to plead with him. She knew where she was heading from here.

But Rob was at the door, turning the key.

Tuesday laughed bitterly. She was floating. It all came back to her. All of it. It had never gone away. Sores at injection sites, mouth ulcers, bronchitis. Thirst and vomiting and the runs. Shitting yourself and pissing yourself and bleeding into your knickers the few times your body had the energy to menstruate. Sleeping on a cardboard box with a news-paper for a pillow, damp cramping your muscles, the cold cracking your bones.

But no pain.

No obligation to anyone except yourself.

Neighbours with no expectations. Who understood you. Tolerated you. Left you alone.

Not lonely. Too fucking out of it to be lonely.

What was she thinking? She should be thanking him, not pleading with him. Since she'd found Campbell, found Campbell out, is this not what she'd been looking for? Permission not to give a toss? She'd kept going because of the two people who'd believed in her. But Dr Blythe had made it clear where she stood. And now Rob had done exactly what she'd come here for. Helped her. Given her permission. Finally let her off the hook.

He yanked up the security shutter. Outside, it was dark.

'See ya, pal,' Tuesday whispered as she ducked back under the shutter.

But even as she said it, she knew that she wouldn't. It might take motivation to do yourself in, but self-destruction was effortless.

COPPER RESINATE

26

Omnia Vincit Amor

Once it was over, Finn claimed it was actually quite funny, like he'd been caught out by some kind of sick, premature April Fool's joke. But at the time, he wasn't laughing.

It started as a tale about a girl and a haircut.

'No my girlfriend. In my dreams, but.'

'Oh aye.' Finn was painting Michael. Just as Maurice had promised, the kid had agreed to sit for a painting without getting paid and, although Finn was delighted to have another subject to test his skills on, at that point he had still to realise it would prove to be Maurice's last contribution of any merit. What he did know, and what engendered in him a measure of unease, was that Maurice and Caravaggio were currently roaming the streets of Partick unsupervised (a certain amount of reciprocal man-love blooming there, Finn had noticed, although most likely they would have both denied it), but it wasn't up to Finn to take responsibility for their every move. And quite honestly, he worked better with the pair of them out of the picture.

The painting Finn was working on was a version of Caravaggio's youthful, victorious Cupid and his creepily misplaced libido. It was one of Finn's favourites. There was, he felt, something magnificently perverted about an image of a swaggering prepubescent with slapped cheeks and a baby scrotum lewdly triumphing over the establishment symbols of respectability. Finn's interpretation was arranged with a sheet draped over the trestle table and Michael – angel wings snaffled from the nativity box hooked over his bare shoulders – half standing, half perched on the table edge, with his left leg hooked behind in a semi-kneeling contortion.

'First thing she says about me, right. Cheek baines tae die for. Couldnae actually believe it. Reckoned she meant track-suit boy or his wee pal.'

'Is that right?' Finn said, not properly listening and wondering instead at what late hour his tranquillity would be disturbed by the reappearance of Maurice and Caravaggio. Finn was still stinging from the near blows that he had come to with Caravaggio earlier in the day. In a fit of petulance (the man's habitual unpleasantness aggravated, Finn reckoned, by the rapidly depleting supply of sleeping pills), Caravaggio had said he was sick of the rain that pissed on the city every fucking day (a slight exaggeration, both Finn and Maurice protested, as this month alone they had already counted one fine day) and was sick of waiting for Finn to do a painting worthy of his (Caravaggio's) mentoring skills and was sick of Finn telling everyone they were related, so Finn pointed out that Caravaggio had mentored shit and anyway what was wrong with St Jerome, at least he was all in fucking proportion (although it was possible that Finn hadn't actually made that particular dig out loud) and of course they were related because the family tree on the inside of Finn's granny's Bible quite clearly traced Finn's unmitigated descent from Caravaggio's bastard offshoot – it was there in black and white any time he cared to take a look – and anyhow, if they weren't, what the fuck was Caravaggio doing here? And Maurice explained that the reason Caravaggio was so het up was because he wanted Finn to paint the lassie, and Finn said he wasn't the only one but they had been through that a million times already. Problem *numero uno* (Finn decided to help Caravaggio by enumerating in his own language as the man was apparently having problems getting his fat head round plain Glaswegian), he wasn't ready (plus, Finn wasn't ready to admit even to himself – never mind to a quasi-incarnate manky slob in ill-fitting tights – that the truth was more that he was terrified of trying) and *numero due*, how was he supposed to persuade Kassia to model when she was presently not on speaking terms with him?

Finn wasn't entirely sure which of his well-enumerated points set Caravaggio off, but the man started flouncing around the studio calling Finn for everything. Thankfully, before it got any more physical than the aforesaid flouncing (Caravaggio was, after all, in possession of not one, but two chibs), Maurice persuaded Caravaggio that the city had its advantages, not least its drinking hours, and the two of them had toddled off to the Vaults for a quick half. That was at opening time and Finn hadn't seen them since.

'And again. Cheek baines tae die for. Ya utter, utter beauty.' Michael was holding a brace of arrows at arm's length, grinning like the juvenile halfwit Finn took him for. 'She says I should show them off. Mebbe get my hair cut. What d'you reckon?' He turned his acne-splattered face from left to right for Finn to get a good look at its geometric lines, and his bright-eyed eagerness gleamed in the semi-darkness of the blacked-out studio. The windows of the studio were papered over with the pages of Maurice's *Gazette* to cut out the unwelcome duration of the evenings post-equinox, but even in the semi-gloom, Finn reckoned, the kid's enthusiastic innocence and unmerited openness was nauseating. It spoke of a hapless naivety which –

considering the criminally inclined drunkards who'd recently left the building – was frankly unhealthy.

'I don't know,' Finn said wearily. 'How the fuck should I know?'

'You're an artist. You see what's nice, what isnae.'

Finn's brush slipped and he muttered to himself. Nice? What did nice have to do with anything? Nice was a word that he would have sold his granny into slavery to avoid being associated with. Nice was insidious and stole between your sheets and fucked you over the second you stopped paying attention. People said that Rob was nice.

'See the lassie, by the way. It was Uncle Maurice that started it. Wouldnae shut up about Auntie Leanne, how he met her when he was my age, telling me all sorts about what they got up to. I was like, *Jeezo, Uncle Maurice. Too much information.*'

Cupid's arrows were weighing heavy in Michael's hands. He put them down and shook out his arms. 'Ya bass.'

'For fuck's sake. Keep still.'

'Fifty years. A whole half century. You know. Uncle Maurice and Auntie Leanne.' Michael picked up the arrows again and repositioned himself. 'I could see straight through him, but. He was only telling me all that stuff cos he was fishing. Wanted to know if I was seeing anybody. Which I'm no, by the way.'

Finn grunted. It hardly ranked as a big reveal.

'It's no that I don't meet girls, but. You mebbe wouldnae think it but the chippy is a total babe magnet. You know, all thae lassies coming in for an emergency chocolate fix or a late night poke of chips.'

'And you're the man to give them a late night poke. Is that what you're saying?'

Michael blushed. 'Naw, no me.'

Finn worked quickly to capture the precise shade of virginal mortification.

'To be honest, I'm a total fail when it comes to women. See when they smile at you, right, how are you meant to tell if they fancy you or no? Mebbe they're just being friendly. It's complicated. That's what I says to Uncle Maurice. I says, *Uncle Maurice, things are no like the olden days. It's way more complicated than when the pair of youse were winching.*'

As he worked on the last touches of Michael's embarrassment, Finn refused to think about Maurice and Leanne. Refused to marvel at how long they had been together. Refused to contemplate how even after fifty years Leanne still cared enough about her man to beat the living daylights out of him when she thought it would do him some good. Lizzi reckoned that it was a weird type of love, a love that lacked strength, but what did she know about sticking with it for the long haul?

'All this was on my birthday, by the way. I was down the pub with my dad and Uncle Maurice. My mum was like, *I'll do you a nice party at the Legion*, but I was like, *Mum, that's mebbe acceptable for your eightieth but no for your eighteenth*, and she was like, *You cheeky wee so-and-so*, but I didnae actually mean I thought she was eighty. I let her bake me a cake, but.'

Imagine shagging the same person for fifty-odd years. Finn cringed at the thought of crinkly skin and sagging flesh. True enough, there might be some comfort in growing old together, but you'd want your eyesight to fail faster than her tits dropped, and her memory to go before you couldn't get it up any more.

'You should've seen what happened, right. I was wetting

myself. Auntie Leanne says she'd help me blow out the candles because the smoke makes me wheezy. Only she goes and sets her fringe on fire. Honest tae God. She's pure dancing round the kitchen, giving it all the sweary words in the sweary dictionary and my mum is like, *Lee-annne*, and me and Uncle Maurice are totally ending ourselves. Uncle Maurice, he goes, *Leanne, pet, you'll put the heebies up your customers with a hairdo like that.'*

Michael had dislodged the wings with his pathetic trills of laughter. He twisted round to sort them.

'For fuck's sake. If I have to tell you again . . .' Finn said. Each time Cupid frolicked, he fucked with the carefully staged illumination. Now, he was leaning in too close to the candlelight and it made the skin of his torso alabaster white. And not, Finn thought, in a good way. He put down his brush and went over to reposition the wings. Up close, he could feel the warmth of acne pimples exuding from Michael's back.

Nothing was going to stop Michael telling his tale, though. Not even Finn's dagger eyes as he readjusted the candles. Finn stepped back to check the newly positioned flame and the fresh light spilt on to Michael's pale arm and across his sternum, and slipped over his skin folds leaving ink-fine shadows across his obliques, and trickled over his abs and quads to stain them with a blush of gold. Exactly as Finn wanted.

By now, Michael was back in the pub with his dad and Uncle Maurice, and drinking his first legal VBL (which he helpfully explained to Finn was vodka, blackcurrant and lemonade in case he didn't know; *but you dinnae actually taste the vodka*). And he got a laptop from his folks for his birthday, did he mention that? (As if, Finn thought, someone gave a flying fuck.) Apparently, it would be good for if he ever went to college.

'What I was really wanting was a Wii but my mum wasnae having it. I telt her, but, there are loads of games that she could play on it – you know, like Just Dance and Just Dance 2 – but she was like, *Not at my age. Are you trying to kill me?* (even though she's no anywhere near eighty) and that was the end of it.'

In an effort to blank out the boy's wittering, Finn concentrated on the subtle variations in Cupid's skin tone. For both their sakes, Finn had compromised on semi-nakedness (for Cupid obviously; Finn was comfortably attired in his usual T-shirt and jeans) rather than the full frontal nudity of the original. In a spirit of over-helpfulness familiar from his uncle, Michael had rolled the legs of his football shorts up over his thighs for an aspect he obviously considered to meet Finn's exacting requirements. The end result was something approaching a polyester nappy, which was, Finn felt, charming in its own way, but rather countervailed the lad's delusion.

'. . . says to Uncle Maurice I'd show him how to do the accounts and whatnot for his business, only for a laugh I went on this dodgy website. You should have seen him, right. He turned all sweaty and was trying to stop me seeing, saying, *That's no right*, and I was killing myself because me and Spence, we're always watching that kinda stuff. That's what made Uncle Maurice determined to fix up a date for me. He was giving it, *Life isnae a porn film*, and saying I'll end up with unrealistic expectations and whatnot. Although you'd mebbe think if that was the case, he'd've fixed me up with a proper lassie and no one you pay for. But then again, that's classic Uncle Maurice. He probably didnae know anyone who'd do it.'

While the story slopped around the studio in tune with the gurgles of rainwater from the gutter outside, Finn sank into his work. He was proud of what he'd done with the set. A mess of props was scattered around Cupid's feet and elsewhere. Props that had been improvised or borrowed or both. A crown from a three wise nativity king, a laurel wreath of leaves from Maurice's potted bay tree, a fiddle that belonged to the teuchter-folky-singalong group who met in the hall on Thursday evenings and, although he was missing a lute, Finn had found a guitar owned by the same group that would substitute (in one of his rare lucid moments, Caravaggio had suggested snapping the fret board to replicate the lute's angled neck but, thankfully, had been diverted by a particularly compelling cartoon in the latest of Jed's comics before he'd had the chance to follow through). Props to represent every archetype of virility, all of them discarded and trampled and disregarded. Knowledge and power and other such manly pursuits laid to waste by a naked wee runt. An arrogant wee fucker with no respect – no fucking concept that he should even have any respect – for anyone or anything else. The type of wee fucker who would happily give your best pal a medal for shagging your girlfriend. And who probably already had.

'We found this site, right, where the lassies were total class and it says they're escorts, no prossies, so we went with this one called Crystal who was proper amazing-looking. Proper amazing. And I'm no just saying that, by the way. Uncle Maurice was the same. Weird thing was, he says he'd seen her some place before, but I reckon that was him with a bad dose of the havers. You know what his eyes are like.'

Omnia Vincit Amor. Love conquers all. Which to Finn's mind – if this painting was anything to go by – roughly translated as *Fuck Everything and Bugger the Consequences*.

'Shift back a bit,' Finn said. 'Your foot needs to be level with the helmet.' The shiny black steel of the soldier's helmet had been recreated in the shiny black plastic of Finn's cycle helmet.

'Gonnae let me stand for a sec? My leg's pure agony.' Michael shifted and the sheet slipped.

'One sec. No more.'

Michael unfolded his twisted knee from the trestle table and stretched it out.

'It was murder while we were waiting for her to get back to us. I was like, *No way is this lassie gonnae go for it. She's way too sophis.* I near enough died when we got her message with it all fixed up.'

Finn gathered up the sheet.

'I telt my mum I was staying with Spence.'

'Sorry?'

'Spence. My pal,' Michael said, climbing back on to the trestle table. Finn refolded the sheet exactly as it had been. 'We've been best mates since we were weans. Like proper wee weans.' Michael examined the puckered sheet between his thighs. 'Is this meant to be a fanny?'

'For fuck's sake,' Finn said disingenuously, squirting fresh paint on to his palette. Truth be told, the kid wasn't wrong. The whole tableau was filled with fannies and phalluses if you took the time to notice. The neck and bow of the violin. The sceptre piercing the crown. The compass straddling the triangle. And not just that. In all corners, the letter V, straining and contriving to be found. In his art book, these orgiastic Vs were proclaimed as Caravaggio's way of honouring and celebrating the man who commissioned the picture, a certain Vincenzo Giustiniani. Finn didn't buy it. Caravaggio wasn't the patron-honouring type.

These Vs weren't the Vs of Victor or Vincenzo. They weren't the tokens of one man trying to flatter another. They were the sex-obsessed, self-obsessed signs of the artist's self-love. Caravaggio? Too fucking right. The painting literally had Vadge written all over it.

Lulled by the hypnotic syllables of the boy's tedious story, Finn went back to the painting. Michael chattered on about the chippy, about not smelling of fried stuff and how his boss never shut the door when he was out the back getting supplies and fat fumes creeping through the holes in the plastic bag that stop you suffocating so even his new shirt from Auntie Leanne wrapped in a carrier ended up stinking like a greasy haddock. And Michael complaining and his boss going, *Get over yersel, ya fucking wardrobe.* Finn stopped listening. He had work to do. The wings were next for their transformation. What you might call a de-vamp, he said to himself. Dark eagle feathers where angelic plumes had once fluttered.

'Did you ever do that?'

'What?'

'Try out the holes in a placky bag. I did it once with one fae Asda's when I was eight or something. Generally, I'm no such a divvy as to stick a bag over my heid to see if it kills me, but for some reason that day the holes were asking to be tested.'

What followed was some other gibberish about looking like a vacuum-packed kipper and the only time his mum ever belted him and Michael arranging to meet the girl outside the shop and his boss wanting to get an eyeful and doing that thing against the inside window where you cup your hands round your face to cut out the reflection but from the street side it made him look like a blind goldfish. Finn concentrated on the texture of the feathers, the flexibility of the quill, the fragility of the space between the barbs. He'd only been at it for a few seconds, but already Michael was on Dumbarton Road and a couple of neds were kicking in the window of the amusements.

'I was hoping tracksuit boy and his pal werenae gonnae tap me for a fag or something cos I'm no a smoker but it's a pure red neck to admit it. See the amount of abuse I get for trying to lead a healthy life. Only once I let on I work at the chippy, I'm usually okay, cos they leave me alone on the promise of a free pie supper. It gets taken out my pay, but.'

Finn stepped back from the painting. It was almost there. Almost finished.

'See when she showed up, I couldnae actually believe it. That's when she says the thing about my cheek baines. The fact it was dark was an advantage because she couldnae see my skin. Makes a change fae, *Should you really be serving food, Pizza Face?* which is what I get all the time in the shop. See the number of times I've wanted to gob in someone's chips. I've never done it, but. Nae need. The boss tests the fat by spitting in it anyway. Take that, ya roaster.'

Finn squidged a dollop of white on to the palette, irritated by the modern-day fakery of the innocuous pigment. A pale and toxin-free pretence of lead white.

'It wasnae until later that I saw how much mair stunning she was in real life even than in her picture, which was mebbe just as well, or there was no way I would've even been able to say, *Don't mind*, when she says, *Good evening. You are the birthday boy, no?* and, *What would you like to do?*'

The white was for the highlights, for the silver-white shafts of the black feathers. Finn wiped his brow with his wrist. He was sweating, but from the goosebump contraction of Michael's bare nipples he could tell the boy was cold. Not just cold but freezing his tits off.

'It was only when she asked that I realised I didnae have a clue what was meant to happen next. My head was pure swimming because I was hyperventilating and I was thinking I should be breathing in to a paper poke. See if she noticed, she didnae let on. She takes my hand and says, *I show you a nice bar where we can drink fizzy.* Even though it was cold out, her hands were warm, and I was like this to myself, *This is probably the first time anyone has held my hand since my mum used to see me across the road to get the bus to St Andrew's when I was in infants.* We dondered along to Partick Cross holding hands and no speaking. She was probably gieing me a chance to get used to the situation. We mebbe even looked like a real couple.'

For the touches of white, Finn needed his finest brush. The white on black. The deepest black shining the brightest white. It was bizarre and yet so easy to see. When he thought about it, it wasn't so much that he could see what was nice and what wasn't as Michael had put it. It was more that he could see how black was white, white was black. The veins of the feathers. The shine of black steel. The deep folds of the drapes. Not a change from one state to the other. Not the purification of the impure or the sanctification of the amoral. And not the virginal being defiled or the profane being purified. What he was talking about here was an absolute coexistence. A concurrence. Both black and white *at the same time.*

Michael was happily rabbiting on, seemingly unaware of Finn's profound insight. '. . . turned the corner to Byres Road, she starts chatting a bit. It's no that often I go up Byres Road, by the way, cos it's full of students and West End trendies. I like the Botanics in the summer, but. Better than Kelvingrove. You know, the greenhouses and whatnot. My dad used to take me there to look at the flytraps and the orchids when I was a boy and when we got hame, we'd tell my mum and she would be like, *Ooh, don't say another word. It's creepy.* And my dad would laugh and say he got why she didnae like the flytraps but orchids were pretty. The thing my dad forgot to mention was that orchids grow on the back of other plants. They dinnae feed off of them, but, so they dinnae count as parasites.'

Both divine and diabolical. Chaste and depraved.

'Move your foot a second. It's too far to the right. No, the other way.'

'That's left.'

'Your left. The painting's right.' That was exactly what Finn was talking about. Take any position on the canvas, any prop, any single point – the arrows held in Cupid's right hand, the tip of the wing that brushed the boy's left thigh in a disconcertingly erotic way, the compass point that almost pricked the edge of his right foot – and it was both left and right at the same time. It wasn't like looking in a mirror where your reflection stared back at you from the wrong side, where left became right, right became left. This wasn't an *either or*, a reflection or inversion. It was both, simultaneously. A consummate duality. Ambivalence in its most head-warping form.

'What else? Oh aye, an ambulance screeched past blue-lighting to casualty which made her tell me that she was gonnae be a nurse when she'd saved up enough to go to uni, and then she says, *I have buyed the uniform already*, which was very funny to her. No so much to me, but.'

Finn was proud of himself. Proud yet humble. Confident yet modest. His gift for this was remarkable. Not everyone had the skill.

'We headed up the road and past the university caff which does the best ice cream in Glasgow according to my mum but it was shut and I says that was a shame because we could have tested it out and she says if I was an ice-cream fan I should go to Italy because they do the best ice cream in the world. A bit further along there was a coffee bar that was still open and she goes, *The manager in there is a wank-merchant*, which was no really a word I would've thought she'd use. She says she knew cos she used to work there and says, *In fact, that is how this happens.* She held up the hand I wasnae holding, and her ring finger was bent.'

It was only afterwards Finn realised he'd been trussed up all along. Like a frog in an experiment in Rob's book, paralysed and twitching, alive and not alive. He was so caught up in his work, absorbed by the magnificence emerging from the tip of his brush, he was oblivious to the danger signs.

'Are you okay?' Michael stopped suddenly and was staring at Finn strangely.

'Huh?' Finn was totally lost. He had no idea where the conversation had turned. 'Aye, no probs,' he replied, because an answer seemed to be required. He leant in to the canvas to work on the punctate highlights of the bolts in the helmet.

'When we got to the place, two bouncers with suits and walkie-talkies were guarding the rope across the stair but they let us past when she smiled at them. They were pure thinking, *What the hell is she daeing with him?* But I was so high I may as well have been on another planet. Or in Italy, for that matter.'

Finn didn't notice his skin peeled back.

'When we got inside, we decided – well, it was her who decided – that it would be best if she ordered the drinks cos she'd get served easier. I had my money all clipped together in my wallet with one of my mum's paper clips so I takes a twenty fae my wad and hands it over. She looks at it and says, *If we drink fizzy, we need more.*'

Every nerve-ending raw and alert.

'Thing is, she was right about getting served quick. Even though the place was heaving and it was shoving room only at the bar, the barmaid served her straight off. She pays and says something in the barmaid's ear and then waves away the change. I'm thinking, *That's my cash, but*, but when she comes back, she's like, *We have special VIP seat*, and we go through a velvet curtain into a wee side room with leather armchairs and whatnot and you could hear yourself speak. The only bad thing was how the light was brighter. She takes off her coat and I cannae actually breathe cos of how amazing she looks in her jeans and spangly top. The barmaid brings the bottle in a silver wine bucket with ice in it, and two glasses on a tray with a bowl of dry roasted peanuts. I love dry roasted peanuts, by the way, but they always make me choke so I was telling myself to mind no to eat them. The barmaid pops the cork and lets the champagne foam in the glasses and doesnae look at me once the whole time.'

Muscles ready to kick with the bolt of electricity.

'When the bubbles have went down a bit, she picks up her glass. I'm thinking she was away to take a drink but she was looking at me like I was supposed to do something. Clink. Only I'd been holding off picking up the glass because my hands were shaky and mebbe a bit sweaty but then I goes to myself, *Well, this is it*, and I pick up my glass and clink it with hers. She goes, *Cheese*, and starts pishing herself and says when she first got here, she thought that's what everyone was saying and she couldnae work out why.

'I was wanting to laugh too but, to be honest, I was a tad

on the nervous side so instead I takes this massive gulp and the bubbles go straight up my nose and I'm coughing like a sixty-a-day-er. When I could get a word out again, I asked her where she was fae even though I knew already because it says so on the website. So we chat about Poland for a wee while and then I ask how old she is, and she says nineteen. I was a bit taken aback, to tell you the truth, cos she seemed older. No to look at. Her manner. Then I was worried that I'd came across rude so I changed the subject and asked her if Crystal was her real name because it doesnae sound Polish.

'She says, *No, it is not my real name. My friend is telling me to make up a name to protect myself from weirdos.*

'At first I'm thinking, *She thinks I'm a weirdo*, but then she says, *My real name is Kassia and I—*'

'Aargh!' Finn yelled. A shock of a thousand volts. A crackle of current that fried his bollocks and turned him blind. He dropped the palette. His paintbrush fused to his palm. His brain contracted, his heart went flabby. He couldn't breathe.

'What's up?' Michael said innocently.

Finn dropped to the floor. He couldn't believe what he had heard. Choking, twitching, he scrabbled to pick up the palette and, with enormous effort, pulled himself back to his feet. His legs had turned to phlegm. He placed the palette on the table, clutched the strut of the easel, paintbrush almost snapping in his other hand.

'Kassia? Are you sure?' The words stuck on his teeth. His tongue had shrivelled. His throat had closed.

'Aye, hundred per cent,' Michael said cheerfully. 'Are you sure you're okay? You look like you've been pure malkied.'

'Fine. I'm fine.' Finn gripped his brush. He had nothing left to paint but he couldn't let go of his crutch.

'D'you know her?' Michael said.

'Aye, no, sort of . . .' The words were claggy. Clung to the roof of his mouth. 'I asked her to model once,' he lied, his thoughts convulsing from the words already spoken. The time lapse between stimulation and contraction. *Wank-merchant. Her ring finger was bent.*

'Will I carry on?'

Michael took Finn's lack of response as encouragement. He started up again. This time choking on peanuts and the champagne going to his head and leaving the club.

Paralysed, Finn closed his ears, trying work out if some-how he had misheard, misunderstood. If the shock had made him deaf to reality.

'Her bit was further than she'd made out. We walked over University Avenue past the building with the anatomy museum in it. Me and Spence went in there once to look at the two-headed babies and pickled willies but we got chucked out when the security guy cottoned us as no real dentist students.'

Watching the boy's mouth chew over the words.

Something about sitting down on the toilet to be polite because his legs were wobbly and he didn't want to whizz on the painted floorboards and looking out the bathroom window at the children's hospital next to where he'd been born and where he'd been in an incubator for ages because he'd been premature or ill or something but which was shut down now which was kind of sad. And then in the kitchen and searching for vodka.

It was unbearable, incomprehensible. If Caravaggio were here he would say it made perfect sense. Fillide was a cour-tesan and, convinced as he was that they were one and the same, it followed that Kassia should be too. And while that might make some kind of perverted logic in Caravaggio's world, what made no sense at all – not one drop, not one iota, not in any fucking world – was that Kassia would spend an evening with a spotty adolescent who choked on peanuts and sat down to piss.

Despite his effort not to hear, Finn was hideously aware of what the boy was saying. He wiped the white paint from his brush with a sheet of kitchen roll. Found the voice to say, 'This was in her flat?'

'I reckon she didnae mean to take me back there. It's just how it ended up.'

The room was filled with the rush of plumage. Black wings of envy in full flight. Finn flinched from their beat. It wasn't that he wanted Kassia for himself, not in that way. All he wanted was to paint her. That she could debase herself like this, with this peri-pubescent virgin, but not even be prepared to speak to him was insane. It was too much to bear. To shut Michael up – for a second, for a minute, for longer – Finn took the arrows off him and unhitched the angel wings. 'We're done, more or less.'

'Ta,' Michael said, getting down and unrolling the legs of his football shorts. 'Can I have a squint? You should've seen her room, by the way. Compared to hers, mines is mint. Hers was a squat. There wasnae one molecule of floor where you could've stepped. If you asked me what colour the carpet was, I'd no be able to tell you.'

While Michael studied the painting, Finn decanted the old white spirit in the jam jar into his waste bottle and poured fresh to clean the last traces of white from his brush. The boy's story was still swirling through his brain, a reality diluted by paint thinner, certainties as swishy and fey as watercolour, making him dizzy, disorientated. His reason was marked with splodges of anxiety, tidemarks of disbelief.

'No bad, no bad at all,' Michael said. And then, as if Finn had asked him, kept going. 'There wasnae anywhere else in the room for me to sit so I dived fae where I was so as no to stand on any of her gear, which was a dive of mebbe a metre and a half, and landed on the bed besides her.' He grabbed his jeans from a pile of his stuff under the trestle table and changed out of his football shorts. The jersey of his boxers bagged over the hollows in the side of his buttocks. He was still talking, chuntering on, but Finn couldn't focus his ears. All he could hear were absurdities, flecked with the odd word that meant nothing.

He lined up the tubes of oils in his box.

Michael pulled a long-sleeved T-shirt over his head. His stomach was pulled tight. His words were muffled under the cotton. 'I telt her that she was the most beautiful girl I'd ever seen which was true but easy to say when the other person is pished. I thought mebbe she could be a model instead but she said she didnae have a portfolio, only she called it a portrait album, and other stuff about needing dosh for rent. Then she says, *It is not too bad if they are all being as nice as you*, and that I was quite handsome and that's when she says to make the best of my cheek baines with mebbe a new hairstyle and a bit of *newlooking* which I thought was a nice word. I wasnae offended, by the way, but I'll no tell Auntie Leanne that she didnae like my birthday shirt.'

In one short afternoon, Finn had aged. His back was stooped like an old man. His limbs were frail. With difficulty, he pulled the sheet off the table and folded it. Then he picked up the props one by one and piled them on the table.

'No word of a lie when I says she was the most beautiful girl I've ever seen,' Michael said, sitting on the floor to pull on his pumped-up basketball trainers. 'Even when she fell asleep and kind of slumped to the side and was dribbling, she was still totally stunning. You know, like Snow White.'

It wasn't right. This childish innocence. It was distasteful. Finn could no longer contain himself. He was filled with rage.

'Did you think about what you were doing? Did you think about how terrible it must be for a lassie to sell herself like that?' He stood over Michael as he put on his shoes. 'Terrible. You've no excuse.' He booted a trainer under the table.

There was a heavy pause.

'Hold on. It wasnae—' Michael began, reaching under the table to grab his shoe. Finn stood on his hand.

'You justify it however you like but it doesn't make it right.' Finn's voice was low. He lifted his foot.

'It's no what you think. Honest. I was just standing beside the bed watching her.'

'I don't want to know,' Finn yelled.

Michael cowered away from him. 'No, really, but. I thought if I left her like that she'd get a cricked neck, so I tried to put her to bed.'

Finn kicked the easel over. The canvas clattered to the floor. Michael shut his eyes, kept talking, faster and faster, going on like he was reliving it all. Finn didn't want it relived. He wanted to shut the boy up, to strangle him with the laces from his ridiculous trainers.

'. . . her shoes, grey suede boot things, but I managed to undae the laces and haul them off. Honest, I didnae do anything. I was just looking. I was trying to figure out how she could walk in heels that high, and then I couldnae help it . . .'

'What the fuck?'

'No, no, nothing. All I did was stick my nose in her shoe,

no even really sniffing. Honest. I just wanted to get closer.'

It was no use. He wouldn't shut up. Finn slumped in the chair.

Michael opened his eyes. 'I didnae do anything wrong. I didnae.' He gave a nervous laugh, but his face was split in two. 'She was sleeping and dribbling and I tugged her a bit so she was lying down properly and stuck a pillow under her head and covered her with the downie.'

'Did you touch her while she was sleeping?'

'No! No, I swear tae God. She nuzzled into the pillow and her hair was falling all across her face and I pushed it back behind her ear so it wouldnae tickle. That's all. You've got to believe me. I really, really wanted to kiss her – no in a pervy way, just because she looked so peaceful – but I didnae. I didnae even kiss her.'

It took more than a few instants for Finn to realise the truth of the situation. To be sure he made the boy repeat it. Twice. And then verify it when he recounted it back. Finally, when he was convinced, he thought his body would puddle under the chair, drip on to the floor, sink into the boards from the relief of it. The torture was over, experiment concluded. It was not what he had feared. Nothing had happened. He wanted to dance, wanted to sing, wanted to leap across the fucking rooftops, but he was incapable of even standing. Instead, he massaged some life back into his neck, his shoulders, his jaw and temple. Nothing had happened. Kassia wasn't tainted by the shame of shagging an imbecile. It was cause to rejoice.

Eventually, when he was able to speak, Finn apologised to Michael. 'I know you didn't mean to hurt her,' he said. 'Not deliberately. Only I can't stand to think of how these things must affect a girl like Kassia. Each time . . .' He let the silence speak.

'But I didnae do anything.' Michael's voice was flat, dead. 'All I did, right, all I did was get my anorak fae the hall and take out all the money fae my wallet – apart fae one pound fifty which I needed for the night bus hame – and leave it beside the baby lotion on her bedside table.' He sighed, like his guts were spilling. 'I didnae think that I was doing anything wrong when I signed up. I just thought . . . well, you know . . . that it was her job. I didnae mean her any harm. I never thought about how she ended up daeing what she was daeing.' His whole body was shuddering. 'I didnae even think . . .'

Finn went over to him, put his hand on his shoulder. With a sympathy he didn't feel, he said, 'It's okay, Michael. It's okay. You know you can do something to make up for it?'

Michael gazed up at Finn gratefully. 'I can?'

'Yes, I'd really like her to model for a painting. You could contact her. Ask to meet up.'

'Eh? I'm no sure, but. I don't think . . .'

'I could look her up myself, I guess. It wouldn't be difficult.' Finn picked up the overturned easel. 'But it would be better coming from you. Think about it. You'd be saving her. Saving her from having to, well, you know. It would be like making amends.'

Michael was shaking his head. He was almost crying. Stuttering, muttering, that he hadn't done anything wrong.

'Fair enough,' Finn said briskly, picking up Michael's coat from the heap under the table. 'If that's what you want to believe.' Michael started sobbing. Finn took the boy's phone from the coat pocket, turned it around in his hand. 'Shame though. It sounded like she really liked you, trusted you.'

Slowly, painfully, Michael took his phone from Finn.

Finn explained how the plan was going to work. 'Arrange

to meet her and I'll go instead.' The idea was so simple, it was genius.

Michael nodded reluctantly and messaged her. There was silence while they waited for a reply. Eventually, the phone bleeped back. It was done. Michael showed Finn the message, and finally Finn laughed.

27

Sleeping Cupid

The Saturday before the Easter weekend, after their usual trip to the library and as an extra-special treat for the start of the holidays, Esme dragged her two oldest boys to the barber's before they went to the park. Frankie broke his customary silence to argue with her the entire length of Byres Road – libraries were for kids, haircuts were for girls, the park was for losers – but they arrived at the barber's before he'd reached the part of the refrain where he hated her, hated Dermot, hated everything and everybody, and so they had to hang about outside for him to finish off. If Esme hadn't already heard it so many times as to be thoroughly bored with it, she might even have found the strength of feeling vaguely touching. As it was, she made sure she'd bundled the boys inside the shop before she throttled Frankie right there in the street, knowing it would be harder to finish him off inside where there were witnesses.

Once inside, the owner took charge of Frankie straight away, and Paddy sat himself in the row of seats along the side wall to read his library book. Esme sat down beside him, trying to ignore the melodrama her oldest son was creating as he climbed into the barber's chair, and glanced around to see if she recognised anyone in the shop. There was no one she knew.

The barber draped the nylon gown over Frankie's chest and lifted his hair from the nape of his neck while he secured the Velcro fastening and Frankie skulked behind his over-grown fringe. Esme picked up the copy of the *Partick Gazette* someone had left on the seat next to Paddy and glanced at the local headlines. In the background the monotone radio was churning out the same news as in the paper.

At the next chair, Leanne was cutting Michael's hair, fin-ishing off the last touches with the clippers. Tufts of mousy-brown hair lay on the tiled floor around the toes of her knee-high tan boots.

'Head down, pet,' she said. Esme sneaked a peek at the two of them over the top of the paper. Leanne's tweed mini-skirt was tight and short, and when she bobbed down a little to neaten off Michael's cut at the neck, her hemline slipped up over her sturdy thighs. She leant in to shave the last wispy strands, and it looked to Esme like she was breathing right on the boy's skin. Her face was so close her blonde hair must have been tickling him and her bosom so close it must have been touching his back, but he didn't flinch. Before moving on, she brushed away the stray clippings with her fingertips before they escaped under the collar of his football shirt, and tipped his head part the way back up. It wasn't just the tenderness, the closeness, the care, invested in those simple acts that made Esme realise they must be related. It was the readiness of the boy to accept them.

The contrast with her own son couldn't have been more galling. Frankie was wriggling around, squirming in his seat, each awkward move accompanied by the squeak of worn leather and as many glowers in the mirror at Esme as he could fit in.

'Sit still, Frankie, and do what the gentleman tells you.' Esme grimaced at the barber. 'I'm really sorry. He's not too happy about this.'

'Don't want to lose your good looks, son, is that it?' The barber pumped the chrome bar to lift the chair to cutting height and sprayed Frankie's hair with water to dampen his dark waves. Frankie sank into the black nylon. Esme's view of him in the mirror was partly blocked by the bulk of the barber in his plaid shirt and camel leather trousers, but she could see enough to make out the faintest hint of shadow above the tails of Frankie's lips. Sometimes she tried to persuade herself that all his nonsense – all his sullen awkwardness, his outright bad manners – was nothing to do with her or Dermot, but was solely a result of the swinging levels of testosterone his poor body was having to adapt to.

Michael, meanwhile, was peering out from underneath his creased forehead. Esme could see him taking deep breaths, looking at Frankie in the mirror, as if he was winding himself up to chat.

'I reckon we can do something that keeps your old mum happy without compromising on style,' the barber said, pulling a comb and scissors from his holster-style utility belt.

Frankie nodded gratefully. Michael exhaled, temporarily robbed of the opportunity to speak.

'The cowboy said you were old, Mummy,' Paddy said, without looking up from his book.

'Just make sure it is out of his eyes,' Esme said. 'I'm sick of never being able to see his face.'

The barber winked at Frankie and started cutting.

'You're awful quiet today, Michael pet,' Leanne said. Holding the clippers aloft, she turned round to speak to Esme. 'Normally we cannae shut him up.'

Michael's neck turned the same red as the stripe in the barber's pole and, when Leanne asked him something about a painting and then with unmistakable pride boasted to

Esme that her nephew had been modelling for a portrait, the colour spread to his ears.

'Auntie Leanne!'

'Sorry, sweetie.' She lifted his head to shape around his ears. And to Esme again, 'I'm embarrassing the poor kid.'

Esme smiled back. If only embarrassment was the worst of her own sins.

The barber snipped away at the back of Frankie's hair, from time to time showing him the bits he'd trimmed to demonstrate that it was only the very tips he was cutting off. Once Frankie was reassured that he wasn't going short, he relaxed and turned his attention to Michael in the mirror. He had the desperate look he got whenever he decided he wanted to make friends, Esme realised, and it made him so vulnerable, and not simply because in this case he was only eleven and Michael was a lot older (although exactly what age Esme found it difficult to tell) but because it happened so rarely he didn't always remember how to go about it.

Eventually, to Esme's relief, Michael spoke first.

'I just want to say that you have nice hair, by the way. You shouldnae get it all chopped off.' And Frankie grinned, fit to burst, and once Michael had started, there was no stopping him. He told Frankie that all mums were the same, they just didn't get it, had no idea about what was trendy, what wasn't. Said his name was Michael but his friends called him Midge, and his mum liked his hair when it was long, but he was getting a passport and for his photo he was going for a whole *newlooking.*

Esme saw the tiniest flinch from her son.

'What the devil do you want a passport for?' Leanne said, standing back to check the evenness of the cut. Satisfied, she brushed down the sleeve of her black polo neck. 'Glasgow not good enough for you these days, you wee so-and-so?'

Michael laughed. 'It'll no work, Auntie Leanne.' He spoke to Frankie again. 'My mum and my auntie dinnae want me to go travelling. They say it's because they want me to go to college, but I know really it's because they'll miss me too much. Eh no, Auntie Leanne?'

'If you say so, sweetheart.'

'Soon as I get my passport, I'm away to Italy. Best ice cream in the world.'

Frankie said, 'Did you hear that, Mum? Michael is going to Italy.'

'Midge. My mates call me Midge.'

Paddy shut his library book with a bang. 'Finished,' he said.

'That was quick, Pads.'

'Almost done,' Leanne said, styling the long parts of her nephew's hair with wax. When she lifted off his gown, she made sure she kept any hair from falling on his jeans, dusted his face with a shaving brush to rid him of the last strands, and held up a hand-mirror to show him the back. Our souls are in the tiny gestures, Esme thought, and a swirl of vertigo threatened to overbalance her.

'What d'you reckon?' Midge said to Frankie. His hair was still reasonably long on top with a side parting, but shaved in close at the sides. 'This lassie I know telt me I should show off my cheek baines. Make the most of them.'

Frankie started raving about how great Midge looked, using words like sick and doss and others that similarly seemed to say the opposite. Esme hid her smile behind the pages of the *Gazette* while Midge thanked him and called him bro and examined his own hair again from the back and then straight on, side on, straight on again, pouted his lips and finally blew himself a kiss. The kiss made Frankie burst out laughing.

The barber was trimming close to his temple with scissors. 'Careful, son,' he said, steadying Frankie's head with his hand that held the comb, 'or you'll end up with a skinhead.'

'Who's next?' Leanne asked.

'This one,' Esme said. She pushed Paddy towards Leanne.

'Can I have a skinhead, Mummy?'

'No, you cannot.'

While Leanne sorted Paddy out on the booster chair, Esme pretended to read the paper, making only the smallest effort not to eavesdrop. Midge was chatting away to his aunt as he zipped up his anorak. He said that she and Uncle Maurice were invited to his mum's for lunch on Easter Sunday. Leanne tugged at the hem of her skirt, told him to say thank you and that she'd be there.

'But if you want your Uncle Maurice to come, you'll have to ask him yourself.'

There were stories hidden behind every family, Esme realised.

Midge leaned over, kissed Leanne on the cheek. 'Keep the change.'

'Cheeky monkey.'

'Bye, folks,' he said as he was leaving. He caught Frankie's eye in the mirror. 'See ya, bro.'

Fifteen minutes later, Esme and the boys met up with Dermot and Charlie in the play park backing on to Dougal Street. Esme leant against the swing post with Paddy's hand in hers and watched Dermot push Charlie high into the air. Charlie's feet soared above Esme's head and made footprints in the sky. There were patches of blue among the cushions of white and all the trees were wearing halos of spring green.

She breathed in deeply to taste the scent of new leaves and growing grass, and Paddy skipped over to join his dad.

Dermot ruffled Paddy's freshly cut hair. 'Skinhead or what?'

Paddy beamed at Esme.

Esme smiled and perched herself in the middle of the seesaw. Scattered all over the ground, on the slide and the swings, on the rubbery surface under the climbing frame, were petals of cherry blossom blown down prematurely in the spring storms, and the air was full of the happy cries of children playing and busy tweets of nesting birds. In the midst of it all, Esme heard Dermot mention something to Frankie about keeping his wig after all.

'Yeah, very funny, Dad.' Frankie's words were missing their usual razor edge. 'You just don't get it, that's all. You and Mum. No idea.'

Esme look round in time to catch Dermot grin sideways at her and she smiled back. Neither of them were so daft as to think that Frankie was permanently back in the land of the articulate, but it was a pleasure to have him visit now and again.

After a while Esme took over pushing Charlie in the swing. Dermot sat on the bench to thrash his phone while Paddy flung himself down the slide, spun on the round-about scooting the toe of his shoes along the ground, jolted the seesaw up and down, and scrambled over the climbing frame with his laces undone. Frankie wandered over to the banking and sat down among the spears of the crocuses.

Eventually – reluctantly – Esme decided they should go. Dermot went to fetch the car and arranged to meet them opposite the gate five minutes later.

It took a while for Esme to round up the boys. It was when she was calling Frankie over that she first saw Finn.

He had jumped the fence and was cutting up the side of the park and along the top of the crocus banking. He turned when she shouted to Frankie. She didn't know him. Not then. What made her remark on him was the way he looked at her. Straight on, unflinching, uncompromising. She felt pleased and uncomfortable at the same time. Most of the looks she attracted these days were just other parents making their silent comparisons.

Esme fastened Paddy's shoelace and brushed sticky petals of damp blossom off Charlie's trousers while they waited for Frankie to reach them. Finn was still watching her. She thought he looked like Jesus. A scruffy and slightly malnourished Jesus, but Jesus nonetheless. And beautiful in an unsettling way. After a minute, he turned away and disappeared.

Paddy ran ahead and Frankie followed. Esme yelled at them to wait inside the gate until she got there. Charlie wanted to walk but his progress was so slow that eventually Esme put her foot down and carried him. By the time she caught up with the two other boys, they were hanging on the gate, messing about. Finn was sitting on a fire hydrant at the corner of Dougal Street, watching all of them through the pruned rose bushes that encircled the park. Unwittingly, Esme caught his eye and he half smiled. His smile was knowing and indiscreet.

Esme grabbed Paddy's hand more roughly than she intended and followed Frankie, manoeuvring them all through the gate together. All the time she could feel Finn's eyes on her. She couldn't shake the idea that he was sizing her up, and she felt uneasy and peculiar and flattered. She shifted Charlie on her hip and steered the boys towards the pedestrian crossing.

Across the road, a taxi had growled to a halt and was

spluttering diesel exhaust while it waited for its passenger to disembark. The taxi door slammed shut. At precisely the same moment, Esme collided with Frankie. Immediately she knew something was wrong. He had stopped directly in front of her and she had stepped on the back of his new trainers and he had nothing to say about it. No muttered swearing, no heavy sighs, no whiplash glower of disgust. His only response was to stand rigidly in the middle of the pavement and stare silently across the road. Esme turned to follow his gaze.

Kassia.

On the other side of the road, miles from the crossing, she was dipping her toe on and off the kerb as if she was testing the water, waiting for the traffic to break.

It took a few seconds for Frankie to come round. The moment he did, he waved frantically and shouted. Esme told him to hang on, to cross at the crossing, but he wasn't listening. Kassia glanced in their direction and, briefly, her eyes clashed with Esme's. Esme reached out to grab Frankie's shoulder, but he slipped out from under her protective grip and hopped off the pavement. He was skipping along the double yellow lines, waving madly, desperate for Kassia to acknowledge him. Paddy, meanwhile, was scolding his brother for walking in the road.

From the other direction, a car was approaching, its engine roaring, music blaring. It was going too fast. Much too fast. Esme snapped at Frankie to get back on the pavement and clutched Paddy's hand tighter. She shifted Charlie again, repeated her demand. But Frankie wasn't listening. He wasn't watching the road. He was staring at Kassia. Deaf to Esme's calls. The car was close, too close, but Frankie was blind to the danger. Bemused by Kassia's disregard. It was right on him. He hadn't seen it. It was going to hit him. In that terrible second, a second that froze time, a second that changed everything, a second she would revisit over and over again, Esme saw Frankie consider every alternative course of action. She saw him decide what he was going to do. Choose his moment. Step out in front of the unseen car. Fear lurched from her toes to her fingertips. She couldn't stop him. Charlie was in her arms. Paddy holding her hand. Frankie was out of her reach. She couldn't stop him. She couldn't.

She screamed. Frankie half turned, hesitated. Paddy let go of Esme's hand, and grabbed Frankie's jumper. The wool stretched. A screech of brakes. The fibres tore. The slam of an emergency stop. The car skidded. Tar trails. Brake fluid. Esme dragged the two boys back on to the pavement. Frankie was staring around, wild-eyed, bewildered, disorientated. Charlie was whimpering in Esme's arms. Yards from them, Dermot was slumped over his steering wheel, eyes closed, panting. Numb with shock, Esme pulled Frankie to her with her free arm.

The rest unfolded as if it was a dream. She was vaguely aware of Dermot getting out of the car and shouting at her for letting Frankie out on the road, and of Frankie stiff under her desperate embrace, and of Charlie crying and Paddy trying to comfort him. But it was all in the background. Instead what she saw, all she saw, was Kassia give Frankie a quick glance to check he was safe before she skipped across the road in the direction of Dougal Street, and Finn stand up to greet her and then vacillate as if he was unsure whether or not to kiss her. And Kassia gesture at him as if she was angry and fold her arms across her waist. And Finn take out his wallet, hand over a bundle of notes, and then some more, and Kassia slip the money into the inside pocket of her jacket and link arms with Finn.

And as the two of them set off down Dougal Street, Kassia glanced back over her shoulder to Esme. The message was clear.

All of this was your doing.

28

Crowning with Thorns

It took all Finn's powers of persuasion, all his not (in his view) insubstantial personal charm, his entire repertoire of apology lines and a large percentage of his monthly allowance to stop Kassia disappearing the minute she clocked it was him not Michael at the meet-up. After a few seconds of hard negotiation, she agreed to model on the condition Finn upped the fee. Which of course he did without hesitating, distracted as he was by the family drama unfolding further up the road.

To Finn's relief, when they arrived back at the studio Caravaggio was still sleeping off the copious quantities of contraband whisky Finn had topped him up with the night before (once he'd staggered his way back through the perilous backstreets of Partick after the all-day session he'd put in with Maurice). As a cunning plan to prevent too many questions on his morning whereabouts and lacking as he was in other stuporifics, Finn had resorted to this magnanimous sacrifice, despite having intended to keep both bottles entirely to himself. The plan had worked a treat. The downside was that in a room the size of a store cupboard the wet snores coming from the corner were unavoidable, so it was inevitable that Kassia spotted Caravaggio sprawled among the fire curtains, his moist red lips quivering on each in-breath and the half-drunk bottle of whisky clutched in his sleeping fist.

Kassia pulled a face. 'Who is that man?'

Finn glossed over it. Said he was no one, a distant cousin, he'd introduce him if he woke up but honest, she was better off not knowing. The fact was, Finn wasn't ready to acquaint them. There was always a degree of difficulty in explaining the presence of a seventeenth-century half-deceased renegade in the hinterland of Partick, but some folk were more receptive to the notion than others. And although Finn was pretty certain Kassia was the sort who would run with an idea until it became clear, in truth he couldn't be bothered to have to make excuses for Caravaggio's prodigious ill-breeding.

For the next few minutes, coaxing and cajoling and banging his head against Kassia's unabating strop, Finn gave her a quick tour of the studio and the simple set. In his eagerness to start, he wondered if he dare suggest that they get on with painting straight away but, in the end, he chickened. He settled for showing her the picture they would be working on and asked her to bring a dress for the proper sitting.

'One with a tight bodice,' he specified, and then reddened up like a pervert.

Kassia tutted. 'I come back on Good Friday.'

Finn prayed he would be able to survive that long.

There were several options available to occupy the intervening days, but none of them filled Finn with any particular desire. He had a type of sickness, he decided, brought on by spring and everyone else's (with the exception, quite clearly, of Caravaggio) unhealthy seasonal cheeriness. Even Maurice had been infected, fixated as he was on the garden and planting and cleaning the place up. Finn required an escape, a diversion, away from Dougal Street and its taxations, but a bike run was out of the question since his biking partner had transpired to be Judas.

It went without saying it would break him too much to see Lizzi.

Which basically left Tuesday McLaughlin. Her chat had exactly the edge he needed to deflect his thoughts from the onslaught of anxiety engendered by his own existence. A circumventary pain.

He'd been meaning to catch Tuesday anyway, ask her for more pills for the slobbering inebriate in the corner because supplies were done and there was the serious question of how he was going to tolerate Caravaggio without pharmacological assistance for one, if not both, of them. The whisky was a stop-gap, a desperate measure, never intended as a definitive solution. Finn prised the bottle from Caravaggio's hand before he spilt it, and sniffed the heavenly vapours. Peat and mist and chimney smoke. The scent of Scotland's opium. Heather mountains and air so crisp you could taste it. He'd bet his last twenty quid that Tuesday McLaughlin had never been north of Maryhill, west of Clydebank. That she'd never had her sinuses seared by the wind or her feet frozen off by a mountain stream. He should take her out of the city, to lochs and mountains, take her on a trip to put some life back on her bones. They could start with a cinch. Conic Hill. A gem on the edge of the fault line that hung across the country like a snapped necklace.

Finn stowed the whisky safely under the trestle table and grabbed his jacket, delighted with his plan. Him and Tuesday were off on a mountain hike. A two-birds-one-stone situation. And a treat for them both.

The drawback to Finn's proposal was that it was weeks since he'd clapped eyes on Tuesday McLaughlin. Given the way that everything else was turning out, there was a possibility that she had got it on with her boyfriend and was living it up in the capital, but he felt it was doubtful. His other acquaintances might have made him question his understanding of the world, but he could pretty much count on Tuesday.

In the garden, he rolled himself a fag and smoked it sitting on the wall, keeping a hopeful eye on the comings and goings at the pharmacy. The walk he was considering was as familiar to him as the jelly inside his eyeballs. He'd done it with Rob often enough. He only had to blink to picture it. Start out in pine forest where the tree trunks slice the sunlight like scalpel blades and the needles rot imperceptibly underfoot. Track a bit higher to where the forest changes to something less surgical – arthritic oaks, ash trees doing their best to live down to their name, bracken thriving in the muddy shade, primroses and bluebells fighting it out for the gauzy patches of light that sink between the branches of the trees. Above the tree line, spongy mountain heath and a graze of scree before the limestone scar. At the cairn, buzzards circling overhead, where even the lightest breeze can lacerate your skin. And below, the gaping wound of Loch Lomond stretching out – banks as rounded as the edges of an ulcer, water as tarry as coagulated blood. You didn't have to be a medical man to understand the healing power of the place. It was the only cure for this spring sickness.

A jasmine bush sprouting at the foot of the wall was beginning to flower. Absent-mindedly, Finn snapped off a sprig and shoved it in his shirt pocket. Above him, a capricious breeze was pulling the clouds around the sky, opening it to sunshine and closing it off again as quickly, but the atmosphere below was uncannily settled.

Maurice was toddling around the garden amusing himself, seemingly unaffected by the toll of the previous day's session. 'All right, Finjay, lad?'

'Sure thing, Mo.' Finn twisted round so he straddled the

low sandstone wall – one foot in the garden, one foot in Dougal Street – and watched Maurice unlock the door of the outhouse. His toolbox was on the path beside the garden bench.

'Did you get hold of your lassie?'

'Aye. She was here today,' Finn said, thinking how fortunate it was that Maurice was so ignorantly unaware that Kassia was the lassie intended for his nephew. For reasons that Finn couldn't quite compute, he had an inkling it would be better if it stayed that way.

Maurice nodded happily and fetched a ten-litre tin of paint from inside. He lugged it two-handed over to the bench.

Finn took a drag of his roll-up and spoke on a held breath with a lungful of smoke. 'We're starting the painting at the end of the week.' On the out-breath, he blew a wispy smoke ring and watched it dissipate against the white sky.

'Och, son. That'll be music to Vadge's ear-holes,' Maurice said, dumping the tin on the gravel. 'Did he no say you should paint the lassie? Good on you, listening to his advice.'

Finn took a sharp inhale to stop himself violently contradicting his friend. He hadn't listened to Caravaggio's advice. As far as Finn was concerned, there hadn't been any advice to listen to. It wasn't like he was deaf to it. He'd been waiting, ready, primed to receive it, but Caravaggio hadn't bothered his bulging backside. Finn was beginning to suspect that Caravaggio wasn't quite so ready to share his genius as he'd hoped. Considering the man was supposed to be penancing his way out of purgatory or whatever it was he claimed, you'd have thought his acts of mentoring would be more forthcoming. But forth they hadn't come, so there was no way Finn was giving him any glory for the work on which he was about to embark.

'You know he's no such a bad lad after all, Finjay. Should've known, what with him being a relly of yours and whatnot,' Maurice said, prising the lid of the paint tin off with a chisel. 'Oftentimes has the tendency to talk some arty gibberish, but. A bit like yourself, I suppose.' He stirred the pot of paint with the handle of an old wooden spoon. 'He's stuck on this painting saving his soul or some such havering. You boys dinnae half take the whole caper seriously.' Maurice shook his head in wonder. 'She must be some looker, this Fillide lassie. To save a man from damnation.'

'Her actual name is Kassia and painting her was my own idea,' Finn said. He was not going to martyr himself in Maurice's opinion when Caravaggio was doing eff all to help. 'I worked hard to pull this off. It took a great deal of effort and personal charm to persuade her over here today and I can tell you for nothing, I didn't do it to keep Vadge happy.' Finn snapped out the last words at the very moment a dishevelled, whisky-blurred Caravaggio staggered out of the porch door.

'She was here? And you chose not to arouse me?'

Where Kassia was concerned, the less arousal the better, Finn reckoned, remembering all too vividly Caravaggio's shortcomings that day in the church. He paled at the memory and went back to watching the pharmacy. Meanwhile, Caravaggio regaled Maurice with stories of his past life and his philanderings with Fillide, and how he was prepared to put past difficulties behind him and what they were going to get up to the moment they were reacquainted. All of it said with slurps of such appalling lecherousness that, even though he wasn't listening, it made Finn literally want to throw up.

When he couldn't stand it any longer, he said as much. *Literally* want to. And he told Caravaggio to call Kassia by her real name because it was doing his nut.

Maurice interrupted before Caravaggio had the chance to riposte. 'Lads, lads. Nae fighting. She'll be back in a few days and you can sort it out then. In the meanwhile, youse could mebbe gie's a helping hand. I've heard it said that youse are both quite adept with the paintbrush.'

'Sorry, Mo,' Finn said, stubbing the fag end he'd sucked dry into the sandstone. 'Some of us have work to do.' He would put the plan for Tuesday temporarily on hold as she didn't seem to be about the place, and have a shot at something new. If Maurice was willing to take Caravaggio off his hands, out of his hair, out of his face, Finn wasn't going to say no. Maurice may have been lacking in the discernment department when it came to choosing acquaintances, but he was a good lad. That was undeniable. There were parts of the man that were genuinely saintly. Finn left Maurice teaching Caravaggio how to paint the woodwork and went back inside.

The days that followed Finn spent dabbling in self-portraiture. Using the mottled mirror and the nearly rotten eel as a snake replacement, he painted his reflection first as Medusa (during which he was obliged to hold his breath for long periods because of the overwhelming stink of dead fish), and secondly as Sick Bacchus. Sadly, he wasn't entirely satisfied with either result. One a woman (of sorts), the other a smooth-skinned jaundiced layabout, both were supposed to be without beard but Finn couldn't be bothered to shave. Plus, in the end, he didn't like the fairground effect of the distortions in the mirror, so he moved on to a brooding St John the Baptist that was less a portrait of his physical self than a portrait of his state of mind. Between these efforts, he wiled away the remaining hours sitting on the wall, staring out over Dougal Street, hoping to catch Tuesday while Maurice and Caravaggio cemented their relationship with gloss paint.

It was towards evening on Good Friday when Kassia eventually turned up. Unfortunately she timed her appearance perfectly to be subjected to Caravaggio's return from another full-day session with Maurice to celebrate the conversion of the garden bench to five star accommodation. Moments after Kassia's arrival, Caravaggio barged into the studio leaving the door open behind him, so bladdered, Finn realised, that he could barely elocute even his customary expletives. Somewhere along the way he had lost his pal.

On this occasion, it was less easy to brush over his presence. 'Have you met my . . . cousin—' Finn began, but stopped abruptly when Caravaggio pulled him aside.

'A gentleman does not approach a courtesan in this manner,' he said. 'Please inform her that I await in my chamber.'

'Gentleman?' Finn said. 'Don't be such a tosser.'

Caravaggio, however, had already installed himself behind the door and begun to undress. The light intruding through the open door was enough to show his flabby man boobs and his back matted with hair. If the sight hadn't been quite so revolting, Finn might have found Caravaggio's presumption slightly amusing. As it was, he was praying Kassia would keep her eyes averted.

Whatever the etiquette of soliciting in seventeenth-century Rome, Caravaggio quite clearly hadn't realised it didn't work that way in present-day Glasgow town. Plus, there was no way Finn was acting as intermediary. If Caravaggio expected him to debase himself like that, to let himself be bullied into message-passing like some dick-sucking flunkey, he was pissing in the wrong pot. Errand-running made you subservient by definition. An undeclared acceptance that you weren't in the same class as either the lassie you were asking or whoever it was you were procuring for.

'Your cousin is impolite, I find. To not say hello.'

While by now Finn would happily have denied the bloodline, he couldn't deny that Caravaggio was impolite. Not just impolite. Totally fucking uncouth. And he couldn't help but admire how cleverly belittling it was of Kassia to remark only on the lack of greeting and not on the fact that Caravaggio was already half-naked with his belly hanging over the waistband of his breeches.

'You're not wrong there,' he said. 'Shall we get on?'

Kassia had her dress stuffed in a school kid's rucksack. The dress was a nasty strapless number that at first sight completely underwhelmed Finn, but she took her rucksack and her cheap party dress and, after insisting that neither of them peek (*you peek I leave now*), changed behind the fire curtains Finn had rescued from Caravaggio's sleeping quarters and strung between the badminton posts. The transformation was astonishing. In her presence, the defiled curtains transmuted into the velvet drapes of a seventeenth-century bordello and the creature who emerged was magnificent, captivating and indecently beautiful. Finn could not have been more appalled. Despite all the practice he'd put in with St Jerome and his spotty nephew, despite all the error-trialling and technique-perfecting, he realised (with an unwelcome and uncharacteristic uncertainty of his own technical ability) that there was a hideous and soul-wringing probability he might not fully do her justice.

Indecency aside, attire-wise there was one slight problem.

Without considering the associated body odour, Finn grabbed Caravaggio's chemise.

'You need to put this on under your dress.'

Kassia took the shirt with her fingertips and sniffed it in disgust. 'Repulsive.'

'Just wear it, please.' For Finn, the blouse was a question of authenticity. For Kassia, it was altogether more degrading.

In his drunken haze, around about the time Kassia put on the soiled chemise, it apparently came to Caravaggio that she wasn't there to fuck him. When Finn next looked in his direction, he was slumped in the corner, morosely swigging back what was left of the whisky, and occasionally lifting a rotund buttock to fart. Finn cringed. The splayed legs and obscene groin-bulge, not to mention the disc of coarse skin peeking through the burst inside seam of his breeches, were offensive to an infinite degree. To spare his eyes the risk of further insult, Finn shut the door to cut out the external light. In the murky darkness that followed, the crimson of the velvet curtains withered to old blood and Caravaggio receded into the blackness.

'It is not possible that you make me wear this outfit,' Kassia said, once she was attired as Finn had instructed and he was showing her the correct pose to sit on the prayer cushion. 'I tell you. This is not at all how it is meant to be looking. I am ridiculous.'

The mildew-stained rustle drifted towards Finn and a second later Caravaggio lurched over and crashed into the trestle table. 'No, it is . . . you are perfect,' he slurred, his words slipping out on a breath loaded with rank and libidinous debauchery. The musky scent was overpowering even for Finn who had had weeks to become accustomed to it.

'Aye, it's meant to be like that,' Finn said, turning his face away from the smell just as Caravaggio slid, comatose, under the table. Kassia watched the performance with benign disinterest.

'We get on with it, then,' she said. 'I have enough of waiting.'

'Last bit.' Finn took his time arranging the candles.

'Really, I tell you, it is boring already. You take so long to prepare.'

Nervously, Finn breathed in the stagnant air and weighed his lighter in his hand, feeling the gentle slosh of lighter fluid against the clear blue plastic. He stooped to light the candles around the periphery of the tableau. Shadow fingers tugged at his hair, his scrawny beard, his frayed jeans, and tickled the dusty corners of the studio.

'Okay, okay. We're good to go.'

The candles were burning lazily in the still air. Kassia's cheeks were flushed with irritation and her pearl earrings glistened like tear drops. But it was only the imitation of sentiment, Finn realised. Her dark eyes were dull and insouciantly bored.

'Hang on, I forgot.' The sprig of jasmine cut from the garden was still in his pocket. He pulled it out, and his fingers brushed the pollen traces of lipstick on the cigarette he had been guarding for months. The sprig was limp from lack of water, and the April buds were tightly closed. A more potent symbol of the erotism emanating from the room Finn could not have imagined.

Kassia sniffed the closed flowers. 'Cat's piss,' she said, letting the stem droop between her fingers.

'Please, Kassia,' Finn begged. 'It isn't that hard. Hold it to your chest.' She lifted it nonchalantly. He was beginning to believe she was tormenting him on purpose.

'Wrong hand.' Finn snatched the stem and shoved it into

her left hand. Her crooked finger folded underneath her palm and she spat with pain.

'Ai, you hurt me, dickhead.'

'Sorry, I'm sorry,' he said. More gently, he positioned her hand at the neckline of the chemise. His paint-stained fingers brushed bare flesh. Ripples of distaste ruffled Kassia's creamy skin.

'Come on, K,' he pleaded. 'Engage with me.'

'You joke with me, no?' Kassia said. 'First you trick me for portrait. Next you are asking for marriage?'

Without the ball-breaking contempt, Finn might have laughed. As it was, he sighed heavily. 'No, no, you've misunderstood. I wasn't proposing. Engage as in connect. Look at me. Like you want to entice me to your boudoir. You're supposed to be a courtesan. We're talking seduction, temptation, eroticism.'

'Not possible. I am ugly, like a farm-maid.'

Considering her natural splendiference, Finn thought, it was surprising how preoccupied Kassia was with her appearance. More than surprising. Utterly incomprehensible. Although at least it meant he had something to milk.

Vanity.

And her simpering lover, Flattery.

Reasoning that below a certain level of attractiveness even the most deluded must be aware of their own repugnance, Finn had always been a firm believer that the pair were concepts of no relevance to the patently ugly. Likewise, he'd always assumed they were of equal if opposing irrelevance to the incontrovertibly beautiful. That the pair were nothing more than superficial acquaintances of the staggeringly average. Astonishingly, he realised, when it came to women, there were still things he had to learn.

'Okay, I think we should go back a step.' Finn picked up

a candle, did a brief sweep of the under-table scenery to check that Caravaggio was still breathing, and opened his book where he had left a thin paintbrush between the pages as a marker. On the glossy plate on page 157: Fillide Melandroni. Insolently checking him out. *Portrait of a Courtesan*. Prostitute. Lover. Muse.

'Take another look.'

With no enthusiasm whatsoever, Kassia smoothed down her skirt and went over. The tulle of her petticoat brushed through the rip in Finn's jeans and prickled against his skin. He swallowed hard before he spoke.

'Stunning, eh?'

Kassia didn't reply.

'Can you see? Can you see how intense this painting is?' Silence.

'K? Come on. Give me something here.'

Eventually, Kassia gave a strained laugh and shook her head. Some of her dark curls fell loose from the clip that bound them. 'I cannot be like that.'

'Yes, you can. Of course you can.' Urgently, Finn thrust the book closer to her, passed her the candle. Her fingers wound round it, pale as the wax.

He watched her as she leant over the book. The candle-light danced and flitted over the whites of her eyes. Her mouth was slightly open and Finn could see the tips of her opal teeth. Her tongue flicked the cushion of her lips. Between her eyebrows, a silk-thread crease of interest. Eventually, in a voice so low he had to lean in, she said, 'But she is special, no?'

'No more so than you,' he whispered back.

She shook her head, roughly handed the book back to him, and said, in a voice too loud for the small room, 'You have a wrong. I am not that person. I do this for the money.'

Under the table, Caravaggio stirred fitfully.

'So did she,' Finn said. 'And more.'

'This girl?' Kassia's black eyes were burning, her sultry breath stealing in and out of her lungs. 'She is whore? In real life, I mean? Not only in the painting?'

'Aye.'

'And you can make me look like that?'

'I can make you look better than that.'

She stared at him, challenging him, disbelieving. 'You promise?'

Finn nodded. He was taking a dangerous gamble. 'Can we start again?'

'Okay, we start again. But that is not to say I entirely trust you.'

This time when she sat down, she connected with him. Opened her soul. Finn's heart stopped, and yet he could hear his racing pulse. His blood pooled in his ventricles, and at the same time coursed through his veins. His breath froze in his airways, but his lungs burnt. This was it. Time to test his talent, his courage, against her beauty.

He picked up a brush.

He dipped it in the oily black.

He brought it to the canvas.

And before he made the first mark, it was over. The door opened. The studio flooded with the false light from the corridor. Under the table, Caravaggio groaned and pulled his cloak over his head.

'What the . . .' Finn put the brush down. He wanted to cry.

Michael was hovering on the threshold, holding back with a politeness just below bursting. He was flushed and flustered.

'Finn. I . . . Oh, hi, Kass.'

'Ooh, hello little Midge.' Kassia leapt up and bounded over to kiss him. 'I should be angry, no, for the trick you played on me?'

The boy blushed. 'I'm sorry . . .'

Finn chucked the paint palette on the trestle table. It skidded to the centre. 'I thought your name was Michael.'

'His friends are calling him Midge,' Kassia said, chucking him under the chin like a child.

The name was saying something to Finn, but he was too gutted to listen. He had been so close. So very close.

'Kassia, gonnae sit back down.'

'Do not do this stroppy with me, please,' Kassia said. 'You know what, I finish for today.' She twisted round for the boy to unzip her dress. 'I like your new hair, little Midge. Tell me what you are doing here.'

'Help. I need help,' Michael-Midge said, once he'd unfastened Kassia's dress. She stepped out of it. 'Finn's help.'

Kassia pulled Caravaggio's chemise over her head and draped it on the badminton post in disgust. She pulled on her jeans and her T-shirt. Shoved her dress into her bag. Sniffed under her armpits. 'That shirt it makes me smell. It is disgusting.'

'What?' Finn snapped. The kid was jiggling up and down. Like he needed a pee.

'Uncle Maurice.'

'What about him?'

Midge's face wrinkled and split. 'He's collapsed. In the garden.'

Finn sighed in relief. Maurice was always collapsing. 'Christ, I thought it was something serious.'

Midge spoke to Kassia. 'Please. I havenae a clue what to do. He said to get Auntie Leanne, but she willnae answer her phone.'

Sometimes Finn was astonished at how slow the boy could be. If it was bad enough to call Leanne, it must really be serious. They needed to do something. Get out there fast. Honestly, the kid was morotic. Which Finn would have said, only it wasn't worth another lot of baby tears.

Caravaggio's moans accompanied their leaving.

They found Maurice outside, head down in the holly bush with the bay tree knocked over beside him. For a moment or two, the three of them – Finn, Midge and Kassia – stood transfixed, staring at Maurice's boiler-suited backside. He was mumbling incoherently and from time to time throwing a limp arm out to grab on to something. His sleeve had ridden up, and Finn's watch was weighing down his exhausted wrist, and each time his arm landed back among the thorns, his papery skin slashed a little more.

'Oh, Jesus,' Finn said. 'He's trollied.'

'No, he's no,' Midge insisted. 'He doesnae drink.'

'Course he fucking does.'

'No. He stopped ages ago. When Auntie Leanne kicked him out.'

'What about when he goes to the pub?'

From deep in the vegetation, Maurice's feet twitched. His brown nylon socks were thinning at the heels.

'Actually, these days you can buy beer with nae alcohol,' Midge said, retrieving his uncle's slippers from under the bay tree.

'You don't say,' Finn said tetchily, and grabbed Maurice by the ankles to haul him out of the bushes. His grip slipped and Maurice's bad foot squelched under his fingers. He dropped it in horror.

'Careful. You'll hurt him.'

'Together we do this,' Kassia said. 'Come, Midge, take

here. You' – Finn realised she was talking to him – 'you take under the arms.'

Finn climbed over the edging stones into the flower bed and parted the branches of the holly bush. Together they lifted Maurice out gently and sat him on the newly painted bench. Kassia went to fetch the first-aid kit from the porch. Maurice was dazed and barely conscious. His face was scratched. His scalp was grazed. His skin was clammy. His lips were grey. Whatever words he managed to slur were incomprehensible and stank of dehydration. Finn tutted to himself. The Midge kid could say what he liked, but he was wrong about Maurice not drinking.

Across Dougal Street, the tenements above the shops loomed up and hid the sun, and an even shadowless dusk fell over the group. Midge sat down beside his uncle and held his hand, and stroked his quivering cheek. Kassia knelt at his feet, peeled off his glaury sock, unwound the grimy bandage, and wiped the worst of the pus from the wound with antiseptic. And Maurice stared ahead, more vacant than Finn had ever seen him.

'We've got you, Uncle Maurice,' Midge kept saying, his words as dull and repetitive as the cooing of collared doves. 'We'll get you sorted.'

It made Finn mad to see them like this. There had never been any need to call Leanne. Maurice would be fine. They underestimated him. 'All he needs is a cuppy and a biscuit and he'll be brand new.'

'I dinnae think so,' Midge said. 'I'm pretty sure . . .'

'It is okay, little Midge. I phone for ambulance.'

'A taxi might be quicker.' Midge checked his wallet, and then in panic said, 'I've no got any cash.'

Kassia nodded her head towards Finn. 'This is no problem. He is loaded.'

Resigned, Finn opened his wallet and handed over his last twenty.

Midge ran off to flag a black cab on Dougal Street. The three of them and the driver manhandled Maurice along the path and bundled him into the taxi.

'Are you coming with us?' Midge asked Finn.

'Nah, not today.' He couldn't stand to pass another minute with the kid.

The taxi departed. And Finn went back inside to mourn his unbegun masterpiece.

29

Madonna of the Rosary

Maurice wasn't the only one to come to the attention of the medical profession in the days following the Easter weekend. After weeks of putting her headaches down to stress and generally dismissing all other signs that things weren't right, Lizzi was caught out by the practice nurse at the GP when she popped in for a check-up on the way to a crisis meeting with her study advisers (armed against bad news with her lucky beads).

With a great deal of tutting and frowning, the practice nurse recorded Lizzi's blood pressure and handed her a specimen tube for a urine sample to dipstick. The pine air freshener in the toilet clogged Lizzi's mouth and nostrils. Like breathing cotton wool, she thought, as she strained to force out a dribble of pee. For the last couple of days it had been like this, her urine practically dried up in her kidneys and all the fluid collecting around her ankles. In the evenings, she sat with her feet up on her dad's footstool, but her ankles still rivalled the ones in Finn's picture. *Legs Eleven.* She fiddled with her beads. The Bingo pictures seemed a lifetime ago. She wished she'd given Finn more encouragement, wished she could go back and be more enthusiastic, more involved, stop him leaving his studio in the Art School and give him the chance to do things differently. If she really could turn back time, she'd go back to the evening in the church hall when she'd first seen his studio and they'd tidied up the hall and laughed about the unpainted ceiling. Or maybe further back. To the night in November when they helped out Maurice, and Finn had come back to her house. She'd replayed that night in all its different versions in her head so often. The version where she sent Finn home. The version where he stayed but she'd been sensible about her contraception. Or where she hadn't and they discussed it afterwards like grown-ups.

The world tilted on the smallest of actions, the most trivial of inactions. And once done, or not done, did your future follow an unrelenting path, she wondered, or was it more like a network, a web of possibilities, where you could take the odd diversion and still end up where you were meant to go? She supposed it depended on the size of the deviation. Failing her placement, getting pregnant, losing Finn to drugs – maybe they were diversions, digressions from which you could never find your way back.

Rather than dwell on it, Lizzi read the fire drill instructions pinned to the back of the toilet door, her face tight, her head throbbing from the overpowering air freshener, straining to pee, until eventually she managed to catch a few drops. She screwed the lid back on the pot and clutched it tightly, anxious not to lose the barely adequate sample. Her urine was pale and unremarkable, and the plastic tube warm against her palm. The misplaced body heat felt unpleasant.

The nurse compared the dipstick with the colour code on its container and said three plusses of protein as if it was something to be proud of. Lizzi didn't need to ask if that was bad or not. The nurse checked her dates, asked about her last scan. Twenty-four weeks now and, yes, everything had been fine at the last scan. Rob had come with her and held her hand and got excited when he saw the baby's heartbeat. He was happy for her, happy that at least this was going well.

Lizzi was told to take a seat in the waiting room. A short while later, the doctor bustled her into the consulting room and asked her to jump up on the couch so she could examine her tummy.

'Lizzi.'

'Sorry?'

'My name. Lizzi. You called me Elizabeth.'

For a moment, the doctor's friendly cheerfulness gave way to a brisk 'I see,' as Lizzi hauled herself up on to the examination couch. She didn't have the energy to regret her snappishness. She could just about accept being weighed, measured, poked and prodded, but she couldn't cope with the fake familiarity in the doctor's voice. It was a false intimacy that wouldn't outlast the duration of the appointment. Lizzi knew because she used the same cheap trick herself.

The doctor rubbed her hands together. 'Cold hands,' she said. 'Professional liability.' She pushed her palm and the flats of her fingers firmly into Lizzi's abdomen, palpating the top of her growing uterus, working her way around the quadrants of her belly. The coolness of the doctor's hands gave Lizzi some respite from the over-comforting heat of the surgery.

She shut her eyes and breathed deeply. She was tense, frustrated, worried that she would be late for the meeting. No wonder her blood pressure was up. The meeting was important. There was so much to discuss. Whether she could appeal her mark for this placement, if she could defer the rest of her exams for this year. She tipped her head up to tell the doctor she had to get going but, as she did, a searing pain shot through her abdomen, her chest, into her right shoulder. She gasped and sank back down.

The doctor lessened the pressure but left her hand resting on Lizzi's belly. She tested the same part again, pressing more gently this time, easing her fingers into Lizzi's muscles, down into the organs below, working from the midline to the angle of her ribs.

'Aah, aargh, there.' The pain bore through into Lizzi's back, up into her shoulder and her neck. She wanted to vomit.

For the second time that morning, a cuff was fastened round Lizzi's arm and the machine clicked into action. Her elbow, forearm, the edge of her hand tingled as the cuff inflated. As the pressure increased, the pump rattled, forcing out air until the resistance was too great. When the cuff began to deflate, loosening slowly, her pulse hammered at the crook of her elbow as her blood battered its way past the dwindling obstruction, and then nothing again as it ran freely. With a cough, the cuff expelled the last of the air.

The doctor ripped open the Velcro fastening and untangled the rubber tubing.

'Well?' Lizzi shook her hand loose, imagining her blood being shaken to her fingertips. She flexed her fingers two times, three times. They were sore and swollen, she couldn't bend them properly, as if the air in the sphyg had been ballooned into them.

'Still on the high side.' The doctor's voice had changed. Less practised congeniality, more stern professionalism.

While the doctor prepared tubes for blood samples, Lizzi stared at the ceiling tiles. One of them was slightly out of place, tipped up on the lip of its aluminium frame, like someone had been caught peeking behind it and replaced it in a hurry. She wondered what was hidden above the fake ceiling, what was there that wasn't supposed to be seen. The health centre was only a few years old. It must be electric cables and venting systems, telephone and computer lines, the mechanics no doubt deemed too unhygienic for this antiseptic environment. Instead, a skin of bland synthetic tiles and plasterboard covered the shameful workings.

Lizzi barely felt the needle going into her arm but there was a dull ache as her blood spurted into the pink-topped vacuum tube. A second, bigger tube followed, this one with a light-green lid.

'I'm checking your blood count and that your liver and kidneys are working properly.'

Lizzi nodded. She didn't actually care. She wanted to get to her meeting.

When it was done, she sat up and tucked in her blouse. A scintilla of lights sprayed in front of her eyes. A meteorite shower. The third today already. Her head was pounding. She was sure she was getting a migraine.

'I think we should get you looked at properly.'

'It's nothing. Stress, maybe.'

'There is more going on than that.'

Lizzi climbed off the couch. The doctor checked some details on the computer.

'So, we'll get you over to the Southern.'

'When?'

'Today.'

'But I've got a meeting at uni in a minute.'

'It's important.'

'So is my meeting.' It was more important. If she didn't sort things out, everything she had worked for was in jeopardy.

'Elizabeth, Lizzi. It is vital that you are assessed at the hospital as soon as possible. You have pre-eclampsia. It is dangerous for you and for your baby.'

Lizzi knew the doctor's words were meant to impress on

her the seriousness of the situation but she was too wound up to care.

'I'll ask reception to call a taxi for you. Did you come alone? You ought to let the father know.'

'My dad works overseas.' Lizzi saw the confused expression on the doctor's face. 'Oh, I see. Sorry. I'm not with the father.'

The doctor checked the computer files again. 'Your birthing partner. Robin Stevenson. Shall we contact him?'

'No, it's okay. I'll let him know later. Once I know what's happening.'

'Wait in reception for the taxi. Drink some water while you're waiting.'

'I don't need a taxi. There are buses that go straight to my house.'

'You don't understand. I want you to go directly to hospital. And I'd be far happier if you were accompanied.'

Lizzi shook her head. There was no one to go with her. Her head was woozy. 'What about my things?'

'Someone can pick them up later.'

'No,' she said weakly. She had a picture of Rob going through her drawers and wardrobe, through the bathroom cabinet and her work stuff, trying to decide what he should bring. He looked confused and uncomfortable, too big and out of place in her bedroom. He wouldn't know which knickers she would want, which of her bras still fitted her, where her emergency visiting pyjamas were. He wouldn't know where her moisturiser was or that she needed a new head on her electric toothbrush or that the tube of Colgate wasn't hers. He wouldn't know that she was allergic to the lime shampoo that was still sitting next to the bath. Or that the Molton Brown shower gel was for special occasions only and it was Boots for every day. Or that she would need her dental floss and her razor for shaving her legs. And that she wouldn't be able to sleep without the photo of her mum she kept in her bedside cabinet. The only person who would know all that was Finn.

'Try not to worry,' the doctor said, guiding her out of the examination room. 'Most cases of pre-eclampsia have a positive outcome.'

Lizzi swallowed hard. There was a threat in that *most*.

30

Portrait of a Courtesan

The last day of the Easter break arrived too soon for Esme. Half the things she had intended to do were still left to be done. Top of this list of intentions was to spend time with all the boys together, but so far that had amounted to a single visit to the cinema. With Paddy and Charlie she'd taken trips to the park and to see their grandparents and up to Loch Lomond, but it had been almost impossible to coax Frankie from his room.

For years now, Esme had worried about her feelings for her oldest son, worried that he could see how difficult she found him compared to the others, worried that what she felt for him was a love born from duty rather than a love for the child himself. But the seconds when she thought she'd lost him had made everything clear. It was not duty. Her love for him was absolute. Integral to who she was and whoever she would become. The horror of almost losing him had been a gift. She tried telling him but he wasn't ready to hear. But she would keep telling him. And keep telling him.

Dermot worked the two weeks of the school holidays. At night when he came home, he retreated to his basement den to play console games or listen to music and Esme was glad of it. She couldn't look at him. Whenever she did, what she saw instead was the image of him slumped over the steering wheel of the BMW. Each time she thought about it, each time she saw Frankie stepping out in front of the car, she got palpitations and tunnel vision and played the scene through to a fictional end where it did not end quite so happily. And it wasn't the terror and relief that had been on Dermot's face when he had braked in time that Esme saw in this version, but the adolescent leer in Kassia's direction that had been on it the instant before. She would never forgive him. Not for that. Not for driving like a boy-racer, or for what he nearly did. And if Frankie's near accident had taught her something about her feelings for her son, it had also taught her another thing much less welcome. How suddenly, precipitously, easily, it was possible to fall out of love with someone.

Gradually over the course of the week, a plan had taken shape in Esme's mind, a half-formed idea to make some right of the terrible situation, an idea that might make some amends for her part in it. So, that afternoon, while the boys were playing downstairs, she sneaked up to her office, quietly shut the door, and opened her laptop.

Her heart was thumping and her cheeks were burning as she typed the words into the search engine. *Kassia escort glasgow.* In truth, she had no idea if her plan would work. She scanned the page of results. There was nothing obvious for Glasgow. Some generic sites. A couple of profiles of girls called Kassia based in London or elsewhere. One or two links to stories that were completely unrelated.

She went back a step, tried a different approach. If she thought about it logically, it was unlikely that Kassia would use her real name. She deleted *Kassia* and searched again. This time she was flooded with results. All Over Scotland, Number One in UK, Incalls, Outcalls, Independent Escorts, Adult Companions, Europe's Best Girls. For no other reason except to be decisive, she rejected the first few and ran through the list, arbitrarily choosing a site that was Glasgow-based. When she clicked the link, she was plunged into a gallery of almost naked girls, pouting and posing in high heels and black micro-lingerie.

Esme scrolled through the pictures, fascinated, transfixed, acutely aware of her own voyeurism. Some of the girls were beautiful, with perfect bodies, their photos tasteful and discreetly erotic. There were girls with their faces in extreme profile or partly obscured behind long hair to hide their true identity, but others were not shy about pouting directly at the camera, faces and everything full frontal, only their private parts hidden behind a strategically crossed leg or fingers that were pretending to masturbate. An ad popped up at the side of the screen giving Esme the chance to upload her own profile. Briefly, she imagined herself in her sexiest underwear, classy but sexually revealing, posing for the gallery. She let her hand linger for a moment on her breast and felt the tingling in her nipple rush through her body, turned on by the idea of some handsome stranger finding her sexually irresistible. It didn't last. When she reached the bottom of the page, she saw some girls had posted selfies. Squeezing their breasts together or offering up their pert young backsides while they twisted to look at themselves in the mirror with their phones visible in their hands. It was so amateurish, it was heartbreaking.

Out of curiosity, Esme checked a few of the girls' profiles. There were students, housewives, girls from all walks of life. Mostly in their early twenties but some older, some younger. Local, French, Italian, South American. Oriental, Black and Asian. Not entirely what she had expected. In one profile, the girl said her day job was an estate agent. For her, it was a lifestyle choice. Like Anna, perhaps.

Hoping for something less amateurish, Esme returned to the search results and had a quick glance through what else was on offer. What she found when she did took her aback.

She'd expected it all to be less explicitly sexual, more coy about the definition of escort, but here there was no pretence that they were selling anything other than full-on sex in all its forms. Some sites offered *high class* expertise. Another site written in flowery ungrammatical English, complete with misspelt clichés and exaggerated promises, said they would *endaevour to give you the best arousing experience from our beautiful ladies*. Another stated proudly that they offered *cheap companions for the modern man* as if it was something to boast about. And all the girls horny and up for fun. GFE and OWO included in the price. Esme had to open another tab to find out what the abbreviations stood for. One site she came across offered a directory – a sex directory – of hardcore pictures of prostitutes recently arrived in town. She had a flashback to the days when she lived in London and every phone booth was crammed with flyers for prostitutes. She used to steal them and post them on her flatmate's door to tease him when his mother came to visit, thinking it was harmless fun. She remembered leaving a party in an industrial unit in Hackney at four in the morning and finding the deserted streets covered with the strangest confetti. Hundreds and hundreds of the flyers had been spilt from a delivery van, flyers produced at the printing press in the same industrial estate. At the time it had seemed pretty racy. Now it seemed so innocent in comparison. The flyers had moved online and they weren't handdrawn pictures of provocative silhouettes any more.

Esme told herself she would check one more site because she couldn't face much more of it, and chose one where the Glasgow section was only part of a much larger organisation. Click to enter and agree to the disclaimer. She could hardly bring herself to look at the page. Not just because it was pornographic, truly pornographic, but because the presence of the organisation behind the camera was so evident. This was prostitution as big business. Whatever the claims, these girls were being exploited. There was no screening of clients. You could sign up there and then. Consult the price list and the time slots available. Pick your girls. Bra size, dress size and genuine verified photos. Bodies for sale to be used as desired. And what made it even more shocking, utterly distressing, was that in every case, no matter how intimate or anatomical the pictures, the girls' eyes were whited-out or their faces pixillated.

It was too much. Esme was disgusted at herself for her naivety. There was a chasm between a harmless fantasy of fabulous sex with a handsome stranger and this sordid reality. She should be thankful that she hadn't found Kassia.

Behind her, someone flung open the office door. Esme started. It was Frankie.

'What's that?' he said.

Flustered, Esme folded down her laptop. 'Nothing. Stuff for work.' She smiled. She was pleased to see him. 'Are you okay?'

'Charlie's asking if we can go to the park.'

'The four of us? Lovely. I'll be down in a sec.'

Frankie hung around at the door for a minute. When she didn't open the computer, he left. Esme waited until she heard his footsteps on the stairs and then unfolded the laptop and hurriedly closed down the pages. She shut down the browser and then quickly reopened it. And erased the day's history.

31

The Resurrection of Lazarus

A couple of weeks after his admission, Maurice was transferred from ITU to the high dependency ward to await his operation. And it was the first time since he'd been admitted that Finn had seen him with his eyes open. On Finn's previous visit, Maurice hadn't had an awful lot to say for himself. Something to do with the plastic tube rammed down his windpipe.

'Nice PJs, Mo,' Finn said. The faded blue nylon added a fetching washed-out effect to Maurice's already dishcloth-grey complexion, he felt.

Maurice tweaked the nasal cannula that was hissing small quantities of oxygen directly up his nostrils. 'Infirmary's best. At least I'm out of that damn nightie.'

'I'd shake your hand . . .' Finn said, grinning, but neither was in a fit state to be touched. One was hooked up to a drip hanging from a rickety stand at the head of Maurice's bed, and the other was smudged with bruises and stuck with a ball of cotton wool where a previous drip had died.

'Gonnae help me sit up, son. I'm sprawled here like a paraplegic,' Maurice said, wriggling under the thin cover. Both his pyjama sleeves were splattered with bloodstains and rusty haemorrhagic swirls were heading the wrong way up the plastic tubing of the current drip. An effect, Finn guessed, related to the cushion of saline leaking between the layers of skin which was making the back of Maurice's hand puff up into a cushion and create a blockage. Which was in turn due to the venflon having almost wriggled free of its feeble vein. Haemorrhage. Saline. Venflon. Finn knew all the terms. He was a verified, certified, medicinal expert. Had had the lecture, read the posters, flirted with the nurse. And, as such, his informed opinion was that, in a direct comparison of the clapped-outness of all things venous, Maurice O'Donnell's vessels were on par to rival Tuesday McLaughlin's.

'Come on then, big man.'

Finn hooked his arm through Maurice's and yanked him to a sitting position. Maurice's pyjama jacket flapped open. Small cushioned pads with press studs were stuck to his skin between odd straggles of white chest hair from when he'd been plugged into the heart monitor in ITU, and a gauze dressing was taped above his collarbone to cover the wound where a central line had been when Finn first swung a visit to ITU. His first and – as previously mentioned – only visit up to now, when the nurse specialist had mistaken him for Maurice's nephew, and explained to him the intricacies of the hacksaw traces scraping across the monitors, and the significance of low oxygen saturation and risks of assisted ventilation in a patient with emphysema. In tones loaded with professional sympathy, she'd detailed the complications of septicaemia and how it could make your kidneys pack in and send your blood pressure through your meta-phorical boots. And she'd mentioned other stuff he didn't like to admit to not entirely following about platelets and clotting. Mentioned venous insufficiency which Finn heard as Venus and had set him puzzling over whether his own life had also been blighted by similar insufficiencies. Told him about the drugs they were flooding through Maurice to support his failing systems, and the various different antibiotics they'd tried, and how everything was complicated by concomitant diabetes.

Finn had stood at the end of Maurice's bed, watching the machine breathe for him, and in his head practised using words like concomitant for when he was next in a medical situation requiring gravitas and expertise. He had wanted to tell the nurse that in this case the complex words weren't necessary, that he'd got the hint as soon as he'd copped the ventilator, but he didn't want to trivialise the situation. Finally, in a well-rehearsed whisper of concern, she asked whether the family had considered organ donation. No, not until she'd mentioned it to be honest, Finn had told her, but said that he was more than willing to consider it – even though you couldn't say he was related in the strictest sense of the word – overcome as he was by an altruistic rapture at the thought of donating an organ to pump some life back into his flagging pal (and, to be fair, by a certain degree of confusion engendered by the constant high-pitched bleeping and unremitting high-grade lighting that saturated the ITU). It was ironic that when the call had come this time he'd been more than ready to sacrifice a bit of himself (albeit a kidney or a varicose vein or some other equally expendable appendage), which was either a tremendous reflection on his relationship with Maurice or, given that Lizzi had asked the same of him, a rather tragic retrospective predictor of the outcome of their romance. It was only when Finn read over the consent form that he understood the donation was *from* Maurice, not *for* him. At which point he ripped up the papers and left the unit in disgust. Last week, that was, when all the bods who knew about this sort of caper didn't reckon on Maurice making it. Clearly, they'd never seen the man's recovery capability after an all-night, park-bench bender.

Surrounded by the relative calm and subdued atmosphere of the high dependency ward, Finn sniggered to himself. When you thought about it, you had to pity the poor reprobate who'd been in line for Maurice's parts.

'Bet you're glad to be rid of all that high-tech shenanigans.' Finn plonked himself in the Parker Knoll chair guarding Maurice's bedside. 'All the monitors and shite.'

'To be honest, I cannae say I particularly noticed. Was a tad out of it there for a while.'

'You're telling me.' Finn was surprised to hear the cracks in his voice. He wanted to tell Maurice how he'd barely left his side, how he'd stuck by him and maintained a constant and faithful vigil, but he couldn't fully trust himself to lie.

'Hey, laddie. Dinnae get yerself worked up. It's going to be fine.'

Finn sniggered and wiped his nose. 'It's not that, you daft git. I'm not worked up. I'd sorted a deal on your body parts, that's all, and you stuffed it up by rallying.'

Maurice smiled at him with eyes so vacant and watery that Finn wondered if his cognitive abilities were being diluted by all the fluids that were flowing into him. Except, of course, they weren't.

'Is this supposed to be running?' Finn said, checking the non-functioning infusion. 'Will I get a nurse? Get her to sort you out?'

'Och, no, son. Leave them. Busy saving lives.' Maurice shifted a bit to get comfortable. 'Say what you like about the NHS, the poor buggers who work here are grafters. They've been really good to me, so they have, what with all their fancy medicaments and whatnot. Pity it means I'm getting my foot chopped aff, but.'

All sorts of suitable sick adjuncts were skirting Finn's tongue but somehow he couldn't find the will to spit them out. Instead, he sat in silence for a while, listening to the sounds of the ward. The chatter of visitors over the hum of the TV, the swish of curtains and the scrape of chairs being pulled closer to beds, the rustle of polythene-wrapped supermarket flowers.

'Is it just me, Finjay,' Maurice said eventually, 'or does ahbody in here look like the living deid?'

'Nah, there's one or two who are definitely the dying dead.'

'Aye, precisely. Talking of whom, where's Vadge today?'

'I tell you what, Mo. I'm missing you, man. I need you to take him out of my hair. He's doing my head in.'

As Finn went on to explain, Caravaggio was making his life an unmitigated nightmare. No exaggeration. Without Tuesday's pills, he was even more of a pain in the arse than usual. Of course, Maurice knew already how Caravaggio had taken to the drink, but he didn't know that the man had polished off both bottles of whisky and yet wasn't prepared to step a foot outside the church hall for replenishments without his buddy Maurice to accompany him (two chibs and the wimp was still scared of the locals). Maurice didn't know how the odorous insalubriate hung about stinking like a sewer, putting Finn off his work and whining incessantly about one exaggerated inanity after another. He'd even had the audacity to accuse Finn of procrastination and other such profanities, and, worse (impossible though it was to credit it), of being an underachiever. Underachiever? Get to fuck. That from a loser who had sucked every seventeenth-century Catholic dick he could get his lips round and still not got a papal commission. The truth (as Finn made a point of pointing out) was that Vadge had underachieved for the whole of post-Renaissance Rome. Plus, Maurice didn't know how, on the personal hygiene

front, things had actually deteriorated if that was even possible (had he mentioned that already?) and that if Vadge
didn't take a bath soon, even the lice inhabiting the seams of
his cloak were going to leave in protest. Finn broke off
before he got to the part about how the priest had banned
them from entering the church in an attempt to protect his
supplies of candles and liquor, and stood up to give a young
woman in surgical scrubs access to Maurice. It turned out
she was the anaesthetist.

'Aye, hen, I know,' Maurice said. 'The gas man.'

She checked Maurice's venflon, fiddled with the giving
set, closed off the drip. Told him she'd re-site the whole
thing before the op and that she'd be back shortly with his
pre-med. On the way out, she passed Midge lolloping across
the ward with a bunch of grapes in his hands and a *Gazette*
under his arm. They smiled at each other.

Midge eyed Finn warily as he greeted his uncle and kissed
him on the forehead. He dumped the grapes and the *Gazette*
on the bedside locker and sat on the edge of the bed. 'What's
with the stick-on nipples, Uncle Maurice?' he said.

'Hey, hey, laddie. Hands aff. And mind the plumbing.'

'Huh?'

'You're sitting on the man's catheter,' Finn pointed out.

'Oops, sorry.' Midge jumped up and spotted the collection bag. 'Wow, look at all that pish. How much d'you think
that is?' He picked the bag up on its stand and read the scale.
'Two thousand, three hundred millilitres. Is that good? It
seems like a lot. Is it okay to pick it up? It's no going to go
back in, is it?'

Finn clenched his jaw. Since the latest drama with Kassia,
even an infinitesimal instantaneous instant in the kid's company was a lifetime too long. Quite frankly, the boy was a
cret-tard.

'It is good though, eh no? Considering they said your kidneys had near enough packed in when you were in ITU.'

And just because he understood the connection between kidney function and urine output didn't, in Finn's opinion, make him any less of a cret-tard.

'Tell you what, it's amazing how much can come out without you feeling a thing. At least until some wee tatty like young Michael here interferes with it,' Maurice said, playfully clouting his nephew's ear. He lifted up the covers and rearranged his nether regions. 'Drags on my Jap's eye, if you know what I mean.'

Finn leant over the bed and grabbed a handful of grapes from the locker. Given what the docs had said about how close Maurice had come to his grand finale, he would have thought any reminder at all that he was alive – however racist – would have been reassuring. He sat back down and languidly tossed grapes into the air as a demonstration of skill for Midge's benefit. Unfortunately not a single one landed in his mouth. The misfires accumulated on the linoleum.

'Can I have a grape, Uncle Maurice?'

'Of course you can, you divvy. What are you asking for?'

Midge bit into a grape and held it up to show Maurice. 'Look at this, right. They are meant to be seedless but I can see a pip.' He dug out the offending item with his fingernail and squidged it between his fingers. 'It's soft. Look. Grape sperm.' He held out his fingertip for Maurice to look at. 'At least they'll be able to make baby grapes.'

Finn scowled. What was the kid doing bringing up seeds and sperm and babies when Finn had specifically put thoughts of Lizzi and Rob to the back of his mind and beyond? Frankly what Michael knew or didn't know regarding Finn's ex-girlfriend and ex-best mate was not the issue here. There was no excuse. Despite his best effort, though, Finn found himself unable to avoid listening to Midge witter on about where Maurice was going to stay when he got out of hospital, that Maurice should come and stay at their house, that him and his mum could look after Maurice, that Uncle Maurice should do this, Uncle Maurice should do that. All in all, Finn was happy to remark that Uncle Maurice didn't look overly convinced.

'Do you not think he'd be better off in his own gaff,' Finn said. 'Leanne'll look after him. She'll be in her element, keeping him under control. It's not as if you'll be nipping off down to the Vaults for a quick one, is it, Mo? After the butchers have been at you this afternoon, you'll be too legless to get legless.' Finn sniggered at his own joke and took another handful of grapes. He caught Midge glaring at him. 'What's up with you?' The kid had a face on like Finn had just eaten a kitten.

Before Finn had the chance to have the nature of his crime fully elucidated, the ward doors squeaked open and the surgeon swept in. His appearance was accompanied by a communal intake of breath. Finn could have sworn the man was literally sucked down the ward by the anticipation of his expectant amputees.

Casually, he tossed another grape into the air. Maurice farted. Midge grinned at the anaesthetist who arrived at the bed seconds before the surgeon. She had brought a cardboard tray with a fresh venflon, a glass vial of saline and two syringes – one of which was still in its wrapper, the other, half filled with chalky liquid.

'Maurice O'Donnell?'

'Aye.'

'Mr Khan, consultant surgeon. I'll be doing your operation. I take it you understand what's going to happen?
We'll take the foot off directly below the knee—'

'That's no my foot. That's half my frigging leg.'

Mr Khan looked at the anaesthetist for help but she was
busy with Maurice's drip, pulling out the spent cannula,
checking the rest of his arm for an undamaged site.

'As I was saying, we'll take the leg off below the knee.
You'll be back in ITU for a day or two, and then – all being
well – back on the ward soon after.'

'All being well? I have to say, doc, you're making me a
tad nervous.' Maurice winked at Finn and Midge. 'Mr Khan,
you say. Mister not Doctor? Are you sure you're qualified
to do this?' Maurice's oxygen cannula slipped from his nose
on to his upper lip. He shoved it back in and turned to the
anaesthetist. 'You can tell me, hen. Is he properly qualified?
Mr Khan or Mr Khan't.'

Finn tossed another grape into the air and again failed to
catch it. Bored of the effort, he shoved a handful in his
mouth and popped open the skins. A carnage of jelly flesh
and sweet juice sloshed over his tongue. In the background,
the surgeon was ranting on about the gravity of Maurice's
situation and fulminating septicaemia and gangrene and
titrated insulin infusions and other medical terms and how
if they didn't amputate the offending limb it was basically
(at least in Finn's interpretation of the surgeon's
medic-speak) curtains for Maurice.

Maurice was listening carefully, nodding wisely as was his
habit. When the surgeon reached the end of his spiel,
Maurice glanced quickly at Finn but, when he saw he
couldn't speak from the number of grapes crammed in his
mouth, turned instead to his nephew and said, 'Young
Michael, is my leg offending you?'

'I'm pretty sure I heard it swear when the doc came in, Uncle Maurice. I wouldnae say I was actually offended, but.'

'There's no doubt you two comedians are related,' the anaesthetist said, flushing Maurice's newly inserted cannula with a syringe full of saline. Maurice and Midge exchanged grins. All at once, Finn's blood ran cold. It was his vein that had been sluiced, his vessels abluted. The cold liquid swilled through his circulation, leaving eddies of swirling blood cells in its wake.

It wasn't on. He wasn't here to get sidelined. They owed him big-time. He'd been ready to donate an organ. If the actual family wasn't going to take the situation seriously, he would have to take over in their place. Finn gulped down the half-chewed grapes and bombarded the surgeon with questions about risks, complications, recovery, rehabilitation and, importantly, when Maurice could next go down the pub.

'With your permission, Mr O'Donnell, perhaps the young man would like to have a chat with me. You are . . .?'

'Finn J. Garvie. Artist.'

'I see. I meant, are you Mr O'Donnell's son?'

As good as, Finn was on the point of admitting, but Midge interrupted him. Played the next-of-kin card. The fucking joker.

The surgeon swept Midge into a side room to have a chat. Dejected, rejected, abjected, Finn watched the registrar push Maurice's pre-med into the new venflon. The liquid was plaster thick. This time, it didn't swirl. It seeped and creeped, dribbled and dawdled, burning the walls of Finn's veins as it crawled through his body ablating his nerves.

When the anaesthetist had gone, Maurice asked Finn if he didn't think it was kind of funny.

'What?' Finn wasn't finding anything kind of funny any more.

'How she thought me and wee Michael were related.'

'You are.' Like nephew like uncle. The pair of them fucking imbetards, creteciles. The docs wouldn't need much of the pre-med to anaesthetise Maurice. Between him and his nephew there was probably less than one neurone to knock off.

Maurice didn't seem to be aware of how little Finn wanted to listen. He rambled on, muttering and stuttering regardless. And it turned out that, after all the next-of-kin stuff, Maurice and Midge weren't blood-related at all. Young Michael was adopted. Or sort of adopted, Maurice said. Sort of. What the fuck? As far as Finn was concerned the *sort of* was irrelevant. Adopted meant adopted. Bottom line: the kid had no more claim to Maurice than Finn did. So much for their kindred spirit and family ties and shared gift for comedy. Maurice and Midge were no more alike than two peas and a fucking trombone. But Finn didn't care. Why should he care? He had his own family issues to contend with.

'It just goes to show.'

'Goes to show what?' Finn wasn't in the mood any more. He'd gone out of his way to visit when he could have been – should have been – using his energy to get Kassia back on board. He wanted to tell her he had reconsidered the picture, that he had chosen a different subject, one where she could wear her dress and flaunt it. He'd promise further financial remuneration even if that put him in a tricky spot. After the splurge on Maurice's taxi ambulance, he was in a delicate situation, that was to say completely fucking stony, and his old doll had refused to advance his allowance.

'Goes to show what?' he repeated snappily.

'It's who brung you up what counts. No who popped you out.'

'If you say so.' It made no odds in Finn's case. One and the same, and neither who he wanted them to be. Even the bloodline he'd been proud of had turned to shit. And all this talk of families and babies was too aggravating. Like picking a scab without any of the pleasure of eating it. He had to stop listening before he thought about Lizzi again.

Maurice was still blethering, his tongue made flabby by the pre-med. No wonder Leanne cracked from time to time, Finn thought. All he wanted now was for Maurice to give it a rest, quit harping on and on about his precious nephew. Did he not realise how insulting it was? Finn demonstrated his interest by yawning loudly while simultaneously listening for a break in which he could make his excuses and run. There was some nonsense about the boy wanting a passport, filling out the forms, adoption certificate.

'Problem is the adoption certificate doesnae exist.' Maurice stopped. Evidently an interlude where Finn was expected to participate.

'How not?' The question was an automatism. Finn had no desire to enquire. No desire to be informed.

'Never officially adopted.' Maurice was wide-eyed at his own punchline.

Finn was failing to find even a modicum of appropriate astonishment.

'Folk say my wee nephew is a bit slow, a wee bit on the daft side, but I've never seen it.'

That was because, Finn reckoned – diabetic retinopathy by the bye – on this subject Maurice was wilfully visually impaired. You only had to look at the boy to see what an absolute tool he was.

'It may have taken the lad eighteen years to work out that his parents never properly adopted him, but that doesnae make him thick.'

If it didn't, Finn wondered, what exactly did it make him? He couldn't be arsed even to answer his own question. Another adoption story was itching his memory.

'You know, he still calls himself by the name she gave him. Makes it tricky for his ma and da.'

Finn was still at it. Scratching a festering, scabby tattoo of a tiny blood-sucking insect.

'It's all he's got of her. A wee note she left for him. That's where the Midge business comes from.'

Fuck, fuck, fuck. Of course. How could he have been so blind? So blind he couldn't see what was tattooed on the inside of his eyelids or, to be exact, on the inside of Tuesday McLaughlin's elbow crook. Finn grinned. Inside he was hooting. He could barely contain himself. He was bursting to interrupt but Maurice wouldn't shut up. Chuntering on about how it had all been kept secret, who the kid's real mother was.

'From all accounts, the lassie was only a wean herself.'

While Maurice recounted what he knew of the story – drug addict, baby in intensive care, the lassie disappearing – Finn matched all the significant points with his theory. Every piece fitted.

Time was a sneaky bastard when you thought about it. Forget maternal instinct and all that shite, the sad truth was there was no way Tuesday would ever have recognised her kid if she'd only ever seen him for a few days when he was born. Especially if she was out of it. How many folk were recognisable from their baby pics if you hadn't seen them grow up over the years? Tuesday would never have recognised her boy. Not ever. Never. Even if she met him in a chip shop.

'Why wasn't it official?' he asked Maurice. 'Was it illegal or something?'

But Maurice was fading. His eyelids were fluttering. He was fighting the artificial sleep of his pre-med. Finn had to lean in to hear. He heard stuttering phrases that started and didn't finish. Phrases that looped off into irrelevancies. He glanced over to the nurses' station. Midge was chatting up the anaesthetist.

'Leanne's sister always wanted kiddies,' Maurice said.

Finn bit his tongue. He wanted to shake the information out of Maurice, grab it, store it. He had a strong sense that he could use it but he hadn't figured out entirely what for. There was something about money changing hands between the lassie's teacher and the lassie's mother, and the teacher not so innocent as he made out.

From the nurses' station, Midge glared at Finn suspiciously. Finn tried one last push to extract the final details.

'Come on, Mo. What else?'

'Young Michael only came to Leanne's sister because she was best pals with the teacher's missus . . . needed to keep her sweet . . . must have guessed he'd been putting it about.'

In summary, then, if Finn understood correctly, Tuesday's old doll sold the kid for lunch money to the PE teacher and he passed it to his wife's best friend, who just happened to be Leanne's sis. Fuck. You really had to pity Tuesday McLaughlin. The lassie had been searching for her son down all the official channels, reckoning the teacher bloke had sorted it properly, legally. But if this Michael was her Midge, and he wasn't actually adopted, there were never any records of him for her to find. And no record of her for him to find. However much either of them wanted it – if they wanted it – they would never have found each other.

It was lamentable, pitiful, tragic.

And a fucking magnificent result for Finn. In one stupendous swoop, he had a way to sort his predicaments. Even when they'd simply been talking child abuse, it had seemed pretty far-fetched that the gym teacher would want to abet Tuesday in any way with her search. Now it had turned out he'd brokered the kid, there was absolutely no chance. Which meant Finn basically had the monopoly on the critical info, and left him free to trade Midge's whereabouts with Tuesday for pills (to drug Caravaggio back to a stupor), and induce Michael-Midge-whatever-he-wanted-to-be-called to entice Kassia back (without the fear of Caravaggio disgracing him) in exchange for the gen on the requisite papers for his passport.

It was genius.

'What is it, Finjay?'

'All good, Mo. All good.'

And it was. The day could not have turned out better.

A second later, the porter came crashing through the doors with the trolley. Midge rushed over to join them.

'Okay, Uncle Maurice.'

Maurice started, suddenly alert to what he had given away. 'But I wouldnae be able to say one way or another.'

'Say what, Uncle Maurice?'

'Nothing, nothing, he's wittering.' For the first time in his life, Finn had the urge to start a sentence with 'I say.' *I say, young man, you wouldn't like to pimp out your young lady prostitute friend on my behalf in exchange for the lowdown on your heroin-addicted, fucked-up, birth mother, would you? Would you?* There was something in the way Midge was glowering at Finn that suggested to him the answer would be no.

Gently, the porter and nurse transferred Maurice on to the trolley. Midge leant over and hugged Maurice and whispered something in his ear.

Maurice turned to Finn with a strange light in his eyes. 'I want you pair to look out for each other, mind.'

'It's okay, big man,' Finn said. 'We can talk when it's over.'

VERMILION

32

The Burial of Saint Lucy

Maurice's funeral was the Wednesday of the third week of May. The delay was due in one part to the inconvenience of dying over a bank holiday weekend, in another part to the palaver of the obligatory post-mortem demanded by the procurator fiscal after a hospital death, and in a final part to the case review that was organised for the departmental audit. Investigations showed no suspicious circumstances, no clinical error, no negligence, or so Finn was led to believe. The conclusion was that Mr Khan probably *could*, given the right material to work with. Which sadly Maurice had turned out not to be. In the end, nobody – no body – got his organs, which was regrettable, Finn felt, but on balance probably the most seemly outcome, especially if you took into account the state of Maurice's parts after the pathologist had been at them with his scalpel. (Plus, he was pretty sure from episodes of *CSI* that there was also something to do with a blender.)

The memorial service was the slot before lunch, an antecedent to the main event at the crematorium. Finn was surprised that it was to be a burning. He'd have thought Maurice was more a hole in the ground kind of guy, although allegedly the cemetery was full to bursting and you had to book your spot well in advance, so it was entirely possible that Maurice hadn't been organised enough. According to

Caravaggio, even though it was against the rules, he'd specified his ashes were to be scattered on the church garden to fertilise the climbing roses. When he'd ever specified that Finn couldn't imagine. The Maurice Finn knew wasn't one to dwell on the mundanities of death.

Because the laws of space and time (as Finn understood them) dictated that those with the shortest distance to travel were always last to arrive, everyone else was seated by the time Finn and Caravaggio made it to the church. Defying their ban, they sneaked in moments before the show began, just as the deadly organ music reached its final crashing chords. Caravaggio was all for storming down the front for a premium seat, but Finn didn't feel like socialising. Instead, he made them sit at the back, from where he could soak up the atmosphere unobserved and watch the proceedings unfurl without being troubled.

The front few stalls were filled with mourners, and Jed floated between them in his ghostly robes chatting to Leanne and others. Someone had placed a hand-picked posy of late spring flowers in a jam jar on the altar and the violet of the bluebells glowed brightly against the altar cloth despite the grey haze that had crept through the rose window and was blanketing the priest and the congregation. Through the rows of heads Finn could just about make out the grinning face of Maurice in the disconcerting photograph Leanne had placed on his coffin. The photo stood next to a wreath that said – shouted, Finn would go so far as to say – HUSBAND. It hadn't occurred to him until that moment that, if indeed he had happened to want to stake his right to a front-row seat, he ought also to have arranged a wreath. (NEIGHBOUR? PAL? SURROGATE DAD?)

'. . . welcome you all to Our Lady of the Assumption to celebrate the life of our friend and neighbour, Maurice

O'Donnell.' The familial mourners nodded along to the priest's words. Midge was on the very front row, sitting with an old couple Finn guessed were the law-breaking impostor parents, and another pair who were almost certainly the paedo teacher and his missus (their presence enough to suggest that Finn had been correct to assume that Tuesday's manhunt had not resolved itself exactly the way she would have wished).

In his official capacity, Jed's pitch was perfect. A consummate blend, Finn felt, of drone and compassion, particularly as he led the congregation in prayer. Prayers were followed by a short reading, then a hymn (to which Finn and Caravaggio moved their lips but succeeded in not producing any sound by virtue of not expelling a whisper of air from their lungs; the pair of them were both unfamiliar with the hymn and acutely aware of their own limitations when it came to holding a tune), which in turn was followed by a question and answer session to which everyone bar Finn knew the correct responses (although Caravaggio insisted on responding in Latin which was more than a little conspicuous). Finally, Midge gave a reading of such astonishing stiltedness that Finn was unsure whether it was a reflection of his intense emotional discord or his appalling level of literacy. Once the torture was over, Jed thanked him and Midge sat down. Crimson, as per.

'And now I'd like to invite Maurice's wife, Leanne, to say a few words.'

If only Maurice had been there to see how stunningly Leanne was mourning, Finn thought as he watched her stand up and smooth down her skirt. How perfectly dressed she was for the part of the grieving widow without having compromised on the particular style that Maurice found irresistible. In her tight black pencil skirt that hobbled her knees so she couldn't take a pace of more than a few centimetres, and a matching black jacket that was only a touch on the over-tight side. Maurice wouldn't have noticed the several spare back-tyres under her bra line that were visible from behind as she waddled up to take the stage because he would have already been blinded – dazzled – by the anticipation of the amount of bosom to be displayed the moment she turned to face them.

Jed held out a white and gold draped arm to assist Leanne with the steps up to the lectern. Her own white-gold hair crowned her plump cheeks, and her mulberry-painted lips pouted magnificently as she unfolded the arms of the reading glasses hanging from a gold chain around her neck and read a poem she had written herself. Finn sighed wistfully. Leanne didn't hold back on the rhyming couplets. She was out a tad on the metre but Maurice wouldn't have cared. It was truly touching, Finn thought – his eyes stinging a little at the corners – in a crass and corny kind of way.

The Eucharist followed. While Jed recited the prayer and blessed the bread and wine, and took some of it himself, Finn contemplated the meaning of life and death, religion and atheism, and other such trivialities. In the past, he had often wondered what kind of jiggery-pokery could turn wafers into flesh, wine into blood, but, on further consideration, decided it wasn't too different from his own profession. Finn himself had the ability to turn scorched earth and metal ores into flesh and blood, so perhaps there was not such a great divide between himself and the priest as he had always imagined.

While the congregation queued for a snack, Finn picked at the holes in his fraying jeans. He'd fully expected Caravaggio to join the picnickers, but when he asked in hushed tones, Caravaggio sulkily told him that, for now, he wasn't permitted. From what Finn understood, there was still the small detail of mortal sins to fully repent.

Minor distractions by the bye, throughout the entire performance Finn had barely been able to take his eyes off the coffin. Whether it was because he was hoping for a soap-opera-style resurrection, or because it seemed to him that the real Maurice O'Donnell had simply left the building (nipped out for a piss behind the rhododendron bushes no doubt), he couldn't get his head around the fact that the person who had been Maurice really *was* there, inside the box. Before he allowed himself to metaphorically lift the lid – to actually picture Maurice lying inside – there were some questions to be considered. Like, for example, whether they had actually got round to amputating Maurice's bad foot before he popped his clogs. And related to that, whether they had put his pieces back together again after the post-mortem. It was troublingly feasible that Maurice's journey to the afterlife would be impeded by single-leggedness or by having had his bits put back in the wrong order. But, then again, maybe it didn't matter if they were just going to chuck him on the fire. Finn decided he would discuss the matter with Caravaggio after the service. For reasons unfathomable, it felt like something he would know.

Once he'd put his existential (or more precisely, non-existential) questions to one side, Finn settled down to enjoy the closing scenes. He was pretty taken aback at how much Caravaggio was enjoying the show (in a weepy, overtly sentimental way). The only minor spoiler for Finn was the clear view of the back of Rob's shaved head throughout, but he cheered himself up by aiming pot shots with an imaginary slingshot at the soft bit under his occiput where the two knobbly bits of skull jutted out. Finn had half expected Lizzi to come as Rob's plus one but, thankfully, she was conspicuous by her lack of being there.

As the memorial grew to a close, the priest said some words about the enormous contribution Maurice had made to both the spiritual and communal well-being of the church. About how Maurice had always been ready to lend a hand, offer his practical skills and his time, his thoughtfulness and his care. About how God would accompany him on his journey to heaven. Despite the sobriety of the occasion, both Finn and Caravaggio couldn't help but laugh. Out loud. Physically doubled over in their pews so that Caravaggio's sword clanked off the ventilation grille. In unison, the front two rows turned to glower at them. Except for Rob, who wouldn't even look at Finn. A flush of righteous indignation passed from Finn to Caravaggio. They knew Maurice better than anyone and the man would have been the first to laugh at the shite being spoken about him (once Finn had explained why it was funny) had he not been a little too indisposed to share the joke.

Finally it was the hostility and hypocrisy of the mourning crowd that made Finn decide not to attend the crematorium. Or at least that's what he told himself. He didn't particularly relish the idea of going alone, especially given the way the undertaker's lackey was firing looks in his direction, and although he wasn't squeamish in that way himself, he had a suspicion Caravaggio might find the whole fire and brimstone element a little too close to the flame. Finn was pretty sure that once you were reduced to ashes, it fucked your chances of making a comeback.

For want of a better idea, the two of them made their way back to the church hall over the low sandstone wall (Caravaggio taking it with a jaunty vault, spirits entirely invigorated by the service). Overhead, hazy grey clouds had wrapped the sun in cuckoo spit and an early summer drizzle settled on Caravaggio's cloak and Finn's bare arms, and together they moseyed across the blooming garden where, in the beds under new sprouts of fern, the last of the primulas were curling at the edges, their petals stained brown where the rain had dragged them into the earth, and rhododendron bushes weighed with buds balled into tight fists were poised to explode into slaps of violent colour.

In the hall, the after-gig party was already set up: several bottles of blended whisky (a lesser quality than that to which Caravaggio was habituated, as he pointed out with disgust) and a couple of bottles of sweet sherry for the non-drinkers; crisps in paper bowls and platefuls of triangular sandwiches. Caravaggio ploughed right in.

'Death certainly wets my appetite,' he said, chomping his way through a fish paste sandwich, and wedging the sherry bottle between his stocky thighs to unscrew the lid with his free hand. Doughy white bread lined his teeth.

'I think you'll find it's *whets*,' Finn said, feeling quite ill.

By the time he'd polished off a plateful of sandwiches and tanked the best part of half of the bottle of amontillado, Caravaggio was slurring. After his perky start, he came over all maudlin. Said he had clearly been discriminated against if his comrade-in-arms had gone straight to heaven (Finn assumed Caravaggio meant Maurice, although if you were talking arms, Finn was pretty sure that Maurice wouldn't have known one side of a blade from another until he sliced his own off at the elbow) when he, Caravaggio, hadn't been afforded the same lenience. Wouldn't let up about how nobody had taken into account the mitigating circumstances, how poorly judged he'd been (on earth as it was in heaven), and how it was unfair, unjust and unmerited that he was stuck in this miserable purgatory with only Finn Garvie for company (especially when purgatory was pretty much out of fashion these days).

Frankly, Finn thought Caravaggio only had himself to blame. He'd murdered his best mate after a to-do over a lassie, so he couldn't really complain if he was asked to do the time. Finn wasn't that keen on Rob these days, but he wasn't sure he'd go quite so far as to kill the bloke.

'I'd venture to suggest that the big man upstairs is all-seeing, all-knowing,' he said, 'so the circumstances can't have mitigated too strongly.'

Thus ended the temporary truce established over Maurice's coffin. Caravaggio got unjustifiably shirty, blaming Finn for having to be in Glasgow in the first place, especially given there were serious questions over Finn's descendancy (Finn demanded angrily if Caravaggio was calling his granny a liar, but didn't follow it through because Caravaggio had his hand on his pommel). Caravaggio churned on and on: about how he was well down on the indulgences he was supposed to have earned; how he hadn't penanted enough, mainly because Finn's work – in his not-uninformed consideration – was basically beyond redemption (a claim that Finn put down to artistic rivalry and didn't allow to upset him greatly); and, much as he missed his drinking buddy and not to speak ill of the dead, it was indisputable that Maurice had led him astray.

'And I cannot even numb the torture with a satisfactory repose. I am cursed to endure the remainder of my sentence being sucked off by a slavering nonentity with less backbone than a leech.'

'I think you'll find it's *sucked dry*,' Finn said. 'Or *sucked up to*,' he added after a pause, so appalled at the image of himself on his knees in front of Caravaggio's scrotum-hugging breeches he didn't have the wherewithal to counter the other insults. 'Prepositions. Nightmare. I have the same problem in Italian.'

'A slavering *pedantic* nonentity who refuses to sort my medication,' Caravaggio said, ignoring Finn's half-hearted attempt to find some common ground.

Regarding the drugs, Caravaggio's comment wasn't entirely fair and Finn said so. He had spent all his spare hours between selfies and praying for Kassia to return watching out for Tuesday at the pharmacy, but she'd clearly ditched the programme and pissed off who knew where. Which was regrettable on several counts, but there wasn't a hell of a lot he could do about it.

'Surely you have a postulation of her whereabouts.'

'You know what?' Finn said, pouring the few crumbs of smoky bacon that Caravaggio had left straight into his mouth from the bowl. 'If you cut the abuse for more than two seconds, I might have the head room to think.'

Aiding Caravaggio's sleep wasn't the only reason Finn had to find Tuesday McLaughlin. Maurice's precipitate departure had distracted him from his well-construed plan. Notwithstanding the slight issue that Midge refused even to exchange pleasantries with him these days, there was still a possibility, Finn reckoned, that if he reunited Tuesday with her Michael-Midge boy, he would have the kid in a stranglehold of obligation (enforced he would hope by Miss McLaughlin herself) and Midge would be compelled to contact Kassia on his behalf.

'Come on, laughing boy. Time to track down our pusher friend.'

As Finn expected, Caravaggio put up a forceful argument to stay put, the basis of which was that the bottle of sherry was only half empty. There was a persuasive element to his reasoning, but Finn wasn't awfully keen for the righteous family to meet Caravaggio when they got back from stoking the pyre. There was no way he was drowning in the reflective indignity of other people's assumptions when they met the delinquent close up. A fleeting wisp of anxiety that Kassia might show while he and Caravaggio were out made Finn come out briefly in goosebumps but they didn't last. He had long since forced himself to stop expecting her to turn up spontaneously. Had had to stop daring to hope, because with every passing no-show, his spirit had disintegrated a little more.

'Take the bottle with you, if you must. Maybe consider leaving the chib?' Finn wasn't particularly keen to court trouble with major armoury. Even in seventeenth-century Rome, it was illegal to carry such heavy weaponry. He made it clear that if Caravaggio got stopped by the feds with a chib that size, he was up shit creek, so to speak, and there was no way Finn was paddling to the rescue. Predictably, Caravaggio chose to dismiss the advice and flounced off to the garden to behead the rhoddies.

Finn was on his way out of the front door to find him when he bumped into the funeral party returning from the crematorium. Literally, give or take a few inches. It was Rob he encountered first. He was holding the door open, smiling and chatting with his hand lightly resting on the suited arm of the funeral director's assistant. When Rob saw Finn, he lifted his hand, hung back. 'I'll catch you up,' he muttered, and the assistant straightened Rob's tie and smiled at him. In a manner which, in Finn's opinion, was unnecessarily pally.

Next up were the fake adopters, the Spences and Leanne. They trooped past Finn without acknowledging him. Only Leanne glanced his way.

Finn took the opportunity to pass on his wishes. 'Sorry for your loss and all that shite,' he said, leaning towards her to kiss her cheek. Leanne gasped. Behind her, Jed shook his head in despair, and took Leanne's arm. He swept her away and fired a glance of sympathy at his brother before the fire doors swung shut behind them.

Rob coughed. Squeezed over his tight collar, the thick rope of his carotid artery hammered under one of the mythical beasties.

'Finn.' Half question, half accusation.

Finn shrugged. He had nothing to say to the guy. Rob was a hundred times more dead to him than Maurice was. He might as well not exist. A fleeting expression of genuine hurt crossed Rob's face when Finn said as much, and Finn only just stopped himself sniggering. For such a brute of a man, Rob could be surprisingly comical.

Outside, the air was still and balmy. The rain had stopped and the sun was making an attempt to batter through the cloud. Caravaggio was near the bay tree, taking sword swipes at its bendy branches. Finn spotted Midge sitting on the garden bench halfway down the path. His head was bowed, and he was turning his phone around in his hand, and his face was even more blotchy than usual. It appeared he had been crying. Finn sat down beside him and rolled a cigarette.

'Want one?'

Midge shook his head. The blotches on his face merged to one scarlet stain.

Finn lit his cigarette. Puffed dramatically on it, looking at the tip every now and then to ensure it was still burning. Midge, meanwhile, drummed his leg nervously, making the garden bench rattle.

After a few minutes of stalemate, Midge stopped his leg-drumming and shifted to stand. Wordlessly, Finn persuaded him to sit back down. The old hand on the shoulder

approach had a high degree of success, he noted, as he signalled to Caravaggio to come over. The shots of amontillado
had done nothing to sharpen Caravaggio's wits because he
entirely failed to understand what was required. It was, Finn
decided, no biggy. The boy he could manage without
back-up. After one final long drag on his cigarette, he ground
the stub into the gravel. Single-handedly rolled a second
(that was to say, using only one hand; it made no sense to
describe a job done by one person as single-handed, Finn
contended, unless that particular person was lacking on the
upper limb front). Lit it. Felt Midge sweating. Decided to act
before they were all swept away in a flood of perspiration.

'Phone.'

There was a squeaky minor protest, but Midge handed
it over. Finn zipped through the contacts to find Kassia. It
would have been faster to have checked the last call, but the
thought didn't cross Finn's mind, distracted as he was by
the sight of his watch – Lizzi's watch, Maurice's watch –
on the boy's bony wrist.

In a few seconds it was done. A message was on its way
asking Kassia if she would model again, telling her how
much Midge liked Finn and that Kassia had a false impression of him, that Finn was a great guy blah blah, and a whole
load of other nonsense.

A couple of nerve-racking minutes later, Kassia beeped
back. *I think about it.* Don't think too long, Finn said to
himself. He chucked the phone back to Midge who shoved
it in the pocket of his anorak. Finn flicked his fag end into
the heather.

'Don't go messing it up now, young Michael,' he said,
giving the boy's knee an affectionate pat.

Michael waited until Finn was almost at the gate before
he fired back with his riposte. 'Fuck off.'

Finn could barely unlatch the gate for laughing.

With the pressure off, Finn was feeling buoyant. Finding Tuesday was now a simple act of charity, of extreme benevolence, on his part. It would benefit both her and Caravaggio, and for that they would be eternally grateful and for ever in Finn's debt. Plus, once Tuesday chucked some tabs in Caravaggio's direction, Finn could get back to work without the whingeing commentary.

United again, Finn and Caravaggio started their hunt in the dosshouses of the West End. In one particularly unappealing place, the arsehole behind the glass partition, who appeared to have his feet glued to the desk, eventually told them (Caravaggio's weaponry a useful aide-memoire) that Tuesday had pissed off. Jumped before she was pushed.

If she was sleeping rough, Finn knew exactly where to find her: beyond the wasteland at Kelvinbridge, where the river tunnelled under Gibson Street. It was the place where Tuesday had once told him she'd spent half her previous life. The place where alkies came to piss away their days, where addicts came to share their blood-borne infections, where rent boys came to blow their earnings. If Tuesday McLaughlin was to be found anywhere, it had to be there.

At the entrance to the tunnel, Finn paused to let Caravaggio catch up. From above, the hum of traffic to and from the university, and breakthrough shouts of students high on the adrenalin kick of finished exams or afternoon sessions in the Union bar came floating down to the river bank. Finn basked a moment in anticipation of the damp underworld ahead. Water trickled over the moss-covered stone walls and the Kelvin flowed into the darkness. It was brisk but not threatening.

'Anyone there?'

Silence apart from the rush of water.

The tunnel stretched ahead an unknown depth. Finn could feel his pupils dilating, sucking in the gloom. He pushed ahead. 'Anyone there? Tuesday? Tuesday McLaughlin?' His voice echoed back at him, thin and damp.

'Wait for me, you precipitous ejaculate,' Caravaggio shouted. 'I might get lost.'

Finn turned round. Caravaggio was silhouetted against the arc of daylight at the mouth of the tunnel, beard unkempt, hair dishevelled, waving the sherry bottle, and looking – despite his protestations – for all the world as if he was completely at home.

'Move your arse,' Finn said.

'I'm hindered by my huge appendage,' Caravaggio double-entendred as he staggered along the towpath, sniggering, with his sword clanking in front of his knees.

Doing his best to ignore him, Finn pushed further into the tunnel and edged his way along the damp arches. The weapon was superfluous. The place was deathly quiet and utterly drained of energy. It was restful, peaceful and Finn wanted to sink into the comfort of it. But there was no sign of anyone. No Tuesday. None of her waster pals who could tell them where she might be. This wasn't the plan. The plan was to find her, to tell her his news, to rejoice in the triumph of her appreciation and humbly accept her heartfelt thanks and her sleeping pills. It was too early in the afternoon for the plan to be a write-off.

Caravaggio clunked to a halt beside Finn and burped loudly. Called Finn a herpes-infested anus for not waiting. His leery sweet sherry breath was sick-making. It was too much. Finn had had enough. A flush of resentment threatened to unhinge him.

At some point fairly soon, he would have to admit that Caravaggio was not the man he wanted him to be. But where was the surprise in that? Nothing ever turned out the way it was supposed to. Everyone let him down. There wasn't a single person he could rely on. Lizzi and Rob had betrayed him. Kassia had deliberately misread him. Tuesday had fucked off to God knows where. Even Maurice had buggered off and left him. Instead he was stuck here with a pissed-up, howfing, social outcast who had turned out to be the antithesis of the bawdy, violent, exorbitant talent he had hero-worshipped for all those years, and it made him feel sick and stupid to admit it. Unwittingly Finn thought back to his conversation with Lizzi, a conversation that had happened in a different life. *Ogni pittore dipinge sè.* If he had learnt anything by this experience so far, it was that that concept was clearly bollocks. For it to be true Caravaggio would be doing the post-Renaissance equivalent of the greeting cards his old doll liked to send. This Caravaggio – this vacuous, slovenly, nauseating fabulist – must have had some PR machine at work to succeed in painting himself as the vicious desperado of the accepted mythology. That and a huge dollop of artistic licence on the self-representation front.

Finn stared into the river, not blinking. A family of ducks paddled past in the gloom. Apart from the odd still-downy feather, the full-size ducklings were as good as indistinguishable from their parents. Unruffled on the surface, below their propeller feet were paddling frantically to steer a route in the drag of the current.

Suddenly, Finn was on the brink of collapse. He was overcome with exhaustion and the effort of fighting. For the last weeks, months, he realised, he had been not so different from those ducklings. Using all his energy to stay afloat while life – inhabited as it was by inconsistent women and renegade accomplices – had constantly dragged him off course.

He groaned and the surface of the river billowed gently like swathes of black silk. At that moment, all he wanted, all he possibly desired, was to fall into its soft folds.

But before he could, a smothered cough crept along the river bank and sank into the moss nearby.

'Was that you?' Finn whispered to Caravaggio.

Caravaggio did not reply.

Cautiously, Finn stepped into the void, patting the dripping walls to feel his way, unable to shake the sense that they weren't alone. His mood swung so violently upwards that he almost retched. He could barely contain the mounting excitement as he pressed ahead into the expanse of black, thinking of his hero's welcome when Tuesday clapped eyes on him, and the astonishing notion that he might actually be genuinely pleased to see her. As he advanced, his ears adapted to the muffled underworld and his skin began to prick from the warmth of other bodies, until he could hear the faintest breeze of displaced air when someone shuffled in their louse-infested bedding and feel the trickle of a cocaine sniff across his skin.

'There are folk here,' he whispered. He could taste the must of stale clothes, smell the rustle of paper bags and the hiss of solvent. He strained his eyes to see what his other senses were telling him.

'I inform you that I am armed and dangerous,' Caravaggio said loudly. His words grated against the steel reinforcements gouging out from the concrete pillars supporting the road above. He performed an elaborate swipe with his sword.

It suddenly occurred to Finn that Caravaggio was bricking it. He reached out a hand to quieten him. 'I don't think we're in danger. I think maybe they're sleeping. It seems a shame to disturb them.'

'I will give you time to reconsider that ridiculous proposition while I find a spot to urinate in peace.' Caravaggio pushed past Finn. Grunts and curses as he tugged his shirt and fiddled with his breeches prefaced the burn of piss. The nerves had clearly got to him, Finn realised. And having hung around with Maurice for so long, he was obviously under the impression that relieving oneself in public was acceptable.

Which evidently it was not. Proof, if it were needed, came in the form of a mild expletive from somewhere under Caravaggio's feet. Which in turn was followed by a rustle of bedding and a scrape of cardboard. A click of a lighter, and a wash of petrol flame swirled past Caravaggio and across the graffitied columns, over Finn, only to settle back on Caravaggio who was standing stupefied over a bundle of bedding and empty lager cans in the angle of the tunnel wall with his dick in his hand. Rudely exposed by the flickering light, Caravaggio let out a high-pitched squeal. Deep in the tunnel, there was a flurry of bats.

Behind the flame, a bare arm covered in tattoos was poking out from a decomposing, pissed-drenched sleeping bag. It belonged to a young guy, sleep-fogged and drug-calm. Gently, he shook his sleeping girlfriend awake and climbed to his feet. The emaciated girlfriend roused herself and slouched amicably beside her boyfriend. Side-on, she disappeared between the cracks in the stone walls.

'We don't want any fuss,' the guy said, kicking one of the empty lager cans towards the river, with an air of such untroubled casualness that it was clear to Finn that he was in fact an extremely proficient and gifted kicker. The can scraped across the paving stones and landed with a cushioned splash in the thick water. It jolted Caravaggio from his dick-holding stupor and he tucked himself back in.

'Do we know you?' the lad said. 'We know you, right?'

Finn half nodded. He knew them all right. They were the missing numbers in the Bingo series. Number Seven: David Beckham. And the girl was as upright and stick-like enough to be Number One. And as he looked around at the row of wasted faces staring up at him from the cardboard city, Finn felt consumed by happiness and regret. Some he recognised, some he didn't. There was Legs Eleven knocking back the Special Brew. And Sweet Sixteen high on crack. Two wee ned boys, their eyes spinning from glue, their grey track-suits grubby with mud, ransacking an old lady's handbag. Not gulls after all, but cygnets. Twenty-two. Finn was laughing and tearing up. It was a truly magnificent display of humanity. Both tragically out of time and beautifully familiar. If only he had another chance.

But the Bingo project was an indulgence. He had to let it go when there were more pressing concerns. 'We're looking for someone,' he said. 'A friend of ours. A lassie. Tuesday, her name is, if you can believe it.' He stopped. Decent again, Caravaggio was clanging his sword off the tunnel wall.

'Wee lassie. So high.' Finn's hand at waist level. 'Skinny. Bleached hair. Tattoo of a midgie on her arm.'

'Tuesday McLaughlin?' (Inside, Finn rolled his eyes. Like there were hundreds of other lassies called Tuesday in this part of town.) 'Aye, we know her. Try the old school at Dowanhill. She's been holed up there for weeks.'

From the tunnel mouth, a set of stone steps cut up to Gibson Street. Caravaggio took them three at a time, re-enlivened by the prospect of imminent pharmaceuticals, and Finn followed in the swirl of his cloak. As they climbed, they were hit by a blast of fat-laden air from the bins in the back lane that ran behind the restaurants. They took Gibson

Street at a pace and turned into University Avenue. The place was crawling with students and Caravaggio was tanking it, weaving between the saunterers, barging shoulders, treading on the heels of shoes, shouting to the crowd to get out of his way. For once, Finn could barely keep up.

By the time they reached the crest of University Avenue, Caravaggio was panting. Dark patches of sweat stained his breeches in the crook of his knees and in the folds of his groin. The warmth of the late afternoon made the smell emanating from him particularly rank, and there was an oily sheen across his face. A glaring contrast to the well-dressed kids lounging on the grass outside the Reading Room in the late sunshine or sitting on the wall beside the library texting, chatting, comparing notes. Confident, privileged, a false sense of their own worth. Finn was as attracted to them as he was repulsed. He tried not to think of Lizzi.

At the bottom of University Avenue, the beeps of the pedestrian crossing harried them to go.

'Get out my frigging way,' Caravaggio shouted into the hordes.

At the entrance to the school grounds, a locked gate barred the way.

'Give me a leg-up,' Caravaggio said. Finn squatted down and interlocked his fingers. It was either the sensation of Caravaggio's sweaty, stinking moccasins resting in his palms, or the anticipation of seeing Tuesday, but Finn's gut looped with nausea. Caravaggio scrambled over the gate, thrusting his round arse uncomfortably close to Finn's face. Finn shook his head to loosen his queasiness, scaled the gate himself, and wiped his soiled hands on the seat of his jeans.

The school grounds were deserted. Soulless, Finn thought. Void. It was the perfect place to let your life unravel. No wonder Tuesday had retreated there.

'Let's check it out,' he said.

All the lower windows and the front entrance to the school were boarded up. It proved too much for Caravaggio. He seized his dagger from his breeches and plunged it into the blockade. Finn left him trying to extricate the blade, raw sewage flowing from his mouth while he, Finn, went off to circle the building and search for a way in. On one of the side windows, the nails had been prised from the plywood board and it was resting against the sash frame. Cautiously, Finn lifted it away. Underneath the window was smashed and the latch accessible. He swallowed to dampen the rush of anticipation. Tuesday was there.

Finn unlatched the window and squeezed head first through the narrow opening into a derelict classroom. His hands scrabbled to reach the floor, and he pulled himself through and scrambled to his feet. There was no furniture, only an old wall clock torn from its wires and propped in a corner. Mouse droppings and pigeon feathers carpeted the spaces between scattered files and exercise books. Behind hidden doors and inside the walls he heard the scratching and scurrying of rats, but there were no human sounds to be discerned. Finn dusted himself off. Among the debris under his feet was a pile of old class registers. He picked one up and blew a cloud of dust from the buff cover. In the sinking daylight, he read the heading. Year VII. Mrs Spence. Inside, columns of neatly printed names and crosses and noughts. Gerrard Stevenson, yes, miss. Robin Stevenson, yes, miss. Further up. Shirley McLaughlin. Shirley McLaughlin? Not here, miss. Years before she had earned her nickname. But Shirley? Finn laughed. The punchline was too obvious.

On cue, the classroom door squeaked open.

'See you still havenae learnt the meaning of privacy,'

Tuesday said, picking her way across the detritus towards Finn. As she neared the window, the shafts of late daylight cut right through her.

'Nice to see you too,' Finn said, although it wasn't. Her matted hair was tied back roughly with an elastic, inches of dark roots showing at the dogleg parting. There were holes in her leggings, her boot had lost its sole completely, and window-side, her face was overexposed and corpse-like. 'Revise that. You look fucking abysmal.'

'Don't look so hot yerself, doll.' Tuesday peered out of the open window, searching for the board to trap in the darkness. 'What d'you want?'

Finn shook his head. There was a smell from her. The sweet smell of opiates. It had the same smell as sex.

'Fuck off,' he said. 'I'm here to see you.'

'So, now you've seen me,' she said, drawing her head back in, empty-handed, glowering at him, latching the window shut. In her pinhole pupils, there were dirty needles and rusty spoons and burnt foil. For the first time since they'd met, Finn saw her as a genuine bona fide lost cause. He turned away to save his eyes.

Fortunately, before he could dwell on the tragedy of it, Caravaggio's round face appeared at the broken window. Tuesday flinched.

'How do I proceed through there without sacrificing my bollocks?' He poked at the spurs of jagged glass.

'You don't,' Tuesday said.

'How are you paying for it?' Finn said, too distracted to pay attention to Caravaggio. 'The smack?' It wasn't what he'd meant to ask. He'd meant to ask how she was, if she wanted anything, food or whatever, why she had left her digs. If she needed them to give the B&B guy a doing or fancied coming out for a cuppy. But he hadn't.

'You're kidding me? Are you my social worker now?'

'No, not at all.' But, Finn realised, he was. More or less. With his knowledge of her situation, his special information. It was a job he didn't want. A responsibility that was too hard to bear. He couldn't tell her what he knew. He couldn't. It would be hideous if Midge met her like this. He didn't want the righteous mob influencing the kid, didn't want Tuesday to be rejected or despised by her own son. It wouldn't be right. Not at all. Whatever the ramifications, he had to withhold for her own good. Cruel to be kind and all that shite.

Outside the window, an impatient Caravaggio demanded that Finn make arrangements to sort out his supply of medication.

'What are you after?' Tuesday asked. 'More of the same?'

'Aye,' Finn said.

Tuesday sneered at them both. 'Youse are fucking transparent. This time, but, cash up front.'

Finn pulled his hair off his face. It was all going wrong. A landslide of fucking wrongness. This month's allowance was reserved to pay Kassia. But if he didn't get the drugs, Caravaggio would be intolerable. He decided to trade on Tuesday's good nature. 'Thing is,' he said. 'I'm a bit short of readies, for the minute.'

'In that case, chubs, you're wasting my time.'

Caravaggio, in response, swore loudly and banged his fist off the window frame. Finn racked his brain for a way to stall.

'Can I paint you?' he asked, surprising himself.

'What?' Tuesday said. 'Have you lost it? Look at me.' She bared her teeth, showing the raw gap, the black neighbours.

Caravaggio leant in through the smashed window to catch a look and snorted. Finn groaned. For some folk, life pissed on you and then pissed on you some more. In Tuesday's case, it had pissed on her an infinite number of times.

'It's distinctive,' he tried. 'Unusual. Plus, you've got sharp features, good definition. You'd be great to paint.'

'Nae fucking chance, matey. Distinctive.' Tuesday shook her head. She was on the verge of tears. 'How could you no have left me be?'

'Look on the bright side,' Caravaggio said offhandedly. 'It's not as if it spoils your looks.'

'Get tae fuck.'

In other circumstances, Finn might have sniggered. But he didn't. Not this time. There was no fire in Tuesday's words.

Caravaggio didn't take the hint. 'Furthermore, it will without doubt improve business. From personal experience, I can attest that fellatio performed by a tart without teeth is infinitely preferable to that performed by a duchess with a full set. And the price should be inflated accordingly.'

Finn was furious. 'For fuck's sake,' he said. 'Why did you have to go and say that?' The lassie had been so close to putting things right. One turn away from a happy ending. It could have all been so different and yet it wasn't. It was too cruel. Too tragic. Too fucking desperate.

'I sought to encourage the woman.'

'She isn't a tart, you titfuck.' Finn turned to Tuesday. 'You're not, are you, T?' He grinned stupidly. He hadn't meant it to sound so much like a question.

'What the hell . . .?' It was almost a whisper.

'Honest, I didn't mean anything by it. I want to help.' The encounter could not have gone worse if Finn had rehearsed it.

'Help? You're kidding, right.' Tuesday spat the words in Finn's face. 'I thought mebbe you'd came here because you possibly gave a toss. But what? Did you come to torture me for laughs? Go on then. Go for it. Finish it off. Break my legs or something. Gouge my fucking eyes out. You're sick, you know that. Sick.' She tapped her finger viciously off her temple. 'You are one fucking sick bastard. Both of youse.'

'No, no, you're wrong,' Finn wailed. 'This stuff, the drugs, the heroin, whatever. You don't have to do it.' He didn't want to leave her here. He wanted to save her.

Tuesday curled her lip over her missing tooth. When she spoke, it was the growl of a cornered rat. 'You know *nothing* about what I have or havenae to dae. You with your piddling wee life and your mammy's money and your fucked-up sense of what is acceptable.'

'No, listen,' Finn started, but Caravaggio leant in further and snatched Tuesday's arm.

'Forget him,' he leered, his chest dangerously close to the jagged glass. 'We can work something out. Maybe, if you can get me some—'

Tuesday shook her arm free and went for Caravaggio. Hands round his neck, practically dragging him off his feet and on to the barbs of glass, screeching right in his face for him to piss off, fuck off, get out of her fucking life, and for a moment Finn thought she might impale him, strangle him. Or that Caravaggio might use his sword against her. But her grip loosened before he was forced to defend himself.

'You rabid bitch,' Caravaggio said, ducking out under the pane, rubbing the bruises round his neck and checking the damage to his shredded chemise.

'I'm so sorry, Tuesday,' Finn said. He didn't know why it sounded like he was begging. 'I could have helped you if you'd let me.'

'You're deluded, doll. D'you know that?' Tuesday shook her head bitterly and trailed out of the classroom, and Finn followed, dragging his feet through the years of debris and animal droppings. At the front door, she slid back the bolts and kicked the plywood board off its nails. A gust of wind rattled along the corridor and the white light from the evening sky sliced through the dust.

'Tuesday. Please. Don't do this.'

'Get lost, Finn,' she said. Her hand was trembling as she held open the door.

Finn didn't have the energy to protest. What was he supposed to do? It was tragic but you couldn't help folk who didn't want to be helped. A blinding firmament beyond the door pierced his eyes, made them stream. Before he could adjust, before he could focus to say goodbye, Tuesday disappeared behind the scrape of plywood and the screech of bolts. It was the last he ever heard of her.

33

Madonna of Loreto

There were half a dozen people at least in the room – reading monitors, adjusting infusions, flicking through notes – and in the middle of it all, Lizzi was lying in bed, propped up on a pile of pillows, her mind vacant with fear and confusion while the staff ignored her in efficient tones of controlled panic.

There was a knock at the door. Rob came in and squeezed through the crowd to reach her bed. He put a bunch of freesias on the cabinet.

'What's going on?' He was another one trying to hide his alarm.

'They think they'll have to do a Caesarean,' Lizzi whispered. She had overheard the staff discussing her options. A bystander in her own tragedy.

'But it's too early,' Rob said, and all Lizzi could do was nod weakly in agreement. It *was* too early. Much too early. She wasn't prepared.

On one side, a senior midwife was reading the foetal heart monitor, examining the trace, showing it to the obstetrician. A student was poised with his pen cocked, ready to record the next blood pressure reading, his eyes glued to the deflated cuff. Everyone blinkered by the seriousness of the situation.

Lizzi shifted so she wouldn't have to notice the troubled glances passing between the staff. She patted the edge of the bed for Rob and asked how the funeral was. And then half laughed. 'Sorry. Stupid question.'

Rob sat down on the bed. Under his bulk, the mattress dipped. Her weight tipped towards him. He was so solid, so reliable, so unlike Finn.

'You know how these things are,' he said. And then, after a pause, 'Finn was a complete twat, but the undertaker's sidekick finally gave me his number.' He laughed without smiling. 'Seems wrong to score at a funeral.'

Lizzi wanted to smile through her headache but it was blinding her. 'I can't remember. Is he handsome?' she managed.

'Very.'

She squeezed his hand. It was about time one of them got over Finn.

'D'you think the men are called mid-husbands?' Rob whispered to her, tipping his head in the direction of the male student.

The obstetrician interrupted to tell Lizzi they were taking her to theatre. The baby was having difficulties. At the same time, the anaesthetist gave orders to a panicky-looking junior to get ready for a spinal.

Lizzi protested feebly. She wasn't ready. It was too soon. Too fast.

A different midwife asked Rob to step outside. He kissed Lizzi on the forehead 'Step outside?' he whispered. 'Is she asking for a fight?'

There was nothing left in Lizzi to joke. She clutched his fingers. Her chin was trembling.

'Please. Can he stay? I don't have anyone else.'

'Are you a relative?' the obstetrician asked.

'It's okay,' the senior midwife said. 'Rob is Lizzi's birthing partner.'

'Fine, just keep out of the road,' the obstetrician said.

Rob stood at the top of the bed, staying clear of the professionals, stroking Lizzi's hair from her face and quietly giving her an account of the deputy undertaker's attractions. She closed her eyes and let the story float over her. She imagined Rob and his friend, saw them snatching glances across the church aisle, smiling, reading each other's unspoken flirtation. She saw the packed church and heard the hymns. She saw the priest and the coffin and the wreaths. Saw Finn without wanting to. And when she left the church before the mourners, Maurice beckoned to her from the bottom of the garden.

Something was happening. An alarm on the monitor was pealing. The trace had slowed up. Her arm was squeezed by the blood pressure cuff. The student recorded the result. 'A hundred and fifty over a hundred and fifteen,' he said proudly.

The obstetrician shouted above the din. 'Come on, folks, we need to get this show on the road.'

The anaesthetist took over. 'Elizabeth, can you roll over on to your side for us?' A trolley was wheeled to her bedside. A midwife helped her move over. Half propped up by the pillows, she clutched Rob's hand. The floury smoothness of vinyl gloves prodded her hip bone and her lumbar vertebrae. She felt the swish of cold alcohol, the swipe of sterile swabs. Heard a clatter of medical instruments, the suck of a syringe flange.

'Knees up a little more, please, Elizabeth. That's good. Okay, a wee scratch now. This is just the local.' The tone the anaesthetist used with Lizzi was different to the stern instructions she was giving under her breath to her junior.

'I don't feel right,' Lizzi whispered to Rob. Lignocaine

424

sting at the base of her spine. Blebs in the top layers of her skin.

'Don't panic,' Rob said. 'They know what they're doing.'

But she wasn't panicking. She was calm, tranquil. It was bizarre and out of place and she realised what it meant.

Rob clutched her fingers.

She nodded, fastened her fingers around his, sucked in air from the room.

'Okay, Elizabeth. This is the spinal coming up. You'll feel some prodding, some pressure maybe, but it shouldn't be painful. Ready now. Hold as still as you can for us.'

Lizzi smelt the anxiety of the junior tasked with the procedure.

'Rob,' she whispered. There was no pain. 'I'm going to die.'

'You daft bint. Get a grip.' Rob's attempt at levity was ruined by the scrape in his voice.

'Will you tell Finn?'

'Cut it out, Lizzi.'

She shut her eyes again. This time she was outside her house. Walking away. Carrying her school bag. Dragging her feet along the pavement. She looked up at the living room window where her mum should have been, but she couldn't see her. Hidden by the clouds reflected in the window. Or gone. Panicking, Lizzi waved but she didn't know if her mother could see her. And then called to her but no words came out. Only a gurgle. Lizzi put her hands to her throat. It sounded like she was choking. But it didn't feel like that. She was floating. Floating close to the ceiling and the strip lights. Looking down on blue scrubs and necks bent in concentration. Several pairs of hands rolled her to a half-prone position. Others fiddled with the anaesthetic pump. The blood pressure cuff chugged to inflate again, and the student concentrating at her bedside poised himself anxiously for the reading.

Lizzi's hand loosened in Rob's and her body stiffened. Her eyes gaped open. Her body jerked. Rob leant over her. He was holding her. Trying to hold her still. He shouted for help but his words caught in his throat.

'Oh, shit. She's fitting,' someone said. Pulled Rob away.

'Come on, people. Magnesium sulphate. Quickly.'

Quickly. Quickly.

Another jerk. A pillow fell to the floor. Her eyes rolled. Jaw clenched, teeth grinding, spit foaming from the angles of her mouth. Her arms spasmed. Her head hammered against the metal bed frame. Her left leg kicked against the thin sheet.

The rush of the drug bolus into her cannula.

All around there were voices. The clatter of equipment. An oxygen mask. The new toy smell of flexible plastic.

Lizzi could see Rob – paralysed among all the activity – watching her helplessly.

'Get the boyfriend out.'

Rob was shepherded from the room. The door shut in his face. Lizzi watched him – confused, disorientated, wondering if he should go back in. Peering through the slatted window in the door. Her bed was pulled into the middle of the room. Monitors, syringes, injections, infusions. She was still fitting. More violently now. Teeth gnashing, tonic clonic jerks. The anaesthetist at the head of the bed, checking oxygen saturation, heart rate. The obstetrician with her hand on Lizzi's tummy, keeping an eye on the baby monitor. Someone closed the blind.

Lizzi was on her way home. Running down the road. Rushing up the close stairs. Piling though the front door and charging into every room. First the kitchen, then the living room, bathroom, her childhood bedroom, each time expecting to find her mother. Watching for her. Waiting for her.

Another cold bolus into her arm. Steady drip from the infusion. Someone took blood from the crook of her elbow. Slammed through the door with blood samples. Rob stood up and filled the open doorway. A midwife spotted him, guided him to a seat in the corridor, gave him a cup of water to hold. He sat staring without seeing. And then gradually, gradually the fits subsided. But Lizzi was still watching, still floating overhead, looking at her exhausted body and her struggling baby. She stayed like that for ten minutes, fifteen minutes. It felt like for ever.

'Good to go,' the anaesthetist said finally.

The senior midwife phoned to inform theatre they were on their way. Someone else called to reserve a cot in the special care baby unit. A porter came in, took the brake off the bed, wheeled Lizzi out of the room. Her auburn hair was pulled in over her temples by the elasticated straps of the oxygen mask, and the rest of it spilt across the pillow. Her eyes were blank, infusion bags piled on top of her, monitors and pumps wheeled alongside. Rob stood up, unsure if he was supposed to follow. Someone flicked a waffle blanket over her chest and shoulders. It partly covered her face. The cup of water slipped from Rob's hand.

Only her parents' room was left. She opened the door. There was no one there.

34

Saint Catherine

The fact that Lizzi didn't actually die (and neither, thanks to the timely intervention of the obstetric team, did her thirty-week gestation, two-pound-two-ounce daughter who for the moment didn't have a name) had very little bearing on Finn. Primarily because no one told him. He didn't know Lizzi was in hospital. He didn't know she'd had pre-eclampsia. He didn't know the baby had arrived. And to be fair, as far as Finn was concerned the baby was Rob's.

When Lizzi recovered enough to make her wishes known, and the baby had been stabilised in her incubator with continuous positive air pressure to help oxygen enter and leave her lungs without her alveoli collapsing or the walls of her bronchioles sticking together (aided by the detergents her little spongy lungs were eventually able to make a few days after her birth, courtesy of the steroids Lizzi had been dosed with minutes before the emergency section), and her dinky heart was pumping vigorously (albeit with a hole between her aorta and her pulmonary artery which would close slowly over the coming few days) and the grape-blue bloom of her lips gradually changed to a delicate pink blush, and her wrinkled new-born body had been baked by phototherapy lights to bleach her jaundice (with the cutest little mask over her eyes; eyes that were checked and rechecked and later zapped with coagulation lasers to stem her impending premature baby retinopathy), and Lizzi had learnt to pump her breast milk and feed it to her through a tube that passed up her minuscule nostrils and down into her walnut-size stomach, she made Rob swear he wouldn't mention any of it to Finn. Not yet. Not until she was strong enough to resist the disruption Finn would bring to their hard-won equilibrium.

Finn, meanwhile, was preoccupied. Too preoccupied to notice the looks of pity the priest threw his way on the rare occasions their paths crossed (almost invariably in a morning when Jed made his way up Dougal Street to the church while Finn sat outside on the garden wall smoking roll-ups and snatching the few moments of respite from a sulky and sleep-deprived Caravaggio; invariably, save the once when, to Finn's astonishment, Jed came sniffing around the back rooms and corridors of the church hall, checking up on him, fussing, and generally being annoying); looks of such withering pity that, had Finn remarked on them, they would almost certainly have reduced him to fag ash.

The problem, Finn decided, was that he was grieving. And honestly, who could blame him? It didn't occur to him (well, strictly, it did occur but he chose to ignore the occurrence because he was mad at the entire bunch of them) that the source of his grief sprang from his recent and tangible losses – Maurice, Tuesday, Lizzi, Rob. Rather, he felt, his grief was the result of something much more substantially abstract, much more weightily intangible. It wasn't something he could demonstrably demonstrate, so to speak, and yet at the same time, it was evidently evident.

The thing was, in the last few hideous days, Finn had finally admitted what he had been unwilling to face for so long. All that had anchored him to his otherwise pitiful existence had gone. His entire belief system – philosophy, creed, guiding principles, call it what you will – had basically fucked off and left him bereft, and regarding the departure, he placed the blame squarely in Caravaggio's wide and off-puttingly stained lap.

The culprit, of course, was oblivious, wrapped up as he was in his own pathetic affairs, but the truth was that more than ever Caravaggio was flaunting his true colours and they weren't the forbidding bone black or perilous lead white that Finn had always imagined. Caravaggio, it turned out, was a man of limp pastels and insipid greys. There was nothing of the artist Finn had worshipped in the man who flounced around the studio in a peevish insomnia. And it was killing him to admit it.

And so, to survive each tortured hour of each equally tortured day, all Finn could do was make a semblance of business as usual, and to that end he busied himself constructing the set for his next picture. It was to be *Saint Catherine* and it was to feature Kassia or it was not to feature at all. Without letting himself reflect too deeply on the likelihood of the picture ever coming to fruition, Finn was at present fashioning a martyr's palm from the long grass that had recently shot up the length of the garden borders, while Caravaggio lounged on the chair scratching his balls, his horny-nailed, leather-skinned bare feet up on the trestle table.

'She's not coming, that tart of yours.'

'She'll come,' Finn said, because she had to, unaware until the words were spoken that he had already recanted his promise to himself, the promise where he would not hope for Kassia to come for risk of spiritual disintegration. He tied off the last loops of the palm and laid it on the trestle table. Broken promises aside, it was some reassurance to discover he was not as done for as he had believed. Better a spirit that was merely disintegrating, he felt, than one that had taken leave of him altogether.

The brainless call of a cuckoo flapped in through the open window and, offended, Finn climbed on the table to shut out the intrusion. The fresh-air lark was Jed's call. When the priest had come visiting – fussing, prying, whatever it was he'd been doing – he'd flung open every window in the church hall including the one in Finn's studio with the instruction to leave them like that for the moment. He had said something about the scent of summer air, and stench of unwashed hair, and Finn had committed the words to memory. Since the funeral, since remarking the non-nephew had inherited his watch, Finn had been collecting rhyming couplets for Leanne in the hope that she would see her way to apportioning in his direction his rightful and deserved share of Maurice's patrimony.

'I need more space. I'll have to shift the table,' Finn said, securing the blackout pages of the *Gazette* back over the window pane. 'Gonnae move your feet.'

Caravaggio refused, without elaborating. A corner of newspaper peeled itself away from the frame. Finn glanced down. The handle of Caravaggio's dagger was protruding from the waistband of his breeches like a lapdog's willy.

'For fuck's sake.' Finn jumped down and tugged the end of the table to move it. Caravaggio's sturdy legs plopped to the floor, all but unseating him.

'Pustulous hag tit,' Caravaggio said without much venom, once he'd settled himself back into the chair. Doing his best to pay him no attention whatsoever, Finn dragged the table to clear some space for his set and turned his hand to detaching the front wheel from his bike. With a deft and almost mechanical reflex, he loosened the quick-release lever and shook it free of the frame.

'I'll need your sword,' he said, placing the wheel upright against the wall that formed the limit of the set. Along with the wheel, a prayer cushion and the martyr's palm, a sword was an essential accoutrement for *Saint Catherine*. A detail Caravaggio knew well. His painting had her caressing a rapier with the same partiality he obviously hoped would later be directed towards himself.

'And again. No,' Caravaggio said.

The flap of newspaper peeled itself further from the window frame, and a globule of sunlight weaselled its way through and ricocheted off an empty whisky bottle lying on the floor by the foot of the easel. It transformed into a focused beam that bore straight into Finn's navel. Beyond the imitation ray, Caravaggio was rubbing his palm along the shaft of his sword.

'I reserve the right to select who handles my blade,' Caravaggio sniggered, with his usual degree of lecherousness. Outraged, Finn snapped two of the spokes on the wheel and blinked away the sordid image. The man was a bona fide wanker.

Leaving Caravaggio to toss himself off, Finn went to fetch a skewer from the kitchen. As a sword substitute, it had to be admitted that it was a tad on the thin and inadequate side, but he had been left with little choice. While he was at it, he grabbed the broom handle, also required for the set and, on his return, found Caravaggio flicking through Finn's art book and snickering to himself in an orgy of self-congratulation.

The scene was, for Finn, pretty much the death knell for any traces of admiration that remained. It wasn't only the artist whose true colours he had seen. The paintings too were showing their true form and Finn didn't want to look. Painful though it was to acknowledge, the works he had admired for so long were at best a mere postcard-grade pastiche of the oeuvre. Blacked-out backgrounds done because Caravaggio was a malingering incompetent who couldn't paint scenery. The same subjects all his mates were painting, repeated time after time after time, because he didn't have an ounce of originality. Figures either head-shots or deformed mutants because he had no understanding of the human form, no sense at all of the beauty of anatomy. Finn's awakening may not have been quick but it had been rude to the point of obscene. And if he had had to endure such a thing, it was only fair that Caravaggio should too.

'For fuck's sake, wake up to yourself, man. Look.' Finn snatched Rob's textbook from among the assortment of stolen goods lying on the floor by the badminton net and opened the pages at random. 'Hands, shoulders, feet. See the way they articulate. The way they speak to other parts of the body. The way they are all in fucking proportion.' He slammed it on the table and snatched the art book from Caravaggio's hands, jabbed one colour plate after another.

Pointedly ignoring Finn's prodding finger and the anatomical distortions in his own pictures, and with a self-deprecating smugness that practically made Finn's toenails detach, Caravaggio said, 'And yet still you endeavour to recreate my masterpieces.'

'You're kidding. I'm not trying to *recreate* them. We're talking reinterpretation, reinvention, refinement.' Finn stopped. He kicked a prayer cushion in front of the broken wheel. It was no use. He would never get beyond Caravaggio's conceit.

'The problem as I perceive it,' Caravaggio said, 'is rather

that it is *you* who is fallacious, *you* who is living in a realm of perverted fantasy.'

Was that perhaps the truth of it? Finn wondered bitterly. He couldn't bring himself to look at the finished paintings of St Jerome and the feverish Cupid and the half-completed self-portraits propped in the corner for fear they would agree. The doubts Caravaggio was insinuating under Finn's skin had set every one of his hairs on end. Truth was, a few selfies, a dead saint and his spotty nephew were never going to cut it, whether you were talking graduating from limbo or graduating from Art School.

Finn shoved the broom handle through the spokes in the direction of the axis of the wheel, desperate not to submit to the creeping doubts, and for the next few minutes worked with his head down, arranging the last of the details, digging out candles, lining up his paintbrushes, not ready to face what was not going to happen.

'Much as it pains me to elucidate your self-deception, the girl is not to be relied upon,' Caravaggio said in a tone of sickly fake concern. 'I beg you to consider an alternative.'

Preoccupied by his diversionary tactics, Finn blanked out Caravaggio's wheedling, simpering entreaties (and the under-breath profanities that escaped him when Finn continued to disregard him), and he didn't notice Caravaggio weasel up beside him. It was only when Caravaggio tried to take Finn's hand that Finn came to and flinched from the warty touch.

'Blacken the canvas entirely if you have to,' Caravaggio said, clearly trying to rise above his own inclination to huff at Finn's revulsion. 'Shit on it. Piss on it. I believe that's what they do these days. It isn't difficult. I entreat you.'

'St Catherine. End of.' Finn lifted the chair on to the table and placed a single candle on the seat. They were both going to have to face the fact that Finn's work was no longer about his portfolio or his degree or his reputation, or even easing Caravaggio's passage through purgatory (if it ever had been). As far as Finn was concerned, Caravaggio could sort his own bail terms. Finn's own redemption was what concerned him now. And it depended entirely, utterly, simply (or not at all simply, he suspected) on capturing the essence of Kassia on canvas. It was, he explained, the only thing left that could save him.

Caravaggio kicked the easel in disgust. 'Then, you self-righteous simpleton, you are fated to join me in this eternal wait.'

Uneasily, Finn steadied the easel and set the prepped canvas straight. Unfortunately, he suspected there was a measure of truth in Caravaggio's unpleasant certainties and Cupid's leery grin seemed to affirm as much. However hard Finn willed it, Michael-Midge was not going to be working his case with Kassia, that was sure. And even if it wasn't sure, Finn hadn't been able to track Michael down to confirm. He hadn't seen the kid since Maurice's funeral, despite heading down the chippy on a recce (casually scoffing a pie supper sitting on the gashed stool and fondly recalling his trip there with Tuesday) where quite unnecessarily the owner had chosen not to let on where Michael had disappeared to, and so, in a fit of repressed frustration, Finn dug his fingers into the foam stuffing between the edges of the seat wound, accidentally extending the injury and had subsequently found himself (unjustly, he felt; the damage would have been infinitely more substantial if he hadn't demonstrated such an admirable level of self-control) barred, thus severing his only genuine but tenuous link to Kassia.

'I cannot stay any longer in this cesspit.'

'Well, piss off then,' Finn said. 'Nobody asked you to come.'

'But that is not true,' Caravaggio said morosely. 'You know as well as I do that I am the answer to all those snivelling prayers you made when you thought no one was listening. Why me? Why did it have to be me?' He was almost wailing.

'But I didn't. Pray. Not for you. Not you.' Finn shook his head to dislodge the hideous notion that he had brought all this on himself. He studied the finished set, battling an almost intolerable sense of futility. He hadn't brought it on himself. He absolutely hadn't.

'It is still feasible the situation could be redeemed. Still conceivable, wouldn't you say? Neither party is satisfied with the contractual arrangements. We could request an annulment. Demand a resilement. Declare a recantation. Please.' Caravaggio whimpered and clung to Finn's shirt sleeve. 'Look at me. I'm not cut out for a northern climate.'

Finn shook him off. 'For fuck's sake, get a grip.' Caravaggio wasn't there because of Finn's prayers. Caravaggio was there because, unfortunately for everyone involved, the course of his purulent blood ran straight from the umbilicus of his bastard child through however many lost generations there were between him and Finn, tainting them all along the way. Which Finn pointed out, in terms that were not quite so reserved.

'I am sapped by your continual reiteration of this drivel,' Caravaggio wailed.

It wasn't drivel. And it was about time the truth was painted in colours Caravaggio would understand.

'See that time in Rome when you butchered your pal on the tennis court after your pathetic duel and then pissed off to God knows where to save your own skin?' Finn said. 'Remember? Aye, of course you do. Well, your woman was up the duff. That's right. Pregnant. If you'd hung around to face the consequences, you'd have known. But you didn't think about that, did you? When you were brawling with your pals, amusing yourselves with your adolescent play fights, doing a runner the minute it got out of hand?'

Caravaggio slumped against the table. Finally the message had penetrated.

'But this is horrendous,' he said, with almost a whimper.

Finn laughed bitterly. 'Horrendous, you reckon? How do you think I feel? Finding out I'm related to nothing more than a second-rate Raphael, a minor Michelangelo.'

Without another word, but with a heavily accented intake of breath, Caravaggio pulled on his moccasins, sheathed his sword and draped his cloak over his arm.

'Aye,' Finn shouted at his disappearing back. 'The truth fucking cuts, doesn't it.'

A moment later, the studio door slammed shut.

In the silence that rebounded, Finn picked up the prayer cushion and pummelled it between his fists. He was glad Caravaggio had gone. Glad. With any luck, without Maurice as his guardian angel, he would end up in a fight with the locals and get the fuck kicked out of him and die for good this time. Unconsciously, Finn tossed the cushion back down, unable to credit how devastated he was. Not so much that Caravaggio had fallen off his pedestal – to that, he had had more than enough time to become accustomed – but more that the pedestal itself had turned into a stinking pile of shit.

There was little he could do now. The set was perfect. A shrine to what might have been. It hardly seemed to matter whether Kassia came or not. Destroyed, Finn knelt on the prayer cushion where she would have knelt, and leant into the wheel as if he could be saved by its steely embrace, and let the flimsy kitchen skewer hang from his grip. After a while, he lay down and put his head on the cushion, placed the skewer-sword across his chest and closed his eyes. He had done everything he could. It was over.

35

Death of the Virgin

'Knock knock. You are there, no?'

Finn woke with a start. The door opened and Kassia breezed in with the electric light from the corridor, carrying her party dress in her schoolboy rucksack.

'Ready to begin again?'

He sat up. He had no idea how long he had lain there. Long enough for dusk to descend. His muscles felt like slabs of granite from sleeping on the floor but otherwise he was brand new. Resurrected. 'I didn't think I would see you again,' he whispered.

'For that you must thank little Midge. He asks me before he goes away. He does it for the sake of his uncle, not for the stupid phone rape thing you do.' Kassia put out her hand to turn on the studio light, but Finn scrambled to his feet to protect the switch. A spark of static leapt from his hand to hers. Kassia flinched.

'Okay, okay. We stay in the dark if this is what you prefer.'

It was what he preferred. Exactly what he preferred. Dumbly, Finn shoved the door so only a sliver of light squeezed through. After so long working himself into a frenzy of no expectation, he didn't know if he could cope with Kassia's beauty full on. He rescued the curtains from Caravaggio's pit and reattached one corner to the badminton post.

'The stinky cousin, he is gone?'

A feeble affirmative was as much as Finn could stretch to.

'Good. I have my dress. This time, I wear it alone?'

By now, all he could do was nod and hold up the corner of the curtain screen, hoping that Kassia wouldn't notice his shakes, his sweaty pits, the way his voice was lodged in his gullet.

While she changed behind the screen, Finn stared at his feet, listening to her take off her jeans, step into the folds of the dress, and wondered what celestial loveliness had decided to give him this break. Triumphantly, he realised it didn't matter that he had taken inspiration from works he no longer respected, from an artist he had seen through. It didn't matter that Vadge was a talentless charlatan or that the family tree was rotten. None of it mattered. Like his wee granny, Finn would thrive despite his roots. He was his own person. With his own talent. He didn't need props. He didn't need costumes. He didn't need themes. He could paint Kassia wearing nothing but a sackcloth (or even, nothing at all) and she would still be astonishing. He didn't need sacred codes or hidden messages to force his work to say what he wanted it to say. Art should speak for itself. That's all there was to it. And as far as Finn could hear, it was pleading with him, entreating him – it was down on its fucking arty knees and begging him – to get on and paint her.

'Tonight, you are not speaking, I can tell,' Kassia said. 'Is it because I have not come sooner? It takes a while to forgive you.'

'I'm sure you've been busy with other clients,' Finn croaked. He hadn't intended to sound so sullen. Sullen was unbecoming. Sullen didn't win friends. Sullen was the enemy of social integration. He knew that from his mother.

'I hear in your words you are jealous. You think I am

working some other place? Actually, no. It is only that I pass time with Midge. I spend the last days in the park with him before he leaves on his travelling.'

So he got his passport after all, Finn noted as a side-thought, after he cleared his throat of its intrusive sullenness.

'I take a little sun.'

'I hope you didn't get too much of a tan,' he said, sifting through his bank of memories to select one that best recalled the whiteness of her skin. 'You know, for the painting.'

'Not too much.' Kassia came out from behind the screen, one arm folded across her chest to hold the bodice of her dress in place, the other lifting her dark hair from her neck. She stood with her back towards him. An echo of the sublime. Finn dropped the corner of the curtain and fastened her dress, pressing his hand into the soft skin of her upper back to tease up the zip. As he leant in, his face hovered over the nape of her neck. She smelt of orange blossom. He was falling from the highest branch.

When her dress was fastened, she stopped to admire her reflection between the strips of light and the mottles of the convex mirror. 'This is better, no? My dress.'

'Aye,' Finn said. He wasn't lying.

'When I am in the park these nice days, I see some girls with legs who are orange.' Kassia lifted up her skirt and stretched out her leg from under the hem, her bare toes pointed ballerina-style. 'I ask myself, how is this possible?'

'A Glasgow tan? D'you not know it?' Finn said, taking down the curtain screen and arranging it in folds around the wheel and prayer cushion, blatantly stalling with the functional stuff while he did some gathering of nerves. He would crack on with the painting as planned. That wasn't to say that he hadn't meant it when he'd dissed Caravaggio's pictures, but now that Kassia was here he had to do something. And it was as good a one as any. Except the naked one obviously.

'Yeah, a Glasgow tan.' He patted his pockets for his lighter and stretched to light the candle on the chair. 'Two ways to acquire that particular skin tone.' In parentheses, he offered to show Kassia *Saint Catherine*.

'This saint I know,' she said, plaiting her hair while she inspected the open page by candlelight.

'What was I saying? Oh aye. Obviously, *numero uno*: fake tan. Salon or home version depending on cash availability and the level of streakiness you prefer.'

Kassia threw her plait over her shoulder and stepped on to the set.

Even as a tortured martyr and under the dim hue of a single candle, she was radiant. Whatever image Finn had in his memory bank could never match the truth of it. He handed her the skewer-sword and laid the martyr's palm at her feet.

'Alternatively,' he said, returning to the easel and his commentary, 'see how some folk eat loads of carrots? Helps them see in the dark or whatever but makes their skin a tad on the carroty side?' He marked her position with nicks in the canvas, went back and adjusted her foot slightly. 'Well, what you encountered the other day is the Glasgow interpretation.' Back at the easel, he took his time preparing the palette from the paint tubes arrayed on the trestle table.

'Irn-Bru. Drink enough, it turns you orange. Head to toe.' Steadily, this time, he picked up a brush. 'Doesnae help you see in the dark, but helps others see you on a dull day.' He forced a laugh, determined not to cave in to performance anxiety. Kept up the patter for the same reason. Fully immersed in self-distraction. 'Makes up for the year-round lack of rays,' he said, dipping the very tip of a brush in the black paint, and then in deeper. This is how he would work. Slowly. Calmly. From dark to light. 'Plus, it's the only proven explanation for the number of gingers in Scotland.' Just for a second his hand stuttered when he saw Lizzi's auburn hair fanned out across his pillow, but he forced himself to continue. Even in his days of arrogant innocence, of innocent arrogance, the first stroke was always the hardest. 'A bit more towards the wheel, please.'

'I understand only half of your talk,' Kassia said, draping herself into the wheel, 'but I like it when you are playful with me.'

When the paint-sopped bristles stroked the canvas, Finn's entire body shuddered, his brain liquefied, his muscles spasmed and his nerve fibres furled themselves into a frenzy of knots. Only by the most masterful effort of self-control (and by remembering with distaste Caravaggio's performance in the church several weeks previously) did Finn stop himself shooting his entire load.

The ecstasy, however, lasted less time than it took for Kassia's next sentence to depart her lips and scurry along his ear canal.

'It is more funny than the serious man who only wants to paint and who bullies me to be ugly for the sake of a silly picture.'

The metaphorical scream that Finn made had him clutching his temples while his face stretched into a monstrous pear drop and his eyes widened to quarry pools and the background swirled in swirls of multicoloured swirling torture. In reality he simply stood there. Frozen with his brush midway between the palette and the canvas. Feeling his dick shrivel and his skin shrink. Was that what he had become? A bully? No better, in the final measure, than Caravaggio, with his belligerence and overbearing conceit? Or Rob, with his passive-aggressive self-righteousness? Or even the priest, with his firm-handed shepherding of his wayward flock? Please. After everything he'd been through, it was too cruel.

'Shit, Kassia,' he said, when he eventually managed to dislodge the words of explanation that were threatening to gag him. Or make him gag. 'Work. Important, you see.'

'What is so important that you become that horrible person?' she said, tugging fitfully at the bodice of her dress.

Lost, Finn gestured at her, at the canvas, at the paint tubes laid out on the trestle table. How could he put it into words? His art was everything. The first and last and only thing. Quite literally, quite tragically, the only thing he appeared to have left these days.

'But that is too silly. The pictures they are not worth this much. They are giving only pain. It is not necessary to be here in the dark all the time. You should be outside and see the sunshine.' Kassia giggled. 'I think you prefer to be like me. To be free of trying to be the very best.'

If she was aware of how her words collided with everything Finn had valued his entire life – his way of making sense of the world, his mission against his mother's sanctimonious prudery or the terror of turning into a nondescript like his father – Kassia gave no sign of showing it. But collide they did. Slap-bang, head-on, right into the frown crease between his eyebrows, and left him reeling from the impact. However, once he recovered sufficiently to realise that although battered, he was not actually critically injured, Finn applied a bit of logic to the situation. The fact was – though it pained him to admit it – he'd been wrong about Caravaggio. Totally wrong. Wrong in every conceivable sense of wrongness. Therefore, it wasn't too far-fetched to imagine that it was entirely feasible he was slightly mistaken about this too. Maybe you could exist happily without being the best. Perhaps you could fail slightly without necessarily being worthless. Good enough was good enough, isn't that what they said? As a philosophy, that particular piece of wisdom had always sickened him. But maybe Kassia was correct. Maybe he didn't have to be like this, slave to this terrible ambition. In the end, all it brought was disillusionment and dissatisfaction. He could never be as good as he wanted. So maybe it wasn't worth trying.

'I'm scared,' Finn said, resting the brush on the palette. 'Scared of not being the person I was meant to be.'

'Ridiculous,' Kassia said. 'Who is this person you were meant to be? This sorry boy who looks so hard at things to paint he cannot see life happening to him. No, no, no, no. It is most important to make the best of things. Like me. I live my life. I am very much more alive than you.'

There were things that were incontrovertible truths and, for Finn, Kassia's words were among them. Involuntarily, he placed the palette on the trestle table and pulled his hair off his face and turned his face up to an imaginary sun. The way she spoke to him, the way she let her glance settle on his skin, let her smile soothe him, caress him, her voice enfold him, was like being lifted by air currents. He was gliding on thermals, above the treetops, above the mountain peaks, above a glittering sea.

'I don't know . . .' Only the faintest ripple of guilt unsettled him and he shut his mind to the deadly undercurrents: Caravaggio loose on the streets; Maurice burnt to a crisp; Tuesday holed up in her refuge. Lizzi. Wherever she was.

'Are you crazy? You have everything. You have nice family and money and girls who like you.'

Girls who like you. Finn laughed. He was beginning to

feel, even if she let him go, he would be able to fly by himself. 'You know what, K,' he said. 'I don't want to do this any more. I don't want to be the person who takes this shit so seriously.'

'Seriously?' Kassia grinned. She put down the skewer, clapped her hands. 'I think you make good decision.'

'I hope so.' Finn held out his hand to help Kassia to her feet.

What happen next was unexpected enough to be vaguely unsettling to a man of Finn's sensibilities. Kassia took a paintbrush and the palette off the table.

'What?' Finn said. 'Are you the artist now?'

'You watch.' Kassia dipped the brush into the deep red and flicked it at the work in progress. 'Do not look so pained. I help to free you from yourself. More please.'

Hypnotised, Finn squeezed more red on to the palette. Kassia stuck the brush in and smeared a thick dollop across the canvas.

'Your turn,' she said, sliding the palette near to him.

Guardedly, Finn took a fresh brush, dabbed it in the green and cupped a trembling hand under the bristles to catch the drips. His insides were skittering with disbelief. For a second he held back – Maurice's saintly entreaties from the finished canvas in the corner begging him to reconsider – but for lack of alternatives and the fact that Maurice was too far dead to hold him to account, he talked himself round. Without further vacillation, and before Kassia could cop him for a wimp, Finn swept the thick paint across the bleeding canvas and then – as near as was possible without the messy follow-through – shat himself.

Tactfully for her, Kassia pretended not to notice. Or maybe her not noticing was genuine. While Finn was grappling with his churning intestines and the possibility that he was not of tremendous importance in Kassia's regard, Kassia grabbed the tube of yellow and manoeuvred around the trestle table to reach the other paintings. Dispensing with all unnecessary preliminaries (like asking Finn's permission or even merely acknowledging the poor saint's presence) she squirted the paint straight into St Maurice's pallid face and swirled it with her fingertips until his cadaverous visage transmuted to a child's sun.

'Oh shit,' Finn said, half laughing, half appalled, not at all sure whether his protest was genuine or a response conditioned by the fact that at some point fairly soon (if the lengthening days were anything to go by) he was due to submit his portfolio. A practically unbegun painting was one thing. His recently deceased pal another. The practice paintings were back-up. Fallback if he didn't measure up to Kassia. Although not any more, he realised, considering St Maurice-Jerome's newly weathered state.

'You could've asked . . .' he started, but Kassia pouted so violently that he hurriedly added he was joking. Honestly, he stressed. Several times to pre-empt a sulk. To demonstrate his extreme and gravitationally free levity of mood, he flicked the bristles of the paintbrush in her direction and a colander of green peas spattered her dress. 'See.'

'Hey, dickhead, this is my party dress. It is not for a joke.' Kassia tore a fistful of paper towels from the kitchen roll and smeared streaks into her skirt. 'Look what you've done.' In revenge, she grabbed the burnt umber and squirted it at Finn. It missed and landed on the floor where it wobbled between them like a proud jobbie. For reasons entirely related, an image of Caravaggio flashed into Finn's head and a smirk bubbled under his liver.

'Honestly, this situation is only funny for small boys,' Kassia said, chucking the roll of paper towels at Finn, but he was too busy gauging the imaginary Caravaggio's reaction to their handiwork that he failed to catch it and the roll headed under the table leaving a trail of light-blue tissue paper behind. Happily for Finn, Kassia was looking at him the way a tolerant mother would regard a wayward five-year-old, and inside he hugged himself. That was exactly how he felt. Like he had been cheeky, mischievous. An episode of minor misdemeanour deserving only the most appealing of punishments. And for the next short while, with a grin carved on his face and his blood tingling with the after-effects of unexpected rebellion, he watched Kassia squirt paint on the rest of the pictures. There were pucker lines between her eyebrows and she was biting her bottom lip. Her prim concentration was quite funny to watch. Very funny actually. Totally hilarious if you took into account what Caravaggio's actual reaction would be if he ever clapped eyes on the vandalised paintings.

Either she didn't hear Finn's warning, or she had decided to pay him no heed, so caught up was she in her task. Either way, when Kassia stood back with a flourish to display her *newlooking*, she slipped on the paper towel trail.

She squealed as she went flying, and landed on the floor with her petticoats puffed up around her and her legs splayed and her skirt covered in skid marks. Finn giggled.

'Dickhead,' she said.

'I tried to warn you,' Finn said, covering his mouth with his hand to catch the rest of the sniggers as they escaped.

At first, Kassia scowled but then, reluctantly, foolishly, hiccuping at first, she too started to laugh. Slowly. And a bit more. Then more, until both of them were giggling, laughing, properly cracking up. Somewhere in the midst of it, Finn found the composure to realise he should help her up. And as he clambered over the obstacles in the studio, he found himself marvelling that this breathtaking girl, this girl who *literally* took his breath away, was the person who had shown him – was showing him, would show him – the light. Everything that had gone before – all the grief and disappointment, the treachery and backstabbing, the doubts and letdowns – was all for this. This chance to be reborn. His own genuine bona fide renaissance. A magnificent rebirth without any obligation to his parents. He would be free. Freed. Finally, with thoughts as profound and moving as these, he pulled Kassia to her feet and, with uninvited tenderness, wiped splatters of paint from her cheek.

At the touch of his fingers, the temperature in the studio plummeted. Immediately, Kassia sobered up, recoiled.

'What's up?' Finn said, glancing round. The studio door was open but the light from the corridor was blocked by the bulk of a thickset form. Caravaggio was back.

'I have returned to elicit clarification on the delicate matter of the paternity of the illegitimate offspring,' Caravaggio said decisively. 'It shames me to admit it, but it appears I have been a cuckold.' He stepped inside the studio. 'Ah, I see I can ask the lady herself.'

Kassia made a nervous, mirthless noise that might in other circumstances have passed for a giggle and freed herself from Finn. 'I hope you were not thinking to kiss me.' With one eye on Caravaggio, she gave a coy smile. 'I kiss only when I am paid.'

Finn gave a weak laugh of denial. He was crashing against a rock face. 'I wouldn't have expected anything else.' He lifted the candle down from the chair to hide his despair behind its light.

'Well?' Caravaggio asked brusquely.

Kassia shrugged warily, as if uncertain why Caravaggio

was addressing her. Finn was too weary to explain that Caravaggio was pissing on the wrong lamp-post as usual. Kassia had fuck-all to do with anything. And as for the bastard offspring, kind of inevitable, the way Vadge had put it about back in the day. But what was the point of going over it again? The stupid bastard was deaf to it all. In the end, the chance did not arise anyway because Caravaggio's attention was quickly diverted by the sight of the destroyed paintings.

'Frigging Jesus,' he shrieked. The candle flame stuttered and he flounced past Finn and Kassia to survey the carnage. Not a single canvas had escaped Kassia's *newlooking*.

'So, I am happy for your new ways,' Kassia said to Finn, wiping her hands on her skirts, 'but now I have enough.' The tiny diamond on her left hand caught the grain in the fake silk of her dress. 'I can go? You do not mind, no? You have my money? Perhaps you give me money also to clean my dress?'

Mind? Finn thought. Mind? Of course he fucking minded. Who the fuck would guide him through his newfound nonchalance if Kassia fucked off? The attempt he made to say so, however, was drowned out by a flood of obscenities that swept around their ankles. He raised the candle an inch and glanced over to where Caravaggio was squatting to view the damaged paintings. Despite the agony of Kassia's imminent departure, Finn still had the presence of mind to note that fat thighs and hanging bollocks should not be seen in tight breeches. The sight was worse than the language emanating from it.

'I prefer to take all my money now so there is no need for me to bother you again.' Kassia was speaking calmly, slowly, but Finn heard a wobble of uncertainty in her voice. Carefully, so as not to betray even to himself how immense was his desolation, he placed the candle on the table, gutted it was all going to end like this, and fumbled for his wallet, pleading with her to come another time, but she simply tore open the worn leather and snatched a wad without counting and shoved it in the pocket of her rucksack.

The cartilage in Caravaggio's knees farted under the strain as he sprang to his feet. 'Wait. I demand an explanation.'

'Okay, I go. Later you pay me more if it does not add.' Kassia snatched up her clothes and bolted for the door.

Still reeling from the shock of being cleaned out by the laundry bill, Finn sank against the trestle table, already resigned to her departure. Caravaggio, however, had other ideas. And, for once, he was ahead of the game. He anticipated Kassia. Sidestepped the trestle to bar her way. Grabbed her arm.

'Who else did you fuck?' Resentment was glistening on his fleshy lips. Or maybe it was just drool, Finn decided. Whatever, it was pretty revolting.

Kassia recoiled from the rank breath and snatched her arm away. 'Fuck off, dickhead. I do not fuck anyone. I do this modelling. Nothing else.'

'Commendable. The only tart in this piss hole of a city who does not fornicate.'

'Finn. I wish to leave. Please.'

Given the way Kassia had just laid waste to his financial and future well-being, Finn later admitted that at that stage he hadn't been immediately ready to leap to the lassie's defence, but the dissing of his adoptive home was enough to shake him from his stupor of self-pity.

'Let her past,' he said sharply.

Caravaggio gave Finn a smarmy smile. 'You and I shouldn't bicker, *Finjay*,' he said. 'Whether it pleases us or not, our fates are intertwined.'

Finjay? The smack of the nickname on lips of such glossy moistness was an affront to Finn's every treasured memory of Maurice. Worse, it was clearly nothing more than a deplorable attempt by Caravaggio to ingratiate himself and Finn wasn't about to be taken in. Insults were par for, but as far as the casual familiarity went, the man could intertwine his own fucking fate.

'Intertwine your-fucking-self,' Finn said, taking the candle off the table and waving it threateningly (or as near as threateningly as was possible to avoid meteorites of molten wax scorching the back of his hand). The candlelight trembled over Caravaggio's face, thickening his brow, accentuating his scar, twisting his smirk to a grotesque scowl. Finn flinched at the sight of it. This wasn't the harmlessly degenerate Vadge he had come to despise. The man staring at him between the flickers looked properly vile. Depraved. Dangerous. An image Finn recognised from numerous self-portraits. He shuddered and for the first time felt something akin to fear.

'Come off it, man. Let her go,' he said, backtracking a little on the aggression front and hoping the rest was a trick of the light. 'I'm serious.' And he was. Serious. Totally serious. For all the difference it made. Because by that time, Caravaggio was otherwise distracted. From the extent of his facial contortions as Kassia's paint-spotted dress was caught by the quivering flame, Finn guessed he'd surmised the main culprit of the painting carnage. A genuine crime to add to the imagined ones.

There followed a minor interval when everything in the studio was unnaturally calm. That singular precious moment during an eclipse when, after long minutes of patience, of sunlight seeping through the fingernail aperture of moon screen, of the day refusing to submit, that moment when the

moon obliterates the sun and the dogged twilight trans-
forms, and finally, finally, you are engulfed in blackness and
the air becomes night-cold. Or so Finn would have said
if you'd asked him. But it didn't last. Without warning,
Caravaggio grabbed Kassia's face and squeezed her cheeks
between his warty fingers. She squealed in surprise and
dropped her belongings to the floor.

'Get off me, you filthy pervert.' Her words were squashed
in her mouth as she twisted to free herself, clawing at the
rough fingers that were bruising her cheeks. Finn could
hardly credit it. For all Vadge was a mincing neurotic in a
flouncy blouse, he did actually have a strong right hand.

'Hey, Vadge, mate . . .'

'Don't you see? Don't you see what she really is?'
Caravaggio yanked Kassia closer to Finn. So close that Finn
could smell the self-righteousness, the infantile indignation,
the churlish sanctimony of the fanatic who believes he is
wronged.

'Man, come off it. Please. Let the lassie go.'

'Let her go? You are pulling my leg, I assume. Mistaking
me for a dainty lady-part. Surely you realise I have a reputation to uphold.'

It was at this point that Finn decided the introduction of
a touch of humorous banter might go some way to defusing
the tension in the room. 'Lady-part? I have to say, pal, not
that I want to cast aspersions, but you haven't done yourself
any favours in that department. Vadge? We did warn you.
Fanny by name, fanny by nature.'

A fatal misjudgement, in retrospect. Whatever self-
restraint Caravaggio possessed (not a great deal, Finn would
attest) imploded. He dragged Kassia towards the set and
flung her against the broken wheel. She sank to the ground
with a yelp of pain.

'This devil-whore ruined me. Ruined me.'

While Finn didn't like to question Vadge's interpretation of his own life, the autobiographical details were at variance with what was written in black and white in Finn's granny's Bible. Kassia-Fillide-whoever-she-was wasn't the ruination of Caravaggio. Fact was, you didn't have to look further than Caravaggio's own misdirected sword skills, so to speak, to find the real reason for his undoing. He'd pretty much instigated his own downfall way back, when he snaffled Fillide from his pal. Shagging the same pal's missus (whose name currently escaped him) at a later date all but ensured it. Small wonder said pal was miffed. And if you went duelling with your besty with blades that sharp, of course it was going to turn out bad. Even Vadge would have to admit it lacked something on the satisfaction front if you were aiming to chop off your pal's bollocks and finished up by killing the chap.

Finn tried to say as much but Caravaggio wasn't listening. He had whipped out his dagger and was swooping it erratically close to Kassia's face. With each wild brandish, his sword clunked against his stocky thigh. And the swipes were coming dangerously near to where Finn was loitering behind the candle.

'Finn,' Kassia wailed. It was both a plea and an accusation. And she was right, of course. He should do something. Certainly. Only he wasn't quite sure what he could do. The man was armed, after all. Doubly armed.

'Vadge, mate . . .' Finn's protest petered out when Caravaggio started fiddling with the buckle on his scabbard belt.

The prodding bulge of his erect dick was straining against his breeches, tenting the manky material. It was one of the most sordid things Finn had ever seen and lately he'd seen sordid things aplenty. His skin slithered over his muscles and he shrank against the easel. This, he hadn't bargained for. That Caravaggio would go that far. That he would desecrate her. Defile her. That he would actually . . . It didn't make any sense. The Caravaggio Finn knew was as wet as a Scout camp in Millport. For a moment, Finn thought he was going to retch. Fear or disgust, it was hard to tell.

And it was surely the retch-inducing sight of the protuberance in Vadge's breeches that caused Finn's difficulty in following the man's polemic. That plus the fact the wanker looked more like he was groping himself with his stumpy fingers than unfastening his belt, all the while belching out an eruption of self-justification that made Finn quite queasy.

When at last the buckle unfastened, Caravaggio flung the sword and sheath aside. 'Well, *signora*. What do you say? Surely it behoves me to commit the deed that led to my being extradited to this dung-heap of mumbling inbreds, does it not?'

A grip of panic seized Finn as, finally, he fathomed the depths of the misunderstanding. Vadge, it would appear, was after revenge on the bloodline that brought him here, to Glasgow, to Finn, to his own personal purgatory, and he assumed it had come through Fillide. But Kassia-Fillide wasn't the mother of Caravaggio's bastard kid. It was the other wifey. His pal's missus, whatever she was called. Maybe Finn hadn't made that clear. He ought to make it clear. He ought to. He opened his mouth to speak but choked on his words, trapped by the fear of making things worse.

Meanwhile, Caravaggio tucked his dagger back in to the waistband of his breeches and leered at Kassia.

'You do not touch me,' she screeched and kicked out. Her bare foot flailed uselessly under her skirt.

Caravaggio's mocking laugh stained the walls. Finn took cover behind the canvas still resting on the easel. Not cowering. He wouldn't say cowering. Biding his time. He pulled his hair off his face. Wiped his forehead. The angles at the edge of his nose. Flicked the sweat off his fingers. Rubbed the bristles above his lip with the tip of his middle finger. Eventually, he forced himself to peer around the edge of the canvas.

Caravaggio was looming over Kassia, dribbling spit into her face, his hand in his breeches, grabbing his cock. He pulled it out. Held it contemptuously in his fist. Kassia was scrabbling around in her panic. Her bodice slipped down an inch. She grabbed the rim of the broken wheel. Tried to pull herself away. Caravaggio coolly stamped her fingers free.

'Is that all you've got?' Kassia said.

In reply, Caravaggio kicked her in the temple. Sent her sprawling across the floorboards. She cracked her head against the badminton post. Finn winced. Any thought that he had had that Vadge was a joke had long gone. A finger of blood was trickling down Kassia's forehead. Stunned, she touched her brow. Gazed in confusion at the stain on her fingertips. Finn tried to stand. Made it as far as his knees. His head was light. Anxiety scintillating in his peripheral vision. He was sure he was about to collapse. He steadied himself against the easel and when he blinked and looked again, Caravaggio had straddled Kassia, had his arm rammed across her throat, had her pinned to the floor. Kassia was choking, gasping, barely even struggling, her hands trapped underneath her own body. Caravaggio yanked up her skirt and petticoats. Tore down her knickers. This couldn't be happening. It couldn't. It wasn't credible that Kassia had stopped fighting. Caravaggio clearly thought the same.

Loosened his grip, leant in to kiss her. Kassia lunged for him and sank the skewer-sword into his thick torso.

'Jesus, you demented succubus,' Caravaggio said, leaping away, and staring in awe at the skewer sticking perpendicularly through his filthy chemise. Finn took a much needed gulp of air. Thank fuck the lassie was resourceful.

(As a lexicographic aside, it was at the moment of impaling and the several subsequent moments that Finn saw for himself the literal definition of *livid*. Caravaggio's face turned deep red, purple, puce. It appeared his blood pressure would burst his skull, his scalp, further mess up his wild hair by the force of the expulsion. The man was going to stroke out, and despite his medical training at Maurice's hospital bedside, Finn did not feel adequately equipped to deal with it. Another fleeting heart tug as he thought of Lizzi's first-aid training, before he rapidly came to his senses, wondering why he was showing any concern for the health status of the debauched lunatic.)

By the time Finn had taken a couple of good breaths, an ink-blot of blood had seeped from Caravaggio's puncture wound into the coarse linen of his shirt. He was muttering to himself, tentatively prodding around the skewer. Finn used those moments to will Kassia to flee, but she was staring at Caravaggio in shock, as if horrified by what she had done. Before Finn could encourage her, Caravaggio yanked the skewer from his flank and tossed it aside and crashed his full weight down on to Kassia's thighs. He was crushing her, breeches straining at the seams over his rotund backside, chubby knees bent at her sides, stubby fingers tearing at her bodice while, under him, she jerked and fought and resisted. Finn caught a glimpse of her erect nipples, her pale breasts, a flash of deep pink between her legs. Caravaggio drew his dagger from the waistband of his breeches, pressed the blade between her thighs. The tip of the blade punctured her creamy skin. A drop of blood ballooned from the wound. She laughed. A taunting laugh, loaded with hate.

'You are desperate, no, when you have to do this to get me to fuck you.'

'Shut up, you foul-mouthed harlot.'

'Or what? You rape me with your piglet tail?'

Caravaggio said nothing, only yanked down his breeches. The dagger slipped from his hand and clattered to the floor. Finn's balls lurched violently into his armpits at the sight of the clenched buttocks, the dirty wrinkles of scrotum, the coarse hair on his thighs. Kassia was screaming, twisting, biting, thrashing. It was horrendous. Horrendous. Finn had to do something. Do something before it was too late. Silently, he lifted the canvas from the easel, preparing to act even before he knew what he could possibly do. Using the canvas as a shield, he edged around the table. Picked up the tube of red paint. Unfastened the loosened lid. Advanced towards the set.

With a battle cry, he launched himself at Caravaggio. The corner of the canvas frame sank into Caravaggio's eye socket. Caravaggio pitched briefly but then brushed Finn aside, refusing to relinquish his grip on Kassia. Finn jumped to his feet and squirted the paint into his face. The studio pealed with squeals of a slaughtered pig. Caravaggio lashed out, toppled. Kassia dragged herself away and slumped against the wall, hair hanging in wild strands in front of her face, in her eyes, in her mouth, and compulsively tugged at her ripped bodice to cover her naked breasts.

Finn took shelter under the trestle table to assess the enemy. Caravaggio, disorientated, eyes screwed shut against the invasion of paint, breeches round his knees, bollocks on display, was swirling his sword hand around him. It was,

Finn realised, his chance to get Kassia to safety. Using the underside of the table, he propelled himself into the open, just as Caravaggio blindly seized his scabbard. Finn dived forward. Reached out. Felt Kassia's cool fingers brush his. Grabbed them. Pulled. Dragged her to her feet. A scrape of steel and Caravaggio aimed an unseeing swipe. Finn dodged the swinging blade. Kassia's hand slipped from his. Half stood, half crouched to find her. Caught the full thrust of Caravaggio's arm on the backhand stroke. The blow sent him flying against the easel. The easel crashed to the ground. The crossbar snapped. A warm stab of the broken wooden strut in his flank. He had enough sense left to be thankful it wasn't the blade.

Caravaggio staggered to his feet, smearing his eyes free of paint with his sleeve. Curses slithered out on his rancid breath as he placed his sword on the trestle table and pulled his breeches over his flaccid penis. He tucked himself in, found his dagger, buckled his scabbard in place and tore reams of paper towels to wipe his face and pad his wound. When he was done, he picked up his sword again and limped over to the corner where Finn was prostrated, suffocating on air curdling with profanities. In the soft candle-light, Finn trapped Caravaggio's stare. The hostility set between them like amber.

Out in the main hall, the fire doors squeaked. Heavy footsteps plodded over the badminton court. Caravaggio cursed and spat, flexed and loosened the fingers of his sword hand, while every laboured breath of Finn's snagged on a stab of pain that was almost as pleasant as it was unexpected. Eventually, he covered his head with his arms, curled into the corner. Tightened his eyes so hard all he heard was the hiss of the arteries in his ears. Prayed, after a fashion. Expected the end to come.

But nothing. Nothing. He didn't hear the slice of the sword replaced in its sheath. Didn't hear the studio door slam or moccasined feet pad quickly down the corridor. Didn't hear the draw of held breath hiding in the thickness of the shadows.

Finn waited for his pulse to settle before he opened his eyes. In the last flickers of candlelight, the chaos in the studio looked peaceful, studied, and save for the splatters of crimson, no hint of the violation that had preceded it. In the corridor, the heavy footsteps were closing in. But in the studio, there was silence. An exquisite silence, broken only by Finn's own uneven breaths and the sound of paint drying. Across the spattered floorboards, Kassia gazed at Finn, her dark eyes wide, the faintest trace of a smile on her lips. With the last dregs of his strength, Finn dragged himself across the splintering floor and took her in his arms. He put his lips to her temple. Tasted salt in his tears. Iron in her blood. Her black hair poured over the boards. And her skin – flawless, sculpted marble.

CARBON BLACK

36

Entombment

Esme stood in front of the one-way glass and studied Finn with her psychiatrist's eye. Forehead on the table; long, greasy hair hiding most of his face; straggly beard just visible; police-issue paper jumpsuit; elasticated shoe protectors over bare feet. One arm clutching his side. The other hanging loose. As if, Esme thought, the cuff of the jumpsuit was weighted down with lead. There was something about the way he sat there – motionless and empty – that was desperately familiar, but it was the image of mental suffering that she recognised, she realised, rather than the person himself. Behind her, the duty sergeant fussed about the room. He dropped a file of papers on the desk. It was crazy busy outside, he said. Coming in here for a bit of respite. Weapons amnesty. Tonight of all nights. Esme murmured only a half-felt sympathy. 'Has his wound been dressed?'

The sergeant sneered at Esme's concern and put his face right up to the window. Told her the lad was at it. The wound was no more than a graze. Beat the lassie up badly before he killed her. Wouldn't have thought he'd be capable to look at him. Too weedy. Just shows you. Sick bastard.

But they weren't seeing the same person. As the sergeant was keen to tell her, the case was open and shut, a foregone conclusion, done without the need to dust for fingerprints. Where Esme saw a young man in difficulty, unwell, distressed, a danger to himself, the police sergeant saw a psychopath, a murderer, a vicious killer. Where Esme saw confusion, self-neglect, despair, the sergeant saw a filthy, lying, low-life. Well, the piece of scum didn't fool him, the sergeant let Esme know without even trying to hide his contempt for her liberal light-handedness. They had him on rape as well as murder, even though the samples hadn't left for the lab yet. Weren't in the least concerned about his denials. Said it was par for the course, seen it, heard it, written the bloody manual. Blaming it on some third party or pretending to be mad. These sickos trying anything to get out of being charged. It was only a nod to procedure and the intervention of the priest that had led to them calling her.

'Is the friend with the tattoos still here? The one who found him?' Esme said. 'Make sure he stays. I'd like to speak to him when I've finished.' She scanned the police report. 'And track down his next-of-kin, parents, siblings, whoever. We may need them when the time comes.'

The police sergeant grunted.

'Who was the girl?' she asked. 'Girlfriend?'

The faintest niggle when the sergeant told her the victim was a prostitute. Not well known. No previous as far as they could discern. But they didn't have a proper name yet, only a working name from the escort website. Crystal. Eastern European, most likely, weren't they all? (No, Esme thought. They weren't.) When he told her you couldn't take what it said on the site as gospel but most likely the girl was from Poland, Esme had to frame the facts in statistics to keep her anxiety at bay. How many girls were working in this city? Hundreds.

'We need him out of there. Examination room, please.'

Through the one-way glass, Esme watched the sergeant and his two colleagues escort Finn from the interview room by his paper-covered arm, one each side of him, the third stooping to reposition the protectors on his feet. The image was strangely intimate, she thought, and though Finn's head drooped wearily and he seemed barely able to hold himself up, there was a presence to him that was almost beatific and which cast shame on his jailers who seemed to recognise it too, and was more than simply the glow of the fluorescent strip lights accenting the white of his jumpsuit.

By the time Esme tracked down the exam room, Finn was already there, sitting with his head bowed and his hands twitching on the table. She dismissed the sergeant, assured he would be outside if needed.

Esme filled a plastic cup from the water dispenser. 'Do you want some?' Finn shook his head without looking up. She gulped the water down. Anxiety mouth. Sand and bleach.

'My name is Dr Blythe and I'm a consultant psychiatrist,' she said, shifting her chair so it was at right angles to Finn. The police file said he was twenty-six. He looked younger, she thought. Maybe it was because he was so lost. 'Because of everything that's happened, I've been asked to make a psychiatric evaluation of you.'

A nod.

'Whatever passes between us is confidential. My job tonight is simply to determine whether you are fit to be charged. I am not here to provide evidence to the police for their case. Only to give my professional opinion on your mental health.' If she did reach a diagnosis, it was unlikely that the police would let him go, but for the moment Esme didn't think it was helpful to complicate matters. 'Okay, Finn? Do you understand?'

Finn licked a finger. Rubbed it over a splinter of dried blood on the back of his hand. It turned brown. Melted to crimson. He looked at his hand without recognition. Slim, long-fingered, with well-defined tendons and bony wrists. Esme handed him a tissue from the box on the desk.

'Finn?'

Another nod. Staring at the blood he'd wiped from his hand.

'It would help me if you could say yes or no. Just so we are completely clear.'

'Yes.' Barely above a whisper. He had the tang of ketones on his breath, the sign of muscle breakdown, the giveaway of someone who hadn't eaten properly for a long time.

Esme took a clinical notes sheet from the tray and scanned the desk for a pen. None. She tried the drawers but they were all empty. 'You'd think they could stretch to a Biro,' she said. Nervous laughter. Her own. She rummaged in her handbag. Car keys, house keys, mini-packs of biscuits, a toy car. Finally, a black roller-ball.

'Do you think you can tell me a little bit about what's been happening?'

He looked up. Pale-faced, drawn. Twisted the tissue between his fingers.

'Finn?'

'It looks to me like you've been having a few difficulties,' Esme said, when he didn't reply. 'Have you been struggling a bit?' She wondered if he had been living on the streets. He smelt like he hadn't washed for a long time.

'Finn?' she said gently.

He looked up at her. Behind his eyes, a whole scenario was playing out.

Esme tried a different tack. 'The police sergeant told me you were an artist. That's interesting. How about you tell me a bit about that?' The file said there had been paintings at the scene.

He said nothing. Screwed the tissue into a ball, threw it towards the bin.

It looked like they were here for the long haul. Esme had promised the boys she would take them to the cinema, a promise made when she'd been counting on the fact that she was never called in, that most of the crises that were likely to arise could be managed by the registrar. 'What does being an artist entail exactly?'

'Aye,' Finn said, staring at her properly, like he was seeing her for the first time, 'you might well ask.' He didn't elaborate. Tears trickled over his cheekbones.

Esme scribbled some notes. Basic things. Appearance, attitude. None of the proper stuff. 'Finn, I can see you are upset. Can you tell me why you are feeling so upset?'

'Let's see.' He pushed up the sleeves of the jumpsuit, absently scratched at the tattoo on his forearm. Esme couldn't make out the writing. 'Oh, I know. Maybe because everyone thinks I'm a psychotic murdering lunatic.'

Esme nodded slowly. She didn't feel threatened. The tough words were negated by the monotone pitch, the silent tears, the hand twisting.

'But that's not what happened?'

'It wasn't me. I keep telling them, but no fucker will listen to what I'm saying.'

'I'm listening.'

'I didn't kill her. I swear. Why would I? It doesn't make sense.' He had that look again. Reliving the pictures in his head.

'But Finn, the police sergeant said—'

He slammed his hands on the desk and shot to his feet. His chair tipped over behind him. He clutched his hand to his side in pain. 'Are you not listening to me? Are you stupid? As stupid as all these other fucking stupid fucks in here?'

The door opened. It was the sergeant, checking on them. He told Finn to sit back down or they would have to restrain him.

'It's fine,' Esme said. 'He doesn't need restraining. Do you, Finn? Honestly, we're fine here, thank you.'

The door closed again. Finn picked up the chair, sat back down slowly. He muttered something that Esme didn't catch.

'I can't hear you, Finn.'

'Sorry,' he repeated. 'Sorry. For the swearing.'

'Do you want something to take the edge off the agitation? Something for the pain?'

Finn shook his head. 'But it's hardly worth me going on, is it? If you've made up your mind.'

'I haven't made up my mind.'

For a few moments, he stared at her. Right inside her, like he was reading her most hidden thoughts. It was a feeling she recognised.

'What happened, Finn?'

'You won't believe me.' He was dry-eyed now, and cautious.

'Try me.'

'I know it seems mental. I know there is no rational explanation,' Finn said. 'But that means I'm not crazy, right? If I was crazy, I'd think that it all made sense.'

'Maybe,' Esme said carefully. 'But sometimes things are more complicated than that.'

'I knew you wouldn't believe me.' Finn sniffed, coughed.

Esme pushed the box of tissues across to him. 'I didn't say that. How about you tell me now?' She put her pen down.

He wiped his nose, took a deep breath and held it. Esme could tell he was deciding if he could trust her to listen. And then he spoke with hardly a pause. Speaking as if she wasn't there. As if he was speaking to some higher judgement. She wondered if he was religious.

'There are folk who live their entire lives in another . . . I don't know . . . let's call it an alternative present, and yet nobody would ever even think to say they were nuts. Prime example: my girlfriend. Or rather, ex-girlfriend. For her, it's like the past is with her all the time. She's always wanting her mother's advice or guidance or whatever, but it isn't like the woman is going to help her pass her exams or sort out her relationships because she's been six foot under for the last ten years. And then this kid I know. With him, it's the other extreme. Obsessed with all the things he's going to do, talking, always talking, about the next thing he's going to do before he's even done with the first, ignorantly unaware of his actual life passing around him. Do you see what I'm getting at? Or other folk with such a distorted view of their own circumstances that, if you didn't know better, you'd swear they were deluded. I had this friend, right, whose missus beat the crap out of him but he convinced himself she did it for love, not because she was fed up of his dubious hygiene and decrepit physique, or because she wanted him to pull the finger out and earn some money for once in his pitiful life.'

'I see,' Esme said slowly.

'Not to mention another pal, a druggie, who thought she could beat her habit by swapping her drug of choice for one equally as addictive but without any of the pleasure. How fucking barmy is that?'

'People have different ways of coping with their lives,' Esme said, scratching her palms. 'It doesn't mean they are deluded.'

'What about this tattoo-artist bloke who used to be a pal of mine who seriously believes his work is an art form? Yeah, really.'

'But Finn, just because—'

'Exactly. We're all at it. Imagine. Like the priest who doesn't even love the God he serves, but has signed up to chastity regardless. Or the physician who makes out she can handle anything that gets thrown at her and blames her eczema on allergies when it's obvious to anyone with eyes that it's stress, pure and simple.' Finn shrugged. 'I'm just saying. Depends on your viewpoint, wouldn't you say?'

Esme stopped scratching and clasped her hands. 'And what about you?'

'I'm the sanest fucking person I know.'

'Be that as it may, you seem to have been having a tricky time lately. You mentioned an ex-girlfriend. Is the break-up something that happened recently? How have you been coping with that?'

But Finn had drifted again. Esme tried a few different approaches but couldn't get any proper answers. This was the part of the job she found the hardest. When people were so distressed and yet convinced that there was nothing wrong, but everyone else looking on could see how much their lives had fallen apart. Not just their lives but the very essence of who they were. When their personality had changed, and their actions and thoughts belonged to a stranger. She tried asking him about his mood, how he coped with anger, had he ever been in trouble before. She asked if he felt safe. Whether he'd ever felt the need to pro-tect himself.

'I know what you're getting at, but you're way off,' he said eventually. 'It wasn't me with the chib. I've told them that already. It was my cousin.'

'Well then, tell me a bit about your cousin.'

'To be honest, he isn't exactly a cousin. It's more complicated than that. Basically he's from the Italian side of the
family. From Rome. Well, not originally, but that's where he
lived for most of his life. Part Italian. Me. Did I say?' Finn
held his hair back with his hands either side of his face,
framing his high cheekbones. The dirt under his nails could
have been paint. Or it could have been blood. 'He was staying with me. Only I didn't expect him to turn out to be such
a psycho. From the beginning he had the wrong end of the
stick. The wrong end of a whole fucking pile of sticks. One
minute he's poncing about in his flouncy shirt and his tight
trousers. Next he completely turns – I'm talking proper
comic-book schizo stuff – and comes over mentally psychotic and is battering her, raping her, stabbing her. I tried to
stop him. You've got to believe me. I tried. I honestly did.
How do you think I got this?' Finn clutched his injured side
again. 'It was truly fucking horrible.' He swallowed hard.
'Can I have that drink now?'

Esme filled a cup for him. He drained it in one, wiping
his mouth with the sleeve of the jumpsuit.

'You know he's been in trouble before? Got done for
murder.'

'We'll look into that later. For now I'd like to find out a
little more about the attack. It must have made you angry to
see all of that?'

'Aye, of course it did. What sort of question is that?
But that isn't the point. Did you not hear me? You need
his details. So you can check him out. It's all there. I can
tell you who he is.' Finn took a deep breath. 'His name is
Michelangelo Merisi da Caravaggio. Caravaggio. Or Vadge,
as Mo and I like to call him.' A pause of a beat or two. 'You

know who he is, right? Moody paintings, sword fights, all that shite.'

Despite her years of training, Esme still hadn't worked out how best to handle the patients with the most persistent hallucinations, the most entrenched delusions. How to get the information she needed without aggravating the situation or colluding with the fiction.

'I can see this is hard for you, Finn,' she said. 'Can you tell me the first time you became aware of this Caravaggio?'

The question opened something in Finn. He launched into an art history lesson, told her things about his past, about college, about his family. There were things in there that Esme could use. A reference to his mother that she wanted to come back to. She made notes to herself in the margin. The story was difficult to follow.

'I really meant the Caravaggio you saw attack the girl.'

He was quite forceful in his argument that it was one and the same person. And about how disappointed he was. Caravaggio had been his hero. But there were other artists he admired, he said, although no one had ever thought to ask him. He listed a few for her. Some of them she'd heard of.

'Different eras, different styles and all that, but they all had one thing in common,' he said. 'All of them visionaries. All masters of technique. Masters of psychological penetration. And other types too, which probably accounted for the syphilis.'

Esme laughed.

'Do you know?' Finn said, smirking. 'All we learnt at Art School was how to speak wank and suck dick.'

Esme wondered whether his language was supposed to impress her.

Finally, she risked the question. She spoke tentatively, as

unthreateningly as she could. 'I wondered if at any time you had considered that your Caravaggio might not be real?'

He laughed bitterly, shook his greasy hair. His paper jumpsuit scrunched as he shifted in his seat. 'I knew it. You think I've lost it but you're wrong. I'm totally together. Couldn't be more fucking together. I know I'm in the shit but I didn't do it and I'm not fucking crazy. All I wanted to do was paint her.'

'I was wondering though, Finn, do you think it is at all possible that you asked her there for another reason? Perhaps after the problems you'd had with your girlfriend?'

He sighed with exaggeration and more than a hint of irritation. 'I don't mean to be rude or anything, but I think you're only visualising part of the picture, so to speak.'

'I see,' Esme said. She scanned the notes she had scribbled.

'No, I'm not sure that you do,' Finn said. He was agitated again. 'Thing is, Kass wasn't a real prostitute.'

'Kass?' Esme gripped her pen so hard her fingers turned yellow. Her writing swirled into patterns in front of her eyes.

'Aye, Kassia. That was her name.'

Finally, Esme recognised him. A blast of bile rushed into her mouth and she thought she would vomit.

Finn was still talking, saying how as far as he knew, apart from himself, Kassia had only had one other client and from all accounts he was *still* a virgin.

But Esme couldn't decipher the words through the confusion of her own guilt. All she saw was his mouth moving. Heard his words come at her as if through mud. Slowed down. Sickening. She'd known all along of course. Known it would end badly. Known when she'd watched Anna and Kassia leave the house on Christmas Day, known when she'd seen Kassia that day in the park, the day Frankie nearly got knocked down and his heart got broken by Kassia's disregard. Known and yet done nothing.

Hurriedly, she resumed writing her notes, jotting whatever she could transcribe. Something, anything. To keep herself from falling apart.

The rest was a formality. Drugs? Some. A fair bit of weed in the past but stopped about six months before, bit of coke though not for ages, the occasional sleeping pill, but they were mainly for Caravaggio. No one in the family with mental health problems, if you didn't count his old doll who had chronic social-climbing disorder, he said, and the old man who had been completely emasculated by his bossy wife. No ops, no meds, no other illnesses. No, not suicidal. Did he need a lawyer?

When she put her pen down, he was lost again.

Later, Esme spoke to the friend. He confirmed what she already suspected, what she had already observed. Lack of self-care, bizarre behaviour, infantile almost. Hardly ate a thing, didn't leave the studio, started out sociable and outgoing, ended up practically a recluse. And this obsession with Caravaggio.

'What's he looking at?' Rob asked.

'Murder, if I find him fit.'

'He's no, though, is he? Fit.'

Esme didn't reply. 'Can you tell me anything about this cousin he's calling Caravaggio?'

Rob looked at her with pity. 'I want it to be someone else as much as you do. But there wasnae anyone else. But it wasnae Finn, either. No the real one. The real one – behind all the posturing crap, behind the myth and the fantasy – the real Finn—' He broke off, choking back tears.

The duty sergeant found Esme in the inspection room, writing up her notes. It's like Paddy's Market out there, he told her. Wondered what she'd got for him. Could they charge the wee shite yet, lock him up, throw away the key?

Esme shook her head. Finding Finn fit to stand trial wouldn't alleviate her culpability.

'Oh, doc, you've got to be kidding me.'

'Put him on suicide watch until we can arrange the transfer. A couple of days, probably.'

'For fuck's sake. We're short on uniforms. Come on, doc. You've been had.'

But he was wrong. Esme dated and signed the case notes. Wherever Finn had found himself was a worse place than either she or the sergeant could dream up for him. She quickly wrote up a separate report for the police and handed it to the sergeant. 'I'll get their duty registrar to see him. They'll want to speak to his next of kin. Oh, and you'll have to organise the transport when they are ready for him.'

When she left the room, Esme could hear the police sergeant muttering behind her. More paperwork, more admin crap, more bollocks, all because of a wee murdering fucker who would be better off rotting in the cells. Esme pulled her work phone from her handbag and called the central switchboard. 'Hi, it's me. I've got one for High Security. Psychotic. Fatal stabbing. Probably schizophrenia. Disorganised. What? No, not me. Disorganised schizophrenia. Hebephrenic. Who's on call? Can you put me through.'

Once she'd hung up, she called home. Too late for the cinema but not too late for pizza. She'd pick one up on the way. She was drained. She'd done her bit. The others could sort the rest out for tonight. All she wanted to do was go home to her boys. Some time soon she would have to tell them about Kassia. Tell Frankie before he saw it on the news. But not tonight. Let him have one more night of innocence before he had the last of it stolen from him.

At the front desk, Esme told them she was leaving. The strap of her security pass caught in her hair clip as she pulled it over her head. The WPC was nattering to her, saying how she couldn't believe all these chibs coming out of the woodwork for the amnesty. Still if it would stop another horrible incident like the one in Dougal Street, it could only be a good thing. Esme freed the tangled strap. Across the station, she heard the slice of metal against metal. An oath to turn the night blue. The WPC pointed at the knife bin in the foyer. Esme glanced over. The swirl of a dark stranger. A glint of steel. A sword going into the bin.

'Sign here please, ma'am.'

Esme signed the form, handed over her pass. Looked again.

But the stranger had gone.

Acknowledgements

In 2015, I had a moment of exceptional good fortune when I met Unbound's editor-at-large, Rachael Kerr. One part editor extraordinaire, one part fairy godmother, one part guardian angel, her belief and enthusiasm for *The Backstreets of Purgatory* buoyed me along as we undertook to turn my manuscript into the book that it has become. I offer her my heartfelt thanks.

The original idea for *The Backstreets of Purgatory* came to me while I was reading Andrew Graham-Dixon's *Caravaggio: A Life Sacred and Profane*. This book became my principal reference source for the details of Caravaggio's life and work that are woven into my novel, and without it I would have been incapable of writing Finn's analysis of Caravaggio's paintings. The expertise is not mine. The mistakes, deliberate or accidental, most certainly are.

Writing, it turns out, is not a solitary endeavour. *The Backstreets of Purgatory* would not be the novel it is if it hadn't been for the input of several writing friends and colleagues who read and commented on early drafts, laughed where it was tragic, wept at my best jokes and wielded the sword for the cull of superfluous characters and chapters that transformed it into the slimline tome that it is today. Bearing in mind that they did not actively discourage me from continuing but rather positively goaded me into it, they must share part of the blame. Melissa Bailey, Claire Black, Margaret

Dolley, Petra McNulty and Conor O'Callaghan, I hope you are suitably ashamed of yourselves.

I am extremely lucky to have such an incredible family and phenomenal bunch of friends. Your kindness and generosity over the years, and extraordinary moral and practical support along the way, have been my source of strength, love and happiness. I cannot fully express how important you all are to me. For patiently listening to me drone on about my writing and forgiving my preoccupations, for letting me check my out-of-date medical knowledge against your current expertise, for offering to be a character in my next novel, for suffering my practice pitches and presentations or starring in the audio clips on my Unbound page, for helping with the nitty gritty of my crowdfunding campaign, organising events, lending venues and persuading friends to be part of the *Backstreets* crowd, I cannot thank you enough. I couldn't have done it without you.

Very special thanks go to my dedicated and trusted first readers, Rachel Holden, Ruth Taylor and Monique Wass, who let me believe that their appreciation of the book wasn't simply based on family bias and friendship, and who gave me the courage and confidence to submit this work for publication.

I'd like to give a particular mention to David Brown, Angela McLaughlin and David Scott, who may or may not realise the part they have played in the genesis of this book and to whom I owe a debt that cannot be repaid.

Huge credit goes to the editorial, design and production team at Unbound, who not only produced this astonishing finished product but who were a delight to work with.

And finally, my sincerest gratitude to every single supporter who pledged their hard-earned cash in advance and helped bring this novel into existence. You are amazing.

About the Author

Helen Taylor was brought up in the Lake District and the north-east of Scotland. She studied medicine in Glasgow and worked for a short time as a junior doctor in the city. Research took her to Oxford and London, but she later returned to Glasgow to take up a fellowship at the university. She has a diploma and an MA in creative writing, and currently lives in France. *The Backstreets of Purgatory* is her first novel.

Supporters

Unbound is a new kind of publishing house. Our books are funded directly by readers. This was a very popular idea during the late eighteenth and early nineteenth centuries. Now we have revived it for the internet age. It allows authors to write the books they really want to write and readers to support the books they would most like to see published.

The names listed below are of readers who have pledged their support and made this book happen. If you'd like to join them, visit www.unbound.com.

Moira Adam
Geoff Adams
John Adams
Margaret Adams
Lulu Allison
Catherine Allsopp
Angela Anderson
Anne Ardica
Joelle Arnott
Mary Rose Atkinson
Michelle Ayling
Lisa Badger
Melissa Bailey
David Baillie

David Baker
Derren Ball
Jason Ballinger
Jo K Barber
Nathalie Baret
Anthony Barnett
Edward Barrett
Simon Barrett
Dave Barry
Pauline Beattie
William Beattie
Paul Beatty
Ewan Bell
Helen Bennett

Sandy Bennett-Haber
Julie Benson
Catriona Birnie
Claire Black
Tom Blackie
Cathleen Brady-O'Hagan
Peter Bull
Clare Bulman
Kate Bulpitt
Kimberly Burke
Kathryn Byrne
Marni Cabrelli
Tiani Callwood
Alison Cameron
Dominique Cameron
Stuart Cameron
Helen Carlile
Paul Carlin
Solenn Carnac
Sean Carr
Geri Carroll
Cazzikstan
John Luke Chapman
Sue Ciechanowicz
Robert Clafferty
Barbara Clough
Janie Collie
Margaret Colyer
Marilyn Corrie
Alister Craig
Claire Crossland Naujoks
Alastair Cunningham
BJ Cunningham

Deirdre Cunningham
Jennifer Cunningham
Sam Cunningham
Tom Cunningham
Annette Danaher
Angela Davey
Jenny Davies
Will Davies
Roy & Linda Davis
Sheena Davis
Olivia Dawson
Rick de Zeeuw
Helene Delbouys
Lucia Delgadillo
Anne Dewar
Jackie Dewar
Janis Dickson
Christian Doerig
Jane Doig
Margaret Dolley
Kirsten Donald
Derek Dougall
Tony and Michele Dropp
Esther Dubrey
Alan Duckworth
Pauline Dunn
Steven Dunn
Robert Eardley
Mark Earnshaw
Catherine Easton
Morag Ellery
Katherine Ellis
Sarah Ernillsdottir

Linda Ferguson
Mo Fisher
Colin Forrest-Charde
Kirsten Forrester
Aileen Forsyth
Naomi Frisby
David Fyffe
Dominic Gallagher
Geraldine Gallagher
Marie Gallagher
Morag Gallanagh
Laurie Garrison
Manuela Garutti-Foley
Andrew Gavin
Paul Gibson
Irene Gilbert
Doug Gillen
Jane Gilmour
Joanna Goldsworthy
Rita E. Gould
Moira Gourlay
Karen Grant
Susan Granville
Posy Greany
Jo Greener
Diane Gregson
Jenny Guthrie
Fiona Hackett
Rory Hadden
Patricia Giangrande Hamila
Tansy Hammarton
James Hampton-Till
Ali Harper

Melissa Hawker
Meike Hensmann
Charles Herd
The Herd's
E O Higgins
Carol Hinchliffe
Peter Michael Hobbins
Paul Holbrook
Rachel R Holden
Roger Holden
Tony Holder
Michael Lewis Homer
Sylvia Howe
Mark Howseman
Jeanne Humber
Ros Hunt
Fiona Hunter
Nevil Hutchinson
Maria Huybens
Donna Imlach
Sarah Jacob
Jayne Jamieson
Christine Jarra
Susan Jeremy
Sandra Johnson
Gail Joughin
Graeme Kaney
Charlotta Kastensson
Mallika Kaviratne
Fiona Kennedy
Christy & Shahid Khan
Imran Khan
Dan Kieran

Shona Kinsella
Lucy Kirkland
Philip Korsah
Sue Kyes
Mit Lahiri
Rachel Lake
Jerry Lambert
Brian & Monica Laundon
Ewan Lawrie
Sarah Ledingham
Susanne Liddle
Michael Luffingham
Anson Mackay
Fiona Mackenzie
Gladys Mackenzie
Heather Mackenzie
Jan MacKenzie
Lesley MacKenzie
Seonaid Mackenzie
Seonaid Mackenzie-Murray
Alison Macleod
Annette MacLeod
Jo Macleod
Finlay Macrae
Catherine Main
Kirsteen Main
Malcolm Main
Ross Main
Gautam Malkani
Julie Mallon
Jenny Malyon
Soohie Mancey-Jones
Tünde Mathe

Jacqui Matthews
Veronica McBurnie
Barbara McCabe
Pamela McCabe
Janice McCall
John McCall
Lynn McClean
Suzanne McClelland
Mark McColl
Richard McCulloch
Sophie McDade
Millissa McDonald
Jacqueline McKay
Petra McNulty
Seamus McNulty
Julie Meikle
Alan Menzies Bell
Cathy Meunier
Simon Miller
Fiona Mitchell
John Mitchinson
Liz Monument
Wendy Moore
Alison Morgan
Alastair Morris
Angus Morrison
Elaine Morrison
Dianne Mostier
Alison Mottram
Carol Mueller
Teresa Munn
Linda Murgatroyd
Alison Murphy

Orla Murphy

Jenni Murray

Carlo Navato

Kathryn Naylor

Hugh Neill

Nina Neill

Chris Newbold

Maria Nicolaou

Conor O'Callaghan

Caroline O'Connell

Elaine O'Grady

Martin O'Neill

Pat O'Neill

Sola Ogun

Ericka Olsen Stefano

Justin Pachebat

Scott Palmer

Madeleine and Tom Park

Nastasya Parker

Linda Paton

Lynda Paton

Hugo Perks

Robert Pinches

Sabina Pirie

Justin Pollard

Beki Pope

Tom Pow

John Poziemski

Ruth Prendergast

Laura Price

Stewart Prodger

Mary Quinn

Alan Rae

Christy Ralph

Ann Ramelin

Lorna Ramelin

Ronald Read

Ian Reeves

Angus Reid

Islay Reid

Eileen Reilly

Fabien Richaud

Ian Robb

Thelma Robb

Dave Roberts

Jude Roberts

Elizabeth Robertson

David Roche

Amali Rodrigo

Auriel Roe

Laura Rorato

Alison Rouse

Alex Rowe

Saj

Pamela Salmon

Catherine Seguimbraud

Lizzy Sempill

Tinni Sharma

Pam Sheen

Lindsey Shields Waters

Caroline Shutter

Alison Sim

Avril Simpson

Joe Skade

Ian Skewis

Claire Slade

Christina Smart
Angela Smith
Lorraine Smith
Steven Smith
Susan Smith
David Somers
Susan Soutar
Kirsty Spink
Rebecca Staheli
Gordon Stark
Katarzyna Stawarz
Chris Stenzel
Laura Stewart
Pauline Stewart
Tabatha Stirling
Sarah Stradling
Audrey Stuart
Catherine Taylor
Gabrielle Taylor
Georgette Taylor
Irene Taylor
James Taylor
Jo Taylor
Lesley Taylor
Margaret Taylor
Ruth Taylor
Sophie Taylor
Toby Taylor
Claire Thom
Craig Thomson
Douglas Thorburn
Richard Todd

Paul Tompsett
Solitaire Townsend
Robert Turnbull
Paola Urbina Barnes
Eva Vermandel
Valeria Vescina
Fiona Walker
George Walker
Danielle Walton
Vicki Waqa
Emelda Wass
Louise Wass
Monique Wass
Lisa Watson
Lesley Watt
Don Weir
Ruth West
Diane Wilcock
Ilene Williams
Alan Williamson
Roy Willingham
Clare Willocks
Derek Wilson
John Wilson
Mrs M Wilson
Norman Winterbottom
Gretchen Woelfle
Caroline Wood
Rowena Wood
Beryl Woodger
Chris Yuill
Simon Yuill